THE POWER OF LOVE

Mac spoke again, his tone serious. "Your life essence is getting weak, Artemis. Dangerously so."

"I know. That blow I took from Malachi before the elevator closed—"

"I can help with that." He drew her into his arms. "Make you strong in light again. If you'll let me."

She nodded. "And you—you need a stronger death shield if you're going to get through Hell without attracting every demon along the way. I can do that. But we have to work quickly. Who knows when that door will open? Or what we'll encounter on the other side."

"Right. Quick." His hand smoothed down her back. "I know a very quick, very effective way to swap power. I say we go for it."

She went still. "You don't mean...you want to make love? Here? Now?"

MORE RAVE REVIEWS FOR JOY NASH!

THE GRAIL KING

"Not since Mary Stewart's Merlin trilogy has the magic of Avalon flowed as lyrically off the pages. Nash captures the myths of the Druids in a fresh, exciting approach delivering a tale that grabs hold of your heart and reaches deep into your soul bringing forth joy and a belief in the old ways bound with the new."

—*RT BOOKreviews*, Top Pick, 4 1/2 stars

"*The Grail King* is a magnificent journey filled with adventure, magic, friendship, and honor that will make it difficult to put down until the end. It's a brilliantly written tale…with its strong undertones of conflict between good and evil.…Beautifully written with dynamic lead characters and several equally potent secondary players, *The Grail King* will put readers into its magical hold right from the beginning. Don't miss this terrific novel!"

—Romance Reviews Today

"*The Grail King* turned out to be a rare jewel of a book, which grabbed my attention from the beginning and kept me enthralled until the very end.…Wonderful, complex characters, an exciting, adventurous plot, and a great romance…I don't know how I've missed reading Ms. Nash's work before now, but be assured she goes on my auto-buy list. Do yourself a favor and read *The Grail King*."

—Once Upon a Romance Review

CELTIC FIRE

"Nash creates suspenseful, haunting and high-tension romance.… A top-notch read."

—*RT BOOKreviews*

"Joy Nash has created a lush world for senses of all kinds.…This is a wonderfully fast-paced read full of romance, love and fantasy that will continue to burn in the hearts of readers after the last page is turned."

—Fresh Fiction

"Joy Nash is definitely one to be watched. She has great world-building skills, and her own personal magic with the pen is guaranteed to make hers a very strong name on the market in the not too distant future."

—Love Romances

JOY NASH

IMMORTALS: The Crossing

LOVE SPELL NEW YORK CITY

For my family—my first and best fans

LOVE SPELL®

October 2008

Published by

Dorchester Publishing Co., Inc.
200 Madison Avenue
New York, NY 10016

ISBN 10: 0-505-52767-7
ISBN 13: 978-0-505-52767-7

The name "Love Spell" and its logo are trademarks of Dorchester Publishing Co., Inc.

Printed in the United States of America.

10 9 8 7 6 5 4 3 2 1

Visit us on the web at www.dorchesterpub.com.

IMMORTALS:
The Crossing

CHAPTER ONE

Her face was pretty, but he couldn't remember her name. Or why, exactly, he'd let her into his bed.

Manannán mac Lir—known variously as musician, Sidhe, demigod, Prince of Annwyn, Guardian of Celtic Magical Creatures in the Human World, and several other names not generally polite to utter in mixed company—squinted through the gray shadows shrouding his bed and his life. The lilting echo of last night's concert had been overwritten by a repulsive coda of expensive whisky and cheap sex.

It was an epilogue that kept repeating, ad nauseam, like a scratched vinyl record.

On a sigh, Mac swung his legs over the edge of the mattress and stood. The room swayed a bit, but settled down quickly enough. Truth be told, his head was abominably clear. One benefit—or curse—of not being human was that authentic Scots whisky drunk far too quickly in far too great a quantity didn't plague him come morning.

He glanced at the bed. Authentic Scots women, on the other hand . . .

He plucked an empty glass tumbler from the carpet and set it on a gateleg table with the remains of the late supper he'd shared with . . . He frowned at the bed. *Maired? Rebecca? Kathleen?*

Scowling in earnest now, he showered and dressed

himself in clean faded jeans and a fresh sea-green T-shirt, then sat on an overstuffed ottoman and laced up his Doc Martens. Decent once again, he considered the sleeping woman.

Shobhan? Martha? Elizabeth?

Bugger it all, he had no idea. The lass was a real beauty, though, with quite a lot of red-gold hair. Her young body was supple and smooth—*all* over, as he remembered it. She'd had a backstage pass to his Inverness gig, the last show of a six-month world concert tour that had gone on about two months too long. She'd been with friends, two equally nubile young birds. Mac had allowed his loyal—if slightly slack-brained—roadie cousins to talk him into balancing the ratio. It'd been entirely by accident this particular girl—*Edwina? Frances? Sonia?*—had ended up in Mac's lap.

The other two lasses were upstairs, warming his cousins' beds. Full Sidhe as they were, Mac was certain Niall and Ronan had not wasted a minute of the night pondering the uselessness of their long, lazy, sex-filled lives. As for his own bird? He'd done his duty by her, of course—Mac was half Sidhe, after all. She'd been more than pleased. But he had hardly felt a thing.

Mac leaned over and shook her shoulder. Abruptly, so she wouldn't take the contact as an invitation to more sex. "Come on, then, love. Up with you."

Blue eyes blinked open. "Mac?" Her pretty forehead creased. "You're dressed."

" 'Fraid so, love. It's full morning."

He strode to the window and shoved open the curtains. His nameless lover's hand shot up, blocking a brutal stab of sunlight. "So soon? I thought we could . . ."

"No. Can't." He made a circuit of the room, retrieving skirt, knickers, sweater, bra. Stilettos. Fishnet stockings, a bit ripped. Had he done that? "I've got an appointment."

He sent a meaningful look toward the door.

Denise? Nancy? Priscilla? pretended not to notice. Stretching like a cat, she shrugged off the bedcovers. Naked as a jay, she gifted him with a brilliant smile.

He tossed her clothes on the bed.

Her bottom lip pushed forward. "You could cancel."

"I appreciate the offer, love, but no. I couldn't possibly miss this meeting." Not least because there wasn't one.

"I'll wait. When you get back we can—"

"I won't be back. Not any time soon. I'm leaving town today."

"Oh! Right. Of course you are. The tour's over, isn't it? Where will you go next? London?"

"No."

"On holiday, then? France, maybe?"

"No."

"Italy?"

Giving up on good manners, Mac stalked to the door. "Listen, love. Stay if you want. Wait for your friends. Or better yet, join them upstairs. I'm sure my cousins won't mind."

He fled a feminine huff, breathing with relief as he stepped into a sun-washed, blustery day. Freedom at last. He headed to the corner pub for a noon pint and a look at the football scores. He was deep into the *Scotsman*, mulling the Dublin Leprechauns' shocking loss to Vampires United, when a porcine chorus of feminine squeals shattered his concentration.

"Oh. My. *God*! There he *is*!"

"Ooooooooh!"

"Manannán!"

Mac's head jerked up. A brilliant flash assaulted his retinas. Blinking furiously, he made out four lasses pounding on the pub's street window. A tall, grinning bloke with a camera hovered behind them.

Bloody, bloody hell. Didn't take long this time. He hadn't even finished his pint.

With a regretful glance at his ale, he sprang to his feet and dug a hundred-pound note out of his pocket. Money enough, he hoped, to cover both the cost of his pint and whatever damage was about to occur. The pub door banged open. Tossing the note on the table, Mac sprinted toward the rear corridor as his fangirls surged across the threshold on the power of a collective, earsplitting shriek.

The barman, who'd been wiping down the counter, paused in midswipe, looked up, and winced.

"Sorry, mate," Mac called back to the bloke as he ducked under a low lintel. Where the hell was the bloody back door?

"His table's *empty*!"

"Where'd he *go*?"

"Back *there*!"

There was a scrabbling sound, followed by splintering wood and a spectacular shatter of glassware.

The barkeep's voice boomed. "Look here, ye bloody lot of besoms. Ye canna just hurtle through—"

Dead end. *Ballocks*. Mac backtracked and shouldered through a door on his right. The men's loo. He slammed the door behind him and pressed his spine against it just as a body slammed the other side.

The doorknob rattled. "Maaaaaac!"

Mac spun about and blasted a stream of elfshot at the knob. The odor of burnt metal steamed into the air. A paunchy bald bloke emerging from the single stall with his hands on his zipper drew up short, bottom jaw flapping. "What the—"

The door shuddered. Thanks be to all the gods in Annwyn, the ruined lock held. Mac directed his next stream of elfshot at the loo's single window, high on the opposite wall. The glass dissolved in a glittering shower of green sparks.

"Pardon, mate." Shoving past his slack-jawed spectator, he grabbed an overhead pipe and swung both legs up and over the sill. The drumming on the loo door intensified, accompanied by a painful counterpoint of frustrated shrieks.

Bald Bloke's eyes narrowed. "Now, wait just a bloody minute! Fine for a lad like you to slide his scrawny arse through there, but how am I to get out? You've welded the sodding door shut!"

"No worries. The lasses will have it down within the minute."

The door's top hinge splintered.

No time to waste. "Look, mate. I'd appreciate whatever you could do to slow those birds down. Sex-crazed, they are."

The man's eyes widened. His thick lips twitched, and his curved spine straightened a little. "Are they, now?"

"They are," Mac said grimly, and propelled himself through the window.

He landed in a crouch beside a smelly rubbish bin, his boots slipping on muck he'd rather not examine. He was in a narrow service alley that ran between the pub and a grocer's. Dashing to the end, he turned right and sprinted past a row of shops, laying confusion spells in his wake. A glance over his shoulder revealed no pursuit. Yet.

He knew better than to hope he'd get away clean. Fangirls were a bloody persistent lot.

A left turn and a right brought him back to his own place. His vintage Norton Commando motorcycle was parked at the curb, its outrageous chrome beauty glittering like diamonds in the sun. He started toward it, then stopped short.

Was that a *thong* dangling from his handlebar?

Bloody, bloody hell. What had happened to his protective wardings?

He flicked the scrap of red lace into the gutter, muttering under his breath. Still cursing, he swung a leg over the saddle and gunned the engine. Once on the road, he cast

an airtight glamour spell around the Norton. Anyone looking would see a battered diesel lorry.

He gunned for the A96. There was only one place in
the human world where fangirls couldn't find him. Mac
didn't intend to stop until he reached it.

No doubt Kalen and Christine would be delighted to
see him.

CHAPTER TWO

"Mac. You've been standing up here for hours, staring at the ocean. What's going on?"

Mac, forearms resting atop the battlement of Kalen's island castle, kept his eyes trained on the choppy waters of the North Sea. Partly because he loved the ocean. But mostly so he wouldn't have to face Christine's shrewd gaze.

Water witches, he thought with some disgust. The lot of them were wicked perceptive. Christine had been at him almost constantly since he'd arrived at her immortal husband's island fortress three days ago. He'd fled to the battlements specifically to get away from her questions. So what did she do? Follow him and ask more.

He tapped a staccato rhythm on the stone. Three-quarters time, with a descending beat. "Doesn't that child of yours need tending, love?"

She smiled. "Not at the moment. Elspeth's sleeping."

And that was another thing. Kalen and Christine's new daughter. The child gave Mac the oddest feeling. He tried to put a name to it.

Envy. That was it. A human emotion he'd never quite understood, and now it was his. He found himself wondering what it would be like to hold his own son or daughter.

Ridiculous thought, that.

"What about your husband, then?" he asked. "I'm sure Kalen needs you for something." He tossed her a good-natured leer intended to feel like old times. It didn't. "Perhaps for making another pretty immortal offspring? He seems to like the first one you've given him immensely."

Christine laughed, her blue eyes sparkling. "So true. I think he spends half his time on the floor with Ellie. Becoming a father seems to have sent Kalen into a second childhood."

"Quite a feat, considering his first was three thousand years ago."

"Only two thousand nine hundred and seventy," Christine replied with a grin. A breeze caught her dark hair, throwing the blue streak at her temple into her face. She tucked it behind her ear.

For an instant, Mac found himself chuckling with her. The mood didn't last, though. The smile slipped from his face, as if it didn't quite fit anymore. Moodily, he returned to his scrutiny of his divine father's watery realm. Lir, Celtic god of the sea, considered himself something of an artist. Da had painted the ocean a deep gray blue today, with brighter patches where cross currents wrestled through the narrow strait separating the island from the mainland. From Mac's vantage atop Kalen's enchanted castle, the coast appeared as a jagged line of autumn rusts and golds. Pewter clouds huddled over the shore, but directly overhead, the sky was clear and blue. Scottish weather did not dare cross Kalen's perimeter wardings uninvited.

Tomorrow was Samhain, though. The northern days were growing rapidly shorter, and even Kalen's vast magic was powerless against the changing season. Mac, a creature of light, had never been fond of Highland winters. He tended to flee to the continent during the darkest months. But now—disturbingly—he found himself looking forward to nearly endless night.

His drumming fingers quickened.

"Mac." Christine's voice was tinged with something that felt uncomfortably like pity. "You can talk to me, you know."

He sighed. "I know, love, but there's nothing to tell, really. I'm just restless, but I'll be back in London soon. Got a few new songs to record." He forced a grin. "And a lady waiting as well—"

"But no one special."

Mac fought a surge of wholly unreasonable annoyance. Christine was entirely right, his lovers bored him to distraction. His friend's concern should comfort; instead it made him angry. What the hell was wrong with him? Manannán mac Lir didn't *do* anger. He didn't do depressed. He didn't do jealousy. He was the lighthearted immortal Prince of Annwyn, for the gods' sake. He'd spent almost all of his seven hundred years laughing. Life was good, life was endless, life was one long party. He'd never met a problem he couldn't get around. Or at least make a joke about.

Until now.

Vaguely, he was aware of Christine turning to match his pose—elbows on the rough stone, face to the sea. He loved her dearly, but gods, how he wished she'd leave him alone. He was bad company—had been for some time. He didn't like to be reminded of it.

"You're not yourself, Mac. At least admit that."

"Christine. I thought mothers were supposed to obsess over their own offspring." He gave a short, mirthless, laugh. "The gods know my mother does."

"Is that what this is about? Niniane? Has she done something?"

"Something more than usual, you mean? No, can't claim old Mum's hounding me any more or less than usual. Niniane is . . . Niniane. She's full Sidhe," he added with a grimace, as if that explained everything. To his mind, it did. "She wants me to come home to Annwyn. Permanently."

"She's Queen of Annwyn, Mac. It's understandable that she wants her only son at her side."

"She can forget it. I hate the Otherworld. It's so bloody perfect. It's been centuries since I've spent more than a few hours in a row in the place, and I'm not about to change my ways now. I've given up trying to make Niniane accept my choices, but that's a familiar battle, at least. It doesn't have anything to do with . . . what's wrong with me."

There. He'd admitted it. Something was *wrong* with him.

Christine laid a hand on his arm. He felt her water magic, flowing like a question. With a sigh he opened himself enough to provide her with at least part of the answer.

Her eyes widened. "Leanna?"

The sound of Mac's half sister's name set his stomach churning. He moved suddenly, breaking contact. "That's part of it. Damn it, Christine, it's like a scratched vinyl record playing over and over in my mind. I keep seeing that foul demon dragging Leanna into hellfire. I can still hear her screams. Taste her terror." He stared at his hands. "You heard her that night. She called for me. Begged me to save her. Do you know, that was the first time my sister ever asked me for anything?"

"You tried your best to help her." Sympathy etched Christine's expression. Which was amazing. Leanna had been Kalen's lover when Christine arrived in Scotland. When Kalen threw his Sidhe lover over in favor of a human newcomer, Leanna had tried her best to kill her competition. Literally.

"There was nothing else you could have done," Christine continued. "That night at the burial cairns—by then it was too late. Maybe if Leanna hadn't made a pact with an Old One . . . if she hadn't turned demonwhore . . . if she'd accepted your offers of help over the years . . . maybe then things would've been different. But she didn't.

Leanna freely chose death magic over life magic. I know it's a hard thing to come to terms with, but your sister chose her own fate. It's no fault of yours that you couldn't stop her from being dragged into the demon realms."

Mac slammed his palm against the wall. "It *feels* like my fault. Where was I when Leanna was born? Where was I when Niniane abandoned her to her drunken human sot of a father? Where was I when my sister was growing up ragged and poor in the mess that came after Culloden?"

"You can't blame yourself for all that! You didn't even know Leanna existed."

"Damn it, Christine, I should have known. I should have been there for her. I should have raised her myself. How could our lovely, heartless mother have thrown her away? The gods know that if I had my own child—"

He cut off abruptly. His own child? It would never happen. He didn't want a Sidhe wife, and the human women strong enough in heart and magic to mother a demigod's child were few and far between.

Christine touched Mac's arm. "Regrets are terrible, I know."

Mac made a vague gesture. "Regrets are all I seem to have lately, Christine. Maybe . . . maybe it's just the season." He made a vague gesture toward the gold and russet coastline. "Everything's dying."

"It'll come alive again in the spring."

"But it's beautiful now."

And that, Mac realized with a rare flash of insight, was the crux of his angst. He was an immortal Sidhe demigod— a creature of pure life magic. Never, in seven hundred years of life, had he ever once thought of death as . . . beautiful.

He glanced at Christine. Her blue eyes were grave. He experienced a chill of foreboding. "What? What is it?"

"Oh, Mac. I never thought it might have happened to you, too." She looked ill.

He wasn't feeling so well himself. "I don't know what you're talking about."

"When did you start feeling unsettled? As early as last summer? After . . . after the Immortals' final battle with Culsu?"

He considered. "Yeah. About then, I guess."

Last year, when death magic had all but overpowered the human world, Mac had refused to flee to safety in Annwyn. Ignoring his mother's protests, he'd joined the four older Immortals in defeating the powerful demon who'd driven their youngest immortal brother, Tain, completely insane.

Christine bit her lip. "Kalen and his brothers—and you—did everything you could to help Tain regain his sanity."

"So we did. And we succeeded. What of it? That's long been done with."

"No. It will never be done with. The only reason Tain isn't a madman now is that Kalen, Adrian, Darius, and Hunter each absorbed some of Tain's darkness into his own soul."

"I know that, love."

"Did you also know that the damage Kalen and the others took on that day is permanent? There's a darkness in Kalen's soul now that won't ever go away. But we'd thought . . . we'd thought only the Immortals were affected. After all, they were the only ones actually in contact with Tain in the last moments of the battle. But now I wonder . . ."

Mac swallowed hard. "Unhealthy habit, wondering." He tried for a light tone. "Curiosity, cats, and all that, you know."

Christine cocked her head. Mac shifted, uncomfortable with her scrutiny. He had the feeling she could look straight through him.

"You look older than you did a year ago," she said finally. "Something like early twenties rather than sixteen.

Kalen and I noticed it right away when you arrived. You've filled out in the chest quite a bit, too, and your zits are gone. We assumed you'd come to some kind of agreement with Niniane."

When he didn't reply, she prompted, "You didn't, did you?"

"No," he admitted. "Honestly, I'm not quite sure how the aging thing came about. It was rather gradual. Mum's not at all happy about it—I look older than she does now. She complained to Da, but Lir told her there was nothing to be done."

"You aged because you absorbed some of Tain's death magic. Like Kalen and the other Immortals did. You must have."

He stared at her, stunned. Death magic? In his own soul? "No. That just isn't—"

He fell silent. It *was* possible. Likely, even, given what had happened to Kalen and the others. Even worse, it was a perfect explanation for Mac's simmering anger, his restlessness, his envy, his angst. Emotions like that didn't spring from life magic.

Now he felt *really* unwell.

"Kalen struggles with the darkness, too, if that's any consolation," Christine offered.

"Kalen," Mac said in a flash of wholly unreasonable irritation, "has always been a moody bastard. Frankly, love, I can't see how you'd even notice the difference."

Christine, incredibly, didn't take offense. "Moody, yes, but this darkness is something more. It's soul deep. But Kalen wouldn't have it any other way, and neither would the other Immortals. If the four of them hadn't been able to lighten their brother's burden, Tain would still be insane. Not happily married."

Mac's brows lifted. "Tain got married? That's one intrepid bride."

Christine laughed. "Yes, Samantha is very brave. She and

Tain are even talking about starting a family." She shot him a look. "Maybe that's what you need. A wife and kids."

His heart squeezed. "Not so easy finding the right woman, love. Kalen got lucky."

"There's someone for everyone."

Mac snorted. "For an immortal demigod Sidhe prince with an objectionable mother? I highly doubt a lonely hearts advert's going to do the trick."

"You hardly need a personal ad. You're the famous Manannán mac Lir. Please don't try to tell me you don't have thousands of women throwing themselves at your feet."

A sincere laugh escaped. "At my feet? Not usually. At another body part? Regularly. But it's not at all conducive to romance. What it is, frankly, is a bloody nightmare."

Christine chuckled. "And to think, a year ago you were grumbling how hard it was to get a mature woman to take a second look at your zitty teenage face."

"Yes, well, since then I've found the Chinese were right. Be careful what you wish for." He glanced at her. "That was the Chinese, wasn't it? Confucius or some such bloke?"

"I have no idea," Christine laughed. "And quit trying to change the subject. Here we have a healthy, red-blooded Sidhe—"

"Only half Sidhe."

"—*half* Sidhe, claiming he's in a funk because he's getting too much sex. How is that even possible?"

Incredibly, Mac felt his cheeks heat. When she put it like that, he did sound rather callous.

He pushed himself away from the wall. "Christine. Give it a rest, will you? I came here for some peace, not for bloody psychoanalysis."

There it was, his detestable anger, rearing its ugly head again. The slight widening of Christine's eyes told him his barb had hit its mark.

He pressed the heel of his hand to his forehead. "I'm sorry."

"No," Christine said. "I'm sorry. I shouldn't make you talk when you obviously don't want to. Forgive me?"

"Nothing to forgive, love." He forced a smile and offered her his arm. "I know you mean well. Shall we go in search of your muscle-bound husband, then?"

"All right."

He walked her to the tower door, then stood back as she preceded him down the steep winding stair. They were almost to the lower landing when they met Kalen on his way up. The Immortal was dressed in his habitual kilt and white shirt, his tiny, tartan-swaddled daughter cradled against his broad chest. The incongruous sight made Mac's heart lurch. Oh, how the tiniest women could make fools out of the biggest, strongest men.

Then he caught sight of Kalen's grim expression.

"What's wrong?" he asked, at the same time that Christine blurted, "Goddess, Kalen. What's happened?"

Kalen retreated to the landing and gently transferred his daughter into her mother's arms before speaking. Christine cradled the infant's head, her worried gaze fixed on her husband.

"A falcon just delivered a message from one of the inland faerie villages. There's been a death-magic attack." Kalen met his wife's eyes. "It's Gilraen's village, Christine."

Mac knew Christine counted Gilraen, the garrulous faerie who'd helped her when she arrived in Inverness a year ago, a close friend.

"Oh no," she whispered. "Has anyone been . . ."

"Killed?" Kalen said. "No. But several young ones are ill." He turned to Mac. "The village elders are asking that you come immediately."

Of course they were. Mac took his role as Guardian of Celtic Magical Creatures in the Human World seriously, though the job hadn't required much attention in the past year. Life magic had surged wildly since the Immortals had destroyed the demon Mac knew as Culsu. Mac, consumed by his music and his world tour—not to mention his brooding—hadn't so much as spoken to a faerie in half a year.

Which begged the question—how had Gilraen known where to find him?

"Mac?" Kalen was looking at him.

"I'll go immediately, of course," Mac said quickly, flushing.

"I'll come with you," Kalen said.

Mac stiffened. Did his friend think he couldn't handle things on his own? "No. The faeries are my responsibility. I'll go alone."

"I don't think that's—"

"If I need help," Mac cut in, "I'll call you. What's happened, exactly? Does the message say?"

Wordlessly, Kalen handed Mac the scrap of parchment.

"Attack came without warning," Mac muttered, scanning the hastily scribbled missive. "Life-draining spell. Brutal, quick. The youngest faeries affected most of all—"

"Oh my Goddess," Christine breathed. "Tamika."

Mac's head jerked up. "Who's Tamika?"

She stared at him. "Gilraen's niece, of course. She was born just four months ago. Kalen and I went to the naming feast. You were touring in Japan at the time, I believe. But I can't believe you've forgotten, Mac. Faerie births happen, what, about once or twice every decade?"

Mac's cheeks heated. He *had* forgotten. Some bloody fine Guardian he was. Faeries were extremely long-lived—once they reached adulthood. Their children were few, and as fragile as human juveniles. "Right. I remember now."

"Gilraen's not sure the infant will survive," Kalen added quietly.

Christine clutched little Elspeth. "How horrible. Who could have done such a thing? A demon?"

Kalen shook his head. "A demon's death spell would have left a blazing trail. Whoever did this . . . according to Gilraen, they left no trace at all."

"Impossible," Mac muttered, crumpling the parchment in his fist. "Death magic always leaves a mark."

It had damn well left its stain on him.

A gaggle of skinny-arsed fangirls, accompanied by the tall, pasty-faced photog, were camped on the beachhead across the channel from Kalen's island. How the hell had they tracked him from Inverness? Gritting his teeth, Mac glamoured his way around them and extracted the Norton from its hiding place. He hit the road with a squeal of rubber. Enhancing the cycle's excellent motor with a high-speed charm, he arrived in the vicinity of Gilraen Ar-Finiel's village in under an hour.

The little man lay in wait at the edge of a meadow, at a point where the human road ran closest to his village. The instant Mac braked, the faerie darted out from behind a clump of moor grass, waving his hat frantically.

Mac hopped off the cycle and listened to Gilraen's impassioned recount of the death-magic attack on his village.

"You had no warning?" Mac asked when Gilraen came up for air. "None at all?"

Gilraen twisted his leaf hat in his hands, his gossamer wings drooping down his back. The faerie's green coat was rumpled, the tip of his short beard had lost its point, and his normally rosy skin had gone several shades toward sallow.

"I swear on sweet Annwyn, Mac Lir, there were nothing. No hint of trouble at all. No scent of death magic. And then . . ." He swallowed visibly, his Adam's apple bulging. "The clan started falling ill. 'Twas slight at first . . . small pains in the head, minor cramps of the stomach. Then came dizziness, gloom, anger. Elders started fighting, the young ones wouldna stop wailing. But little Tamika—she was too weak even to cry. That's when we knew 'twas a death spell. Thank the gods ye were close by."

"About that," Mac said, "how did you know where I was?"

"Why, your fan blog, of course. MacTracker. Updates daily, it does. Sometimes twice in a day."

Mac blinked at him. "Your village is online?"

"Aye. We got a satellite uplink last spring, so we could follow your world tour. Yesterday's post said you'd gone to Kalen's after that last show in Inverness. Gave road directions and all."

Bloody hell. That certainly explained the fans camped on the beach. But how had the blogger known?

"I e-mailed Kalen, of course," Gilraen went on, "but I know the man never checks his account. So I sent a falcon as well."

"Smart of you." Shoving aside the acute annoyance his unrelenting fans engendered, Mac refocused on Gilraen. "How are the young ones doing now? Tamika, especially. Your healer is attending them, I assume."

"Aye, so she is. The older bairns are recovering, 'tis true. But the wee one . . ." The leaf hat crumpled, and a single tear tracked down Gilraen's leathery cheek. "She's verra bad off, Mac Lir. I fear . . . I fear she's dying."

Mac's gut clenched. "No. I'll take her to Annwyn at once. She'll heal there."

Gilraen shook his head. "We'd have brought her to the gates already, if 'twere possible. 'Tis not. Her heart flutters like hummingbird wings, and her breath is the faintest whisper. She canna be moved."

"Why didn't you bring her immediately? As soon as you realized what had happened?"

"By then 'twas already too late. The spell struck that quickly and caught us unaware. We thought this type of evil finished with, we did. The clan's seen nary a demon or ogre in over a year." The lines bracketing Gilraen's mouth deepened. "Ye assured us it was safe to leave the protection of the city, Mac Lir. We returned to the countryside with high hopes."

The reproach hit home with a painful strike that made Mac feel like the lowest of worms. He'd spent the last year roaming the world—performing, brooding, grabbing stale pleasures. If he'd been home in the Highlands, alert and looking after his responsibilities, he might have neutralized this threat before it occurred.

The spell-caster had left no trail, Gilraen had said. And yet . . . Mac frowned, concentrating. Faeries were highly sensitive to magic, but Mac's senses were infinitely sharper. He inhaled deeply. There was a whiff of spent death magic in the air. The barest trace.

It was a sour stench, like milk left out in the sun. Such rankness was only to be expected where death magic was concerned. But what took Mac by surprise was the accompanying undercurrent of . . . sweetness. Like lilacs in springtime. Like laughter. Like life magic.

Now, *that* was exceedingly odd.

For the first time in months, Mac's curiosity stirred.

"What it is, Mac Lir?" Gilraen's wings lifted and buzzed. "What do ye sense? Demons? Unseelies?"

"Neither. There's a residue of death magic, yes, but there are traces of a life magic spell as well."

"Death and life magic, cast together? It makes no sense!"

"You're right. It doesn't," Mac murmured. "But both kinds of magic were cast here. And I'm certain there was only one spell-caster."

"But who?"

"A human, most likely. Very few races other than humans can handle both death and life magic." But none, to his knowledge, did so simultaneously.

Gilraen gave his beleaguered hat another half twist. A stray leaf fluttered to the ground. "What human would harm a faerie child? Faeries are good luck for humanfolk."

True enough. Which only made the situation that much more bizarre. Mac scrubbed a hand over his face, momentarily startled by the scratch of whiskers. Six months earlier, after seven hundred years of not needing a razor, his beard had come in with a vengeance. He still couldn't get used to it. He felt like a bloody werewolf under the full moon.

The rage bubbling inside him was certainly worthy of a werewolf. What scum of a human would dare harm a faerie infant? He itched to start tracking the villain, but right now the sick child was his first priority. "Take me to Tamika, Gilraen. Gods willing, I'll be able to heal her."

Gilraen's wings buzzed. "I hope so, Mac Lir. I hope so."

CHAPTER THREE

Dear Goddess. She'd gone too far this time. Too, too far.

And now an infant lay dying.

Artemis Black gripped her moonstone pendant, her clenched fist pressing into the hollow at the base of her throat, and held herself very, very still. Bile burned in her throat; the Cadbury chocolate-and-hazelnut bar she'd gulped in lieu of breakfast churned in her stomach. The faerie clan's life essence, trapped inside the pendant, burned her palm.

Her senses were raw; she could feel every nuance of the energy bound to the stone. The panic and fear of the young ones, the grief and anger of the elders. But those sensations were new, and faint. Far more vivid was the life of the faeries before she'd cast her spell: fellowship and feasting, dances under the moon, the exhilaration of flight.

It was all hers now. Stolen in the most underhanded, shameful way.

Her grip on the stone tightened. Pain sliced through her palm. She did not let go.

She *deserved* to be hurt. Deserved contempt and loathing. What she was doing was wrong, but she'd never meant it to go this far. Normally, she excluded the young ones from her spells, but today she'd decided to cast her net a little wider. Time was running out, and she'd wanted this to be the last village.

It hadn't seemed so bad when she started. Faerie life essence was so strong—an embarrassment of magical riches, really. She took so little from each village, relatively speaking. Until now, the effects of her theft had been negligible. A headache here, a pain there. Vague anxiety, soon forgotten. With each magical heist, the moonstone glowed a little brighter—and what, really, had been the cost to the faeries? Nothing. The last six villages hadn't even known they'd been robbed.

But none of those villages had had an infant.

It hadn't even occurred to her to look for a baby in this one. Faerie births were extremely rare. The youngest children she'd encountered so far had appeared eight or nine years old; in reality, they were probably fifty human years or more. Never in a million years had she expected this village to have had so recent a birth.

She'd been wrong.

Gods. She'd made a ton of mistakes since she'd come to Scotland, but this one? This one was off the charts.

She could fix it.

But if she did that, she'd need to siphon an equal amount of life essence from another faerie village, very quickly. There was so little time. Just over a day. And faerie settlements were notoriously difficult to find. Clueless American that she was, Artemis hadn't realized just how difficult until she'd arrived in the Highlands four months ago and started hunting. Sure, she'd been able to map out Scotland's major ley lines easily enough, but what she hadn't realized was that faeries preferred to nestle their villages on tributaries of the main power channels, on magical paths as faint and delicate as spider's silk. Hard to see, easily broken. She'd had to execute some fiendishly complex spell-work in order to reveal them.

It had taken three weeks to locate this last village. She didn't have three weeks—or even three days—to find another. Tomorrow was Samhain. She had to be ready by sunset. If the next twenty-six precious hours passed and she wasn't ready . . .

Her chest squeezed so tightly, she couldn't breathe. The stone in her fingers burned. Stars danced before her eyes. She stared through the streaked windshield of her rented Vauxhall Corsa, fighting back tears of pure panic.

Would she do even this to attain her goal? Let a baby die? What had she become?

She pried open her fingers. The moonstone glittered, luminous with life. Artemis's hand began to shake. Breath hissed painfully from her lungs, like air from a tire pierced by a small, sharp blade.

Everything depended on the life essence contained in the moonstone. *Everything*. But how could she sacrifice an innocent life for her cause?

How could she not?

Mac abandoned the Norton by the side of the road and set off across the meadow, wading through waist-high grass. Gilraen flew grimly beside him, translucent wings buzzing, his pointed-toe leaf shoes grazing the tops of drooping seed-heads. His village wasn't visible to most eyes, though it was not far away at all. A human on a country ramble could easily come within inches of the faerie settlement and have no idea at all that it was there. Unless that human had very powerful magic and was looking very carefully.

The community was good-sized by faerie standards—fifty human paces across. Hidden behind multiple glamour spells, the cluster of huts nestled on the meadow's upper slope, round thatched roofs mingling in perfect harmony with the carpet of yellow-gold grasses laid out before them. Walls of twigs formed a perfect unity with the forest behind. A low peat wall ringed the village and marked the placement of the strongest perimeter wardings.

Mac, of course, had no trouble at all seeing past the glamour. He steeled himself for the village's tears and grief, but as he crossed the field in Gilraen's wake, he became aware of . . . laughter?

He blinked. *What the bloody hell—?*

A buzz of elation filled the air. The entire population, it seemed, circled and dove above the roofs like a flock of happily crazed hummingbirds. Spotting their approach, several of the faeries detached themselves from the group and darted toward them, calling greetings as they flew. Mac recognized the lead flyer as Gilraen's plump wife, Arianne. Her round, pretty face was flushed with joy. "Such fine news! Such blessing! Oh, Mac Lir, 'tis too wonderful. Thank ye, thank ye!"

He stared at Arianne, nonplussed. "Thank you for what?"

"Why, for healing our wee lass, of course. Tamika is well!"

A cheer arose from the circling faeries. Several executed graceful, midair tumbles in tribute. Mac smiled at them briefly, struggling to make sense of this startling turnabout.

A half dozen faeries swarmed about his head, the females tossing him kisses. Arianne dove at him, arms open, careening headfirst into his chest, nearly tipping him over. Mac grasped her shoulders, holding her at arm's length, wings buzzing.

"Arianne," Gilraen said, dazedly, buzzing in the air beside his wife. "Can it be true? Wee Tamika is truly well?"

"Aye, thanks to Mac Lir."

"I had nothing to do with it," Mac said.

Arianne beamed. "So modest. As a prince should be. I knew ye would put things right. I told Gilraen as much. 'Mac Lir will save the young one,' I told him. And ye have! Just as I said ye would."

"I intended to do just that, but I can't claim credit. I haven't had a chance to do anything. Tamika's recovery isn't my doing."

"Where is the lass?" Gilraen put in.

"There," his wife said, pointing behind her. "Laina," she called, "bring the wee one here!"

A dainty faerie swooped low, cradling a squirming, cooing bundle in her slender arms. The tiny child's cheeks were rosy, her eyes bright. Gossamer wings—too young yet for flight—fluttered with vibrant energy. She waved a small fist in Mac's face. He touched her cheek. She responded with a wide, toothless grin. Clearly, she was in perfect health.

Mac exchanged a perplexed glance with Gilraen, who looked just as puzzled. "When did she recover?" he asked Arianne.

"Why, just a few moments past, not long after Gilraen went out to meet ye. 'Tis why I thought—"

"It wasn't me," Mac repeated. "Perhaps your healers . . . ?"

Arianne shook her head. " 'Twasn't any spell of ours. We tried every spell we knew, and still the lass weakened."

"Are you sure Tamika was so close to death? Perhaps you mistook the severity of her illness."

"Nay." Arianne's voice trembled. "I wouldna mistake such a thing. Tamika's life essence was all but gone. If her recovery was nay your doing, Mac Lir, 'twas a gift from the gods. From your own father, perhaps."

"Perhaps," Mac murmured, but he knew it wasn't true. The Council of Celtic Gods had strict procedures governing miracles. First, a formal petition for Divine Intervention had to be made by the hopeful party. Once the plea arrived in Annwyn, debates were scheduled, which had to be attended by a two-thirds quorum of the Celtic Gods and Goddesses. Who did not have a long tradition of agreeing on anything. More often than not, arguments raged interminably, the opportunity for Intervention passing long before any Divine Action was recommended or denied. Even in those rare instances when debates ended quickly, Intervention was seldom approved. Such heavy-handed divine action tended to upset the balance of magic, to the detriment of both life- and death-magic creatures.

Whatever had happened here, it had not been an act of a god.

The faeries, however, didn't seem inclined to question their unexpected good fortune. Like human children, they lived in the moment. The entire clan had come out to the meadow to spin circles in the air. Arianne executed a graceful pirouette and held out her hand. "Dance with us, Mac Lir!"

"Perhaps in a bit," he told her distractedly. "I'll just have a look about first."

Arianne smiled and nodded. Gilraen flew to her side, and together they joined the main dancing circle.

Troubled, Mac approached the village's peat wall. He was as glad as anyone at Tamika's abrupt recovery, but it made no bloody sense. Death magic just did not suddenly reverse itself.

He turned to his right in front of the village gate and began a slow, thoughtful circuit of the settlement, casting his senses—both magical and mundane—in all directions. Searching for another trace of that odd, chiaroscuro magic.

Fifteen minutes later he was back where he'd started, none the wiser. The impromptu *ceilidh* was still going strong. Strains of music—bell flowers and reed flutes— drifted across the meadow. Straightening, Mac rubbed the back of his neck and stared into the forest beyond the village.

He'd found exactly nothing. Which meant he'd missed something. Which in turn meant either his magic was slipping—and he was certain it wasn't—or his quarry was very, very clever.

Squaring his shoulders and setting his jaw, he paced to the edge of the forest. Casting his senses once again, he reached deep into the earth and high into the air, touching the magical patterns that infused the forest with life. A subtle disturbance, so faint as to be almost nonexistent, scraped his awareness. Raising his hand, he spoke a single word. A spark of light glimmered between the slender white trunks of the birches.

Then it died, just as quickly.

His eyes narrowed. He stood stock-still, staring at the place where the light had been. It didn't reappear. He made his way to the site and, kneeling, extended a hand. He spoke the revealing spell a second time.

A spark glowed bloodred against the dark loam. Death magic. It took a moment for Mac to overcome his natural Sidhe revulsion and actually touch the remnant. His palm came down, depressing the spark on the springy earth. Magic pulsed faintly against his skin. He braced himself for a surge of wrenching nausea.

It didn't come.

Oh, there was a reaction, to be sure. A vibration that quickly spread through his whole body. A lick of darkness. Of death. But, surprisingly, it was not at all unpleasant.

On the contrary. It was . . . *arousing?*

He snatched his hand away, shocked to the very core of his immortal soul.

Mac was half Sidhe, half divine. Neither race tolerated death magic well. Touching the remains of that spell should have left him disgusted. Repulsed.

Not horny as all hell.

He was hard and throbbing—no sense in denying the blatantly obvious. He frowned down at his tingling palm, as if he could find an explanation etched among the lines there. Baffled, his senses still buzzing, his arousal slicing through his gut like a sweet, sharp knife, he touched the spot again.

This time he was ready for the raw jolt of carnal aware ness. Shoving the sensation to the back of his mind—bloody difficult, that, considering his current anticipatory state—

he probed deeper, seeking the essence of the spell. Death magic, yes. But—and here the rest of his body went as rigid as the part between his legs—he sensed life magic as well.

Death magic and life magic—joined in one spell? He tore his hand away, utterly and completely gobsmacked. Mind-boggled, in fact.

Most magical races practiced one form of magic or the other, life or death, by virtue of which force gave birth to their existence. Humans had a mix of magic in their souls and could choose to practice either type—or both. Chief among those who dealt in both life and death magic were sorcerers, demonwhores, and vampire addicts. But such spell-casters never mixed the two forces in one spell. What would be the point? When death and life magic were cast together, they canceled each other out.

They didn't merge into a force so strong it sent Mac's mind—and senses—reeling.

What, exactly, was he dealing with here? Closing his eyes, he delved deeper into the fading magical signature, snatching at evaporating whispers. Secrets the unknown spell-caster had tried very hard to erase.

Awareness of the villain's essence jolted through him. Human, as he'd expected. Or mostly, anyway. And . . .

Female.

A new wave of desire coursed hotly through his veins. A woman. A witch. With magic that was . . . unique, to say the least. The spell she'd cast—death and life magic inter-twined completely and seamlessly—should have been im-possible.

And yet here it was, calling to him. Drawing him in. Fascinating him.

Sending sweet, consuming fire straight to his cock.

Gods.

He tore his hand away. Cold beads of sweat chilled his brow. He sat back on his heels, heart pounding.

This unknown witch was stunningly dangerous. Completely undetected, she'd approached a hidden faerie village and cast a life/death spell that had devoured the clan's life essence like a starving wolf. She'd pushed an infant to the brink of death.

And then she'd allowed her spell to . . . what? Evaporate? As if it had never been?

Why?

Mac shoved himself to his feet and paced a series of ever-widening circles around the spark. It took a half hour to find a second clue, a good fifty feet from the first. But the third came easier, and the fourth easier still.

A trail.

One he would follow to its end.

"Mommy? Where are you? Please answer. I'm afraid. . . ."

Artemis's eyes snapped open on darkness, her heart pounding like a herd of elephants on stampede. "Zander? Oh gods, baby, is that you?"

Silence.

Tears burned her eyes. A dream? But Zander had sounded so real. So alive. So *frightened*. Artemis didn't count telepathy among her magical powers, but if she were to have a mind connection with anyone, surely it would be with her only child.

She held her breath, listening, but found only cold, dead silence. Zander was gone now. If he'd ever been in her mind at all.

She shoved herself into a sitting position, her spine screaming in protest of the unnatural position in which it had spent the last few hours. There wasn't much room in the back of the Corsa. And it was damn cold.

She drew her knees up to her chest and huddled under her tartan blanket. The thick wool, combined with her old army jacket, did a decent job of repelling the night air. But the chill in her heart? Nothing could reach that.

The starless night seemed to seep around the edges of

her tightly closed windows. She'd chosen this road for its remoteness. She hadn't wanted to sleep at all, but sheer exhaustion had given her no choice. Her magic was useless unless she maintained her body's equilibrium.

She checked her watch, glowing faintly yellow in the dark. It reminded her of a malevolent eye.

Five-thirteen. The sun would rise at seven twenty-five. With sunset exactly nine hours and five minutes beyond that. Eleven hours and seventeen minutes left until her rendezvous. Her fingers crept to her throat, encircling the moonstone. She'd slipped a charmed silk-platinum woven pouch over the pendant to shield the stolen life essence, but the knowledge of the energy at her fingertips calmed her. At least a little. Whatever it took, she had to resaturate the stone before sunset.

Fully alert, she flicked on the car's dome light. The map was where she'd left it, tucked safely into her pack. She extracted it carefully, unfolding it on her lap. At a casual glance, it appeared to be what it once had been—a simple road map of the Highlands, the kind given out at any tourist office. A brief, whispered spell—life magic alone, this time—turned the document into something more.

Lines of light seeped across the paper like a web spun by a drunken spider. At irregular intervals, green dots appeared. Faerie villages. The ones she'd stolen from, at least.

Beside each village she'd scribbled notes—dates, times, energy. The life essence calculations were fantastically high—and those were conservative estimates of what she'd skimmed. Highland faeries were exceedingly vibrant and long-lived, more so the farther north they lived. Some witches believed this was due to their proximity to the gates of Annwyn, which were said to be located somewhere on the north coast of Scotland east of Inverness. Artemis didn't know if that was true, but she did know there was nowhere else in the world where life essence was so concentrated. Which was why she'd come to Scotland. With just the right balance of life and death magic, she'd been able to siphon the faeries' excess energy into the moonstone.

In four months, she managed to lift energy from twenty-seven communities. Twenty-six, she amended. The last one didn't count. She had to find another settlement, and quickly. She bent her head, searching. She had four likely locations already marked. One was close by, less than a half hour's drive west. She'd head there first, and hope for the best.

She made a note of the roads leading to the village, then sighed and rubbed a kink in her shoulder. Releasing the spell on the map, she watched the bright lines fade, leaving only an ordinary-looking mesh of red and blue human roads. She'd have to burn the document once she had what she needed. Goddess only knew what havoc a vampire or demon could wreak with the information she'd gathered.

Folding the map, she slid it back into her pack and cut the dome light. The eastern sky was still dark, and weighted by the threat of rain. Emerging from the backseat, she confronted the cold, damp gloom that passed for an autumn morning in the Highlands. Drizzle spat tentatively from leaden clouds, as if trying to decide whether an honest downpour was worth the effort.

As she reached for the driver's door handle, a wave of light-headedness caused a momentary blankness in her vision. When had she last eaten? Yesterday morning, the chocolate bar. Since then, nothing.

Stupid. Stupid. Stupid. No sleep, no food—there was no faster way to lose her balance. She couldn't afford that. Balance came first, before everything. Balance was the key to her power. Abandon it, and she might as well slink home, defeated.

She climbed into the car and pulled out onto the road, her knuckles white on the steering wheel as she fought her

American instinct to hug the right shoulder. Even after four months in Scotland, she hadn't made peace with driving on the left side of the road. Depressing the accelerator firmly nonetheless, she sped through one completely dark village.

She slowed at the second town, a bit bigger, and showing signs of early morning life. Stomach cramping, she pulled up in front of a shabby grocery store, where the proprietor was just rolling up a metal security door. A garish plastic jack-o'-lantern hanging in the window grinned hideously.

She bought coffee, with lots of cream and sugar, along with a package of Walker's shortbread rounds and an apple. She ate several cookies and drank half the coffee before leaving the store. Juggling her purchases, she shoved open the grocery door and bent her head against a sudden spatter of rain as she hurried to her car. Which was probably why she didn't realize anyone was near until a man's voice startled her so badly she dropped her cup.

Dark liquid spread over the pavement; the man stepped from the shadows.

"So, love. On our way, are we? Where to next?"

Her pulse accelerated like a jackrabbit. He was tall, lean, and blond, and had materialized from the alley running alongside the grocery. She could just make out the shape of a low-ride motorcycle tucked into the shadows. Hands sunk deep in the pockets of his battered leather jacket, he strolled into the weak light cast by a dying streetlamp. His gaze raked her body.

Her first thought was that he was young. No more than twenty-two, she guessed, and even that was a stretch. Vamp? No, a vampire wouldn't risk being out this close to sunrise. Demon? No to that as well—she could smell a demon at a hundred paces. Did he have life magic, then? He was extremely appealing, in a raw, angular way. Carefully, she cast her senses in his direction.

No. No life magic, either.

The tension seeped from her shoulders. A mundane human. Well. She knew how to handle mundane men. Young ones, especially.

She met his gaze. His eyes narrowed.

He was startlingly fair. A day's worth of blond stubble on his jaw was so light it hardly qualified as a shadow. His longish hair brushed the raised collar of his jacket. Three silver hoop earrings glinted in his left earlobe. His shirt was a simple sea-green tee, worn over faded, ripped jeans. A blue tattoo, reminiscent of the sea, rode high on his left cheek. The mark cast a dangerous aura over his features.

He moved toward her, his long legs eating up the space between them with easy, unyielding grace. She didn't realize she was backing up until her butt hit the door of her car. He snorted; her cheeks heated. Casually insolent, he lounged, half sitting, half leaning, on the hood of her car.

He was very tall. He wasn't even standing erect and she had to tilt her head back to look him in the eye. An odd, tense knot twined in her stomach. A faint Scots burr brushed her ears.

"Where're we going, love?"

"Nowhere with you. Get off my car."

He straightened, but kept one hand planted on the sloping metal mullion where the edge of the driver's window met the front windshield. Only a foot or so separated them; she could see his breath turning to mist in the cold morning air.

His eyes were green, she noticed suddenly. Startlingly so.

A shiver chased up her spine. Unconsciously, she straightened her shoulders. His gaze flicked to her breasts, then back to her face.

And just like that, she knew how to get rid of him. She almost laughed at how easy it would be. But just to be nice, before she humiliated him, she'd give him one last chance to back off. "Look, buddy, I don't know who you are, and I don't want to. Get away from my car."

He didn't move an inch. "American," was all he said.

"Yes," she replied, annoyed. Her accent was obvious.

He shook his head, the slightest hint of a smile lifting one corner of his lips. "Why am I not surprised?"

"I'm sure I don't know."

She set her package of shortbread and her apple on the car roof and slipped her hand into the pocket of her army jacket. Blondie's eyes followed the movement, but he said nothing. Her fingers closed on her car key. She pressed the remote, unlocking the door.

"I wouldn't try leaving, love, if I were you."

"Then it's a good thing you're not me." Her hand shot to the door latch. She wrenched it open; he caught the upper edge and slammed it shut. His momentum brought him flush against her, his chest pressed against her spine, her stomach squeezed up against the car door. His breath puffed on her neck.

Okay, *now* she was pissed.

"Listen," she said through clenched teeth, her hand still on the door handle. "Get off me. Now. Before I get really, really angry. I don't want to hurt you."

"What? You know karate?"

A jerk with a sense of humor. How lovely. "You don't want to find out what I know," she muttered. "This is my last warning. Go. Away."

"Ah, a bird with spunk."

His hand—the one that wasn't holding the car door shut—slipped into her loose hair, cupping her head from behind. He leaned in close, bathing her ear with warm, moist breath as the cold drizzle rained over them both. "I like spunk, love."

Enough already.

She jabbed back with her elbow—hard. At the same time,

she grunted a word, punctuating her physical defense with a quick, highly effective spell.

Death magic.

It hit right on target.

"Oof—" Her attacker stumbled back a step.

She yanked the car door open, already struggling with a pinch of guilt, even though he *was* a jerk. The spell she'd hit him with was extremely disorienting. It wouldn't hurt him permanently, but she could've used a life-magic spell to get rid of him. If she hadn't been so mad.

She glanced his way as she slid into the driver's seat. A gasp escaped; her grip on the car door's inner handle froze. He wasn't where she expected him to be: sprawled on his ass on the sidewalk. His vivid green eyes were inches away, on the other side of the window, snapping with fury.

He took advantage of her split second of shock to insert his fingers between the car's window frame and roof. The next instant, the door tore from her grip. A strong hand imprisoned her wrist. With a distinct lack of care, he yanked her out of the car.

She cried out and tried to jerk away, but his grip was about as forgiving as a locked iron shackle. Stunned awareness of his superior strength pulsed up her arm. He twisted the limb behind her back, forcing her to her knees.

"Aaahhh—" Tears sprang to her eyes. Gods, but he was strong, and not just in the mundane sense of the word. She'd scored a direct hit with that death-magic spell; there was no way a normal human could have recovered so quickly.

He had magic. Powerful magic.

Was it light or dark? She didn't know. Couldn't feel it. He had not only magic, but an uncanny ability to shield it more completely than anyone or anything she'd ever encountered.

He held her down with a punishing grip. Gravel bit

through her fatigues and into her knees. Pain shot through her wrist. She stared up at him, heart stuttering, her mind frantically scrambling for a way out. A quick spell, one she could cast without speaking, before he realized what she was doing. It would have to be life magic; she had to speak her death spells out loud.

She grasped at the first defense that sprang to mind. A powerful distraction spell, particularly effective on young males. She shifted her weight, bracing for quick movement. The words rang in her mind.

The spell shot like white light between them. As she'd hoped, the charm hit before her captor could react, right in the groin. He staggered back a step, an astonished expression on his handsome face. His green eyes crossed.

His grip slackened.

She shot to her feet, circling her arm to twist her wrist out of his slackened grasp. At the same time, she kicked hard at his knee. It was the first defense move she'd learned in basic training, and it had never failed her.

Until now.

He just managed not to let her break free. A slight shake of his head, and his eyes refocused, glittering and more angry than before.

His gaze swept over her with proprietary boldness. Shocked to the core, she felt her body respond. Her skin tingled, as if he'd ripped off her clothes and run his hands over her naked body. The sensation spread like lightning, zinging sparkling darts of desire at her breasts, her stomach, between her thighs. A wave of pure, raw lust blanked her mind.

She blinked up at him, suddenly not understanding—or caring—who she was, *where* she was. Or what she'd been thinking about, just seconds earlier.

He jerked her to her feet. Her mind numb, she went without protest. Was she supposed to fight him? Or was this all just a game? She couldn't remember.

He backed her against the car door. Pinning her lower body in place with his hips, he spread her arms wide. Her jacket hung open; his gaze took in the swell of her chest. The distinct ridge of his arousal pressed hard and hot against her belly.

A shudder passed through her. Suddenly, all she could think of was how empty she felt. And how good it would feel if he would only fill her.

Gods, this wasn't right.

She blinked up at him, through the haze of stars in her vision. "What . . . what did you do to me?"

He presented her with a grim smile. "Turnabout's fair play. Or so I've heard."

"I . . ." What? She hardly knew what she meant to say. It was so hard to think straight. "I . . . I don't understand."

"Don't recognize your own spell, my little witch? I find that hard to believe."

"My own—?" Understanding pierced the fog in her brain. A flood of horror followed. "You reflected the lust charm back at me?"

"First marks for you, love. You know, you really should be more careful about the magic you send out into the world." He smiled thinly. "Karma and all that."

He flexed his hips again. She closed her eyes and fought the urge to squirm. She wanted to beg for his hand . . . *there*. Despite his sarcasm, his reprimand rang true. Gods, how humiliating to be caught by her own spell—and this one in particular. Her entire body hummed with need.

"I . . . I was only using it as a distraction. To get away. I wasn't going to"—she swallowed—"follow up on it. Let me go. Please."

"Is that what you really want?" His hips rotated crudely, his erection stroking her intimately through his jeans and her fatigues. Arms spread and pinned, brain fogged, uncertain of her adversary's power, Artemis cringed with horrible vulnerability. Unsettling green eyes watched her closely.

The undisguised lust she saw reflected there told her he hadn't been completely unaffected by her ill-chosen spell.

A wave of shuddering lust passed though her. Her captor's breathing was just as harsh as her own. Gods. If he shoved her into the backseat of the car right now, she doubted she'd have the strength—or the desire—to stop him from taking what he wanted.

Her gaze shot to the door of the shabby grocery. The plastic pumpkin in the window leered back at her. If only someone would—

"No help from that sodding American jack-o'-lantern, love. I've got a pretty strong glamour on us at the moment. We're all but invisible."

Of course. If she looked at just the right angle, she could see the energy of his concealing spell, rising like heat on a searing summer day. Her throat closed.

"What are you going to do to me?" she croaked.

He frowned down at her. "I haven't decided. Get in the car. And no sudden moves."

Her relief when he released her was so intense she didn't even consider disobeying. She'd felt enough of his strength—both magical and mundane—to know she wouldn't get far. He opened the car door and she climbed in behind the steering wheel.

He got in after her. "Keep going, love. Other side."

She scrambled over the shift to the passenger seat. A desperate lunge for the opposite door handle proved fruitless—the lever wouldn't budge, and the button that worked the lock didn't move. He'd jammed it, magically.

Of course he had.

Her captor made a slight throat-clearing sound. She looked back to find him watching her.

"Running's not an option. You've got some explaining to do."

Explaining? Oh gods. This couldn't be happening. She'd

assumed this was a random attack. But now she wondered. Could he know? She realized her fingers were creeping toward the moonstone and she stilled her hand abruptly. Casually, she let it drop to her lap.

He hadn't seemed to notice. Good. That was good. With any luck, she could keep his attention away from the stone until she got rid of him.

If she could get rid of him.

She swallowed her panic. "Who are you?"

"Me? Just a friend of the faerie village you attacked. That wasn't too wise, you know."

"I don't know what you're talking about."

"My dear little witch. Lying's even less of an option than running."

"I'm not—" The expression on his face cut her dead. "All right," she amended hastily. "I do know what you're referring to. But it wasn't an attack. It was a mistake, that's all. Once I realized what had happened, I fixed it. And I won't be going back, so there's no harm done. So you can just let me go and—"

"Sorry, love. No can do."

"Stop calling me that. I am not your love."

"No? Well, then. You should watch where you toss your lust spells."

His smile was wolfish, and it didn't reach his eyes. Artemis felt herself responding to it, anyway. The effects of the rebounded spell were still raging at full force. When his gaze drifted down her body, igniting a slow trail of fire, she nearly groaned out loud.

She wanted to touch him. Taste him. Instead, she crossed her arms over her breasts like a shield. Lust spells were self-limiting; the sensations racketing through her body would fade in a few minutes. She could hang on to her sanity until then. She hoped.

But could she escape him? She wasn't sure what kind of

magic would be most effective against him. The shield he had on his power made it impossible to figure him out. How could she fight him if she didn't even know what he was?

"Look." She hoped like hell her desperation didn't show. "Just leave me alone. I'm outta here, anyway. You'll never see me again."

"And what a shame that would be. We'd never have a chance to discuss that exceedingly odd spell you cast on the faeries."

Her jaw dropped. "You felt that? But how . . . I thought I'd . . ." She trailed off, biting her lip.

"Thought you'd covered your tracks, did you? Not quite well enough, love."

"No one could have tracked that spell. No one." Except that, apparently, he had. "Who are you?"

"Who are you?" he countered. He reached out and plucked the pack from her lap. The clasp opened so easily she was sure he'd used magic to unfasten it.

"Hey! Give that back!"

He blocked her grab neatly with his left elbow and tugged open the zipper. She watched, stomach churning, as he tossed her driver's license and passport into the backseat without so much as a glance.

"I thought you wanted to know who I am," she said.

"I wasn't talking about your name, love."

"I am not," she muttered, "your love."

He pulled out her map. She held her breath as he gave it a fleeting look and started to toss it after the passport. Then, to her horror, he brought it back into his line of vision, frowning slightly.

He sent her a sidelong look. "What's this, then?"

"What does it look like? A map. I got it at the airport in Glasgow."

"No doubt you did, love," he said, shaking out the folds and setting it on the steering wheel.

"Lost?" Artemis taunted.

"No more than you," he replied, passing his palm over the map.

Artemis's head fell back against the headrest as the tell-tale glowing lines spread across the page. Goddess. How the hell had he guessed? She was screwed now. Big time.

His jaw hardened. He didn't speak as his sharp gaze took in the ley lines and the marks denoting the faerie villages she'd skimmed. The notes scrawled beside them tracked her progress from Glasgow into the Highlands. Names, dates, village population estimates. The numbers denoting the value of the life energy she'd stolen were particularly damning. She'd used demon notation, since demons were the only beings who objectively quantified such resources.

Damn her for her obsessive need for clarity and organization. Stupid, stupid, stupid. She should never have kept notes.

His ominous silence dragged on as he read each and every word and number she'd written. She waited, barely breathing, fighting an unholy urge to squirm. Instead, she concentrated on identifying a spell likely to best him. Since he was so angry on behalf of the faeries, it was likely he was a life-magic creature. Was it best to fight him with a light or dark spell? Should she cast something here in the car? Or wait until they were out in the open?

She was so intent on her plotting that when he did speak, she jumped.

"Explain yourself."

She met his gaze. "No."

His jaw went rigid, his eyes darkening to forest green. Anger pulsed in the space between them, hot enough to burn.

Artemis half turned, pressing her back against the passenger door, her body poised for defense. *Breathe*, she told herself. *Breathe*.

In. Out. In. Out. Balance. That was the key. It always was.

Too bad this stranger had tipped her world on end.

Slowly, carefully, he refolded the road map. Then, with a single, brutal motion, he ripped it in half.

She jumped.

Watching her closely, he stacked the halves and ripped them again. A flick of his finger ignited the paper. Artemis gasped. The map burned to dust in his palm and he didn't even flinch. Four months of painstaking magical detective work, gone in a heartbeat.

She went deathly still. She wanted to cry. She wanted to smash her fist into his face. From the look in his eyes, he knew it. She bit back the curse on her lips.

"So. You've been stealing life essence since the summer solstice. From no less than twenty-seven faerie villages."

"Twenty-six," she muttered. "The last one doesn't count."

"Demonwhore?"

She bristled, even though it was a fair assumption. Demons thrived on life essence. Their human slaves often went to great lengths to secure it for their masters.

"No," she said.

He regarded her thoughtfully, then nodded once. "I think I believe that. Your aura doesn't have that sick gray tinge. Not a whore, then. But a puzzle, even for me. You're not, I think, entirely human."

"I don't know what that has to do with—"

She broke off, startled, when his fingertips brushed her cheek.

He was still angry, but his touch was incredibly gentle. The contrast left her trembling. He traced her cheekbone, her jaw. The line of her neck. The sensation sent a tingle through her senses, faintly sexual in nature, though her misfired spell had faded almost entirely by now. She'd never felt anything like it before, but after a moment or two she understood what he was doing.

He was reading her magic.

She shrank back against the passenger door, but there was

no place to go. He moved with her, his big hand cupping her head, cushioning the smack of her head against the window glass. His thumb brushed over her lips, warm and firm.

She stared up at him. He was far too close, and what he was doing . . . she could feel him, *inside*, brushing the edges of her psyche. It was far, far too intimate a touch.

"Stop it." She hated how her voice trembled.

"Hush, love."

His green eyes gazed at her. Or more accurately, gazed through her. Seeing, she was sure, things she did not want to reveal. She tried to make herself very small. He prevented it, with nothing more than a brush of his fingers on her cheek. She felt as though she were caught in some bizarre dream.

She closed her eyes and concentrated on drawing her next breath. Oxygen didn't come easily. *Gods.* What was he doing to her?

Finally, *finally*, he drew back, breaking the contact. By that time, she'd slid so far down the seat she was practically lying down. He slammed the driver's door shut, closing her in with him. Hastily, she shoved herself upright, gathering her shredded dignity as best she could.

He regarded her with open curiosity. "You're mostly human. But there's quite a bit more. A bit of naiad, perhaps? Or something similar?"

There was no point in lying. "My great-grandmother on my mother's side was a *mami wata*. An African water spirit."

"Ah. Water magic. Explains the ease with which you cast that lust spell."

"Yes."

"And do you have a dryad somewhere in your family tree?"

"Sort of. My great-grandmother on my father's side was a Norse giantess from the Iron Wood."

"Earth magic. And . . . sprite for air magic?"

She sighed. "No. My air magic is much stronger than a sprite's. There's a Native American shaman somewhere on my mother's side. At least four generations back, as far as I know. A shape-shifter who received his magic from a thunderbird spirit."

"Do you have fire as well?"

"Yes. One of my ancestors from India was an atharvavedic priest."

His brows arched. "Quite the cultural mix you are. Born in America, then?"

"Yes. Hawaii. But I've lived all over the world. Army brat," she added at his questioning gaze.

His gaze flicked to her jacket. "Followed your parents into the service, did you?"

"Yes," she grumbled. "Psychic ops. But I'm a civilian now."

His expression was bemused. "I'll bet they were sorry to lose you. Witches connected to all four elements are exceedingly rare."

"I know that."

"And that's just your life-magic heritage. There's more, isn't there?"

She bit her lip. She knew what was coming.

His voice took on a hard edge. "You're part demon."

She forced a terse nod.

"How far back?"

"My father's grandmother was a demonwhore. His mother was the product of that union. And I might as well tell you, there's another demon—a Japanese *oni*—way back on my mother's side. And I have lesser death-magic ancestors, too. A couple of Norwegian trolls, on my father's side."

He was silent for a moment; then, "Interesting family you have, love."

A hysterical laugh escaped. "That's one way of putting it."

"And yet—" His lips crooked in a ghost of a real smile. "You've got the look of an angel."

She raised her brows. "Angels are blond."

"A dark angel," he clarified.

His voice sounded strange. She couldn't interpret the new expression that had crept into his eyes. He cupped her face again, one hand on either side this time.

And then, before she quite realized what he intended, he leaned forward and kissed her.

CHAPTER FOUR

She tasted like honey. Smelled like that wild, perfect moment that rode before a breaking storm. Felt like that breathless instant at the start of a show, when he took the stage before thousands of cheering fans. Mac ravaged the witch's lips, taking full advantage of her startled gasp. His tongue quested inside the slick mystery of her mouth as he maneuvered around the stick shift and pressed her body into the leased car's stained upholstery. He fought the urge to rip her ragged army jacket to shreds.

Gods in Annwyn. What was he doing?

He wasn't quite sure. All he knew was that he didn't plan on stopping any time soon. There was an exquisite buzzing in his head, and a blessed heaviness in his groin. He hadn't felt this turned on—this *alive*—in a very long while.

He plundered her mouth, invading, demanding. Sucked on her lower lip. His senses drank in her magic; it hummed through his veins like the most potent whisky. Heady and rich, she was an angel with a devil's bite. Perfect balance. Life magic and death magic bound together so seamlessly it was impossible to tell where one left off and the other began. It was like nothing he'd ever known, nothing he'd ever imagined was possible.

A perfect storm of power. The woman he'd told Christine couldn't possibly exist. One who was strong enough to intrigue and challenge. It was just too bloody bad she was using her magic for nefarious purposes. The thought angered him. His kiss turned brutal.

He expected her to push him away. She didn't. But neither did she encourage him. Her passivity stroked his anger, and his lust. He speared his fingers through her short, soft hair. It puffed against his jaw like a dark, silky kiss. He clenched his fingers in the curls.

She reacted with a small sound deep in her throat. He lifted his head and looked into her eyes. They were chocolate dark and hazed with desire. Her gaze flicked to his mouth. Her fingers curled on the collar of his jacket and held on tightly. She wanted him, and not just because of the ricocheted spell, which had all but faded.

An intense rush of satisfaction heated his groin. Mac had always enjoyed sex—he was half Sidhe, after all. But this? This coiling dark desire was something new. Something fueled, he was sure, by the dark stain on his soul.

Anger and lust—and the devil only knew what else—took hold. His hand snaked between the open edges of her jacket. Her shirt was some flimsy, soft material; he could feel the outline of her bra—no padding—beneath it. He stroked the upper edge. Lace? Incongruous, that. She didn't seem like the lacy type. He smiled against her mouth and wondered what color. He liked lace.

He brushed a thumb lightly across her nipple. She gasped and cursed in one breath. It sounded like a prayer. He explored more of her. She wore a heavy pendant that nestled in the valley between her breasts. It was warm from contact with her skin.

He frowned. Too warm. Almost hot. Almost as if—

She made a small, wild sound, like a cornered animal. He stilled. Had he frightened her that badly? Misread her body's cues? He started to pull back. He wasn't a completely mindless brute. Then a small, hot hand slid over his groin, cupping him through his jeans, and every last one of his brain cells shorted out.

Frightened? Not by half. Working so swiftly his head spun, the witch slipped open his belt and popped the single button of his jeans. She tugged at the zipper. It slid, then caught. She made a sound of frustration, and—

A squeal of brakes, somewhere behind the car. Then . . .

"Ooooooh!"

"I *see* him!"

"Where?"

"In that *car*! Ohmygod! He's *snogging* that—"

Mac wrenched his head around. His glamour spell was in shambles—he'd lost hold of it a while back, amid a crashing wave of lust. At just the wrong time, apparently. His public had caught up with him.

Ballocks. Why couldn't the paparazzi harass Prince Harry for a change?

A half dozen or more shameless hussies tumbled pell-mell out of a beat-up van. The lead bitch launched herself across the car park. Her pack streamed after her. Behind them came the tall photographer, wheeling a motorcycle from the alley.

Mac's Norton.

Bloody hell! He nearly launched himself at the thieving blighter. Until he realized that if he opened the car door, his adoring fangirls would have him naked in under five seconds.

His fingertips itched. A few well-placed bolts of elfshot would be more than satisfying, but he couldn't risk hurting anyone. Besides being extremely churlish, injuring fans surely was not a good career move.

He turned on the witch. "Key."

She gaped at him. "What?"

"Oh, sod it." He pointed a finger at the ignition and muttered a word. The engine roared to life, hazard lights flashing, windshield wipers clacking furiously.

The fans were almost on the car. Mac spoke a quick

repulse spell. There was a dull thud as a skinny lass hit the driver's-side door and rebounded into the arms of her friends. The lot bowled over like ninepins.

He jerked the shift and slammed his foot on the accelerator. The Vauxhall lurched crazily. Damn manual transmission. He maneuvered the shuddering engine past second and third gears and careened into the roadway, where the cheap hunk of British metal at last gained some confidence. They flashed past his Norton. One of the fangirls was in the saddle now. The photog rode gunner, his camera flashing like a strobe.

Mac spared his baby an anguished glance. The Norton was doomed.

The witch braced one hand on the dashboard and half turned to watch out the back window.

"Two girls down. They actually threw themselves head-first onto the pavement trying to grab our bumper."

"Crazy besoms."

"The others . . ." She rose to her knees to get a better look. "They've run for a white minivan . . . They're behind us. The motorcycle—that's yours, right? It's behind them." She glanced at him. "They're gaining."

"Bugger it. Couldn't you lease something better than this piece of trash?" Mac stomped on the accelerator. Out of the corner of his eye, he saw the witch's fingers twitch.

"Don't you dare help them," he told her.

For a second, he thought she'd defy him. Then she sighed, faced front, and flopped down in her seat.

"Wise choice, love." Mac tossed a confusion spell over his shoulder. Brakes squealed, followed by a horrid metal-grinding sound.

"Oh my God!" The witch popped up and twisted back around. "What did you do?"

"Took out a tire on the people mover. The lasses should be a while changing it."

"The motorcycle's still coming."

Damn. This was it. He muttered another spell, before he could change his mind.

The witch gasped. "Flames are shooting out of the tailpipe!"

Mac couldn't bear to look.

"They're pulling over . . . jumping clear." She let out a rush of breath. "Gods. The cycle just crashed into a tree. It . . . gods! It just exploded."

Mac took the next curve far harder than necessary.

The witch grabbed the strap above the door for leverage as she turned to face front and—damn her—started to laugh. "Old girlfriends?"

"Nope. Don't know them."

"Then why are they chasing you?"

He looked at her with some surprise. "You don't know?"

"Should I?"

Bemusement settled in. He executed right and left turns, then picked up the main road. "You're bamming me. You have to know who I am."

"Why? Are you famous or something?"

Or something. He shot her a look. "You really don't know?"

She shook her head. "Don't think so."

He shrugged. "No reason not to tell you, love, other than for the rare pleasure of anonymity. You'll figure it out soon enough. I'm Manannán mac Lir."

He waited for a reaction.

Then waited some more.

He glanced over at her, irritated. Her brow was furrowed. Clearly, she was trying to place the name. As if his face hadn't been plastered all over the telly and the Internet for more than a year. As if he didn't currently have three hits on the international top ten chart.

He felt insanely insulted.

Finally—*finally*—her eyes widened. "Manannán mac Lir,

the Celtic demigod? The one who helped the Immortals save the world last year? And . . . aren't you some kind of musician, too? Celtic techno stuff? Guitar, bagpipes, and synthesizers?"

Ah, so she wasn't completely deaf, dumb, and blind. His ruffled pride settled a bit. Though, perversely, another part of him wished she'd said she had no idea who he was at all.

"The same."

She eyed him. "But . . . you're Sidhe, right? How come your ears aren't pointed?"

"I'm only half Sidhe," he said irritably. "Didn't get the pointy-ear gene."

"Oh. Manannán, huh? That's a mouthful."

"Call me Mac. And you are?"

She looked out the side window. "Me? Nobody, really."

"Does nobody have a name?"

She hesitated, then sighed. "Artemis. Artemis Alexandria Black."

It didn't sound like a lie. "So, Artemis Alexandria Black. Tell me. Do you often cast lust spells at strange men?"

"Only the threatening ones."

"Could be dangerous, that."

"Not really. It's a quick and easy spell, and very effective in temporarily disabling men. Young ones especially. Once the spell hits, about ninety percent of a guy's blood rushes to his . . . well, you know where. His brain turns to mush for a few seconds, which gives me plenty of time to craft a more complicated defense." She made a sound of disgust. "At least, that's how it's supposed to work."

"You made your mistake in thinking I was young," Mac said. "In reality, I'm an old geezer of seven hundred."

"You can't hold that against me. You look like a college kid, and you hide your magic like nothing I've ever seen. I assumed you were a mundane."

"You should never assume, love."

"Obviously." She grimaced. "Before today, I'd've sworn there wasn't a man alive quick enough to send that spell back at me. Of course," she added, almost to herself, "this is the first time I've met up with a demigod."

"Something to write about in your diary, then."

"I don't keep a diary."

He didn't answer. She didn't move. The silence quickly became awkward, as if they'd both suddenly remembered they weren't friends. He could almost feel her apprehension, winding into a tight, anxious coil. She had good reason to be afraid of him. Artemis Alexandria Black was surprising, yes, and entrancing besides, but all that was not nearly enough to distract him from the issue of the life essence she'd stolen. From twenty-seven faerie settlements. Even if she had released what she'd taken from Gilraen's village, what had she done with the energy she'd gathered from the other twenty-six?

That was the question, wasn't it?

He settled back in his seat, watching her from the corner of his eye as he drove with one hand draped on the wheel and the other resting lightly on the shift. He'd been so intent on her magic that he hadn't noticed much else about her. Now he saw that she wasn't what anyone would call beautiful. In fact, she was rather plain. But that didn't mean she was hard to look at. Not at all. Her complicated ancestry had given her dark, almond-shaped eyes, high cheekbones, and olive skin. Her midnight-dark hair sported gold highlights he didn't think came from a bottle. Though the lust spell was completely spent, his gaze lingered on her full lips and slender neck. The memory of her breasts in his hands—not too large, not too small—would not leave his mind.

And her magic . . . it tingled like champagne blended with some dark, forbidden spice. He wanted to explore her power again, and explore her body at the same time.

He was half hard, his belt open and zipper still half un-
done, right as she'd left him. Thoughts of engaging her in
a horizontal Highland fling were seriously interfering
with his contemplation of her crime.

Reluctantly, he pulled his mind out of the gutter. The
witch's crime couldn't be ignored. Mac was Guardian of
Celtic Magical Creatures, and Artemis had admitted stealing life essence from beings under his protection. The
Sidhe Council had rules about such behavior.

Rules . . . and penalties.

Stealing life essence was difficult and dangerous—it involved death magic, which the Sidhe abhorred. But the re-
wards, for those human witches and sorcerers who could
manage it, were huge. Demons were the primary users.
Often, they forced their whores to gather the energy, but
they also paid top dollar to independent black market
dealers. Most of the contraband bought and sold came
from humans, however. Not faeries. Though faeries had
much higher concentrations of life essence, they were
much harder to steal from than humans. Faeries could
scent death magic a mile away.

But Gilraen's village hadn't sensed Artemis at all.

Mac sighed. He didn't fancy the prospect of dragging
his captive before the Sidhe Council, which just happened
to be headed by Mac's own lovely mother. But what else
could he do? Hop out of her car at the next village and
forget he'd ever found her? Shirk his duty, leaving more
faerie villages vulnerable? He'd destroyed her map, but no
doubt she had other resources.

He could think of only one other option. Admittedly, it
was a temporary measure, but it was strangely tempting.
He could keep her for a while. Keep her out of trouble
and keep her focused on him.

He grinned.

"What's so funny? And where are you taking me?"

He negotiated a tight curve, narrowly missing the front bumper of an oncoming lorry. She gasped and braced her hand on the dash.

"That depends," he said, guiding the Vauxhall out of the curve with one hand. "Where are you headed, Artemis Alexandria Black?"

"Nowhere in particular."

"Then you're in luck. That's where I'm going as well." He glanced at the fuel gauge. "We'll need petrol soon, love."

"I know," she muttered.

He glanced over his shoulder. A tangled blanket and a pillow lay on the backseat. There was a book there as well. Dante's *Inferno*, classics edition. Hmmm. A little light bedtime reading? "You've been sleeping in your car."

"Yes."

"Why?"

"Saves money."

"Cold in the winter, though."

A pause. Then, "Come winter, I won't be here."

They approached a village. He stopped to allow two old crones to inch along a pedestrian crossing, then took a left into a petrol station. He opened his door, turned in his seat, and met her gaze. "Do us a favor, love. Don't try to run. You won't get far, anyway."

She nodded. He got out of the car, pausing to do up his zipper and belt. She sat very still, staring straight ahead.

He didn't trust her. He cleared his throat. When she looked up, he caught her gaze and pointedly cast a keeping spell about the car, tight enough to stop even a gnat from entering or exiting. Her lips thinned. He raised his brows. She huffed, crossed her arms, and gave him her back.

He chuckled.

He filled the tank, checked the oil, and paid. All the while, he kept one eye on her, not quite trusting her not to do something foolish. Returning to the car, he dropped the keeping spell and slid into the driver's seat. He'd bought a bag of crisps at the station's vending machine. He tossed it in Artemis's direction.

She caught it with one hand. After a brief hesitation, she lifted it to her lips and tore off a corner of the bag with even white teeth.

She might as well have dragged those teeth over the stiffest part of his body. Lust kicked into his groin. All that male blood she'd been talking about earlier drained to parts south, leaving him light-headed.

And she hadn't even used any magic.

Unsettled by his appalling lack of control, he snatched her pack off the floor of the car and started rummaging through it, more carefully this time. She stiffened, but didn't try to stop him. Most likely because she knew she was powerless to prevent him from doing whatever he wanted.

She had the usual detritus. Banknotes, credit card, loose change. Chewing gum, a package of nuts, a few petrol receipts, the car key he'd been looking for earlier. A photo wallet.

Curious, he flipped the last open and found a dozen or more pictures, all of what he thought was the same child. First as a baby, then as a toddler, and finally as a lad of about six, a wide grin showing the gap where his front teeth used to be. In some of the photos, the child was alone; in others, he had his skinny arms wrapped around Artemis. The lad shared her dark hair and eyes, and the stubborn tilt of her chin.

Artemis made a soft sound, something akin to a whimper. He looked up to find her eyes filled with such pain that his instinct was to gather her into his arms.

He didn't. "Your son?"

She nodded.

"Is he . . . gone, then, love?"

"No! No, not that. He's just . . . sick." She snatched the photo wallet from his fingers and held it tight against her body.

He frowned. "The life essence you stole—you didn't intend it for him, did you?"

"Yes," she said too quickly. "Yes, that's it."

His eyes narrowed. "It won't work, you know. Healing requires pure life magic. Stolen life essence is tainted by the death spell used to harvest it. But then, a witch of your obvious talent and training would know that." He paused. "Which means you must have another reason for gathering energy."

"No. That's not true."

If he hadn't been watching her so closely, he would have missed her flash of panic. It was there and gone that quickly.

His jaw hardened. "Don't lie to me, Artemis."

"All right. I won't. But what does it matter about the life essence? I gave it back."

"To Gilraen's village, yes. But what about the others?"

Her eyes flashed guilty. "But . . . they had so much! They didn't even miss the little I took."

"That's not the point. What you did is highly illegal. What happened to the magic? Did you sell it?"

"Y-yes."

"To a demon?"

"To . . . to humans. Demonwhores."

"Who turned around and presented it to their masters."

"No. The whores I sold to used the life essence for themselves. To . . . to counteract the effects of their masters' death magic. You know what that does to demonwhores."

Her casual words hit him like a fist in the gut. Yes, he knew what a demon's death magic did to a whore. Leanna had tried her best to shield herself from it, using her muse magic to collect the life essence of her lovers as leverage against her master's touch. But in the end, his sister had fallen completely.

"If your demonwhore friends are so bloody worried about the toxic effects of death magic," Mac said evenly, "they shouldn't have gotten tangled up with demons in the first place."

"Most people don't think things through before summoning a demon. They think they can handle the situation."

She was right about that—Leanna certainly had believed she had the upper hand on the demon she'd summoned. And so, apparently, did Artemis. Because Mac didn't believe the witch's story for an instant. She had to have a demon contact.

"You know, love, somehow it occurs to me that if you were really brokering faerie life essence on the black market, you'd be living a bit less rough than you are at the moment."

"Look." Artemis made a good effort, but she couldn't quite hide the desperate note that had snuck into her tone. "If I give my word I won't steal any more life essence, will you please let me go?"

He cocked his head. "Perhaps I would. If I didn't know you were lying through your teeth."

She sucked in a breath, looking a bit green around the gills, but she didn't deny the charge. With a grim nod, he fished the car key out of her pack and inserted it in the ignition. Starting the engine, he drove out of the petrol station.

He'd just pulled onto the road when Artemis turned and gripped his arm. Her hand shook. He swerved to the curb, braking sharply.

"You have to let me go. I swear I won't bother another faerie village, or any other Celtic creatures. After tomorrow, I won't even be in the U.K. Please. How can I convince you?"

His anger dimmed a bit. Her heart was in her eyes; she was no longer trying to hide her desperation.

"What's wrong, love? What kind of trouble are you in?

Is it your son? Do you need life magic to heal him? Where is he? I could help him myself, perhaps."

She drew back sharply, her eyelashes sweeping downward. "I . . . it's kind of you to offer, but I'm afraid you can't help. Please. I know I can't fight you. Just let me go."

He was tempted, but knew he couldn't do it. Her fervent promises were lies. Artemis might not be whore to a demon, but he'd bet his immortal soul she was doing business with one. For whatever reason, she was desperate for life essence. If he let her go, she'd steal more—from faeries, or worse, from humans. If she overstepped her limits again, someone would end up dead.

"Tell me the truth," he said quietly.

She didn't quite meet his gaze. "I have. As much as I can, anyway."

"If you won't talk, I can't help. And as for letting you go—forget it."

"What . . . what do you mean?"

"I mean I'm not letting you out of my sight. Not until I figure out what to do with you."

CHAPTER FIVE

Artemis wanted to scream. It was only by a supreme act of will that she managed not to. *How* had she gotten herself into such a colossal mess? Found out and kidnapped by an elfin prince of Annwyn. An immortal, no less.

Stupid, stupid, stupid.

For one vulnerable moment, she'd actually considered confiding in Mac. His beautiful eyes had conveyed such compassion. When was the last time a man had looked at her that way? Never, that's when. What Artemis usually saw when she looked into a man's eyes was something much less complicated.

Fear. Of who she was. Of what she was capable of.

Mac didn't fear her at all. He was far too strong for that, both physically and magically. He batted away her spells as if they were gnats. On one level that made her afraid, but on another, it made her feel . . . hope. She longed to transfer the weight of her burden onto his broad shoulders.

Except that she couldn't. She was her own hope. Mac might be vastly powerful, but he was a creature of life magic. He couldn't cast death magic. And where Artemis was headed, death magic was king. Life magic was useless. Mac would be about as much help as a litter of newborn kittens.

She sidled him a glance. He was driving too fast, with only the fingertips of his right hand touching the steering wheel. His right elbow rested comfortably on the open driver's-side window. This, on a road so narrow that a person standing in the middle could have stretched out his arms and touched the stone fences on either side. Gods help them if they met a car coming the other way. Artemis anchored a hand on the dash and a foot on the floor and prayed they wouldn't.

The road curved sharply. Her stomach lurched, but the sensation wasn't completely due to Mac's sudden veer to the left. Her wristwatch had taken on the psychic proportions of a ticking bomb. She shut her eyes so she wouldn't have to look at it. Time was flying by at lightning speed, even faster than Mac's driving. Less than eight hours now until sunset.

Brakes squealed, yanking her eyes open. A black car barreling toward them barely managed to career into a narrow lay-by in time to avoid a headlong crash. A rude gesture and an angry blast of horn chased Mac as he sped by.

Heart slamming against her ribs, Artemis sucked in a breath and tried like hell to find her balance. Unfortunately, Mac had flung it to the North wind. She had to get a grip; without her magical balance, she might well give up. And she would never do that. She'd give her last breath, and beyond, to get to Zander. Her little boy. The only person in the world she truly loved. And who truly loved her back. Desperate tears stung her eyes.

A lump in her throat burned. But giving in to hysterics, tempting as that might be, was not going to get her anywhere. If her stint in the military had taught her anything, it was to face facts. She was, for all intents and purposes, being held prisoner by a demigod. All the jokes and banter aside, Mac was one pissed demigod. And rightly so. What Artemis had done was unconscionable. But she hadn't had any other options, other than giving up on Zander altogether. And that she would not do as long as there was breath in her body.

She fell back on her training. Analysis, then action. All right, then. To-do list. Item one: escape Mac. Status: doable, if the right circumstances arose. If he got distracted, or eased up on his vigilance. Either was likely to occur eventually. She'd just have to be ready to jump when it happened.

Item two: find and raid one last faerie village. Status: tricky. Once she escaped Mac, he was sure to put every faerie settlement in the Highlands on alert. She'd never get what she needed then.

It was possible, of course, to steal life essence from other sources. Humans, for example. Mac, being Sidhe, probably wouldn't care so much about that. But humans hadn't a fraction of the life essence faeries possessed. She'd have to steal from hundreds of people. If she lost her balance and went too far . . . she didn't want to think about it. The consequences could be disastrous. But it was a moot point, anyway. It would take days to skim what she needed from humans. She had seven hours and forty-five minutes.

Sick at heart, she moved on to item three: make her Samhain sunset rendezvous with Malachi. But what if she showed up with less than the agreed payment? Would he still deal? Would she have to offer him . . . additional compensation? The idea made her shudder, but she knew she would do it. What was her own pride worth, compared with her son's life?

She pressed her hand to her chest. The moonstone warmed her palm even through her army jacket. She swore her heart had stopped beating for an instant when the gem snagged Mac's attention. Thank the gods she'd been able to distract him—again, with sex. Even without a spell, they'd nearly crawled inside each other. And when their powers touched . . . that had been incredible. She'd thought faerie villages were the deepest pools of life? They were puddles to the ocean of Mac's immortal soul.

She froze.

Dear gods.

The answer to her desperate prayers was right here, staring her in the face. Or, more accurately, sitting beside her, driving like hell on wheels. She didn't need another faerie village or even a throng of humans to resaturate the moonstone.

She could skim Mac.

She'd only need a drop of his potent immortal life essence. The question was—could she steal from him? Without his knowing? Because she was dead certain that if he discovered what she was up to, *pissed* was only the beginning of how angry he'd be.

She turned the problem over in her mind. The spell she'd used on the faerie villages was out. The victims of that spell had to be unaware of the spell-caster's presence. Mac was only too well aware of hers.

There was another spell she might use, though. One that was much more elemental. Heat flashed through her body; her mouth went dry.

Risky. Very risky.

Did she dare?

The car slowed as sheep pasture gave way to houses. They were entering another village. A tourist sign pointing the way to Culloden Battlefield flashed by her window.

"Where are we going?" she asked, hoping her voice sounded normal.

"Patience, love." A right and a left turn guided them out of the village and onto another country lane, pasture and moorland on either side. A tall iron fence ran along one side of the road, punctuated by stone pillars and topped by an electric wire. Mac braked in front of a closed, locked gate. Security cameras, mounted atop the gateposts, swiveled in their direction.

Artemis sensed magical protection as well, a glimmer of an incredibly complex pattern of wardings. If she wasn't so wound up, she would have enjoyed examining it more closely.

"We're here, love."

"Where's 'here'?"

"One of my homes away from home."

He leaned out the window and pressed a button mounted on a post. "Mac Lir," he said into what looked like a speaker.

Immediately, the gate creaked open, its two halves swinging outward. Mac spoke a low, lyrical spell. Green lightning flashed between the gateposts. A shower of sparks exploded, then twinkled into nothingness.

Mac put the car in gear and drove through. A second spell restored the wardings behind them. The gate shut with a brutal twang. Like a jail cell door. A chill ran down Artemis's spine. Well. This certainly put a crimp in her escape plans.

The driveway was long, lined with stately oaks. After a half mile or so, it branched right and left to frame a ridiculous expanse of lawn, manicured to within an inch of its life. A peacock strutted by, his harem of hens waddling in his wake. A perfect foil for the stately mansion behind them.

Built of honey-colored stone, the structure rose five stories. Lace curtains fluttered from the windows, and graceful eyebrow dormers peeked above the tiled roof. A curved split stair swept from the drive to a set of gleaming mahogany doors.

Mac cruised to a halt at the foot of the stair and turned to face Artemis, one arm draped atop the steering wheel. "Like it? I bought it last year. Used to be an English duke's hunting lodge or some such thing. I've installed brilliant security, both mundane and magical." He gave her a cheeky grin. "As you've no doubt noticed. We'll stay the night here and sort things out."

Stay the night? Did that mean what it sounded like? Artemis's heart tripped a double beat. Mac might be handing her the perfect opportunity to get what she needed. She searched his sea-green eyes, trying to read his intentions. His gaze remained annoyingly inscrutable.

"All right."

He shot her a look. "No argument?"

She smiled. Provocatively, she hoped. "Would an argument get me anywhere?"

His grin widened. "No."

Her stomach did a flip. Goddess, but he was drop-dead handsome when he smiled. He should be locked away. Their gazes met, and lingered.

Two uniformed servants chose that moment to appear, one man at Mac's door, the other at Artemis's.

"Welcome, sir," said the one on Mac's side. "So good to see you."

"And you, too, Fergus." Mac's glance back at Artemis was both amused and apologetic. "They came with the house," he told her in a low voice. "Couldn't very well turn them off, could I?"

"I suppose not," Artemis murmured as she gave her hand to the servant who had opened her door. He helped her from the car as if she were a duchess, his eyes betraying not a hint of censure at her scruffy attire.

Mac's attendant bowed. "Luggage, sir?"

"None for me. But the lady . . ." He sent Artemis an inquiring look.

"Um . . . yes. A blue duffel. In the trunk."

"I'll have it brought up immediately," Fergus said. "To . . . ?"

"To my suite," Mac said promptly.

Artemis flushed, relief and anxiety doing a tap dance duet in her belly.

Fergus didn't blink. "Very well, sir."

She jumped when Mac's large, warm hand settled at the base of her spine.

"Relax," he said. "I don't bite. Well," he amended, "not unless asked."

She snorted, and he chuckled. She didn't protest as he propelled her up the stairs and into a dark-paneled entry hall hung with large, depressing oil paintings of stiff-necked lords in red coats riding to the hounds. Overhead, the chandelier was made of antlers. She studied it dubiously.

Mac looked slightly embarrassed. "I've been busy the last six months. On a world tour. Haven't had a chance to redecorate."

A long line of staff members were already assembled to greet them. Mac addressed the balding butler at the front of the queue.

"Is my suite ready, Giles?"

"Of course, sir. And may I add, it is fine to see you here at Winterlea?"

"That it is," declared the motherly looking lady at Giles's side. "Do you and your lady require a meal?"

"Definitely, Fiona."

"Very good, sir. I'll fetch a menu of choices."

"No need. Just send up one of everything you've got handy."

Fiona beamed. "Certainly, sir."

Mac gave a rueful shake of his head as he steered Artemis toward a wide, forest green-carpeted stairway. The pressure of his fingers on her spine sent a tingle racing to her nerve endings. "I've tried to get them to stop calling me 'sir.' They just won't do it."

Mac's suite was on the first floor, facing the front lawn. In the sitting room, a delicate collection of antique furnishings fought a losing battle with an invasion of twenty-first-century electronic paraphernalia. A huge computer monitor dwarfed a spindle-legged desk, an array of audio equipment had been crammed into a gilded wardrobe, and a six-foot-wide flat-screen TV dwarfed a marble-topped sideboard.

In one corner, furniture had been removed entirely to accommodate an eclectic collection of musical instruments—electric and acoustic guitars, a three-tiered electric keyboard, an ancient Celtic harp, a modern drum set, a flute, bagpipes, and several unusual, medieval-looking instruments. Old and new clashed in dizzying furor, achieving an odd sort of truce. Balance? Perhaps, but it was a violent one. Like a wild seesaw. Like her emotions whenever she looked into Mac's eyes.

Especially now that she'd decided to—here she swallowed hard—seduce him.

She halted on the tiled entry floor and bent to take off her boots, loath to track mud on the silk Persian carpet. She untied the laces slowly, gathering her courage as the strands unraveled. She felt grubby and exhausted, and not the least bit alluring. Mac, damn him, looked as fresh and sexy as if he'd just woken from a ten-hour nap. He shucked off his leather jacket and tossed it on a wingback chair.

Padding into the center of the carpet, she turned a slow circle. There were at least three rooms adjoining the main one—a bathroom, one small cubicle that looked like an office, and a third, much larger bedroom, dominated by a massive four-poster bed. She caught a glimpse of a dressing room and a second bath beyond.

A knock sounded. Mac opened the door to Fergus, who entered with Artemis's sorry-looking duffel. He carried it into the bedroom as if it were made of solid gold. It looked pitiful perched on a carved mahogany luggage rack.

Slow heat climbed into her cheeks. Mac hardly would've ordered her bag brought to his bedroom if he didn't have sex on the brain. But that was good, she told herself. Very good. It played very nicely into her plans. Now, if only she could stop feeling so damn guilty . . .

She plastered a smile on her face. "Nice place you have here. But it's not your main home, I take it?"

"No. I've got a house in Inverness I share with two Sidhe cousins. I picked up this place a while back when the fangirls started getting obsessive. No one comes through those gates, unless I bring them in." He paused. "And no one gets out, unless I allow it."

We'll just see about that. "I'm flattered to be your guest, then."

He snorted. "Don't be. For you, it's more like house arrest than a garden party. You'll stay here until I decide what to do with you."

"I can think of a few things," she murmured.

He glanced up sharply, his eyes glinting with interest. "Sounds promising. Like what, love?"

"Oh, I have a few ideas," she said. "But before we discuss them . . . I'd like to get out of these clothes."

His gaze swept down her body, igniting a tingling trail.

"And take a shower," she added.

His eyes returned to her face.

Definitely interested.

"Have at it, then, love. There's a private bath off the bedroom."

She sauntered past him, lightly running her fingertips over his forearm.

Heat flared in his eyes, along with a look of speculation. "Why so friendly all of a sudden?"

Had she overplayed her hand? "Would you prefer a fight?"

He grinned. "Oh no, love. I like the new Artemis Alexandria Black."

She crossed into the bedroom. For a single terrifying moment, she thought he was going to follow right away. That would be disastrous. But thankfully, he hesitated ever so slightly, long enough for her to smile and shut the door.

She backed up against it, heart pounding. So far, so good, but time was quickly running out. She glanced at the mantel clock, trapped under a glass bell jar. Six hours, three minutes until sunset. She had a shower to take, preparations to make. And one sexy immortal demigod to seduce.

Her gaze fell on the bed.

How fast could she get Mac into it?

Twenty-two minutes later, Artemis wiped a damp palm on her jeans and grimaced. She'd've looked more alluring in a skirt, but she hadn't come to Scotland on vacation, after all, and jeans were the sexiest apparel in her duffel. At least the pants were clean, and the snug scoop-necked black tee she'd paired them with did nice things for her modest bustline.

Her pendant was gone, hidden in her pack with her pictures of Zander and her special knife. She'd take just that one small bag with her when she ran.

She'd tried to tame her hair, still damp from her quick shower. Hopeless, she knew, because her short curls had been nothing but frizz ever since she'd stepped off the plane in Glasgow. She hoped it looked wild and sexy, rather than wild and hideous. Too bad she didn't have any makeup; mascara would have boosted her confidence. Artemis knew she wasn't ugly, but she wasn't pretty, either. Sometimes, perfect balance manifested in perfect boredom.

It had never bothered her too much—her neutral looks had been an asset during her short-lived military career. Now she stared at her reflection in the fogged bathroom mirror and grimaced. The dark circles under her eyes and the tightness at the corners of her mouth were not at all appealing. She looked every one of her thirty-three years. And from the neck down? No major flaws, but no real assets, either.

If she'd been any good at casting a glamour, she would have considered a subtle, appearance-enhancing spell. But glamour was one area in which her talents were weak. No doubt Mac would've detected a glamour, anyway. How humiliating that would be.

She paced into the bedroom. Like a soldier preparing for battle, she inspected the big four-poster bed one last time. It'd taken longer than she'd anticipated to set the stage for the spell she intended to spring on Mac, and there was no room for error. She'd finally gotten everything just right.

Fear spurred her to the sitting room door. Opening it, she located Mac by the aroma of coffee wafting from a bay window alcove. Lounging in a chair next to a small dining table, he cradled a mug in both hands, his long legs stretched out before him. His hair was wet—he'd just emerged from his own shower. Freshly shaven, he looked even younger than he had before. It was hard to fathom he was—what had he said? Seven hundred years old?

He'd replaced his jeans and tee with a green silk bathrobe that deepened the color of his eyes. His feet were bare. Most likely, the rest of him was, too, under that robe. Artemis swallowed hard, telling herself it was all good. If Mac was already thinking sex, everything would be that much easier.

She became aware of music playing softly, stereo lights pulsing in time with the beat. An instrumental piece, Celtic harp and bagpipes electronically blended with the natural rush of a waterfall. It had to be one of Mac's own compositions.

She'd been vaguely aware of the growing international fervor regarding Mac. The music of Manannán had always been popular in Europe, but the musician himself had been elusive, never appearing in concert. No one had suspected the composer was a demigod. But after last year's battle with the Immortals, both Mac's music and his identity had gone global. He'd become a phenomenon and had embarked on a world tour. Artemis hadn't paid much attention.

She should have. Even though it was only a recording, the life magic emanating from the speakers was breathtaking. Tendrils of sound and emotion curled around her heart. For a moment she stood motionless, drinking it in. The sound was so . . . *Mac.* Now that she'd met him in person, that was really the only way to describe it.

During her brief absence from the sitting room, someone had brought the promised food. Mac's table was spread with an immaculate white cloth and laden with eggs, bacon, sausage, stewed tomatoes, sautéed mushrooms, toast, and beans.

From the looks of Mac's plate, he'd started eating without her. He sent an apologetic glance. "Wicked poor manners, I know, love, but I was a bit peckish. There's plenty left."

"I don't mind."

"What took you so long? I was beginning to think you'd thrown me over in favor of a nap."

Artemis hoped her blush looked coy rather than guilty. "You weren't afraid I was trying to escape?" she said lightly.

"Not at all. You wouldn't get far."

That's what you think. She smiled sweetly. "I'll keep that in mind. How long will I be staying here with you?"

"Not sure, love." He set his mug on the table. "What would you like to drink? Coffee? Tea? Chocolate? I've got all three."

"Chocolate, please."

Mac obliged, pouring rich dark liquid from one silver pitcher and adding hot milk from another. Artemis sank into an empty chair, her stomach showing faint interest in breakfast. She should be starved, she supposed—she'd barely eaten in days. But after four months of anxiety gnawing at her gut, her appetite was minimal. Still, she needed to keep up her strength. She accepted the plate Mac offered and took a bit of everything.

Mac easily consumed three times what she did. When his plate was bare, he poured himself a second cup of coffee—black—and leaned back in his chair. His expression was thoughtful, and Artemis would have given a lot to know just what he was thinking. His green eyes gave so little away.

Unnerved, she considered how best to make her move. Her gaze dropped, focusing on Mac's thumb and its gentle, rhythmic stroke on the rim of the coffee mug. How would that touch feel on her body? The thought had her squirming slightly in her chair.

His eyes narrowed.

She forced a nonchalant smile. "So, have you decided yet? What to do with me, I mean?"

His gaze dropped to her chest. Subtly, she straightened her shoulders, making the most of her modest assets. She twined a finger around a lock of her hair.

He looked up. She touched the tip of her tongue to her lower lip. He countered with a quick, brilliant grin, the force of which all but knocked her off her chair. Gods. No wonder his female fans hounded him.

Then he shook his head slightly and cleared his throat. His thumb ceased its gentle caress of the mug. "Right, then. Well, love, let's get everything out in the open. As you no doubt know, Sidhe law forbids willful, malicious theft of Celtic life energy."

Artemis blinked at his sudden shift of mood. Mac was

no longer smiling; it was as if the temperature in the room had plummeted ten degrees.

She scrambled for a defense. "But . . . I'm not Sidhe. I'm not even from the Celtic isles. I'm not subject to your laws."

"That's where you're wrong. Sidhe law applies to all animate creatures in the U.K. and Ireland, living and undead, resident or visitor. And I'm going to be straight with you, love. I'm already out on a limb, delaying your arrest. I should have hauled your lovely round arse straight to the Sidhe Council."

Artemis swallowed. "Why didn't you?"

"The penalty for your crime is no picnic." He paused, waiting until she looked at him again. "At the very least, you'd be stripped of your powers and forced to live the rest of your life as a mundane in the human world."

"And . . . the worst?"

"Let's see. A life of servitude as a mundane in Annwyn. Captivity for life in a Sidhe prison. Or . . ." He paused. ". . . death."

A sick tremor vibrated through Artemis's body. Gods. If she'd known how brutal Sidhe law was . . . Well, it wouldn't have made a difference, would it? She'd acted out of necessity.

She forced a nonchalant tone. "Slavery? Imprisonment? Death? The Sidhe aren't very forgiving, are they?"

"No. We're not."

She lifted her chin, watching him through downswept eyelashes. "Then why did you bring me here, Mac? Why not just throw me to the lions?"

"Good question."

She leaned forward, presenting him with an excellent view of her cleavage, such as it was. "You must have an answer."

The bottom of his mug thumped on the table. His palms flattened on the table. "It must have something to do with my divine, forgiving half. Even though I know you're guilty as hell, I just can't bear the thought of seeing you broken."

"Because . . . of what happened between us? When you kissed me?" Her words were a husky whisper, and she wasn't even acting anymore. Just the memory of his kiss made her dizzy.

"That kiss? Do yourself a favor and forget it. You've got more important things to ponder. You're a powerful witch, Artemis, but you're playing with magic that's deadly. You think you can control the demon you're dealing with—"

"I'm not dealing with a—"

He slammed his fist on the table, making the dishes jump. "Please. Don't lie to me. There's no other plausible explanation for what you've done. You're not demonwhore, not yet, but you're headed in that direction. You may think you have the upper hand, but you don't. I know someone far more powerful than you who—" He stopped, and swallowed hard. "Forget that. Just believe me when I say that it won't work. Sooner than you think, the death magic you're dealing with will destroy you. Tell me. Is it money you need so badly? If so, I can get you all the cash you want. All you have to do is tell me how much."

Artemis's chest contracted painfully. Mac's green eyes were clear. And so sincere. He truly wanted to help her, despite everything she'd done. The thought was humbling.

For an instant, she let herself imagine what it would be like to lean on his strength. To let him shoulder her burden. The desire to confide in him became a physical ache in her chest.

But she wasn't a fool. Where she was headed, his magic was worth about as much as a cheap card trick. And if she told him the truth? If she told him what she planned to do with the moonstone hidden away in the bedroom? He'd haul her ass before the Sidhe Council faster than a nightclub magician could say "abracadabra."

No. She was alone, as she had been from the start. Trust no one: *that* was the mantra that had gotten her this far. If she abandoned that credo now, Zander would be lost forever.

She met his gaze frankly. "I don't need money. I don't need anything except my freedom. If you really want to help me, just give me that."

He rubbed his chin. "I might be persuaded. On one condition."

"What's that?"

"Your promise that you'll stop stealing life energy. And stay far away from faeries, Selkies, brownies, sprites, imps—any and all the Celtic life-magic creatures. And humans, too. Give me that, Artemis Alexandria Black, and you can go on your way."

"Just like that? You'd trust me?"

He snorted. "Not as far as a faerie could toss a ton of bricks. That's why I've taken the liberty of placing a tracking spell on you. You can go, but if you even think of stirring up any death-magic mischief, I'll know immediately."

She stared at him, aghast. "*What?* You spelled me?"

He leaned back in his chair. "I did."

"But . . . you couldn't have. I didn't feel a thing."

He raised one implacable brow.

Swiftly, Artemis scanned her chakra centers, searching for energy drains. *Damn.* Mac wasn't bluffing. The spell was there, bound to her first chakra—the psychic center of safety and stability. What he'd done was clamp the magical equivalent of a mundane house arrest monitor on her soul, similar to the binding spell vamps and demons attached to their most troublesome human whores.

Cautiously, she tested the charm's strength. The jolt to her senses was swift, strong, and painful. She might be able to remove it, but it would take weeks of delicate spellwork. Months, maybe.

Gods. How humiliating. And she hadn't even known he'd done it.

He watched her, a glint of dark amusement in his eyes.

"When?" she demanded.

He grinned. "Just now, while you were contemplating getting under my robe. You were a bit . . . distracted. Angry at me, love?"

Angry? She was livid. But not at him—at herself. For Mac, she felt nothing but grudging respect. And a sharp, urgent stab of lust. He'd spelled her, and she hadn't even known it. Here was a man who was not the least bit put off by her power—because his was so much greater. He'd never be afraid of her. Ever.

It was an incredibly arousing thought. If only she could make love to him under more honest circumstances.

She shook her head. "How can I be angry at you? If I were you, I wouldn't have been half so lenient. Why have you been?"

He sighed. "I don't sense any true evil in you, Artemis. You play with fire, yes, but you returned the life energy you stole to Gilraen's village in time to prevent Tamika's death. I don't believe you ever wanted to hurt anyone. I think it scares you very much that you almost did."

She examined her twisted fingers.

"The Sidhe Council won't care about your intentions, though," Mac continued. "They'll pass judgment purely on your actions. Remember that. I won't even make you swear a false promise to abandon your foolish plans. Just know that if anything untoward happens in your vicinity—anything at all—I'll snatch you up in a heartbeat." He picked up his coffee and took a sip. "All right, then. I find I'm not really keen on keeping unwilling prisoners, and with the tracking spell in place, I won't have to. There's no reason for you to stay. I'll have Fergus bring your car around."

What? She blinked at him. "But—"

"Isn't that what you want?"

"Well, yes, but . . . suppose I also want to stay? At least . . . for a while?"

His gaze sharpened. "*Do* you want to?"

Knees shaking so badly she swore she could hear them rattle, she rose and rounded the table. Mac half twisted in his seat as she draped her arms over his shoulders from behind. Her lips brushed his ear. "Yes."

His muscles bunched under her arms. Awareness spun between them, drawing tighter with each second that ticked by.

"Tired, are you?" He sounded softly amused. "Need a good rest, perhaps?"

She stroked his chest, smoothing the lapels of his robe. "Maybe later."

When he didn't immediately answer, she kissed the hollow beneath his earlobe. "Turn your chair around," she whispered.

He obliged, and she sank to her knees before him, gently kneading his thighs. His taut muscles warmed cool silk. The robe tented beneath its loosely knotted sash.

A genuine smile played on her lips. "I want to thank you," she said, and for once, her words were completely sincere. "For not taking me to the Sidhe Council."

He threaded his fingers through her hair. "You don't have to thank me this way."

"I know. But I want to. Do you mind?"

"I'm half Sidhe, love. We're insatiable. Of course I don't mind."

She stroked him through the silk. He was harder than granite. His breath caught as he framed her face in his large hands.

Lowering her gaze, she parted the edges of his robe. His erection practically leaped into her hand, hot and eager. He clenched his fists in her hair until her scalp tingled.

Other places on her body were tingling, too. She teased her fingers up and down his shaft. His magic flared. Hers answered, just as it had responded to his kiss. He was so powerful. His immortal soul was so vast. And she only needed a drop of his essence.

She kept her strokes deliberately light; his grip on her hair tightened almost to the point of pain. His hips came off the chair as he pressed himself more firmly into her hands.

"*Artemis.*"

His intense green eyes nearly took her breath away. The expression on his beautiful face was strained.

"I'm telling you again, love, you don't have to do this. I don't expect anything from you."

"I want to give you something." And it was true. She wanted so desperately to give him pleasure. Guilt was a driving factor, of course. What she planned to do to him was so wrong, on so many levels. But she couldn't pretend her yearning to gratify him was all about guilt. She wanted to please him. For him. And for herself. She wanted to feel his vast power rise to overpower hers.

She brought her lips to within an inch of his erection and blew a soft stream of air across the tip. He rasped air into his lungs. She kissed the rounded head.

He exhaled a shaky breath. "Well, love, if you're willing . . ."

"I am. Don't worry about that."

She was more than willing. The scent of him intoxicated her. An ache had sprung up between her legs, one that urged her to rub against his body like a cat. Drawn by her needs as much as his, she parted her lips and welcomed him inside her mouth. He groaned, pulling her deep, then pushed her away until she almost lost him. Then he was urging her back again.

She let him set the pace, giving as he demanded until he murmured a low curse and eased her gently away, disentangling his fingers from her hair.

"Too much too soon." He crooked her a smile. "No need to rush."

No need to rush? There was every need! Time was rapidly running out. But it wouldn't do to let him guess that.

She sat back on her heels and smiled up at him. Holding his gaze, she grasped the hem of her T-shirt and slowly pulled the garment over her head.

CHAPTER SIX

If Mac weren't immortal, he'd have thought he'd died and gone to heaven.

Artemis, bare-chested, on her knees, her lips full and wet, was an absolute dream. One he sure as bloody hell wasn't in a hurry to wake up from. Had he thought her not much of a looker? He was rapidly revising that opinion. She was perfect. He itched to touch her smooth olive skin and her perfectly shaped breasts. Take her peaked nipples into his mouth.

She rose to her feet. His eyes followed the movement. With fluid grace, she braced her hands on his chair's armrests and leaned forward, breasts swaying. He waited for her next move in delicious anticipation. Artemis was so very much more than any woman he'd been with in a very long time. She had the rare ability to surprise him. He hadn't realized until just this moment how much he needed that.

Dipping her head, she planted a brief kiss on his lips. But when he reached for her, she murmured, "No" and moved back. Her fingers went to her waist, slipping the button of her jeans. Mac watched with riveted focus as denim slid over lean, tanned legs.

She wasn't wearing any knickers.

He sucked in a breath. Her hips and belly, gently rounded with just the right amount of flesh, beckoned with a seductive sway. The triangle of curls between her thighs matched the hair on her head—velvet night, tinted with unexpected gold. The sweet scent of her arousal sent his lust spiraling. But it was her magic that inflamed him most of all. That mysterious balance of light and dark.

He all but fell out of his chair in his haste to get his hands on her. On his knees, he gripped her hips and canted her forward, pulling her off balance. He liked her off balance, he decided. She gave a small, incredibly sexy cry, her legs tensing, her hands grasping at his shoulders.

"Don't worry, love. I won't let you fall."

The enticing hollow of her navel beckoned. He bent to kiss it. Lust throbbed through his body, hardening him as it hadn't in over a year. He was insane to want this witch so badly. She practiced death magic, and Sidhe abhorred death magic. It should have been the ultimate turn-off.

It wasn't. Rather than repel, Artemis's magic fascinated. It called to the slice of darkness embedded in his soul. Beautiful, strong, and deadly, her dark/light powers glistened like the edge of a finely honed blade. Death and life, perfectly balanced. Coaxing. Tempting. Luring him to places he would not have considered going only a year before.

Her trembling fingers sifted through his hair, blessedly scattering his thoughts. She held him as his tongue swirled in her navel. Fingernails dug into his scalp as he licked a wet line downward. He filled his hands with her generous arse, urging her legs apart. He nuzzled her curls, drank in her scent.

He nipped at the sweet spot hidden in her soft nether curls. She made a beautiful, helpless sound in the back of her throat. He stroked from her buttocks to the backs of her thighs, lifting and parting her legs. His breath was coming heavily now; so was hers. He ducked his head farther and parted her honey-sweet folds with his tongue.

She gripped him hard. Her nails dug so deeply into his scalp he wondered if she'd drawn blood.

"You don't have to worry about getting me pregnant," she gasped out. "I'm on the pill."

He nearly laughed out loud. For all her magical sophistication, Artemis was woefully ignorant if she thought any pill could control his fertility. Mundane birth control was extraneous—no seed would take root in her body unless he wished it. And no human barrier to conception could protect Artemis if he wished to impregnate her.

An image of Artemis, belly swollen with his child, flashed through his mind. He was appalled at how appealing the notion was. True, her magic was incredibly strong. Equally true, she turned him on like nobody's business. But she was also a thief, a liar, and a death-magic practitioner. Not exactly the kind of mother he'd wish for his child.

Even so, he was more than ready for mating; his cock was pounding so violently he thought he might explode before he even got inside her. That wouldn't be very god-like at all. In fact, his divine pride might never recover from such an indignity.

Best to consummate this act quickly. He was half lying on the rug already; rolling completely onto his back, he started to lift her atop him.

Artemis gasped, shoving against his chest. "No . . . No, Mac, stop—"

His grip on her hips tightened; she struggled harder, pushing him away. Blood pounded in his head, and something dark and ugly in his soul roared to life. *Stop?* How dare she back off now, after bringing him this far along?

When he spoke, there was a dangerous edge to his tone he hardly recognized. "Not thinking of changing your mind, are you, love?"

His fingers clenched, pressing muscle and bone. She gave a small cry of distress. "No! No, of course I'm not changing my mind. Please, Mac. Let go. You're . . . hurting me."

She wasn't being coy. She'd gone rigid. He stared at his hands, clamped on her hips. With very little effort, he could snap her pelvis in two.

Sickened he'd come so close to losing control, he forced his fingers to relax. Angry red marks marred her skin; she'd bruise, certainly. Gods in Annwyn. What had come over him?

But if Artemis was offended, she hid it well. Still suspended over his body, she ran a hand down his stomach, ending with her fingers wrapped around his rod. His hips jerked off the floor.

She sounded breathless. "You misunderstood, Mac. I didn't mean I want to stop completely. I just want to take this to your bed. It'll be a lot more comfortable than the floor."

She punctuated her request with a squeeze, in just the right place and with just the right amount of pressure. Sheer relief roared through him.

"Anything for a lady," he gasped.

He stood, lifting her in his arms as he rose. She hadn't expected that; she yelped and clutched at his neck. Her naked arms and legs, all smoothness and warmth, wrapped his torso. His fingers slipped between her legs and stroked slick wetness.

She buried her head in his chest and moaned. "Hurry, Mac."

He wasn't inclined to argue. He strode into the bedroom and tossed her into the middle of his bed. She bounced once, enfolded in the soft puff of the quilt. A shrug of his shoulders sent his dressing gown slithering to the floor. Naked, ravenous as a predator, he crawled to her on all fours. If she was his prey, she was a willing victim. Her hands ran over his back, urging him closer. Her legs parted, welcoming.

Her magic shimmered around her, dark and light and mysterious. He wanted to delve into it, discover its secrets. Discover her secrets. He was sure she had many. He was equally sure there were some he would not like. Far from giving him pause, the thought only inflamed the small dark void in his soul.

She stretched her arms overhead; her legs wrapped around his hips. His head lightened; his groin went heavy. He pressed her thighs farther apart, stroking a finger through her lush wet femininity.

She twisted and moaned, her hips arching, following his hand. "Now, Mac. Please."

"Take it easy, love. I want this to be good."

Her grip tightened on his shoulders. "It is good. It's fantastic. Gods. I want you inside me."

He grinned, his fingers still teasing. The play of emotion on her face held him entranced.

"Not yet," he murmured. "I'm having too much fun."

He stroked a sweet spot. Her hips came off the mattress, her reply lost in a breathy moan. Intense satisfaction heated his blood. He walked his fingers to her navel and circled the tantalizing indentation. She whimpered, her breath reduced to short, sharp pants. He'd never seen anything so lovely as her dark, pleasure-hazed eyes.

"You . . . have this . . . kind of fun . . . on a . . . regular basis?"

"Not as regular as you might think, love." He nuzzled between her breasts.

"I can't . . . believe that. What about . . . all those girls . . . following you?"

If she could talk this coherently, he wasn't doing his job. He slipped a finger inside her and was rewarded with a moan. "Those lasses are far too young for me."

"There . . . have to be . . . older ones."

Would she never cease talking? This babble had to stop. It was quickly becoming a matter of pride. He swooped down and captured one deliciously hard nipple in his mouth, first scraping it with his teeth, then drawing it firmly into his mouth and suckling. At the same time, he slipped a second finger inside her and pressed, finding another, deeper, sweeter spot. She gasped and arched, squirming against his hand, all speech forgotten.

There. That was more like it.

Yet for some reason, he found himself answering her query. "There are older women. I take what they offer often enough. I'm half Sidhe, after all."

Her hands roamed his sweat-slickened body, leaving perfect, impossible magic glimmering on his skin. It felt good. Incredibly good. He was struck with the urge to purr, like a big cat.

"Ah yes," she said. "And Sidhe are insatiable."

"Speaking from experience, are you?" His words were light, but his hand stilled. The thought of Artemis making love with another Sidhe ignited a dark, heated rage.

"I've never slept with a Sidhe. But I've heard the stories. Everyone has."

He lifted his head and looked at her. "As I said, I'm only half Sidhe."

"I don't suppose a god has any problems getting a date, either."

He laughed. "You're right about that, love. Hang on. You're in for a wild ride."

He nipped at the upper swell of her breast. Licked a line along her collarbone. Caught her earlobe with his teeth. Then he covered her mouth in a lush, openmouthed kiss.

She responded like fire before a hot wind, wrapping her arms and legs around him, molding her body to his. He filled his hands with her, his palms gliding over her soft skin. But when she tilted her hips, encouraging him to enter, he held himself just out of reach. When she reached between them, trying to take control, he caught her wrists and stretched her arms over her head, anchoring them to the mattress.

"I want to touch you," she panted.

"Not your turn, love."

He caught her protest with his mouth, chuckling as she twisted and turned, trying to escape his hold. He transferred both her wrists to one hand, leaving the other free to touch her breasts. All the while, he nibbled along her bottom lip, rained kisses over her nose and cheeks and eyelids. His tongue completed a leisurely exploration of her right ear while his thumb and forefinger plucked and rolled her nipples into hard, exquisite pebbles.

She shuddered and writhed, her legs clamped around his hips. Her eyes were closed, her wild curls framing her flushed face. It was all he could do not to give in to her pleas and plunge into her wet heat. But he wasn't ready. Not yet.

First he wanted to see her shatter.

He shifted, allowing her arms to move, but only so he could pin her wrists in a different place, against the mattress on either side of her hips as he drew her hardened nipple into his mouth, suckling hard, then scraping it with his teeth.

"Oh gods." She could barely utter the words. "What are you doing to me?"

"Can't you tell, love? No? I'll just have to do it again." He turned his attention to the other breast.

"But—" Gasp. "I . . . we . . ." Gasp. "Make. Love. Now."

"I am making love to you."

"Not . . . what I mean."

He scraped his teeth across her belly, working his way down her body. "Has anyone ever told you that you talk too much in bed?"

She uttered a sound that might have been a laugh. "Sometimes."

He frowned. "Do you have a lover? Currently, I mean?"

"You mean . . . besides you?"

"Very funny, love."

"No. No, I don't." She swallowed hard as his breath bathed the inside of her thigh.

"Don't worry. It's like riding the London Underground— you never forget how. Now, love, try not to talk for a while. I'm going to be too busy to keep up my end of the conversation."

His tongue slid into her sweet folds. He feasted there, dipping and delving deep inside, then drawing back and suckling. Artemis made a mewing sound, like a kitten. He moved her hands to the insides of her own knees and used them to push her legs apart. The sight was incredibly erotic.

Gods, he wanted her. She was sobbing now. Begging for him to come inside her. She was so close to coming. Lust beating an insane, demanding tattoo in his groin, he moved over her. He positioned himself at the glistening entrance to her body, and with one swift, deep thrust, united them.

She cried out, her brilliant light/dark magic igniting around him. Inside him. Gods in Annwyn. It felt so damn good. He slid his palm under her arse and tilted her hips. His next stroke hit harder, loosening another sweet moan from her throat. Her legs came up, anchoring around his hips, holding him deep inside.

He started a pounding, unyielding rhythm, music to his soul. He caught her on the high plateau of her climax, then urged her higher still. His magic shimmered and flowed with hers, joining, sharing. Her breath came in small, glorious pants.

He slid deep, then withdrew almost completely. "Come for me, love."

She shook her head wildly. "No. I can't—"

"That," he said, plunging deep, "is the most ridiculous statement I've ever heard from a woman." He nipped at her neck. "Remember who you're with, love."

She gulped for air. "As if I could forget."

He smiled as he moved inside her, enjoying the feel of possessing her. She was tight, hot, slick. On the verge of shattering, if his calculations were right. And they were. He'd spent nearly seven centuries perfecting his sexual technique. He was never wrong about such things.

She clung to him, her eyes glazing as the peak rushed at her. Her hips jerked, her inner muscles clenching like a fist. Quickening his rhythm, he angled his body up on his elbows. He wanted to watch her as she broke.

It was as beautiful as he'd anticipated. Like the crash of a wave in a storm. Her head tossed, her body arched, her mouth opened on a soul-deep moan. Satisfaction rolled through him. He thrust deep, spinning out her peak as long as he could.

Eventually, though, the perfect moment had to end. Artemis turned boneless, her body sinking into the mattress. Mac held himself hard and motionless inside her, as her eyelids fluttered open. He took in her dazed expression. A slow grin spread over his face.

"That was lovely," he said, dipping his head for a kiss. "You're lovely."

"I'm . . . I'm not." Her body was suddenly tense in his arms, and something like fear flashed in her eyes. "Did . . . did you come, too?"

"Not yet." He thrust gently, letting her feel how aroused he still was. Painfully so, if truth be told. "But I intend to. Very soon." He grinned. "If you're still willing?"

She closed her eyes briefly, and nodded, almost with relief. "More than willing. Her hips lifted, but the offer was marred by the single tear that escaped from her closed eyes.

Mac caught the drop with a brush of his thumb. "Come, now, love, why so sad?"

"Nothing," she choked out. "Nothing. Just . . ." She shook her head. "That . . . what you made me feel— it was amazing. It's never been like that for me before.

Men never . . . plunge into my magic like that. They're too . . . afraid of it. Of course," she added, humor creeping back into her voice, "a god doesn't have those kinds of hang-ups."

"I'm only half a god," he reminded her with a laugh.

"Half is more than enough." She urged his mouth to hers. He complied, and for the next moment or two, though he was still buried deep inside her, all they did was kiss.

Until kisses weren't enough.

Artemis nipped and licked his lower lip. Her hands moved to his arse, and her hips wriggled.

"Your turn," she said.

He smiled and resumed the dance. He'd take his turn, and bring her with him as well.

He stoked their fire with slow, deep thrusts. Soon he had her moaning. Thrashing. Her magic swirling. She was close to a second fall. He felt the first stirrings of his own orgasm.

Her magic stirred with it, swift and strong and sure. It touched him. Called him. Delved into his soul. He felt her there, close to his heart, close to that dark, unwanted void he'd spent so long denying. Under her touch, the wound didn't seem so ugly, or so hopeless.

Artemis's light filled his darkness. Her darkness fed his light. The nagging sense of incompleteness that had plagued him for the past year vanished like a bad dream. This was what he'd been looking for. This union of light and dark. Not a struggle, but a balance.

Freedom.

He thrust deep inside her. The leading edge of his orgasm tickled his senses. She was close to breaking a second time as well. He could feel her inner muscles tremble as they clamped tight around his shaft. Life magic surged in his cock, and for the first time in Mac's long life, the urge to release all of it—all his immortal soul's life-creating potential—was overwhelming. Artemis's mention of pregnancy had burrowed its way to a place deep inside him. The seed of her suggestion had released tenuous roots. He could do it. Create a new soul, a new life. A child.

There was a reason why that was a bad idea. At least, Mac thought there must be. But logical thought was tricky at the moment, with his hands and soul full of Artemis and her magic. The only thing he knew for certain was how completely *right* it felt to be buried inside her. The woman was a perfect, pure, high note. His long life was like a song that had been waiting for that single tone to complete it. And now he'd found her.

He made his decision. When he went over that final sweet edge, he'd let his creative magic flow free.

The spell. She had to spring it at the exact moment Mac's climax hit.

But—oh gods!—how could she do that, with waves and waves of pleasure and light flowing over her, under her, through her?

Mac's fingers bit into Artemis's hips. His light and life pumped into her body. He was rock-hard inside her, and so incredibly deep. It felt as though his magic had found the very center of her soul.

It was too deep. Too good. Her balance was slipping.

A wave of pure bliss rose. She was a split second from coming a second time. The knowledge stunned her. She'd slept with few men; none had really dared to know her this completely. Sometimes, she'd managed a pleasant climax. But a mind-shattering orgasm? *Two?* Incredible.

It would be sheer disaster if she came a second time now. If she did, she'd never complete the spell. And it had to be finished, no matter what the effort cost.

Falling forward, supporting her weight on rigid arms, she wriggled her hips, trying desperately to tilt away from the devastating sensations. A shudder ran through her, and for one awful second she thought she'd fly right over the edge. Then—blessedly, horribly—the peak receded.

Numbness descended; her pleasure faded to a faint blur. It was the first part of her spell. Thank the gods, she'd regained the upper hand. It was imperative that she keep it. Her lust drained away. The haze of sensual yearning lifted. Her mind cleared like a winter sky.

Mac's wild thrusts continued, but now it was as if she were outside herself, hovering above the bed. Not feeling: watching. Waiting. He jerked hard, gasping her name. His fingers branded her hips as he stiffened inside her.

Now.

She parted her lips and whispered a word so ugly, so foul, her soul recoiled. Bitter regret burned in Artemis's throat. Mac was the most generous, most incredible lover she'd ever known. What he'd made her feel . . . no. She wouldn't dwell on that. Not now, not ever. Their association was over. When he came back to himself and realized what she'd done, he would hate her.

The knowledge brought a stab of pain in the vicinity of her heart, but she shoved the discomfort aside. There would be time enough for regrets later. There always was.

Mac's spine arched; guttural pleasure vibrated in his throat. The spell broke with a sound like a dam cracking. Tongues of hellfire sprang up at the four corners of the bed. From the flames, four death arcs rose, curving gracefully overhead. The leading ends touched down in the centers of the bed's four sides, forming an arched cage above the mattress. Ruthlessly, she tightened the strands of her spell.

Time warped, suspending Mac at the peak of his perfect bliss. Working swiftly, she ran her mind along the edges of Mac's soul. She'd never skimmed someone so powerful. Was he aware of the death magic hovering above him? He didn't seem to be. His soul was drenched in brilliant light.

Orgasm. It was the most powerful light/dark experience. An act that made new human life possible, yet the French had once named it "the little death." Sexual release paved a path straight to a soul's essence. Artemis's death spell had widened that path, giving her leverage to extract what she needed from Mac's soul.

She cast her senses toward him. Mac's divine spirit was so bright she could only view it obliquely. His power stole her breath. He was so strong. So alive. Immortal. She told herself that the drop of his soul she needed was nothing. A penny to a billionaire. Unfortunately, the rationalization did nothing to lessen her guilt. A theft was a theft.

But she wouldn't balk. Not now, when she was so close to the next step in saving Zander. Hardly daring to breathe, Artemis reached out and touched Mac's life energy. Whispering spell words of both life and death, she gathered a single strand of life essence into her body.

The burst of bright-hot energy nearly undid her. White and dazzling, Mac's life essence was far more vast than that of an entire city of faeries. It was so pure. So brilliant. So *good*. Tears stung her eyes.

His soul was wild and free, like his father's kingdom, the sea. Potent and sexual as the earth, the Sidhe realm. Artemis desperately wanted to linger, to know him better, but she didn't dare. It was past time to break their connection.

Except that she couldn't seem to summon the will to do it. The temptation to know him, really *know* him, drew her like a magnet. Such a connection could never happen in love—she was a fool to even think that word. But joined as they were, body and mind, Artemis had the brief power to go deeper into his soul. If she was careful, he would never know.

It was wrong; she didn't delude herself that it wasn't. Artemis was nothing if not honest—at least with herself. A part of her screamed for her to stop. But it was a weak part of her will, and she knew it would lose. She wanted so badly to be close to him one last time.

She shut her eyes and slipped farther down the path her magic had opened. Farther into Mac's life essence. What she discovered there amazed her.

Oh, not the proof that Mac was kindhearted and honorable. He was a creature of life magic, after all, and she'd already sensed his ultimate goodness. No, it was his unexpected vulnerability that astonished her. Such a human weakness was so at odds with his cocky, confident facade.

Here was a demigod whose deepest wish was love—human love. Mac wondered if he deserved it, if he would ever find it, if there was a chance that any human woman would ever look past *what* he was to see *who* he was. At a deep level, he was afraid to find out. His poignant, little-boy fear of rejection tugged at Artemis's heart.

Who would have thought?

She felt Mac's mind stir, stretching for awareness. She'd stayed too long! Hastily, she retreated, drawing back into her own body and soul. It hurt. Badly. She wanted to stay, wanted to hold him, wanted to become part of him.

Wanted to love him.

The thought caused the air to vacate her lungs. Love him? Who was she kidding? She'd just violated his soul in the most terrible, underhanded way. Once he woke, the only feeling he'd have for her would be disgust.

She felt that something precious had died. Which was ridiculous, because from the beginning, everything she'd shared with Mac had been a lie. Pushing her grief aside—by now, she was very good at that—she released her hold on the spell. Mac's orgasm evaporated; his body relaxed. Breath huffed from his lungs. Tension drained from his beautiful face. He softened inside her, a faint smile on his lips.

Fighting sudden tears, Artemis cradled Mac's stolen life essence in the arms of her soul. As she rose to her knees, a keen sense of loss scoured her as his shaft slipped from her body. She was about to move off him completely when his eyelids fluttered and opened. His green eyes, frowning, met hers.

She froze.

He'd caught her out.

How long she remained motionless—naked, guilty, vulnerable, waiting for his anger to coil and strike—she couldn't have guessed. It felt like forever. In reality, it was probably only a few seconds.

Then his forehead smoothed, and his eyes lost their focus. His voice, a mere whisper, brushed her senses.

"Ah well. I hope you won't mind, love."

She stared at him. Mind? Mind what? She was the one who'd done the unconscionable. For a moment, she thought he would say more. Then his eyelids fluttered closed, and his body relaxed into sleep.

It was over. She'd done it. Artemis didn't move for a full minute. She couldn't; she was trembling too badly.

When at last she was able to leave him, she went slowly. Carefully. Their bodies clung with the slight suction their mingled sweat had created, but only for an instant.

She was free. A wave of loss broke over her. She only just managed not to fling herself back onto the bed and into his arms and beg for his forgiveness. Impossible, of course. What she'd done was unforgivable.

Gingerly, feeling as though her heart had sustained a violent blow, she stood facing the window as she reined in her unruly emotions. Where was her famous balance now? She needed it, desperately.

She blanked her mind and concentrated on her mantras. The soothing vibrations helped her redisover a small measure of her equilibrium. Digging her small pack from the bottom of the duffel, she tugged open the zipper and slid the moonstone from its pouch.

She cradled the gem in her left palm. The spark of Mac's life essence glowed in her heart, expanding until white light filled her chest. A whispered spell sent the energy zinging down her arm and into her hand. In the space of a heartbeat, Mac's life essence drained from her soul and flashed into the moonstone.

Some of her own energy drained with it. Knees suddenly trembling, she steadied herself with a hand on the luggage rack. She allowed herself a single moment of weakness. A tear rolled from her eye to splash on Mac's soft carpet. The moonstone, now saturated, was a hot, living presence in her fist.

She slid the stone back into its silk-platinum pouch, tying the strings tightly, but leaving the chain dangling. She slipped it over her neck.

She'd done it. She had what she needed for her rendezvous with Malachi. She only hoped she could get to him on time.

Demons insisted on punctuality.

CHAPTER SEVEN

It was easier than she expected to slip out of the mansion undetected. Presumably, the perimeter wards on Mac's estate were so powerful he didn't feel a big need for internal security. Still, the place was crawling with servants, any one of whom was capable of spotting Artemis's mad dash down the garden path. Crouching low to the ground, she ran like hell.

She drew up short about twenty feet from the estate fence. Iron bars, even tipped with serious-looking spikes and a nasty electrified wire, posed no problem. A relatively simple spell would bend those bars like pipe cleaners, and she could short out the wire with just a couple of words. No, as always, the real difficulty was magical.

A quick probe told her Mac hadn't been bluffing when he said no one entered or left his estate without his permission. His perimeter wards thrummed with vibrant life magic, entirely worthy of the demigod he was.

He'd designed the barrier to repel both life-magic and death-magic attacks. Demons *and* fans. The thought brought a wry smile. Mac's magic was strong, but polarized—set to resist one type of magic per spell. Clearly, he hadn't anticipated an assault by someone casting a merged spell. Still, getting through wasn't going to be easy.

Keeping to the shadows of the garden's lush greenery, Artemis followed the perimeter fence, circling toward the

main gate. That would be the easiest place to break
through. The seam that allowed legitimate visitors to pass
was any warding's weakest point.

A pulsing techno-beat met her approach to the gate. As
she'd suspected—hoped, really—the muddy country lane
outside Mac's estate had become a very popular place. A
half dozen cars, including the white van Mac had called a
"people mover," sprawled in disarray along the road, doors
open, music blaring. Empty beer and whisky bottles littered
the ground, along with candy and chips wrappers. A gaggle
of skinny-assed girls—some atop the cars, others pressed up
against the fence—swayed to the rhythm of Manannán.
The whey-faced photographer who'd wrecked Mac's motorcycle paced behind them. Every so often he lifted his
camera and pointed it toward the mansion.

Mac really was quite the celebrity. Well, no wonder—the
man was hot. His young fans, so thin and careless and free,
caused a twist of envy in Artemis's heart. She'd never been
like them, unencumbered by life and duty. Her magic and
her military upbringing had always set her apart.

Artemis slid into the shadow of a broad oak. She could
just make out the feverish stream of conversation buzzing
from the road.

". . . *has* to come out of there *sometime*, he *can't* just—"

"Could be *days*—"

"I'd stay out here *forever* for a chance to—"

"Did you *see* that *cow* he had in the car with him? I don't
know what *she's* got that *I* don't—"

"If *only* we could figure out a way to get *in*—"

"The spells I bought from that old *witch*—"

"Smoke and a bang. She robbed you *blind*, that ugly
bint did—"

And more of the same. Good. Not a real witch among
them. Artemis blocked the voices from her mind, and they
faded to a murmur.

The oak's low-hung branches shielded the mansion

from view. Hopefully, Mac was still asleep in his bed. Thoughts of that bed led to thoughts of what they'd done there. Which led to thoughts of how angry Mac would be when he woke up and realized what she'd done. *Don't go there*, she cautioned herself. Regrets would only destroy what was left of her balance. And balance was the only way she was going to get through those gates.

Sinking into a crouch, she unzipped her pack. Her hands shook as she withdrew a small, jewel-handled anthame. The blade was no longer than her middle finger. The knife was deadly sharp, and still humming with the magic she'd cast over Mac's bed.

A slight nausea still lingered from the death spell she'd spoken there. She didn't relish the thought of casting another so soon, but what choice did she have? Less than five hours remained to her meeting with Malachi, and with her map gone, she wasn't even sure in which direction the nearest natural power sink lay. If she was late, would the demon reneg on their contract?

She knew the answer was yes. Demons, as Mac had so helpfully pointed out, were skilled manipulators. Malachi was an Old One—powerful and brutally dangerous. He'd exploit any error Artemis made to the fullest extent. Her skin crawled as she considered one dread possibility after the other. But angst, she knew, wouldn't help. With a little luck, she wouldn't be late at all, and she'd retain the upper hand. Demons were deceitful, yes, but even the most powerful Old One was bound by the spell that had drawn it into the human world. And Artemis's calling spell had been perfect. Completely unbreakable. As long as she held up her end of the bargain, the contract she'd struck with Malachi would stand.

She laid the anthame atop one of the oak's protruding roots and scanned the ground for the other items she'd need. Twigs and leaves, newly fallen. Snatches of moss and lichen. A smear of dirt. A small, white pebble.

She arranged the horde of debris on a bare patch of dirt. The lichen and moss she bundled into a ball, forming a rough approximation of a doll's head. A thin, flexible branch served as a spine, with shorter twigs for arms and legs. Leaves filled out the torso and hinted at hands and feet.

The white pebble was the key—as the golem's heart, it would hold the magic of the animation spell. She placed it gently in the center of the figure's torso. A new life, fashioned from death.

Drawing the anthame from its sheath, she pressed the tip to her left ring finger. The familiar dart of pain helped her mind keep its focus. A red bead of blood glistened on her skin. Laying the knife on the ground, she squeezed the wound. Blood swelled like a crimson tear.

Bowing her head, she uttered several low, guttural syllables. They cut like shards of glass on her tongue. By the time she'd reached the end of the verse, her mouth felt raw and foul. Her balance shifted toward the dark side of magic. Her next words were ones of light and beauty. Soothing, like a honey balm. Vital energy flowed. She directed it into the golem's heart.

Now came the difficult part. The two spells she'd called, one light, one dark, would obliterate each other unless expertly blended. Artemis thought of the process as weaving, because that was the mundane activity her magical talent most closely resembled. But the joining spell was much more than that. She wasn't weaving thread into cloth. She was weaving light and darkness into life and death.

The opposing forces, drawn from her blood and from her soul, clashed. Artemis plucked equal strands of good and evil, entwining them by pairs into a magical web.

The cluster of dead leaves and moss began to look . . . different. A mundane human eye might not have noticed, but to Artemis, seeing and feeling with her witch's senses, the change was clear. The golem animation had begun.

The blood-smeared pebble shone and pulsed with steady light. The golem's moss face shifted and smoothed, taking on a human aspect. Eyes, nose, and mouth formed. Hair appeared—green, but humanlike nonetheless. The twig and leaf limbs flexed, testing their newfound cohesion.

The golem soon found its balance, and turned to face its creator. It hadn't opened its eyes. Not yet. Artemis steeled herself. She hated this final segment of the animation spell. The golem's naming. She searched for just the right sound, and found it.

"Tott. Time to wake up."

Mossy eyelids opened, revealing a dark, bright intelligence. Something like a smile quirked the figure's green lips. The golem, fully alive now, bent low at the waist, then turned a slow circle with arms extended. Sheer wonder and gratitude lit his small face. Twig feet executed a jig.

"I am alive!" He grinned broadly.

Artemis swallowed the raw lump in her throat. "Yes. You're alive."

"It's a wonderful feeling." The golem tilted his head to one side. "I'm to be Tott, then? A male? Very well." He bowed. "Tott, at your service, mistress. How may I serve you?"

There was nothing to do but tell him. The entire purpose of a golem's life, was, after all, to serve its creator.

"On the other side of this tree, there's an iron gate. It's heavily warded."

"Against life magic? Or death magic?"

"Both."

"Ah." The single word conveyed a wealth of sadness. And acceptance.

A sick feeling circulated in Artemis's chest. "I need you to open the gate. There are humans on the other side, though. They must not be hurt."

Sober understanding flickered in the golem's dark eyes,

but otherwise his expression didn't change. "Mine's to be a very short life, then, isn't it, mistress?"

"I'm sorry, Tott. If I could give you more time . . . But . . . I can't. I have to get through that gate as fast as I can."

"Your need is my duty, mistress. I want nothing more."

"I wish . . . I wish it could be otherwise."

He paused. "Shall I begin at once, mistress?"

Mutely, she nodded.

Without a backward glance, Tott turned and trotted around the curve of the tree trunk. Heart in her throat, Artemis eased around the oak, keeping the golem in sight. Tott scuttled across the lawn toward the gate.

He made no attempt to hide from the fans on the other side. A girl with purple-streaked haired caught sight of him and squealed, pointing. Her three friends turned and stared. The photographer hopped to attention and rushed the fence, camera clicking.

"What is it?" one of the girls asked.

The purple-haired girl stuck her hand through the fence. "Here, little man. Come on, that's a nice boy. . . ."

A dark-haired girl, who'd been dancing on the hood of a nearby car, stopped dead. "No! Gods! What're you doing? Don't call it. Get away! That thing is dangerous."

Well. At least one of Mac's fans had some sense.

The photographer lowered his camera. "What the hell is it, then?"

"It's a golem, you idiot! Death magic!"

He laughed. "It looks like a doll."

The brunette scrambled off the car and retreated to the far side of the road. "Well, it's not! A golem is a death animation. A slave that concentrates its creator's magic, kind of like a laser focuses light, multiplying the power. And the type of witches and sorcerers who animate golems . . ." She shuddered. "Their magic is strong enough on its own. Just . . . just don't get too close to it. You don't know what it's been ordered to do."

The photographer took a cautious step back. About half the fangirls did, too, retreating to the other side of the road. The rest, good sense lost to curiosity, held their ground.

"Fools," Artemis muttered.

Tott reached the gate. With a jump, he shimmied up the center post, not stopping until he reached the top. Balancing nimbly on the spiked finials, he circled his twig arms overhead. A small whirlwind rose on the ground beneath him, swirling leaves and chip wrappers.

A murmur rippled through the onlookers. The photographer raised his camera, adjusted his focus, and started shooting. A few more fans beat a prudent retreat. But one or two idiots remained close to the fence. Damn.

Artemis stepped out of the shadow of the oak. "Hey! You there! Your friend is right—the golem is dangerous! Get back!"

They retreated a step or two. Not enough. Artemis wiped her palms on her jeans. She had to believe Tott would be able to keep the bystanders safe. The little man was doing his best to concentrate the spell on the gate's wardings. His arms were a blur of movement.

The whirlwind rose, sending leaves and trash flying. The force swirled directly beneath Tott, turning through the closed gate as if it weren't there. Tott's arms circled even more quickly. The car nearest the gate heaved an inch off the ground and skidded across the road.

The last of the bimbos screamed and scurried to safety. *Finally.* Now Tott was free to let the tornado rise. Artemis's magic rode inside it, lifted and expanded by the tiny man she'd created. Undiluted, her magic was strong. Augmented by a golem's power, it was nothing short of terrifying.

Wind buffeted Artemis's body, flinging her hair about her face. Her senses were taut as the gate groaned and bent.

The warding spells stretched, emitting an ear-piercing squeal. Artemis shot a glance back at the mansion. Mac's servants were gathered at the front door.

Hurry.

Perched above the maelstrom, Tott raised his head. Fear contorted his face. "I am ready, mistress."

It was difficult to talk around the lump in her throat. "Thank you, Tott. I won't . . . I won't ever forget you."

"To be remembered is all any creature can hope for."

He bowed his head. The tornado rose, enveloping the golem's small body completely. Artemis forced herself to watch. She owed that much, at least, to the brief life she'd created. Her heart pounded as her magic, multiplied exponentially by Tott, flashed bright as the sun.

The golem's dying scream merged with the explosion—his death *was* the explosion. The blast, though expected, hurled Artemis backward. Her butt hit the ground. Mac's protective wardings shattered, sending shards of magic ripping in every direction.

The fangirls shrieked and dove behind the van. Artemis rolled, covering her head with her arms.

Then . . . silence.

Cautiously, Artemis lifted her head. The tornado was gone. Shoving to her feet, she ran toward the shattered gate amid a shower of leaves and twigs. Something small and hard fell at her feet.

A white pebble, smeared with her own blood.

She resisted the urge to snatch it up. Tott wouldn't have survived more than a few hours in any case; golem magic was that short-lived. The small man, grateful for the sip of life that never should have been his, had surrendered his existence willingly. Would it have been better if he'd never lived at all? Artemis didn't know. She only knew that she would grieve for him. That was more, she supposed, than most golems received from their creators.

The ruined gate swung crookedly on its hinges. A huge hole gaped in the warding spell. She darted through the opening, shoving past stunned fans as she ducked behind the white van. Its new spare tire gleamed.

Wrenching the driver's door open, she slid behind the wheel. Luck was with her. The key was in the ignition.

"Hey!" The purple-haired girl popped up near the front left headlight. Her tiny T-shirt bore an image of Mac's smiling face. "Get out of there!"

Artemis gunned the motor.

The girl threw herself onto the hood. "Stop! This people mover is *mine*!"

Artemis rolled down the window and stuck her head out. "If you have any brain at all, you'll get out of my way. You saw what I did to the gate. Do you really want me to toss a spell at you?"

The girl's mouth formed a perfect O. "It's *you*. The one who was with Mac. This *morning*." She gasped. "Did you . . . ohmygod! Did you *do it* with him? *Did* you? What was it *like*?"

Artemis jammed the shift into reverse. "Get off the hood. Now."

"But—" The girl's expression shot from awed to panicked. Flattening her body, she grabbed hold of the side rearview mirror. "No! This is my da's car. I can't let you take it. He'll have my head."

"I'm sorry. Really. But I need it more than you do right now. Now get off. You'll never stop me, and besides, you're missing all the fun."

"Fun?"

"Yeah. Fun." Artemis angled her head toward the mansion. The fangirl pack streamed across the front lawn, the photographer loping behind. "Mac's waiting. And your friends have got a pretty good head start on you."

"What? Oh, bloody, bloody *hell*!" The girl scrambled

off the van and hit the ground running. "Wait! Waaaait for meeeeee . . ."

Artemis slammed the gas pedal and careened into the road, tires spewing gravel. Making for the highway, she uttered a sound that was half sob, half hysterical laugh.

Poor Mac.

CHAPTER EIGHT

Mac woke to a sound like a rifle shot, coupled with a psychic wave of death. Shuddering, gasping, he clawed at consciousness, scrabbling for any lifeline. His tongue tasted like sheep dung; his joints burned like acid. A sharp iron hammer pounded the inside of his skull.

As bad as his physical hurts were, they were a mere pinprick to the gaping wound in his psyche. There was a hole where a piece of his soul should have been. He had never felt so exposed. So dirty. So . . . used.

By *Artemis*.

He sat bolt upright. Damn it all to hell. The witch was gone. The sour aftermath of her spell clung to his skin, and hovered in the empty space above his head. She'd gotten him good, blinding him with sex, then using the distraction to dig into his soul with a thin, sharp knife blade of death magic, taking what she wanted.

With a curse, he bounded from the bed. Beyond a few steps, the foul aura diminished considerably. Eyeing the mattress warily, he leaned just close enough to snatch a corner of the quilted coverlet and yank it off the bed. The evidence of Artemis's crime stared at him from the four corners of the white bedsheet. Four, small rust-colored stains—each about the size of his smallest fingernail—marked the bases of the bedposts.

The pounding in Mac's head intensified.

Blood. *Her* blood.

She'd spelled him. With death magic. Just as he'd . . . as they'd . . . *gods in Annwyn!* He was an idiot. He should have known a death witch wouldn't offer sex for free. On the contrary. She'd taken her payment. She'd stolen a piece of his soul. And he hadn't even known she was doing it.

But that wasn't the worst of it. Not by far.

Spitting curses, each fouler than the last, he stalked naked into the sitting room. The worst of it was that he'd lost control. Completely. Utterly. In that blinding instant of raw magic and complete bliss, he'd given Artemis something he'd never even considered offering to any other woman.

A child.

Gods in Annwyn. Putting aside for the moment that only an arrogant bastard would have made such a momentous decision without first consulting the lady involved, he was left staring at the stupidity of what he had done. He should be drawn, quartered, and flayed alive. Artemis had played him like a master musician. The melody of her light magic had completely obliterated the ugly counter-point of her dark intentions. How could he have been such an idiot?

How had he thought her worthy of carrying his child? She was the worst possible choice. But perhaps . . . per-haps his magic hadn't struck its mark. Perhaps Artemis's death spell had prevented his seed from taking root. It was a slim hope, but he snatched at it.

He had to find her. Discover if she was, indeed, carry-ing his divine child. And if his magic had created a new life—well, he'd have no choice but to lock the woman away until his child was born. Afterward . . . bloody hell. He didn't want to think about afterward. His emotions were too violent.

Raw anger—along with a considerable dose of humil-iation—flooded heat into his face. Unmanageable anger had been his unwanted companion for the past year, but this—this boiling rage was beyond anything he'd ever experienced. Damn it, he wanted to *kill* something.

Elfshot gathered on his fingertips. He aimed at the mantel. Green sparks shot; an innocent ceramic shepherdess exploded. The thump of her shiny head on the floor was fiercely satisfying. Deliberately, Mac took aim at the accompanying shepherd. Couldn't have the little bloke feeling left out, could he?

The shepherd joined his shepherdess in pieces on the floor. Vaguely ashamed, Mac turned away from the shattered ceramics. What a fool he'd been, to think any of Artemis's tenderness had been honest. He knew she was a criminal, and yet he'd trusted her. Not because she deserved it. Because he'd wanted her, desperately.

With her, he'd felt *alive*, as he hadn't since the battle to save Tain. The sex had been incredible. At least for him. Had it been good for her, too? She'd sure screamed loud enough. Had it been Mac's skill or her own death spell that had gotten her off?

He didn't like admitting it, but he suspected that death magic had been a large part of his own pleasure as well. A year ago, death magic would have shriveled his cock. Now, because of the slice of death in his soul, he had a damn good idea of the obsession that compelled demonwhores and vamp addicts to destroy themselves. He'd worshiped Artemis with his body, had thought she'd been as blown away by their lovemaking as he was. And all along, all she'd been after was a drop of his immortal life essence, to barter to a demon for the gods only knew what.

Still muttering under his breath, he returned to the bedroom and snatched a change of clothes from the dresser. She couldn't have gone far; there was no way she could get past his estate's wardings. He'd have her in hand within minutes. Then, by all the gods in Annwyn, she'd give him some honest answers.

He shrugged into his leather jacket. As he was passing by the window on his way to the door, a chorus of feminine squeals arrested his forward motion.

"Ooooh, *look!*"

"There he *is!*"

"In the *window!*"

Bloody, bloody hell. Fangirls on his front lawn. Impossible. How the *hell* had they gotten through the gate?

The iron hammer resumed its tattoo beat between his eyes.

He knew how. *Artemis.*

"Yoo-hooo!" A pretty redhead with enormous breasts waved up at him. "Mac! Hi! Can I come up?"

A brunette bounced at her side. "Me, too, Mac! I love you!"

The pair was only the advance guard. His gaze shot beyond them. The main pack, two dozen lasses, at least, galloped behind them, shrieking like banshees. The tall photog as well.

Ballocks. When he caught up with Artemis, he was going to strangle her.

Ducking out of his suite, Mac took the servants' stair three at a time, wincing at the sound of breaking glass and Fergus's subsequent shout. With any luck, he could duck out the servants' entrance before any of the girls found it.

No luck. The redhead and the brunette from the front lawn were, apparently, smarter than they looked. The instant he stepped into the sheltered service court, the pair cut him off. The dark-haired lass raised a camera; its flash momentarily blinded him.

"Oh, Mac," her friend breathed. "Crystal and I just *happened* to be driving by, and we thought—"

He sidestepped her grasping hand. "How did you get through the gate, love?"

"Oh. That. Well, some frumpy old witch made a little

man out of leaves. A golem, someone said it was. He blasted it open for her."

Mac's jaw dropped. Artemis had animated a golem? One powerful enough to incinerate his strongest wards?

Well done, woman!

The thought snuck in before he remembered what that same woman had done to him in bed. This proved it. Artemis Alexandria Black was a menace to society. A menace who was most likely carrying his child. Could things get any worse?

A purring sound snapped him back to the present. The redhead was rubbing against his chest like a sex-starved cat.

"Mac." Her tongue touched his neck; her hands skimmed his chest. "Crystal and I would just love to—"

"Er—"

Crystal plastered herself to his back. "—get to know you better, Mac."

"Sorry, lasses. Not a good time. In a bit of a rush at the moment." Deftly, he extracted himself from their enthusiasm. "Tell you what. Crystal, is it? Why don't you send a couple copies of that photo you took round to my agent? I'll autograph them for you."

The pair squealed like giddy piglets. Mac dashed across the lawn, sweeping a wide arc around the fangirl pack, tossing spells of confusion in his wake. His entrance gate was indeed a tangled mess, iron bars twisted like spaghetti, the ground below charred black.

He slowed. Simple golems were death animations. That alone shouldn't have been enough to destroy his wards. Indeed, the dark spell's acrid odor hung in the air, but that wasn't what sent Mac's pulse into overdrive. A fresh scent lingered as well, a perfect, harmonious chord of life magic.

Again, Artemis's unique touch had created a perfectly balanced light/dark force far more powerful than the original death-magic spell. He couldn't help pausing in admiration. It was magnificent, really. Wickedly stunning.

Like the orgasm she'd given him. Like the fascination he just couldn't shake. The unpredictable witch was so far beyond Mac's experience she left him wondering which way was up. Who the hell *was* she, really?

Oh, he knew a few facts. Number one: Artemis was a lying, conniving bitch. Two: she was a brazen hussy. She'd stolen his life essence—after he'd saved her from the consequences of the same crime. Unforgivable, that—but he found himself, inexplicably, racking his brain for a plausible excuse. Because . . .

Facts number three and four: he genuinely liked her, and most likely, she was to be the mother of his child.

He couldn't have impregnated a woman who was evil. He hadn't sensed that about her. But what the hell was she up to? He'd asked if she was in trouble. He'd offered his help—of magic and money. No sane human turned down an offer of assistance from an immortal demigod.

Which left only two possibilities. Either she was insane— and he didn't think that was too likely—or she was involved in something extremely malevolent, something she knew he would never agree to help her with. The latter seemed all too likely.

Even if by some miracle she wasn't pregnant, he had to recapture her. There was no telling what mischief she'd get up to next, or where she would enact her next scam. If one of his charges suffered because of his leniency, Mac would never forgive himself.

He picked up her trail outside the ruined gate. She'd been in too much of a panic to hide it. She'd left in a vehicle—no doubt stolen from one of his fans. The witch had no shame. And no sense of self-preservation, either.

Surely she couldn't have forgotten the tracking spell he'd put on her.

She'd forgotten the tracking spell Mac had put on her.

Stupid, stupid, *stupid*.

Pulling abruptly onto the shoulder of the road, Artemis gripped the van's steering wheel with a shaky hand and directed her senses inward. The mark Mac had put on her was strong. No way could she remove it in time. But weaken it? That she could do. Fracture it? Perhaps that, too.

A half hour later, a grim smile on her lips, she merged back into traffic. She'd split Mac's spell into thirteen separate spells, twelve of which she'd attached to random passing motorists. That should slow him down. At least, she hoped, until sunset.

Acutely aware of each passing second, Artemis followed the twisted road north, then picked up the A96, heading west. Only one hour and forty-seven minutes until the sun sank below the horizon.

I'll be there soon, Zander.

Adrenaline tying knots in her stomach, she stomped on the accelerator, careening into the right lane and skimming past the car on the left with mere millimeters to spare. The driver shook his fist, but she'd already cut back in front of him. Acutely aware of each passing second, she sped toward the strongest power sink in the vicinity she could locate without her map. The site was more well known than she would have liked, but beggars couldn't be choosers.

Gliding off at the next exit, Artemis slowed at the bottom of the ramp and scanned the tourist signs until she spotted one that pointed the way to Clava Cairns. The prehistoric grave site contained three prehistoric burial mounds, each ringed by a circle of standing stones. It was a rare place, where death and life magic met in balance. Tonight, Halloween, the veil between life and death stretched thin, making that power even more accessible.

The road narrowed as she left a small town behind. She entered a cleft of land between two rising meadows. Samhain festivities were in full swing—parked cars and tents lined the road, and black-garbed figures clustered about small balefires. She abandoned the stolen minivan in a low, muddy spot no one else had claimed. The tires sank into muck past the rims, but that hardly mattered. She wouldn't be coming back.

Keeping to the shadows, she made her way toward the cairns, skirting costumed humans—faux vampires, fake demons, stage-worthy goblins without a drop of magic among them. A black-robed, kohl-eyed Satanist—his aura indicated he possessed at best a smattering of magic—cast her a baleful eye. She only hoped he managed to survive the night unscathed by true evil.

She kept her senses open to genuine sorcerers and death witches, and magical creatures of all kinds. Vampires, ogres, werewolves, faeries, Sidhe, selkies—all represented complications she couldn't afford. Best to avoid them.

She ventured as close to the cairns and standing stones as she could. The burial mounds had long been empty of corpses, but the magic that had caused the ancients to lay their dead in this place was eternal. The cairns were positioned on the joining of several ley lines. That natural power, combined with the magic of the long-ago witches who'd consecrated the earth for burial, vibrated beneath Artemis's feet.

Electricity hung in the air, as if a storm approached, though late afternoon sunlight slanted through crisp, clean air. Shadows were long; sunset was only minutes away. Artemis's hand crept to her throat, her fingers wrapping the comforting weight of the moonstone in its protective pouch. Soon the prize would be in Malachi's hands, and she would be on her way to Zander.

She faded into the crowd, a look-away spell providing privacy. She reached into her pack, pulled out her photo wallet, and flipped to the most recent picture of her son. She'd taken it at a playground, last spring. Her heart squeezed with her remembering.

"Watch, Mommy!"

Zander hoisted his skinny body to the top of a knotted climbing rope, a good fifteen feet about the ground. Before Artemis could react, he launched himself into the air, hanging suspended for an instant, arms spread, before landing on his feet, sure as a cat.

Artemis swallowed the soft-landing spell in her throat as Zander ran to her, all smiles. He'd spoken the spell on his own.

"Did you see that, Mommy?"

"Yes. That was great, baby."

"Aw, Mommy, don't call me that. I'm not a baby anymore."

He was right. "Of course you're not."

"And my magic is strong."

"Yes. It is."

And that was the problem. Her son's magic *was* strong—and his talents, like hers, were almost equally split between life and death magic. Zander's potential had caught the attention of psychic ops command. When Artemis realized what was happening, she'd left the military, taking advantage of a wave of troop reductions that had followed the Immortals' victory over death magic last year. She didn't want Zander following in her footsteps. She didn't want him learning the dark arts, as she had. She didn't want him dealing with vampires, death sorcerers, and demons, as she had.

If only she'd realized her dealings with one particular demon had already placed her son in jeopardy. How could she have been so complacent? The Immortals' defeat of a foul Old One didn't mean evil itself had been destroyed. Dark and light were two sides of a coin. Equal forces with a mutual dependency. One Old One might be gone, but there were others, equally depraved, to fill the void.

Artemis, of all people, should have been more wary. She knew better than anyone how demons operated. She'd spent years outwitting them and had made more than one deadly enemy. She should have anticipated the attack on Zander.

Guilt threatened to swallow her whole. If only she'd set stronger protections around her son. If only she'd been more vigilant. If she had, maybe Zander's small body wouldn't be lying in a hospital bed. Alive—the beeping monitors proved that. But there was no light behind his beautiful eyes. His physical form was just a shell.

His soul, his life essence—it was gone. Stolen.

Tears threatened. She blinked them back. She shoved the photograph into her pack—she shouldn't even have looked at it. Not now, when her meeting with Malachi loomed large and everything depended on the next few hours. She needed to be on top of her magical game.

But when she cleared her mind, it was only to make room for thoughts of Mac. Gods. How humiliated he must have been when he'd awakened to the backwash of her putrid spell. How enraged. She could almost see his green eyes snapping with fury.

She slid her anthame from her pack, anxiety rising. Was he still looking for her? She only hoped fracturing his mark on her had done its job in throwing him off her trail.

Sunset was almost upon her. The crescent moon was just visible in the western sky, riding low. The moonstone pendant was a hot, heavy presence between her breasts. She moved into position directly atop the cairns' major ley line. She would have preferred a position closer to the burial mounds, but the fenced-in area and its adjacent car park was far too crowded with magical folk. She'd have to make do.

Bending, she scratched a circle on the bare ground with the tip of her blade. The invisible power line ran exactly through the circle's center. She conjured a ring of protection and stood within it. Calm descended as she pulled the magic of the sacred earth into her body.

The revelers all around grew frenzied in anticipation of sunset. Shucking their clothing, they danced naked around their fires. Only a few minutes now, and it would be time to open the portal and enter Malachi's death realm. If all went as planned, she'd reemerge before dawn with Zander's soul.

She drew a sharp breath as the sun touched the horizon. Extending her left arm, she set the tip of her knife to the tender skin on the inside of her elbow. The activity outside her circle receded to the edges of her consciousness. Sounds fell away; the ground seemed to dissolve. Her lips moved, forming words so ugly, so dark and deadly, the fabric of the human world rebelled. The air grew thin, space itself stretched. The blade pressed to her skin; the point pricked. A droplet of blood dripped down her forearm.

She spoke Malachi's name.

Pure death magic gathered. Her balance faltered, and her stomach roiled. She bit back a surge of bile. It took everything inside her to stop from breaking her circle and fleeing. Tightening her grip on the anthame's jeweled hilt, she turned the blade to the air before her. The fabric of reality, already stretched thin, had been made even more vulnerable by her death spell. A single slice would rip it in two. She angled the blade for the final cut.

It never came. Brilliant green light stunned her vision. The beam struck the flat of her anthame's blade, spinning the knife from her grasp. It turned hilt-over-tip, its honed edge slicing through the outer edge of her circle before embedding itself in the mud.

Her protective spell shattered. In the same instant— before she could move, before she could even *think*— something hit her from behind, sending her sprawling.

"No!" she gasped. Her first thought was that Mac had caught her. Gods, no. Not now. Not when she'd been so close.

Strong magic—life magic—held her facedown on the muddy ground. Artemis struggled, kicking, trying to turn to look at him—but got exactly nowhere. She grunted out a quick death spell and flung it behind her.

She heard the spell hit, but the pressure didn't let up in the least.

"Come, now." A cold, feminine voice dripped with disdain. "That was pitiful. Can't you manage anything stronger?"

Artemis's blood froze. Her captor wasn't Mac.

"Who—oof." She choked as something shoved her face in the mud. "Let. Me. Up."

"I think not, witch."

The force controlling Artemis rolled her swiftly onto her back. She blinked up at her captor. Tall and delicate, the woman appeared to be no more than twenty. She wore a green silk gown, the bodice trimmed in gold braid. A gauzy skirt with a pointed handkerchief hem skimmed her knees and calves. Her bare arms were decorated with gold bangles, and golden sandals shod her delicate feet. Blond hair, intricately braided, wrapped her head like a golden crown, leaving her graceful neck—and pointed Sidhe ears—bare.

Her glittering green gaze was eerily familiar.

"Are you . . . are you Mac's mother?" Artemis whispered. "The Sidhe queen?"

"Silence, witch. You're not fit to pronounce my son's name."

Gods. She was screwed. And the sun had all but sunk past the horizon. She tried to keep her voice even. "You're right, of course."

"I can't believe he bedded you." Niniane's delicate nose wrinkled. "He must be insane. You stink of death magic."

"He . . . he's through with me now. I'll never see him again. There's no reason for you to attack me. Let me go, please."

"Believe me, there's nothing I'd like better than to never lay eyes on human scum like you again. Unfortunately, it's not that simple. I've heard disturbing reports from the faeries. My son has been shirking his duties. Get up."

Artemis lurched to her feet, yanked by Sidhe magic almost before the command had reached her ears.

"Follow me."

The Sidhe queen wove easily through the crowd, a look-away glamour deflecting the attention of the Samhain revelers. Artemis had no choice but to follow, her legs jerking as if controlled by puppet strings as she moved farther and farther from her ruined circle, from her anthame, from the portal to Malachi's realm. From Zander.

Sheer horror squeezed the air from her lungs. There was no question as to where Niniane was leading her. To the place where Mac should have taken her. The Sidhe Council.

"Please. No. I can explain."

"Your chance to speak will come, witch. For now, you will be silent."

Like hell she would. Gathering her magic, she gasped out a death spell.

The charm fizzled like an apprentice witch's first solo charm.

Niniane whirled about, every inch of her body vibrating with rage. "You dare attack me?"

With a flick of a finger, the Sidhe queen pitched Artemis backward. She landed hard on her butt. A tingling curtain of green sparks showered down all around her, forming a shimmering cocoon.

Niniane lifted a hand and murmured a wisp of a spell Artemis couldn't quite hear. The matted grass near Artemis's right hand began to glow. When the light died, Artemis was left staring at what looked like an oversized fox hole, secured by a round wooden door. The Sidhe queen grasped the tarnished brass handle. The door opened easily. The first few steps of a stone stair came into view.

Artemis drew a breath. "What is that?"

"A Sidhe barrow," Niniane said. She cocked a perfect

eyebrow. "Surely a stalker of faeries like yourself knows of the barrows."

Artemis did. And if she weren't so panicked, she would have been fascinated. Sidhe barrows—most likely thousands of them—existed all over the Celtic isles, their entranceways hidden even more thoroughly than a faerie village. According to legend, the mounded earth barrows led to a network of magical underground passages that provided near-instant transportation between entrances, no matter how many human miles apart the doors lay. It was rumored the Sidhe barrow network even included passages to the Celtic Otherworld, Annwyn.

And to the Sidhe Council.

Niniane jerked Artemis to her feet. "Down you go, witch."

"No, I—"

"No arguments."

Mac's mother wouldn't be swayed. Desperate, Artemis eyed the curtain of green sparks. Could she break the spell that bound her and dash through the barrier to safety? She had to try. Working swiftly, she gathered death words and crafted them into a dense, ugly pattern in her brain.

She took one step toward the stair, eyes downcast, keeping Niniane in her peripheral vision. A second step brought her to the doorway. She placed a foot on the top stair.

Niniane's stance shifted; her shoulders relaxed, just a fraction.

Artemis took advantage of the slight opening. She flung her spell, felt the restraints fall from her limbs. She spun about and bolted, through the shower of sparks, across the meadow, cursing the tall grass. If only she could get back to her circle before Niniane caught her . . .

A deadweight struck her square in the back. The next instant she found herself stopped dead, her hands bound behind her with magic that burned her wrists. Niniane appeared in her vision. If Artemis thought the Sidhe queen angry before, it was nothing compared to how enraged she was now. "Please. My lady, let me expl—"

Her words evaporated in her throat. Her lips felt thick; they refused to move, as if they were . . . *sealed shut?* Her horrified gaze met Niniane's satisfied one.

"That's right. No more disobedience. No more death spells. You'll not speak again until I give you permission."

Artemis swallowed thickly. All right. She wasn't completely defenseless—she could cast life magic mentally. She assembled a charm in her mind . . . only to have it unravel before it was well formed enough to cast.

Niniane sighed. "You're a stubborn one, aren't you? But stupid. I'm the Queen of Annwyn! No life magic you could call will help you escape."

She was right. Artemis was truly powerless. But she had to get away. She had to. She'd missed her sunset rendezvous with Malachi—no doubt the demon was furious with her. When she finally managed to reach him, she'd have some serious groveling to do. Groveling and worse.

Her mind blanked as Niniane forced her down the dark stair. Green elflight twinkled to life, illuminating a damp, dark, tunnel. Roots hung from the ceiling, brushing her face. She sneezed violently—once, twice, soundlessly. Her eyes burned. With her hands bound behind her, she couldn't even wipe them.

Niniane propelled her forward, unrelenting. "You stepped into the wrong arena, love, when you set your sights on my son. Mac may be reluctant to serve up your punishment, but you'll find I am not."

She steered Artemis into a steeply sloping side passage. Fifty paces later, the passageway reached a dead end in front of a tall, ancient doorway.

The door's frame was an arch of shining silver-gray granite, intricately decorated with a Celtic knot pattern.

The door itself was oak, hewn from a single slab of that sacred wood. Its surface bore carvings of Sidhe men and women, slender and tall, dancing with arms entwined.

The portal glowed with an ethereal light. Niniane lifted her palm, and the slab swung inward. Bright white light shot pain into Artemis's eyes. She squeezed them shut as the Sidhe queen shoved her over the threshold.

A shiver of dread chased down her spine.

Niniane laughed. "Welcome to the Sidhe Council chamber, witch."

CHAPTER NINE

Why the hell should he feel sorry for her?

The answer was, of course, that he shouldn't feel a drop of pity. The witch wasn't worth it. She'd cast death magic over him while he worshipped her body, intent on giving her nothing but bliss. She'd virtually raped a piece of his soul, blasted through the wards on his estate gate, and, if he'd read her magical signature at the cairns correctly, she'd been a breath away from tearing open a portal to a demon realm when Niniane caught up with her.

And how the hell had that come about, anyway? He dragged both hands through his hair. His mother must have spies everywhere. How much did Niniane know? He'd tracked the two women to the barrows. Niniane was definitely taking Artemis to the Sidhe Council.

Did his mother know Artemis had attacked the faeries? Did she know the witch was a talented sorceress trafficking life essence to demons? If not for the likelihood Artemis was carrying his child, Mac might be tempted to leave the infuriating witch in Niniane's clutches.

Niniane, who had abandoned her own half-human infant, would be beyond appalled if she discovered someone like Artemis was pregnant with her grandchild. No doubt she would sentence Artemis to death all the more quickly because of it. The all-too-real scenario caused Mac's chest to contract so violently it was difficult to breathe.

He dashed through the maze of tunnels, eyes fixed on the glowing trail at his feet. He only hoped he wasn't too far behind. Damn Artemis for splitting the tracking spell he'd put on her. He'd lost an hour of precious time tracking mundanes.

Despite the fact that Artemis had lied to him, had used him in the basest way—had, in fact, ignited his fury to the boiling point—all Mac could think of was getting to her in time to save her from the Sidhe council's judgment. Despite Artemis's disturbing affinity for death magic, and his certainty she was dealing with a demon, he couldn't bear to see her hurt. Child or no.

He was a bloody idiot. Clearly the battle to save Tain had done grave injury to Mac's intelligence and common sense as well as to his soul.

He didn't even pause before the closed door to the Sidhe Council chamber. Shoving the door open, he burst into the room, blinking against its sudden dazzling light.

Eight alabaster columns supported the chamber's sky-blue dome above. Artemis stood atop a platform set in the center of the chamber. Her head jerked up as the door crashed against the wall. Something like hope flashed in her eyes. He suppressed the urge to dash to her side. It wouldn't do. She stood upon the platform of the accused. By Sidhe law, no one could stand with her.

Her hands were bound behind her and her lips were pressed firmly together—sealed shut, he had no doubt. Niniane didn't appreciate back talk.

He swung his gaze to his mother, who stood before her councillor's throne—one of seven bejeweled chairs set in the spaces between the columns. Her lips were pursed with displeasure at his sudden appearance.

Conflicting emotions warred in Mac's chest. He hadn't spoken more than a dozen words to his mother in over a year—since the day he'd told her an Old One had hauled her only daughter through a portal to a demon realm. Mac didn't know why he'd expected to see a glimmer of regret when Niniane learned of Leanna's fate. But he *had* expected it, and it hadn't surfaced. Now, even though Mac cared for his mother, and knew she felt his withdrawal keenly, he could hardly bring himself to look at her.

"Manannán. Whatever are you doing here? Your presence isn't needed."

Mac crossed his arms and popped his shoulder against one of the columns. "I disagree. This woman is my responsibility. I have no doubt that you know that."

Niniane's hand fluttered. "She was not in your custody when I apprehended her. I've already summoned the Council. We will examine the criminal—a criminal, I might add, you should have brought to us a day ago—and issue a verdict. You will have nothing to do with the proceedings."

"We'll see about that."

Niniane huffed. A bell rang, and Artemis stiffened. A door directly opposite the one Mac had entered opened. This second portal led directly to the Celtic Otherworld and opened only for members of the Sidhe Council, the elders charged with deliberating human crimes against Celtic magical creatures.

One by one, the councillors entered, bowing to their queen as they passed. Mac eyed each in turn. The wrinkled face of Saraid, the most ancient of Sidhe, reflected the passing of a half dozen millennia. Even so, her blue eyes were bright as a child's and the points of her ears did not droop in the slightest. Her twisted yew staff rang against the chamber's stone floor, marking each slow step.

Behind Saraid strode her son, Briac, dark and somber, nearly as ancient as his mother. The ermine trim on his robe trailed sparks. Behind Briac glided three telepathic sisters—they'd been born triplets, an exceedingly rare and fortuitous event in Sidhe history. Lustrous red curls cascaded like liquid flame down their backs. Enid, Enys, and Erlina—Mac had the damnedest time telling them apart—were renowned for centuries of fair judgments in Sidhe/human disputes.

Tadc was the last of the councillors to enter, his waist-length blond hair gathered in a queue so tight it had to cause his scalp to ache. Of all the councillors, Tadc's contempt for the human race was surpassed only by Niniane's.

The Sidhe did not so much as glance at the accused. Pacing to their thrones, they remained standing until Niniane's regal nod gave them permission to be seated.

Seating herself, Niniane gave her skirt a final brush of her hand. "The trial may begin."

Tadc was the first to rise. His pinched eyes looked Artemis up and down. "What is this creature?"

Mac uncrossed his arms and stepped forward. "She's a witch."

Tadc raised a brow. "Human?"

"Mostly."

Niniane regarded her son steadily. "Manannán apprehended her a day ago. He should have brought her directly to us. He did not." She sighed. "You're always too soft where humans are concerned, Mackie."

Mac's cheeks heated. Niniane knew he hated that childhood nickname, but she continued to use it as a way of keeping some small power over him. It galled him he couldn't help cringing every time he heard it.

"What I don't understand," Mac said slowly, "is how you came to know of her."

A small smile played on Niniane's lips. "Why, your paparazzi, of course."

Mac stared at her. "You've been in contact with my fans? My *human* fans? I don't bloody believe it."

Niniane hated humans. He couldn't fathom she'd stoop so low as to make an alliance with one of them. But it made sense. Pieces to a nagging puzzle fell into place. His unraveled glamours. The uncanny accuracy of his fan blog. The speed with which the fangirls tracked him. Of course Niniane had helped them. And they, in turn, had helped her.

"That underfed photographer is especially handy," Niniane was saying. "If not for him, I'd hardly know what you were up to anymore." Her lips thinned as she turned a disgusted eye on Artemis. "But really, Mackie, don't you think you've gone too far this time? Consorting with a death witch? What could you have been thinking?"

"A death witch?" Enid cut in. Or perhaps it was Enys. "What is her crime?"

"She's cast death magic against Celtic creatures," Niniane stated. "She siphoned life essence from faeries. I've spoken with dozens of victims since I learned of the attacks. Apparently, since the summer solstice, many, many villages have succumbed to this witch's dark arts."

A shocked murmur swept around the circle. The councillors muttered and shook their heads. Briac regarded Artemis as if she were a particularly disgusting species of slug.

"Deaths?" Saraid's voice was colder than the North Sea.

"None," Niniane admitted. "The amounts stolen were relatively small."

"So as not to draw undue attention to her crime," Tadc murmured. "Clever for a human."

Mac shifted on his feet. "In at least one instance," he interjected, "the accused returned the stolen life essence when it became clear her attack had endangered the life of a young one. The child recovered fully."

Niniane waved a hand. "A minor point. Clearly, the witch is guilty. I propose a death sentence."

Alarm widened Artemis's eyes. She shook her head, her throat bulging. She stumbled forward a step, in Niniane's direction, teetering at the edge of the platform.

Niniane leaped to her feet, elfshot bursting from her

fingers. The bolt hit Artemis. She bent double, staggering
back to the center of the platform. Her lips worked, but
couldn't part far enough to let out a cry of pain.

Damn it all to hell. Bugger Sidhe law. Mac surged toward the platform. Sariad's reedy voice drew him up short.

"Take care, Mac Lir, that you do not do something you
will regret."

Mac barely restrained himself from leaping onto the
platform. Saraid was right; breaking Sidhe protocol would
hardly help Artemis's cause. He settled for inserting his
body between Niniane and Artemis. "Assaulting a prisoner? That's beneath you, Mother. And as for this witch's
punishment—death is not an option. Nor is slavery in Annwyn. I will not allow either sentence."

Niniane's fair brows rose to her hairline. "Why? Just
because you've had sex with this whore?"

Mac's jaw clenched, sending a sharp pain into his temple. "No. Because this witch hasn't caused any lasting
harm to anyone. She doesn't deserve to die."

"You're a grave disappointment to me, Manannán.
Slumming with a death witch. Really! When are you going
to stop your irresponsible darting about the human world,
playing that obnoxious noise you call music, shirking your
responsibilities to your own people—"

Mac's fingers curled into fists. "I have not shirked my
responsibilities."

"No? Then tell me how this witch has been able to assault so many faeries. Because you were not here to protect
them, perhaps? You were flitting around Europe. Asia. Aus-
tralia. The Americas. If you'd stayed in Annwyn—or even
in Scotland—where you belong, it would not have happened."

Mac was in no mood to face the truth of that. The elders eyed him; his face burned. "Where I go and what I do
is none of your business, Mother."

Niniane pointed her slender finger and shook it. "When

will you learn, Mac? The Prince of Annwyn must *rule* from Annwyn."

"Mother." Mac's teeth clenched so tightly pain radiated into his jaw and down his neck. "Can we please return to the subject at hand? The trial of this human?"

The Sidhe queen's rosy lips pressed into a thin, unattractive line. "Very well. The Council will proceed with her interrogation." Her eyes narrowed. "It would be best if you go now, Manannán. This will not be pleasant."

Alarm flashed through Artemis's eyes.

"No." Mac's voice was deadly calm. "I'm staying."

Wisely, Niniane didn't press the matter. Settling back into her throne, she addressed Artemis with loud, slow words, as if speaking to a small, stupid child.

"I will lift the mute spell so you may answer the Council's questions truthfully and completely. Be warned, human— no lie may be spoken in the Sidhe Council chambers. If you attempt to do so, it will be known instantly. The penalty for falsehood is death." Her gaze flicked to Mac. "And there is no recourse. Do you understand?"

Artemis nodded once.

Niniane raised a finger. Artemis let out a choking gasp, as if a noose about her neck had suddenly been loosened. She rubbed her unbound wrists.

"Now, then. Your name, human."

"Artemis Alexandria Black," she rasped.

"You are a witch?"

"Yes. I—"

Niniane silenced her with a frown. "You will answer only the question posed, Miss Black. Now. I sense you are mostly human. What other blood flows in your veins?"

Mac stifled a curse. This line of questioning certainly wouldn't help Artemis's cause.

"Water spirit," Artemis began. "Norse Giantess. Shapeshifter." She swallowed. "Troll . . ."

Niniane's eyes narrowed. "And?"

Artemis's voice dipped to a whisper. "Demons. Several different kinds."

Mac winced as a shocked murmur raced around the circle. Briac scowled deeply, his fingers steepled under his pointed beard. Tadc shook his head in disgust. The three sisters exchanged glances, then turned as one to stare at Artemis. Only old Saraid's expression did not change.

Niniane's shudder was one of pure disgust. "It makes me truly ill to consider the sex acts that produced this creature." She peered at Artemis. "You are a disgusting mongrel. Is there no Celtic blood in you at all?"

Artemis met the Sidhe queen's gaze squarely. "No. There isn't."

"Thank the gods for that, at least! The thought of Celtic magic mixing with that of demons and trolls . . ." She glared at Mac. "I cannot believe you bedded this atrocity."

Mac stared back, stonily, until his mother huffed and turned back to her prisoner. Damn it all to hell. For Artemis's crime, there was only one sentence, other than death or imprisonment, that the Council could hand down. This archaeological expedition into Artemis's antecedents was uncalled for.

He wanted to jump up on the platform and wrap her in his arms. Disturbingly, that emotion didn't have anything to do with her possible pregnancy. It had to do with Artemis alone.

He moved between Niniane and Saraid, physically aligning himself with the circle of elders in a none-too-subtle reminder of his power among the Sidhe.

"Miss Black's ancestors are not on trial here," he said. "The charge against her is simple. Nonlethal theft of faerie life essence."

Niniane's green gaze bored into Artemis. "Is my son's accusation true, human? Think carefully before you answer, and remember the penalty for lies."

Artemis's chin lifted. Her shoulders went back; her eyes met Niniane's, coldly. Mac bit back a groan. A bit of groveling wouldn't come amiss right about now.

"It is true, Your Highness. But, if you please, I can explain. My need is great—"

"Your needs are no concern of ours."

Artemis stiffened, eyes flashing. "But you must hear me! I demand—"

A shocked buzz zipped around the Council chamber. Sidhe elders did not tolerate impertinence. Tadc shook his head, Briac's scowl deepened. The sisters exchanged glances. Saraid gave a sigh.

Niniane surged to her feet. "You are not in a position to demand anything, whore!" Her hand rose, sparks of elf-shot gathering angrily on her fingertips.

Mac moved quickly, blocking Niniane's view of Artemis. "Stop, Mother. Stop now."

Grudgingly, Niniane lowered her hand. "Justice will be served." Turning, she addressed the elders. "You have heard the witch's confession. She is guilty of her crime. Do any of you wish to question this creature further?"

A sudden ring of wood on stone sounded. All eyes turned to Saraid, watching in silence as the most ancient Sidhe used her staff to lever herself onto her feet.

She set her piercing blue gaze on Artemis. "Miss Black. How many faeries have felt the effects of your death magic?"

Artemis blinked. "I . . . I don't know."

"Your best estimate, if you please."

"I . . . about two hundred. But none were permanently harmed."

"But they *were* harmed, I assume? Became ill? Lost their joy for life?"

"Temporarily. Yes."

The elder moved closer. Leaning heavily on her staff,

she made a slow, halting circuit around the accused, her gaze traveling from Artemis's head to her toes several times. Raising her gnarled hand, she pointed a long, twisted finger. "You wear a charmed pendant."

Mac didn't miss the flash of raw fear in Artemis's eyes, quickly suppressed.

"Yes."

Mac's attention sharpened. What was this? He didn't remember Artemis wearing any pendant, magical or otherwise. She certainly hadn't been wearing it in bed.

"You will remove it. Now."

Artemis's hand went to her throat. "No, please, I—"

Saraid spoke a word; Artemis's hand dropped. The elder hooked her forefinger beneath the chain at Artemis's throat. The silver links separated.

A round pendant, about the size of a quail's egg, dangled from the elder's weathered fingers. The ornament had an odd covering—a silk-platinum weave, Mac realized with a start. No wonder he hadn't been aware of it. A silk and platinum fabric, bespelled in just the right way, blocked magical probing.

Old Saraid muttered a second spell. The pendant's protective covering fluttered to the ground, revealing a tear-shaped moonstone. Rays of white light shot from the gem in all directions, giving the stone the aspect of a star.

Shocked silence reigned. For once, even Niniane was speechless.

As for Mac, he could only gape. *Bloody, bloody hell.* Artemis hadn't sold the life essence she'd stolen. She'd hoarded it. Every last drop of it, including his own, was trapped within the gem. The energy packed into that tiny rock boggled Mac's mind.

The faces of the councillors radiated sheer outrage. Stolen life magic had only so many uses, and all of them nasty. No human could be entrusted with such power.

Artemis stood rigid, her gaze fixed on the pendulum swing of the moonstone. She looked up suddenly, directly at him. The raw anguish in her dark eyes sliced the breath from his lungs.

Gradually, he realized that the elders had shifted their attention from Artemis to him. Seven pairs of eyes were regarding him with profound disappointment.

Niniane rose, her body shaking. "Manannán. I cannot believe you consorted with this criminal." She nodded at Saraid. "Destroy the stone."

Artemis's eyes went wide. She lunged at the faerie queen, stumbling to the edge of the platform. Saraid held her back with a word.

Artemis sank to her knees, tears streaming from her eyes.

Niniane's color was high, her gaze pinning Artemis in place. "Never, in all the centuries that I've lived, have I witnessed such a blatant insult to the Celtic races. Nor do I ever wish to see such a thing again. Saraid?"

The elder nodded gravely. Her lips parted; a single word rolled off her tongue.

The moonstone flared with a brilliance that had even Mac shielding his eyes. As if a floodgate had been opened, thousands of sparks streamed upward, whirling like a cloud of stars above the elders' heads.

"No! Oh gods, no!"

Artemis jumped up and stretched as high as she could, as if she could pluck the stolen morsels of life from the air. But it was too late—the bits of souls were already seeking their sources. Mac felt a sizzle, and an accompanying flood of well-being, and knew the life essence Artemis had taken from him had been restored. And the rest—

Niniane waved a hand and the chamber door leading to the human world opened. The dazzling cloud streamed through it. In the space of two heartbeats, Artemis's entire ill-gotten harvest had vanished.

The moonstone went dark. Saraid's fingers opened. The gem fell, striking the floor with a solid ring of defeat.

"No . . . no . . . n—" Artemis swayed on her feet.

Her knees abruptly buckled. Damning Sidhe protocol to hell, Mac leaped to catch her.

He was an instant too late.

CHAPTER TEN

A beam of elfshot leaped from Niniane's fingers, knocking Mac clean off his feet as he stormed the platform. It was the last thing Artemis saw before she crumpled to the ground. For several long, gray moments, she fought to stay conscious. She was far too petrified to faint.

Gradually, lucidity returned. A ball of green light hovered over her head, spilling sparks all around. The moonstone lay at the eldest Sidhe's feet, as cold and empty as a broken promise.

She squinted through the twinkling cage. Mac was just picking himself off the ground. She could hardly believe his mother had dared strike him.

Niniane's voice rang clear. "This witch's crimes are clear. What punishment shall we mete?"

Mac let out a growl. "Mother. Stop this."

"A vote has been called for, Manannán," Niniane replied. "You cannot prevent the Council from speaking its verdict now. As queen, I cast my vote first." She paused. "Death."

"Mother—"

"Death," a second voice intoned.

Gods. This couldn't be happening.

"Death."

"Death."

"Death."

"Death."

"Death."

"*No.*" Mac glowered at the Sidhe. "No. I will not permit it."

"Mac." Niniane's rebuke was sharp. "The Council has spoken."

"I don't bloody care. I made it clear at the start of this proceeding that I will not allow a verdict of death in this case."

Niniane scowled at her son as if he were a recalcitrant toddler. "Mac. This witch is a danger to our kind. You know it's true. Her crimes are proven, and she shows not one iota of remorse. Her power is beyond anything I've ever sensed in a human. And if that's not enough, she's part demon! If she's not executed, she'll likely use her magic for ill again." She spread her hands. "Can you deny it?"

"No," Mac said tersely, his jaw working. "But death isn't necessary to ensure her reform. Stripping her of her powers will be punishment enough."

His declaration struck like a punch to Artemis's gut. "No," she gasped. "Mac, no! You can't let them—"

He rounded on her. His eyes reflected her own pain. "Artemis. You've admitted your guilt before the Council. The elders saw the life essence you hoarded with their own eyes! How can you imagine you'll leave here untouched?" His fist clenched and unclenched. "At least you'll be alive."

"As a mundane?" Artemis cried. "I'd rather be dead!"

"See, Mac?" Niniane cut in. "The witch agrees. She *wants* to die. Why not let her? It'd be for the best."

A muscle in Mac's jaw twitched. "No. The Council will cast the power-stripping spell. Now, while I watch. Afterward you'll release Artemis into my care."

It was like being in a cell, with the walls slowly caving in, and no way out. Stripped of her powers? Artemis couldn't imagine a worse fate. Without her magic, she'd never get to Zander. Her contract with Malachi might be long expired and the moonstone useless, but as long as she had her power, she wasn't completely without hope.

But first she needed out of this room. Out of this glittering green cage. The walls were getting thicker and more opaque with every passing second. But how? Panic spun in her mind. That was no help. It took every shred of discipline she possessed to smother it.

Balance. She needed balance. Desperately.

Artemis closed her eyes and concentrated on her breathing. In, out. In, out. Outside voices faded. She conjured a still pool of calm; a moment later, a possibility dropped into it.

Her eyes popped open. Her pulse accelerated. It wasn't an easy solution by any means. She wasn't even certain she could pull it off; the walls of her prison were still too transparent. But if they thickened farther . . . it might work.

Of course, she could also easily end up dead. Or worse. But it was the only chance she had. If she got the chance, she would take it.

Somewhere on the other side of her glittering prison wall, Niniane was an indistinct form. "Mackie. She should die. You know she should."

"I know nothing of the sort," Mac replied. "The Council will proceed as I've instructed." His tone was laced with unmistakable threat. "Does anyone wish to oppose me?"

Silence reigned for several long seconds. The voice of the oldest Sidhe female broke the quiet. "Beware this path, Manannán mac Lir. I agree with the queen. This witch should die."

"The loss of her powers will be more than enough punishment," Mac said grimly. "The sentence stands."

A soft rush of air sighed from Saraid's lungs. "As you command, Prince."

The elder's staff struck the ground. Artemis caught one last glimpse of Mac's outline before it was lost behind the

curtain of green light. And then she was alone, surrounded by a solid wall of Sidhe magic.

Her heart pumped. Unwittingly, the Sidhe Council had
handed her exactly what she needed.

A chant began, Saraid's ancient voice pitched high. One
by one, the other Sidhe councillors joined her song. The
vibration of their gathering magic shook Artemis to the
bone. Power coalesced, awesome, earth-deep power,
readying for the assault on Artemis's soul.

Time had run out. She had to make her move. Now.

I'd rather die.

Regret burned like acid in Mac's stomach. He didn't
doubt Artemis's words for an instant. He'd feel the same,
faced with the prospect of losing his powers. He enjoyed
the human world immensely, and counted many humans—
even mundane ones—among his friends, but . . . become
one of them? Just the thought made him shudder. But the
prospect of Artemis losing her life? Losing the new life
likely growing in her womb? That fear made him physically ill.

He paced the edge of the Council chamber, berating
himself. How had he allowed things to come to such a sorry
pass? He couldn't shake the feeling that he'd betrayed
Artemis in some fundamental way. It never should have
come to this. And it wouldn't have, if she weren't so bloody
stubborn. And if he hadn't been such a bloody fool.

The elders' spell progressed swiftly. The seven councillors circled the chamber, tracing silver runes in the air.
Their chant had begun in harmony, but with each passing
circuit, a note of the melody shifted into discordance.
Though a few idiot critics described Mac's own music as
less than melodious, this raw dissonance was something
much different. Mac's compositions flowed from the
magic of creation; the elders chanted a spell of destruction. Not death magic, but deadly just the same.

His eyes narrowed on his mother. He wouldn't put it past her to pull some kind of trick. But he detected nothing. Niniane was furious with him, to be sure. But the truth was, she had to obey him. As a demigod, he ranked above her in the strict hierarchy that ruled Sidhe culture. Mac wasn't smug enough to think she wouldn't find a way to get back at him, though. Ah well. He'd just grit his teeth and handle whatever annoyances she threw his way. As always.

The threads of the power-stripping spell were visible now, woven in ugly knots of putrid green, obscene orange, and muddy brown. The elders were showing signs of strain. Their faces were pale, their gaits unsteady. Their voices, however, did not falter on the hideous disharmony they'd created. Mac ground his teeth, wishing it would end.

And then what? Artemis would hate him; he knew that for a fact. He felt like punching something. His power was vast, and right now—useless. He never should have let her get away from him. How had he missed that moonstone? He should have found it and forced the truth out of her. It rankled that she hadn't trusted him.

The spell reached its chaotic crescendo. Niniane's hands moved swiftly, tracing a blur of runes. Magic strands twisted and thrashed in the air. At Niniane's shout, she and the elders spun toward the center of the chamber. Their spell dropped like a writhing net of vipers over Artemis's glowing green prison.

The harsh echoes of the elders' voices faded. Their eyes were bleak, their faces haggard. It was impossible to cast such a spell without feeling its horror.

A hiss of acid and smoke filled the chamber. The strands of magic dissolved, eating away at the walls of Artemis's prison, digesting it, melting it, inch by slow inch.

Niniane sighed. When she spoke, her voice was infinitely weary. "The Council has done as you commanded, Manannán. But I still think it would have been better to kill the witch. She'll probably just take her own life, anyway, as soon as she can manage it."

Mac's gut lurched. He wouldn't let that happen. He'd take care of Artemis—he'd convince her that life, even as a mundane, was worth living. He'd offer her as much of his life essence as she wanted. He'd make things right. At least as right as they possibly could be. He made the vow as the last wisp of smoke cleared from the center of the chamber.

Niniane let out a gasp.

Mac's blood pounded into his ears. He couldn't even manage a gasp of his own—all he could do was blink like a village idiot at the empty platform.

Artemis was gone.

CHAPTER ELEVEN

"Death magic! That foul human dared to cast *death magic*! Here! In the Sidhe Council chamber."

Niniane vibrated with pure outrage. She strode to him, her balled fist striking him so hard on the chest that he actually staggered back a step. But his eyes never moved from the place where Artemis had knelt just minutes before.

He had to fight to keep an idiotic grin off his face.

Niniane's fingernail jabbed his shoulder. He blinked down at her. If looks could cook, his immortal arse would be fried.

"This is your fault, Mackie. The Council voted for death, and you stopped us. What were you thinking? That witch commands an insane amount of power! No one escapes from a Sidhe Council chamber. No one! We—" Jab. "Should—" Jab. "Have—" Jab. *"Killed her!"*

"Gods in Annwyn," Tadc muttered, striding to Niniane's side. His jaw clenched as he stared at the spatter of blood staining the platform of the accused. Wisps of yellow smoke curled above it.

"It's certain none of us here will be going after her," he said. "The witch escaped to a demon realm."

As if anyone needed clarification on that point. The odor of sulfur was unmistakable. Mac still couldn't wrap his mind around it. What Artemis had done—here, in a room bewitched against death magic—should have been impossible.

Damn, but she was good.

"How could she have done it?" Niniane demanded.

"Indeed," Briac put in. "That is the question. The sheer potency of the death magic required to open a demon portal in this chamber should have killed her outright. Her body should be lying here at our feet."

Saraid paced forward, leaning heavily on her staff. She halted, sniffing the air. The corners of her mouth turned sharply downward. "Soul separation."

"Ah," Enid, Enys, and Erlina breathed in unison. "Of course."

Mac didn't like the sound of that. Some witches and sorcerers—very few—could temporarily separate soul from body. A dangerous feat, useful at times, and he didn't doubt Artemis could do it. But he'd never heard of the technique being used to open a demon portal.

"Explain," he told the sisters.

Enid's blue eyes blinked. "Opening a full demon portal in this room would have killed the spell-caster instantly. But a clever witch might have created a small pinprick in reality with no harm to herself."

"Go on."

Enys continued her sister's explanation. "Once the witch had established the pinhole in space, she separated soul from body. Her soul would have been able to slip through the small hole, while her body remained behind."

"But her body isn't here," Mac pointed out.

"In the third part of the spell," Erlina went on, "the witch's soul cast death magic from the demon realm, widening the portal enough to allow her body to pass through. Then she collapsed the passage. All in all, a very dangerous maneuver. Not many humans could have completed it."

Mac's admiration multiplied. Good? Forget it. The woman was amazing.

But could an unborn child, so newly conceived, survive what she'd done?

He started to climb onto the platform. Saraid stopped him with a withered hand on his arm. "The witch is dangerous. Take care, Mac Lir. She may yet drag you into a fight you cannot win."

"Leave me be, Saraid."

Jumping onto the platform, he cast his senses into the curling vapor. His mind touched the barely healed rift in space Artemis had opened and closed. Pure death lay beyond.

His elation at Artemis's escape evaporated. Had she dodged one distasteful fate only to run directly to another? If she had the power to leave the Sidhe Council chamber, couldn't she have gone somewhere more . . . pleasant? Paris? Hawaii? Siberia? Few humans willingly entered a death realm.

Unless they had a very compelling reason. Acid churned his gut. He didn't want to admit it, but all evidence pointed in one direction. Artemis had been planning to deliver the life essence–drenched moonstone to a demon.

Bloody hell. No wonder she'd lied. No wonder she'd rejected his help. If he'd known, he'd have done everything in his power to stop her.

The demon had to be an Old One; he was sure Artemis could trounce any lesser entity. Was the moonstone payment or tribute? For what? What would she risk her own soul to obtain? Something to do with the lad in the pictures. It had to be. He'd seen her eyes when she looked at her son. She loved him, most likely more than she cared for her own life. Had a demon stolen the lad? Was the stolen life essence a ransom payment?

If so, the Old One would not be pleased when Artemis showed up empty-handed. The demon would want alternate payment. Mac had a good idea what that would entail. Abruptly, he rose, pacing the perimeter of the platform. A year ago, when Leanna disappeared, Mac had been powerless to follow her. He'd been a creature of pure life magic then—a trip into a death realm would have rendered him too ill to function. But now . . . now things were different. Because of the slice of darkness that was now a part of Mac's soul.

"Mackie. Get down from there." Niniane had halted several steps from the platform. "This entire chamber reeks of death magic now. It's useless. Contaminated. We'll have to fill it in and dig out another."

Her hands went to her hips. "What an inconvenience! If that demonwhore ever shows her face on the Celtic isles again, she's going to pay."

"She's not a demonwhore," Mac snapped. *At least, not yet.* He hoped.

Niniane sniffed. "After all she's done, you're still defending her? Gods in Annwyn, Mac, I don't know what to do about you anymore. You slum in the human world, consorting with scum. You ignore nice Sidhe girls—even half-breeds! You never come home to Annwyn—"

She choked on a sob. A genuine sob, Mac realized with a start. He stared at his mother, nonplussed. Was that a *tear* rolling down his mother's face? Sidhe, as a rule, didn't cry. The emotions they felt weren't human ones. And his mother was one of the coldest Sidhe he knew. He hadn't thought tears possible for Niniane.

The other councillors appeared just as startled. The sisters averted their eyes, while the males politely turned their backs. Old Saraid leaned on her staff, frowning.

The event called for a response, Mac was sure. If only he could think of something to say.

"Mum . . ." He cleared his throat. "I'm sorry I don't get round to visit more. It's just that . . . Annwyn makes me uncomfortable. Everything's so bloody perfect there."

Niniane sniffed. "If it were really perfect, you'd want to be there."

What kind of warped logic was that? He dragged a hand through his hair. He didn't have time for this. Artemis might be facing an angry Old One at this very moment.

He jumped off the platform and approached her. "Look, Mum, all right. I'll try to stop by more often. Now please. Stop crying."

"Crying? I am not crying. Crying is a human activity."

"Whatever you say, Mum."

Niniane's chin lifted. Eyes perfectly dry now, she spoke in tones of ice. "Councillors, we are finished here. I see no need to linger. Manannán, see that this chamber is destroyed."

Turning, she swept through the doorway leading to Annwyn.

The three sisters glided in her wake. Tadc and Briac followed more sedately. Saraid, bringing up the rear with her measured gait, paused in the doorway.

She regarded Mac with a grave expression. "You plan to follow the human witch into the realm of death."

Mac said nothing.

She shook her head. "I ask you, Manannán. Do not do this. Death . . . it is strong. In the end, it cannot be denied."

A shiver chased down his spine. "I'm sorry, Saraid. Nothing you can say will stop me. I have to do this."

For a long moment, the elder did not reply. Then she inclined her head. "For that, Manannán mac Lir, I am truly sorry."

Stupid, stupid, stupid.

The words were Artemis's new mantra. Couldn't she do *anything* right? She'd planned everything so meticulously.

What had happened to shatter all her carefully laid plans?

Mac had happened, that's what.

No. She couldn't blame all of it on him. She'd been her own worst enemy. If she hadn't lost her balance and taken too much life from that faerie infant, the past twenty-four hours would never have happened.

She'd never have met Mac. Never have made love to him. . . .

She pushed that thought away. No use thinking of love, or of life. She was surrounded by death.

Demon realms were created by death magic, existed in death magic, thrived on death magic. Separate realms were controlled by various of the demon clans. Malachi was the master of this particular realm. Just the thought of facing the Old One here, in his place of power, made breathing difficult.

Or maybe that was just the cigarette smoke.

For whatever reason, Malachi had fashioned his realm in the guise of a garish, smoke-hazed human casino. She'd entered on the main gaming floor—slots to her left, craps to her right. Texas Hold 'Em on a raised platform just behind her. Smoke everywhere. A fit of coughing overtook her. The air was so thick and foul her lungs balked at absorbing it.

It felt as if someone had lit a fire in her throat, but she was so grateful to be alive and whole that she welcomed the pain. Reuniting her soul and body once both had escaped from the Sidhe Council chamber had been a close thing. She almost hadn't made it.

Paradoxically, death creatures fed on life magic and life essence. A human needed strong death-magic defenses to survive in a death realm. The instant her soul had arrived from the other side, a dozen or more lesser demons had attacked it. Fending them off, while at the same time reuniting the two halves of herself, had been a harrowing experience.

She'd done it, though. Now, with a death-magic shield in place, her soul and her life essence were protected. Her magic was strong enough to repel any lesser demon, and most intermediate ones as well. As for Old Ones . . . well, this realm had only one of those. Malachi.

The crossing had cost her, though. She felt as if she'd been mauled by an ogre, drained by a vampire, and tortured by a troll, all at once. Her stomach churned, her muscles ached, and a sharp pain stabbed the base of her skull. Her balance was gone, and the atmosphere around her was hardly conducive to getting it back.

The lesser demons she'd vanquished had slunk away, but not far. They skulked at the corner of her vision, eyeing her with unconcealed hatred. Waiting for her to weaken.

She scanned the room. The casino floor was crowded, and noisy with ringing bells and foul curses. Death metal music screeched from hidden speakers. Demons of all shapes and sizes—some in human form, others in animal or grotesque guises—growled bets amid a cacophony of chinking cash, screeching music, and shrill jackpot alarms. Human demonwhore waiters and waitresses, their naked bodies adorned with chains and leather, circulated among the demon gamblers, bearing trays laden with smoking cocktail glasses.

Artemis watched one black-haired whore approach a particularly hideous demon with pointed ears, a flat snout, hairy human chest, and cloven-hoofed goat legs. Slapping the proffered drink out of her hands, the foul creature grabbed the hapless waitress by the hair and bent her face forward over the edge of the craps table. Pinning the whore in place with a massive claw, the creature rose behind her, its male member hugely red and distorted.

With one vicious thrust, the beast impaled its victim. The whore's screams of pleasure were lost amid the demon's loud, guttural grunts. The creature's two companions—each as hideous as their friend—roared with approval.

Bile burned its way up Artemis's gullet. She staggered backward, legs shaking so hard she nearly collapsed. Was that to be her own fate? Surely not. Even without the moonstone, she had more to offer Malachi than cocktail service. She commanded magic, both light and dark, and she possessed knowledge of spells any Old One would covet. Malachi could make use of her in a variety of ways that didn't include sex.

And he would. But she was equally sure that whatever payment Malachi demanded in return for the service he'd promised her, sex would be part of it. Demons thrived on lust. No Old One would pass up the chance to take another sex slave, especially one as magically powerful as Artemis.

Demonwhore. Just thinking the word made her want to throw up. And if she went so far as to imagine Malachi's touch on her body, his hot lips nipping and licking her skin, his inevitable invasion of her body . . .

Oh gods, she was going to be sick. She darted behind a sickly looking potted palm and deposited her last meal at the base of it. Shaking and light-headed, skin cold and clammy despite the heat, she pressed her forehead against the palm's brittle trunk and tried to regain her equilibrium. There had to be some angle she'd missed. Some bargaining chip that would help blow her out of this miserable dead end.

But in her heart, she knew she'd reached the bottom of her bag of tricks. It didn't matter. To ransom Zander's soul, she'd do anything. Even whore with a demon.

She stumbled along a marble pathway, her gait more zombie than human. A very young demonwhore waitress offered her a smoking drink; she could only shake her head mutely. A few steps later, a demon in the guise of a beautiful human male materialized in her path, wearing a seductive smile.

"Welcome to Shadowhaven, little witch. Come with me, and I'll make you come your brains out." His grin widened at the pun.

It wasn't an idle boast. Demons were experts in lust and pleasure. That was how they lured their human whores.

"No, thanks," Artemis said, sidestepping. The demon shrugged and sauntered past, but not before copping a feel.

Normally, she would have blasted him for it. Right now petty revenge was the last thing on her mind. Her gaze darted around the hazy casino floor. Malachi had to be here somewhere.

She didn't see him.

She turned to find another demon—this one in the guise of a strapping young cowboy, complete with spurs and hat—strutting into her personal space. Not a bad look, she supposed, if a girl didn't mind red demon eyes and a slightly sulfurous odor.

"Where y'all goin', sweet thang? Ladies ain't allowed here in Shadowhaven all by their lonesomes, you know. Y'all need protection."

"I've got all the protection I need, thank you."

"Do ya?" He cocked his head. "Whatcha doin' here, sweetheart?"

"Looking for someone."

Cowboy grinned, flashing even white teeth. "Y'all found him."

"I don't think so." She paused. "But maybe you can help me. I'm looking for Malachi. Do you know where he is?"

Equal measures of fear and hatred flickered in the demon's red eyes. "You won't like Malachi, sugar."

"I already don't," Artemis told him.

"Then stick with Travis here, missy. I'm a real good time." Reaching out, he cupped her breast in his large, warm hand.

Revulsion, intimately entwined with grotesque fascination, shivered through Artemis's body. Demon magic. She struggled to ignore it as she met Travis's gaze squarely. "Malachi's expecting me. Somehow I don't think you want to come between your master and his newest . . . guest."

The handsome demon grimaced. "You're dead right about that, sugar. We're all Malachi's slaves here, and no sane demon wants to get on that bastard's bad side." He gave a short laugh. "Bad side? Who am I kidding? All Malachi's sides are bad. But some are worse than others, if you catch my drift."

She did. "Tell me where he is. I'm late enough as it is. I wouldn't want him to get any angrier than he probably is already."

"Say no more." Travis jerked his chin toward a dark door behind the faro tables. "The lord and master's hosting a Halloween party in his private suite. Very exclusive. Just Malachi and his favorite whores."

"Thank you."

He eyed her. "You won't be thanking me once Malachi's got you."

Travis was right, but Artemis refused to dwell on that. She started for the indicated door, her steps growing sluggish as the distance shortened. When she at last stood before the polished black slab, it took an overwhelming act of willpower and a vivid mental image of Zander's lifeless body to force her knuckles to rap on the door.

"Who the hell—"

The door opened so violently the hinges screeched in protest. An enormous demon in human guise—broad chest, beefy arms, no neck, and a square, uncompromising jaw—glared down at her.

A drop of drool forming at the corner of the demon's mouth as he ogled her. "Well, well, well. What have we here?"

"I—"

He ignored her. "Human," he spat over his shoulder, as if in answer to a question Artemis hadn't heard. "Or mostly, anyway. Young. Female. Dark hair. Tits on the small side, but not too bad." He paused. "Strong magic."

"By all means, Drager," replied a smooth male voice. "Invite Miss Black in. She's kept me waiting long enough."

Drager's fleshy fingers closed on Artemis's wrist. He yanked her into the room so violently she landed on her knees and skidded, burning her skin on the plush, cut-pile carpet. When she tried to draw a breath, she nearly choked on sulfur. The death magic in the room was easily three times the level on the other side of the door. The air pulsed with putrid potency.

Eyes stinging, not daring yet to look up, she studied the intricate red and black interlocking skulls pattern on the carpet. Two humanlike feet, encased in shiny black leather dress shoes, were negligently crossed at the ankles, just inches in front of her right knee.

Slowly, she raised her eyes. Trousers of fine merino wool encased long, powerful legs. A slender-fingered, elegant hand rested on one knee, clasping a smoking crystal tumbler. Fingernails were short and masculine, and neatly trimmed. Gold cuff links glinted above a strong wrist. A sleek black silk shirt, topped by a brocaded black and silver vest and stretching across a muscular torso, was offset by a bloodred necktie. As for the demon's face . . .

Artemis looked into Malachi's eyes. She'd seen him only once before, when she'd summoned him and presented her proposal. Despite her revulsion for what he was, Malachi's physical appearance had stolen her breath. His human guise was so beautiful it made her chest hurt. His rich black eyes showed not a hint of demon red—except when he chose to reveal his true essence. His aquiline nose belonged to a king, his faintly stubbled jaw to a warrior, his lips to a lover.

Artemis tried very hard not to imagine what the Old One's true form looked like.

Malachi reclined on a plush couch, two human female demonwhores, a blonde and a redhead, on either side. A small, implike demon with a curling tail stood on the couch's headrest, massaging his master's neck. The women were naked, or nearly so. The blonde sported a collar and nipple rings; the redhead's leather bustier cinched her tiny waist while leaving her lush upper and lower body bare.

The blonde glared at Artemis with unconcealed malice. The redhead didn't even glance her way. With a start, Artemis took in her pointed ears. The whore was Sidhe. *Part Sidhe*, she amended. The redhead must have at least some human blood, or she wouldn't be able to survive in Malachi's lair.

"So." Malachi's eyes raked over Artemis. "You've come at last. My dear, I had almost given up on you."

"I'm sorry. I was detained." She began to rise.

"No. Remain on your knees. I prefer you there." Malachi's tone, lethally calm, dripped with displeasure.

Artemis sank back to the plush carpet, fear twisting knots in her gut.

Malachi leaned forward, his eyes narrowing. "You do not have my payment."

There was no point in lying. "No. I . . . I did have it, but I encountered . . . difficulties."

The demon stood, slapping away the blond whore and thrusting his smoking glass at the redhead. "You are bold, coming here without the stone."

"My need is great."

"That may be, but my services do not come cheaply."

She tried to swallow, but her throat had gone very dry. "I . . . realize that."

"Are you prepared to pay?"

She looked directly into his eyes. "Yes."

His pupils flared red. "For what you ask, the price is high. Higher, no doubt, than you will wish to pay."

"Don't assume that."

The demon's brows were two slashes above dark, unfathomable eyes. "Even if you are willing to acquiesce to my demands, I wonder—will you be able to please me?"

Oh gods. "I hope so."

He smiled thinly. "We shall see. Remove that rag of a coat."

Artemis hesitated only a second before shrugging off her jacket. It fell to the floor behind her.

"And your shirt."

She stiffened. "No. Not until we have an agreement."

Malachi gazed at her for what seemed a long time, eyes narrowed almost to slits. She tried to keep her desperation from showing, but she suspected the effort was futile. Only a very desperate woman would prostrate herself at an Old One's feet and all but beg to become his slave.

"Very well." Malachi stood and held out a hand to Artemis.

She took it and he tugged her to her feet. His touch tingled, sending zings of blatant lust racing along her nerve endings. Even though Artemis knew no human could resist responding sexually to an Old One, her body's automatic reaction sickened her. Malachi regarded her with a hot, appraising gaze. Artemis felt as naked as if she were already his whore.

Her brain recoiled; her body swayed toward him.

He smiled. "Come along, my pet. We will discuss the details of our . . . future association . . . in private."

CHAPTER TWELVE

The seductive stroke of red-nailed fingers on a deck of cards snared Mac's attention.

"A hand of Twenty-one, sir? Or would you prefer a more . . . *private* game?"

A wide-eyed demon in pouty feminine form stood behind a blackjack table. Breasts the size of small watermelons peeked from behind a fall of lustrous dark hair. The entity's only article of clothing—if one could call it that—was a red bow tied around her slender neck. A perfect match to the bloodred paint on her lips and nipples.

She looked him up and down, undressing him with her eyes. Mac shied away. The demon hadn't even touched him, but already he felt used. The dealer was eyeing him as if he were her next meal. Which actually, he could be. Mac's soul had to be the most potent source of life essence to ever cross into this cursed realm.

A cherry tongue swiped the demon's lower lip. The gleam in her eyes intensified. The creature blew him a kiss; Mac felt like throwing up.

And yet he couldn't tear his eyes from her. His cock, damn the thing, had gone hard.

He clenched a fist. His hand was shaking. Demon sex had never been his idea of a good time—no pure life-magic creature would willingly touch a demon. Or enter a death realm. A year ago, a place like this would have made him violently ill. Now, despite his revulsion, he couldn't deny an undercurrent of energy and excitement.

The change was due to the death magic in his soul. It provided protection from the evil assaulting him from all sides, while at the same time drawing him toward it. How long could he last in this place? Long enough, he hoped, to find Artemis and drag her out of here.

And if he encountered a fight from the demons eying him? Well, he wasn't entirely sure what he'd do then. His life-magic spells wouldn't be worth much in a demon realm. Could he cast death magic? The thought was distasteful, but he was prepared to do whatever he had to.

A buzz of adrenaline kicked in. The prospect of dealing in death brought a kind of perverse exhilaration.

"Well, hon?" pouted the blackjack demon. "Whaddaya say? Should I deal you in? It's Shadowhaven's best game."

"Sorry. Not interested."

"Can't win if ya don't play, big boy."

"Can't lose, either."

He scanned the room behind the blackjack table. Gold, crystal, mirrors, and smoke, vanishing into infinity. How the bloody hell was he going to locate Artemis amid this murky mess?

The demon leaned over the blackjack table, her nipples brushing the green felt. Mac found himself looking. With a knowing smirk, she fluttered her long, false eyelashes.

"Come on now, hon. Just one tiny bet? What's the harm in that? Your life essence is high enough to afford a bad hit or two."

"Sorry."

Her red lips pursed. "Whatchya come here for, if ya don't wanta play?" Her red eyes narrowed. "Ah, I know. You're part Sidhe. Elven. I know what your kind likes. . . ."

The demon dissolved into a shapeless, oily mist. A

moment later, the dirty cloud coalesced into a new figure. Mac blinked at the demon's new guise: a short, squat, bearded dwarf, in full battle armor.

The dwarf-demon hopped up on a stool. "Like me now?" he asked gruffly. "Turn you on, do I?"

"Are you whacked?" Mac demanded.

"Oh, come now, my tall, blond Sidhe-male. Don't play shy. I know what kind of fellowship you crave. Saw it in a human movie a little while back. Some cracked story about a halfling and a ring . . ."

"Bloody hell! *That* movie? Don't believe everything you see on pay-per-view, mate. Besides, I'm looking for a female right now. A human woman."

The demon snorted. "Troublesome creatures, human women. Don't see why you'd go after one." Yellow teeth flashed. "Not when you could have me."

"Maybe you've seen her," Mac said through clenched teeth. "Not too tall, curly brown hair and dark eyes, olive skin. Might have come through here about a half hour ago. Unusual magic. Her death- and life-magic talents are equally strong."

"Oh," the demon huffed. "*That* one."

"You've seen her?"

The demon responded with another smear of oily smoke. This time he reappeared as a broad-shouldered American cowboy. "Damn straight, I saw the little woman. Reckon everyone in these parts did. Could hardly miss a hot little filly like that, now, could I?" He smirked. "Too late for y'all to catch her, though. She skedaddled into the back."

"The back?"

"Malachi's private suite. Y'all know about Malachi, don'tcha?"

"Is he the master of this realm?"

The demon slapped his knee with his ten-gallon hat. "Give the Sidhe-boy a gold star! Yep, Malachi's lord here. More's the pity."

Mac scuttled his annoyance. "Where's this back room, then?"

The demon centered his hat on his head. "Let me give you some advice, partner. Give it up. Y'all would never get through the door." He looked Mac up and down. "Life spells are worthless on this side. Death magic's what a man needs, and, son, you ain't got much. Y'all are about as dangerous as a pup."

"Don't be so sure about that."

The demon rounded the blackjack table, grinning. "Why, shucks, boy. I bet y'all can't even stop the likes of me from bending y'all over this here table and—gack!"

Cowboy choked on his taunt as Mac slammed his fist into his face. The entity reverted to smoke, sending Mac staggering forward, punching through nothing. Red fireworks exploded in his vision; pain stabbed his skull like a dozen sharpened spikes. Before he quite knew what was happening, a drop of his life essence had escaped his soul. The white spark zigged and zagged above his head like a drunken horsefly.

Cursing, Mac made a grab for it, and missed. The demon—back in its naked-woman guise—laughed. Parting her lips, she flicked her tongue, froglike, and caught the bright light on the tip. Catching Mac's gaze, she licked her lips and smiled.

An electric jolt of revulsion/anger/lust shot straight to Man's groin. He wanted to throw up. He wanted to slap the demon's smug face. He wanted to throw her down on the floor and . . .

He was on the verge of launching himself across the blackjack table when sanity kicked in. The sodding little bugger was goading him, and he was falling for it. The wanker would like nothing better than Mac's assault— violence would allow it to get an even bigger drop of his soul. With a low curse, Mac gripped the edge of thc table. The polished wood cracked.

The demon threw back her head and cackled. "Not bad, Sidhe-boy, but you'll need a lot more willpower than that to stop Malachi from stripping your soul bare. He's one mean bastard. What with the shakeup that went down last year, the master's one of the top dogs in the demon realms now. Your tender life-magic ass won't last a heartbeat."

She cupped both her breasts, squeezing and lifting, her bloodred nipples pointed at his mouth. "Now, I have a better idea. Give up your human whore and stay with me. You'll have a lot more fun. I promise."

Mac grabbed her bow tie and twisted. "Listen. I'm out of patience. No more games. Where's your master?"

The demon made a show of choking and gasping, but her eyes gleamed red, her expression oddly triumphant. Hot hands swept over Mac's shoulders and down his arms. "Ooh, you're more dominant than I gave you credit for. Sure you don't want to play? I'll let you tie me up and whip me—"

Mac dropped her as if scalded. He was wasting his time; she wasn't going to tell him a damn thing. Turning without a word, he started walking.

"The other way, hon."

He stopped and looked back. "What?"

"I said, the other way. To Malachi."

"And just why should I believe that?"

The demon shifted forms suddenly, returning to cowboy form. "Suit yourself, partner. It's your own funeral, after all. I just thought that if you've got a death wish, I might as well be the one to get the credit for delivering you to the master. Malachi's suite is behind the faro tables. Through a black door. Do me a favor and tell him Travis sent you, would you? I'd surely appreciate it."

Mac hesitated. He wasn't at all sure the demon was telling him the truth, but since he didn't have a clue where Malachi was, one direction was as good as another. He changed course, heading toward the blinking neon faro sign, slapping away grabbing hands—demon and human—on all sides. Everyone in this gods-forsaken place wanted a piece of him, and the effort to repel them was taking its toll. Another spark of his life essence floated free. A horde of lesser demons fell on it in a feeding frenzy.

Damn. Demigods were not meant to travel through death realms. If only Mac understood the death magic in his soul more fully, he might be able to put it to use. Fighting the death bastards with their own weapon might prove infinitely satisfying. As it was, the cowboy demon was right. Mac's defenses were pitiful.

How the hell was he supposed to rescue Artemis when he could barely protect himself? He couldn't even dim his life essence. It shone though the murky air, attracting demons like flies. If he were smart, he'd get out of this wretched place and leave Artemis to her freely chosen fate.

And let his child die here? Not bloody likely.

He halted at the base of the three steps leading to the faro platform. There was indeed a black door behind the tables. A demon in the guise of a thick-necked human bouncer stood guard. Was Artemis behind that door? Submitting to Malachi's lust? Every instinct Mac possessed screamed for him to vault over the faro tables and bash down the black door.

Luckily, prudence prevailed. He gave the guard a second look. Malachi's goon wasn't an Old One, but he wasn't a neophyte, either. And there were any number of lesser demons between Mac and the bouncer. As much as Mac was itching for a fight, he knew he couldn't take on them all. His usual rules didn't apply here.

Gripping the brass railing with one hand, he directed his focus inward. He'd spent the last year denying the death in his soul. Now, for the first time, he sought out its putrid stain.

He probed it gingerly, as a human might do with a rotted tooth. Its ugliness repulsed, but if he meant to snatch

Artemis out of an Old One's clutches, he had no choice but to make use of the only weapon he had. Death magic. He'd never cast a death spell in his life—hadn't thought he had the knowledge for such a feat. But somehow, as he poked and prodded the small, rotten abscess in his soul, he *knew*.

Words—repulsive, ugly—sprang to his lips. It hurt to utter the syllables. First, fourth, and seventh notes on an octave, the chord slashed at his ears like broken glass. His stomach lurched; he almost retched. He renewed his grip on the railing, and when the nausea passed, somehow he was still standing upright.

He didn't feel so good. But when he took a step, no hands grabbed at him. No red eyes darted in his direction. It was as if he'd faded from view.

Damn, he'd done it. He'd cast a death glamour. All in all, it hadn't been so different from casting a life-magic glamour. Sort of like putting on a shirt backward and inside out. It didn't feel good, or look good, but it got the job done.

No, he didn't feel good at all. But he felt better than he had a moment ago. Definitely better.

With a deliberate tread, he threaded his way between the faro tables, eyes fixed on the black door and its massive guard. With new insight, Mac assessed the bouncer, identifying weaknesses in the demon's magic that hadn't been apparent to him before he'd dipped into his darker side. He cracked his knuckles. He could take the blighter, he thought. And once Malachi's goon was out of the way . . .•

The bouncer turned; the black door behind him swung open. Mac's scheming evaporated when a woman emerged from a pall of yellow smoke.

Artemis.

His knees all but buckled under a tsunami wave of relief. Artemis had lost her army jacket, but otherwise was fully clothed and, as far as he could tell, unharmed. Mac was about to slide into her view when a demon appeared in the doorway behind her, dark energy crackling about his head and shoulders. An Old One. It could only be Malachi.

The demon radiated the absolute, seductive power of death. He guided Artemis to his left, a proprietary hand curled about her nape. The sight of that controlling touch set Mac's blood boiling. Clearly, Malachi considered Artemis his property. Had she whored for him? Moaned with pleasure as the demon poured death into her body? Mac heard a cracking sound and realized it came from the hinges of his own clenched jaw.

Malachi and Artemis advanced. The lesser demons and demonwhores parted in waves before them, some bowing low, others falling prostrate. One even attempted to kiss the toes of Malachi's polished shoes. A vicious kick was the demon's reward for his obeisance.

Mac slipped through the crowd, following, watching for an opportunity to make his move. Damn, but he wished he could be sure of Artemis's welcome when he tried to free her. He wasn't. She'd come here of her own free will. She might very well react badly to his rescue.

His quarry disappeared into a dense haze of smoke. The putrid fog was so thick Mac nearly collided with Malachi's back when the demon suddenly halted. They'd come to the end of what looked like a short, blank corridor. There didn't appear to be any exit. Mac drew back, considering. What was going on?

Neither Artemis nor the demon seemed to be aware of Mac's presence—apparently, Mac had cast a more than competent death glamour. Would he be able to call hellfire as well, in place of his usual elfshot? Experimentally, he extended his palm, but before he could make an attempt, Malachi reached out and placed his palm flat on the blank wall in front of him.

A silver door materialized. A round button appeared on a panel to one side, bearing an illuminated, down-pointing arrow. Malachi pressed it.

Mac frowned. An elevator?

It seemed to be. Malachi and Artemis stood shoulder to shoulder, waiting, the fingers of Malachi's right hand still wrapped around Artemis's neck. Artemis's spine was ramrod straight. She held her arms crossed over her stomach, her hands gripping her elbows. Her eyes didn't stray once to the demon on her left. They remained fixed on the silver door.

Clearing his throat, Mac dropped his death glamour and strolled into place on Artemis's right. "So. Where to next, love?"

Artemis choked. If her head had whipped around any faster, Malachi's grip would have snapped her neck. She stared at him as if he owned two heads—both of them dead ugly. "*Mac*. What are you doing here?"

"Rescuing you, of course. Whatever your problem is, I can tell you right now, love, this smarmy demon bloke here is not your solution."

Malachi's dark gaze met Mac's over Artemis's head. His split instant of surprise quickly transformed into a scowl. Long fingers tightened on Artemis's neck, making her wince.

"Friend of yours?" the demon asked her.

"No—"

"*Yes*," Mac said at the same time.

Artemis stabbed him with a swift, deadly glance. "No. He's not. Get out of here, Mac."

"Not a chance." Damn, but the woman needed someone to save her from herself. He grabbed Artemis's upper arm and, with one swift yank, jerked her out of Malachi's grip. The demon's fist closed on air.

"You idiot—" Artemis began.

"Shut up, love," Mac said, shoving Artemis behind him. He kept an even tone, but inside, his heart thudded furiously. One touch on her arm had told him what he needed to know. A spark of divine life grew inside her. She was carrying his child.

"Mac. Give it up. You can't fight him. Not here."

The demon's red eyes narrowed. "Not anywhere, Sidhe. You go too far, coming here. I don't know how you got in, but the trip may very well be the last one you ever take if you don't step away from this human now. She is mine. We've just executed a blood contract."

Mac met Malachi's gaze. "Sorry, mate," he said mildly. "I had this one first. She had no business coming to you without my permission."

He ignored Artemis's enraged sputter.

At the corner of his vision, he noted figures slipping into the open end of the corridor. Lesser demons and demonwhores, buzzing with excitement. Getting ready to join their master in a little fun, were they? That could get difficult. He was new to this death-magic thing.

Artemis darted a look at the gathering crowd. "Let go of me! Don't you understand? I don't want to be rescued!"

"Too damn bad." Mac's fingers tightened against her struggling, grinding her wrist bones together until she gasped with pain and stilled. Her resentment sizzled, heating the air between them.

"Are you insane?" she hissed. "Please, Mac, get out of here. This is no place for you, don't you see that? Malachi's an Old One, and Shadowhaven is his realm. He'll destroy you."

"With pleasure," the demon agreed. His hand came up.

When the stream of hellfire left Malachi's fingers, Mac was ready for it. He countered with an equally ugly blast. The twin forces met in an explosion of red stars.

Artemis let out a gasp. "Death magic! How . . . ?"

Rage shimmered over Malachi's sallow face. "So. The Sidhe prince has hidden depths. No matter—"

The demon launched a spell. Mac spun, shielding Artemis with his body. The attack sliced his shoulder, painting a fiery streak of pain.

"Aahh!" He lost his balance. Arms flailing, he fell against

Artemis, smashing her between his chest and the elevator door.

"Gods damn it." Instinctively, he threw up a defensive shield, sealing himself and Artemis in the shallow space defined by the door's frame. Bugger it. He'd cast life magic, by reflex. If he'd had time to think, he would have attempted another death spell.

His life magic was weak in this realm of death. He only just managed to hold the shield in place, while the world spun with violent vertigo.

Artemis wiggled against his chest; her elbow connected with his gut. What the hell was she doing?

"Damn it, Mac," she grunted. "Move. I can't breathe."

"Too bloody bad." He wasn't giving her an inch. He didn't trust her half that far. Gods in Annwyn! Maybe his mother was right. A nice Sidhe girl would never have gotten him into a situation like this.

Malachi let out a roar. Hellfire assaulted Mac's fragile shielding. Sweat poured down his neck. So this was what it felt like to be roasted alive. He squashed Artemis even harder against the elevator door, trying to shield her from the worst of the heat.

Artemis—damn her stubborn soul—was still trying to escape.

"Ballocks, witch, untwist your knickers! I am not giving you back to that creature."

"You freaking, arrogant ass! How dare you tell me what to do!" She was almost in tears. "You don't know what you've done. You've ruined everything—"

He didn't know what galled him worse: that she wouldn't tell him what "everything" was, or the fact that she had so little faith in his abilities. "What's the matter, love? Sleeping with a mere demigod turn out to be a bore? A demon's kiss more your style?"

"Bastard," she spat out.

Malachi sent another death surge at Mac's shield. Flames leaped; the temperature soared. Mac let out a stream of profanity, using a few choice words he didn't think he ever before had an occasion to utter.

"Oh gods," Artemis breathed. "That life spell of yours isn't going to hold much longer. Listen to me, Mac. Please. I appreciate you coming after me, I really do, but you have to let me go now. You don't understand—"

"Tell me, then," he ground out. "I'm all ears."

"There's no—"

A bell clanged.

"—time to—aaack!" Artemis's words shattered into a scream as the wall at her back slid open.

No, not the *wall*. The *door*.

The elevator had arrived.

She pitched backward; Mac fell forward. They landed together, limbs tangled, on a smooth, hard floor.

Malachi bellowed his outrage. Hellfire exploded, hotter than before. Mac's shield bowed inward, filling half the elevator cab before bouncing out again. An instant later, Mac felt the spell shiver. A sound like cracking ice filled his ears. A web of fine lines appeared at the top of the life-magic shield, just below the head of the elevator door frame. The fissures spread downward, like a spider's expanding web.

"Ballocks." He lunged for the elevator panel, which sported a single, unmarked button.

Artemis beat him to it. She jabbed the button once, twice, three times. "Close, damn it!"

Mac's shield was disintegrating, crumbling from top to bottom. He shoved Artemis to the floor as a blast of hellfire broke through, but not quickly enough to shield her from a glancing blow to the shoulder. Malachi's wild laughter ricocheted inside the cab.

"Gods in Annwyn, Artemis. Are you all right?"

She winced, rotating her shoulder, her face pale. "I think so."

Another blast hit the wall over their heads. Bounding to his feet, Mac threw everything he had into bolstering the shield. Which meant he had nothing at all left for making the elevator move. Artemis stared up at him, eyes wide. Her mind seemed to have blanked.

"Artemis," he said sharply.

A measure of lucidity seemed to return.

"Anything you can do, love, to close that door, would be greatly appreciated. Death magic, life magic, whatever. At this point, I'm not choosy."

For a second she just blinked up at him, brows furrowed, as if he'd been speaking in troll grunts. Then she gave her head a shake. "I think I can do something. I'll just need . . . some time. Maybe a minute . . ."

She might as well have asked for a year. "Right, then," Mac said, ducking another lick of hellfire. "Do it."

He threw all his concentration into delaying the inevitable destruction of his shield. Behind him, on her knees, Artemis bent double and grunted out a series of hellacious syllables—fingernails on a psychic chalkboard. The noise went on for what seemed like forever until . . .

His shield collapsed.

Malachi let out a triumphant howl.

"Got it!" Artemis cried.

The demon lunged; the elevator doors swished closed in his face, plunging Mac and Artemis into darkness. A muffled shriek sounded. A resounding thump shook the cab.

Artemis jabbed the elevator button. The cab lurched sharply upward, as if a giant hand had jerked on the cable. For one interminable second it hung motionless, as if suspended in midair. Then the force holding them aloft snapped, and the cab plummeted downward.

Mac floundered in the darkness, grabbing hold of Artemis's leg, her elbow, her shoulder. Finally, he managed to wrap his arms around her as the force of the elevator's downward plunge plastered them to the floor. A sound like a tornado's roar battered his skull.

"Do you know where we're going?" he shouted, his lips close to Artemis's ear.

"Now you ask," she shouted back at him.

"Just tell me."

He felt a shudder pass through her. "We're going as far down as we can go, Mac. We're going to Hell."

CHAPTER THIRTEEN

After what seemed like hours, Malachi's elevator to Hell slammed to a stop, jarring Artemis's skull against the side wall of the car. The impact vibrated inside her head like a hammer on a gong. For several moments, the tremors in her brain overrode coherent thought.

Then all sound ceased.

For a brief, heart-stopping moment, Artemis thought she was dead. But no. If she were dead, her head wouldn't be killing her. Or maybe it would—she didn't know. But certainly, if she were dead, Mac's arms wouldn't be clamped tightly around her, and his heart wouldn't be thudding in the same life-affirming rhythm as her own.

He'd come after her. After all the lies she told him, after what she'd done to him, Mac had plunged into Malachi's death realm, intent on rescuing her. She tried, but she couldn't quite get her mind wrapped around that stunning, impossible thought.

She buried her face in his chest and clung to him. He smelled earthy, sweaty. *Alive.* His body was warm and solid and more comforting than she deserved.

And he'd cast death magic. What did that mean?

He rubbed the back of her neck, erasing the lingering soreness left by Malachi's touch. She felt a puff of breath at her temple as his lungs expelled a low laugh.

"Whoever heard of going to Hell in an elevator?" she said.

"Very funny, love. Trolling for a handbasket joke, are you?"

An unwilling chuckle escaped her own throat. "Unfortunately I'm not kidding, Mac. That's where we're headed." She paused, sobering. "We might be there already."

He cleared his throat, but didn't immediately answer. It was too dark to see the disbelief she knew was in his eyes, but she could almost hear the wheels turning in his mind, reaching the only logical conclusion possible.

"You do realize that's impossible," he said finally. "I mean, popping in and out of demon realms—that's one thing. Living creatures do it all the time. Going to Hell— actual *Hell* with a capital H—that's just not done by people who aren't dead."

She eased out of his arms, when all she really wanted to do was stay. But she couldn't afford the luxury of weakness. Or of hiding from what had to be done. *If* it still could be done.

Mac could very well have ruined everything.

A writhing mass of serpents twisted in her stomach. No. She would not believe she'd gotten this far only to fail.

"It's not impossible for living people to go to Hell," she said quietly. "It's just . . . really, really difficult."

She hiked herself to her feet; she heard Mac do the same. She wished she could see him, at least a little, but the darkness was so complete she couldn't even see the shadow of her hand in front of her face. Feeling her way around the close confines of the elevator car, she found the button and pressed it. Nothing. Groping to the right, she found a vertical seam in the door and tried to pry the two halves open. She succeeded only in ripping off a fingernail.

She sucked her cuticle and cast her senses toward the door, trying to determine the nature of the magic that held it shut. She launched one death spell after another, until both her repertoire and her strength were exhausted. Magic didn't seem to work right inside the confines of the elevator. She couldn't even keep a flame of hellfire going, for illumination.

The quiet rasp of Mac's breath sounded behind her. He hadn't moved, hadn't spoken. His breathing was calm. Even. Hers was rapid. Erratic. She found the button again, pressed it even though she knew it was futile. Then another thought struck. She ran her hands up the wall and found a small hinged panel. She tore it open and found an emergency phone. "Hello? Hello?"

The line was dead.

She shouted into it, anyway. "Malachi! Are you there? Answer me! You have to believe me, I had nothing to do with this. I didn't know he was coming after me—"

With a muttered curse, Mac snatched the receiver from her fingers. The next instant it crashed against the wall. Sparks briefly illuminated the harsh lines of his face.

"Oh gods." Artemis slid into a crouch, her back pressed against the wall, and covered her hands with her face. What if they never got out?

"Stupid," she muttered under her breath. "Stupid, stupid, stupid."

She fell silent. Damn, but it was hot in here. Sweat trickled between her breasts. Interminable seconds ticked by. When Mac finally spoke, his voice was flat.

"Want to tell me what's going on here? What's so important you're willing to sell yourself, body and soul?"

A cold, heavy fist clenched where her heart should have been. She blinked back tears. "My son. Alexander. I . . . I call him Zander."

"Named for you, is he?"

"Yes. After my middle name."

"You told me he was sick. Was that a lie?"

"I . . . no. It's the truth, sort of. Zander's . . . not well."

"Is he dead?" Mac asked bluntly. "Is that what this is

about? Some insane scheme to rescue your loved one from the underworld? You know that's impossible. It didn't work for Orpheus, love, and it's not going to work for you." His tone softened, marginally. "There are rules about this kind of thing, Artemis. Absolute rules not even a god can break, no matter how much you may want to."

"Zander's not dead." She barely choked out the words. "He's . . . he's in a hospital. In Philadelphia."

She could feel Mac's puzzlement. "Then why aren't you by his side? Why come to Scotland to assault faeries? You know stolen life essence won't help. Neither will demons. Why make a deal with Malachi? What on earth are you trying to do, Artemis?" His tone roughened. "And why won't you tell me?"

"Because you . . . you can't help me," she said in a small voice. "On earth, in Annwyn, your life magic is awesome. In Hell—life magic is next to worthless." She raised her head. "But—you cast death magic in Malachi's realm. How?"

"Let's back up a moment, love. My questions first. Your son is in Philadelphia. But you're bent on going to Hell."

She nodded, then realized he couldn't see her. "Yes."

"Why?"

She linked her arms around her bent legs and pressed her forehead to her knees. "Zander's body is alive in Philadelphia. But his soul . . . it's not there with him, Mac. It was stolen. By a demon."

"By Malachi?"

"No. Not Malachi. By another demon. But that demon wouldn't negotiate, so I summoned Malachi and struck a deal. Life essence in return for his assistance in rescuing Zander's soul."

"Artemis," Mac said gently. "If Zander's soul was stolen, then he's dead. A body can't live without a soul."

"No. That's not true. Some humans can live without a soul, for a short time. And for a boy like Zander, who has demon ancestors—he could stay alive for months. Half a year, maybe."

"How long's it been, love?"

"Five months," Artemis whispered. "Five months, twenty-seven days, six hours . . ." It was difficult to take her next breath, but somehow she managed it. "He's . . . in something like a coma. But the trauma is psychic, not physical. He's well cared for. The last time I called the hospital, his nurse told me he looked very peaceful, like he was sleeping. I just wish . . . oh, I just wish I was there with him. . . ."

Mac touched her arm. She startled; she hadn't realized he was so close. His arm went around her shoulder. Instinctively, she leaned into him. His touch was a cool oasis in the thick, oppressive darkness.

"He wouldn't know you, love, even if you were there. Not if his soul is gone."

"I know." She sniffed. "But . . . I want to hear his voice. So badly. If I could only hear him call me Mommy, just one more time . . ." She lost her battle with her tears. "I have to get to his soul. Soon. Time's running out. It's being held on the lowest level of Hell."

"How are you so sure it's there and not in one of the demon realms?"

"The demon who stole Zander's soul doesn't have a death realm outside Hell. She reigns in Ptolomaea, a sector in Hell's deepest layer. It's the only place beyond the Styx where innocent, living souls can survive indefinitely. Hecate has a special hunger for living souls. Mostly ones belonging to children. She collects them on Earth and imprisons them in Hell."

"Hecate the hag?" Mac's surprise was evident. "*She's* the demon that stole your son's soul?"

"Yes. Do you know her?"

"Of course. Scotland's been her favorite hunting ground ever since that mess with Macbeth. She mainly haunts humans, but I've encountered her a few times over the years, when she dared to interfere with Celtic creatures. Hecate's one of the few demons who confine themselves to one sex when they take human form. You won't find a nastier bitch anywhere. How did she find your son all the way in the States?"

Artemis closed her eyes. In the darkness, it made no difference to her sight, but somehow she felt as though she were hiding.

"It's my fault," she said brokenly. "I called her."

She couldn't see Mac's face, but she felt his disapproval just the same.

"You summoned her? Gods in Annwyn, why?"

"It . . . was part of my job. In the army. Psychic ops deals with demons all the time."

"But you're a civilian now."

"Yes. I got out, last year, after the Immortals' battle restored the balance of magic. But I was born to the army. My family's aptitude for both life and death magic makes us perfect psy soldiers. Both my parents were psy-ops. Both were killed in action."

"It that where you met your husband? In the military?"

"Zander's father, do you mean? We were never married, but yes, we served in the same unit, and sometimes . . . well, you know how it is. We didn't plan the pregnancy. It just . . . happened."

"An accident, was it?" Mac's voice sounded strained.

"Yes. I suppose you could say that."

"Where's Zander's father now?"

Artemis sighed. "Dead, too. It happened two years ago, at the start of the death-magic surge. Dennis was on a routine mission when he was ambushed by a gang of rogue vampires. They drugged him up and turned him against his will."

"Gods."

She shivered. "It was awful. He came back a few nights

later, pretending nothing had happened. The vamps had set him up as an inside man, so they could get a crack at our armory. But Dennis was pale as death, and when he crawled into bed, his skin was cold and dry. I touched his neck, and found the puncture marks." She was silent for a moment. "He tried to turn me as well. I fought, and somehow managed to call for backup. He died fighting, like he'd always said he wanted. Unfortunately, it was for the wrong side."

"You must have been devastated to lose someone you loved like that."

"I was. Dennis was a good man. But . . . I still had Zander. He kept me sane, even when the world was falling apart. I would have left the army after Dennis died, but with death magic exploding everywhere, I couldn't take that option. I had to stay and fight. That was when I first encountered Hecate. The army routinely made deals, you see, with demons willing to promote our short-term objectives. Hecate was one of those. She helped, but she had more in mind than the payment the army offered. She had her eye on Zander. She'd sensed a glimmer of his soul through mine, and had marked it. It was subtle. At the time, I didn't realize what she'd done."

"What happened then?"

"The Immortals happened. You happened. Death magic took a hit, and everything changed. Suddenly, there wasn't anything keeping me in the military. Psy-ops was downsizing. I took my pension and left. Zander and I settled in Philly. He went to first grade at the local public school, I got a job at a magical arts store on South Street. What I didn't know was that Hecate was watching us. She made her move just after Beltane. Since then, Zander's body has been nothing more than an empty shell." She paused. "I summoned her, of course. I offered to negotiate for his release. She laughed at me."

"So you turned to Malachi."

"He seemed the best bet. I knew he'd been Hecate's rival for centuries. Millennia, even."

"What did he agree to do, in exchange for the faerie life essence?"

"Provide me safe passage to Ptolomaea. And he pledged me an army of lesser demons to use in my fight against Hecate. His own assistance, even, toward the end."

"Brave of him, to wait until it was clear how the battle was progressing, before risking his own arse," Mac commented. "And what if you lost the battle, regardless of Malachi's assistance?"

"Most likely, I would have become Hecate's slave."

She wasn't sure how to interpret the silence that followed. Was Mac angry? Did he think her a fool? Was he just disgusted? She wasn't sure she wanted to know.

Finally, he spoke. "I can't imagine Malachi was pleased when you showed up without the moonstone."

She let her head fall back against the elevator wall. "He wasn't. I had to renegotiate."

"And?" The single word dripped like acid.

She forced the words out. "I agreed to be Malachi's whore for seven years. But Zander will be free. That's the only thing I care about."

Mac's voice vibrated in the dark, low and angry. "Has Malachi had you yet?"

She winced. "No. Not yet. Not until Zander is safe."

"But you signed a contract. In blood."

Thick, hot air filled her lungs on a painful inhale. Now she was damn glad she couldn't see Mac's face. "Yes. I did. And as long as Malachi keeps his end of the bargain . . . I'll honor my word. I'll become his whore."

"No. You won't. As of right now, Artemis, your contract with Malachi is void. You're under my protection. You and—" He cut off abruptly, clearing his throat. "You don't need Malachi's help. You've got me. I'll get you to Ptolomaea and back. I'll rescue your son. I swear it."

"You, Mac? You can't possibly be serious! You're a creature of life magic! What do you know of Hell and death?"

"Not much, love, I admit. But I'm a very fast learner."

"It won't work. Your life magic will be practically useless in Hell."

"I'll wager my death magic works just fine."

"Your—" She broke off. "Yes. Your death magic. I asked you about that before. How did you do it? It shouldn't have been possible. You're a creature of pure life magic."

"Not pure, Artemis. Not anymore."

"I don't understand."

"Here. It'll be easier to show you."

His hand reached for hers, fumbling in the darkness. Their fingers caught and clasped. A spark of dark, ugly energy leaped from his body to hers.

It came from his soul.

She drew back, stunned. "But . . . how?"

"It came from the battle to save Tain. The bloke was mad—driven over the edge by death magic. In order to restore his sanity, his brothers each absorbed a piece of Tain's darkness. Somehow, I ended up with a bit, too. I don't pretend to know exactly how it happened. I didn't even realize I'd been . . . wounded . . . until just a few days ago." He paused. "This is the first time I've considered what happened a good thing. Because it let me follow you here."

"Oh, Mac." She brought his hand to her cheek and pressed his palm flat against her skin. He was so . . . alive. She'd been so entranced by his light, she never even suspected his soul hid darker secrets. But now that she knew, it made sense. The restlessness she'd sensed in him, the vulnerability, the soul-deep anger . . . those were the trappings of death magic, not life.

"You . . . you really think you could help me get to the bottom of Hell?" she whispered.

"I don't think you can get there on your own. Your

death magic is strong, Artemis, but what about your life essence? That's finite, and every demon in Hell will be angling for it. Travel with me, and you'll have an infinite supply. You won't need Malachi's protection. As for any threats we'll encounter—I'm still getting the knack of this death magic thing, but your tutoring will shorten my learning curve, I'm sure."

"You want me to teach you death spells?" She couldn't fathom it. "I don't know, Mac—"

"Thanks for the vote of confidence, love."

"It's got nothing to do with that. Mac, this isn't your fight. Whatever sliver of death magic you possess, it can't be nearly enough to protect you. You can't die, but you could end up imprisoned for eternity. No." She moved away from him, breaking contact. "No, I'll just wait for Malachi to find me. He'll uphold his end of the contract, and you can go home."

"Bloody hell, Artemis. You are the most stubborn female I've ever had the misfortune to meet." His fist slammed into the elevator wall, right next to her head.

She yelped. "Damn it, Mac. Be reasonable—"

"Reasonable? How's this for reasonable? I'm not letting you out of my sight. Not until you and your son are safe in the human world."

"Mac—"

"Stubble it, Artemis. Get one thing through your thick skull. I'm not going anywhere, except with you."

Her heart thundered against her ribs. "You . . . you would really do this for me? But why? I've treated you so horribly."

He was silent for a long moment. Once or twice, she thought she heard him inhale, as if he were about to speak, then changed his mind. Finally, he just gave a rough laugh.

"Glutton for punishment, I suppose."

He touched her then, his fingers slipping through her

damp curls. His big hand cradling her head. His touch was startlingly cool.

"You love your son very much," he said.

"Yes."

"I think he's a very lucky lad, to have a mother like you," he said, his voice hoarse. "I think any child would be lucky for it."

"I don't know about that. If it weren't for me, Hecate never would have found him."

"Shh," he chided. "You were doing a dangerous job. No doubt you've saved hundreds of lives during your time in the military. It's foolish, and counterproductive, to think you could have prevented every ill. If there's one thing I've learned in seven hundred years of living, it's that looking backward never moves you forward."

She sniffed. "I guess."

He traced the arch of her cheekbone with his thumb. "Focus on what comes next. Getting out of this elevator. Finding Zander. Going home. We'll take one hurdle at a time." His thumb stroked again, soothing. Artemis was reminded of that same gentle stroke, on the rim of his coffee cup—it seemed like such a long time ago.

He spoke again, his tone serious. "Your life essence is getting weak, Artemis. Dangerously so."

"I know. That blow I took from Malachi before the elevator closed—"

"Damn bastard." He drew her into his arms. "But I can help with that. Make you strong in light again. If you'll let me."

She nodded. "And you—you need a stronger death shield if you're going to get through Hell without attracting every demon along the way. I can do that. But we have to work quickly. Who knows when that door will open? Or what we'll encounter on the other side?"

"Right. Quick." His hand smoothed down her back. "I

know a very quick, very effective way to swap power. I say we go for it."

She went still. "You don't mean . . . you want to make love? Here? Now?"

His breath kissed her temple. "Why, Artemis. What a fine idea. I'm so glad you suggested it."

She gave a shaky laugh. "I've heard some pretty wild pickup lines in my day, but never one as audacious as that."

"Was it successful, love?"

"I . . . I don't know yet."

His hand slid to her bottom, lifting her with him as he rose. Bracing her with her spine against the wall, he fitted his erection into the cradle of her thighs. "How about now? Any clearer? Come on, Artemis, that door could open any second."

She parted the edges of his jacket and laid her hands on his chest. His shirt was soaked with sweat. His musk made her head spin. He shrugged, letting heavy leather slip down his arms and fall behind them on the floor.

"You're really sure you want to do this?" she asked. "You're willing to let my death magic surround your life essence?"

"It'll make me stronger, won't it?"

"Yes, but . . . it will also make you . . . darker. It might linger, like the wound you took on during the battle to save Tain."

"I realize that. I don't care. Now a question for you, love. Why is it so hard for you to accept my help?"

Tears crowded her eyes. "Maybe because . . . I'm not used to anyone offering to help me do anything. Most of the time, it's the other way around. People need my power, my help. You're the first person I've ever met who hasn't wanted something from me." She felt him shift. "I just can't seem to make myself believe you're real. And . . . you've barely known me a day. And during that time, you've seen me steal, lie, whor—"

He silenced her with a quick, brutal kiss. His voice was strained. "Quiet, love, you're ruining the mood. I'm not . . . so perfect as you make me out to be. As for what you've done, I don't care."

His palms circled on her bottom, leaving a tingle of life magic. The positive energy chased away her fatigue and soothed the pounding in her head. He smelled of male sweat and potent life. And of hope. Hope so sweet, and so precious, it dislodged the last protest from her mind.

A lump formed in her throat. She didn't deserve this. Not from someone like Mac. He was willing to dirty his soul for her—perhaps permanently—and she was too needy to tell him she couldn't accept such a gift. She'd fought alone for so long, and now that he was here, with his arms wrapped around her, ready and willing to fight at her side, she couldn't turn him away.

He awed her, truly. He was so . . . *good*. So . . . noble.

His fingers flexed on her buttocks. He rocked the hard ridge of his erection between her thighs, setting off zings of sensation. His tongue circled inside her ear, making her gasp.

"And don't think," he said, "that I won't be enjoying myself very, very much at your expense."

Okay, well, maybe not quite so noble.

Still—

"You're sure? The death magic—"

He pressed his forehead to hers and groaned. "Artemis— I'm more than seven hundred years old."

"I know that."

"I've seen quite a bit of death in seven hundred years. I've lost count of how many human friends I've seen die. I've loved, I've grieved, but not once have I ever truly understood death. Not instinctively. Not the way a human can."

"Most humans would rather not understand death."

"I know. Humans want to live their lives as if they're immortal. Then one day—bang. It's too late for anything, even regrets. But the humans who face their deaths early on—the ones who acknowledge it and use it to shape their lives—they're the ones who truly live."

"But—you *are* immortal. Life will never be over for you. You don't need to understand death. Why would you even want to?"

He pressed his forehead to hers. "Do you know what it's like to know you'll never die?" He exhaled a low laugh. "No, you don't. You can't possibly know."

"I can imagine. It would be wonderful."

"Sometimes it is. Other times, it's only . . . shapeless. Like random notes that refuse to arrange themselves into a proper melody."

"Human lives can be shapeless, too."

He sighed. "I don't expect you to understand. Just trust me, Artemis. Please."

She forced herself to nod. "All right."

He kissed her again, a soft, comforting contact. His hands began moving on her body—skimming her hips, her stomach, her breasts. Each brush of his fingers sparked a tingle of need.

She ran her hands up his arms. She wanted to surround him, mold her body to his. His lips covered hers, warm and firm and alive. His tongue stroked, tempting and invading. A drop of his sweat dripped onto her shoulder. It felt like a benediction.

She wrapped her arms around him, her body straining to get closer as she speared her tongue into his mouth. His fingers plucked at her jeans' button. Her pants slid down her legs. His hot palms slipped into her panties, cupping her bottom, and then her underwear was gone, as well.

His hands roamed under the hem of her shirt, stroking, causing her belly to clench. The front clasp on her bra sprang open; his thumb found her nipple, and squeezed gently. Then, with a sudden shift of his body, his mouth replaced his hand.

Sweet fire poured like heated honey through her veins. She cradled his head to her breast as his lips, tongue, and teeth teased. Dimly, she was aware of Mac shoving down his pants. He urged her bare legs open and draped them around his hips.

His arms held her steady, the wall supporting her back. The blunt tip of his erection slid over the soft skin of her inner thigh.

Her head fell back, thudding gently against the wall. She felt dizzy, her balance slipping. She wanted him higher. Inside her. When his hand moved between her legs, to touch the place that ached for him, it was all she could do to bite back a moan.

"Don't fight it, love."

Mac stroked into her curls, finding his target with unerring accuracy. Life magic exploded inside her; a wave of pleasure crested. She tried to ride it even higher. Her pulse was racing, and it was damn hard to breathe. Impossible to think. Where was her balance now?

"Let yourself go, love."

She reached to bring him to her, but he shifted his hips, holding himself just out of her grasp. She moaned her protest, the plea sounding foreign in her throat. Blinding need assaulted her. When had she ever wanted a man so badly? Never.

That terrified her. Mac had taken control of her body and her soul and there was nothing she could do to wrest herself back from him. Not until he chose to let her go.

The air in the elevator was a warm cocoon, surrounding them, locking them together. Her body was open to him. Sweat soaked them both. Mac's breath rasped, his scent intoxicated her. His tongue delved inside her mouth, demanding, unrelenting. His fingers probed the hot pulse between her legs. One digit slipped inside on a hot, wet stroke; his thumb circled her clitoris, driving her higher.

She shuddered, clinging to him, too weak to do anything but accept the raw emotion he demanded that she feel.

For him.

She gasped as his hands moved to her hips, positioning her to receive him. His erection pressed against the entrance to her body. Her inner muscles contracted, trying to draw him in. His fingers slipped along the separation of her buttocks, lifting and separating the smooth globes. She arched in his hands, her mind spinning into raw, stunning lust.

Finally—*finally!*—he entered her.

Slowly.

She gritted her teeth, trying to endure it. Every unhurried, searing inch of his plunge branded her soul. Her womb contracted, never wanting to let him go. A surge of light teased the edges of her senses—Mac's life essence, white and hot and more alive than she could bear. This time, unlike the last, the gift was freely given.

With a shudder, he opened his soul completely to her. She sensed its dark stain, the single blot on his perfection. The wound would be wider, darker, uglier, before their mission was over.

She wanted to cry.

"Steady there." His voice was a ragged whisper. He'd buried himself inside her, but wasn't moving. "Cast your death magic. Inside me. Now."

She didn't want to do it.

He must have sensed her emotional withdrawal. "Oh no, Artemis, love. None of that. There's no going back now."

He reached between their bodies and stroked her, just above the place where their bodies joined. She gasped as a wave of dizzying pleasure surged and retreated, leaving her panting. Groaning, he pressed himself inside her even deeper. Her core was alive with his hot, primal pulse.

"Hurry, love. Even demigods have their limits. I won't be able to hold back much longer."

Swallowing her doubts, and her guilt, Artemis dug deep into her mind. Hideous syllables, dark and dangerous, sprang to her lips. Her tongue grazed his neck, tasting salt.

She nipped, hard, and tasted a single drop of blood.

The death spell slipped around their joined bodies like a midnight cloak, her dark magic surrounding his light. Mac withdrew almost completely from her body.

Artemis choked out the spell's final word. He plunged back into her body on a smooth upward slide that seemed to reach the center of her soul. Light flashed behind her closed eyelids. His rhythm quickened to a frenzy.

His lovemaking, fueled by death magic, took on a raw, selfish edge. His restraint splintered. She felt herself slip past pure pleasure into a mix of blinding bliss and pain.

He took her hard and fast against the elevator wall. Their grunts and groans collided, their sweat and musk mingled, their bodies slapped together. Mac cried out as his climax hit; Artemis's came an instant later—stunning, searing, and all-consuming.

Inside the cocoon of Artemis's death spell, the sweet, dark pleasure went on and on and on. The cloak of death enveloped them, sheltered them, but, incredibly, did not dim Mac's light. If anything, the containment Artemis had fashioned allowed Mac's life-magic essence to blaze hotter than ever.

She coasted down from her peak, her mind already struggling to throw off the haze of afterglow. His grip on her hips loosened. Her legs slid down the outside of his thighs until her feet touched the floor. Mac braced his hands on the wall on either side of her head and let out a long, shuddering breath.

He softened and slipped from her body. She felt the loss keenly. She ran her hand through his hair, fingers sifting through the damp blond locks. The smothering heat and darkness suddenly seemed to separate them, rather than unite. She thought she should say something, but she couldn't think of anything that wouldn't sound trite.

She let him go.

She felt Mac's reluctance to part; she thought he was about to speak, but then he seemed to think the better of it. He drew back and muttered a word—a word she couldn't believe he knew. The dark disappeared in a subtle glow of hellfire.

Artemis blinked into the diffuse red haze, cast by a small, amorphous sphere hovering just above Mac's left shoulder. As he'd said, he learned quickly. Power found its own level, whether the medium was light or darkness.

His back was slightly turned. He'd pulled up his jeans and was zipping them closed. He left his leather jacket lying on the floor.

He wasn't looking at her, but she could feel him at the edge of her mind. No. *Inside* her mind. She stared at his back, nonplussed. She hadn't considered the possibility that the psychic touch of their lovemaking would remain once their bodies parted.

She couldn't hear his thoughts, and she didn't think he could hear hers, but the sensation was incredibly intimate just the same. And incredibly uncomfortable. She was reminded of a dream she once had in which she'd inexplicably found herself naked during a military briefing before ten fully clothed male colleagues. The hot embarrassment, the sinking feeling in her stomach, the knowledge that every part of her was on display—the absolute certainty there was nowhere she could hide—that horrible vulnerability was just what she felt now. Except worse, because she knew this was no dream.

Cheeks flaming, she snatched up her jeans and struggled into them. By the time she'd finished lacing her boots, she'd gathered enough courage to meet Mac's gaze. His green eyes reflected red hellfire. The effect was unnerving.

Gods. What was he thinking? She'd seen into the bottom of his soul when their minds joined. What had he seen when he'd looked into hers? Did he regret his vow to help her? Did he hate her now, for accepting his offer?

She was too much of a coward to ask.

They stood staring at each other until the moment stretched into awkwardness. Finally, Mac angled his head toward the elevator door. "Ready, love?"

She nodded.

He pointed a finger. Spoke a word.

Nothing happened. His death magic was still new. Erratic.

He frowned.

"Here," Artemis said. "Let me try."

She spoke a word. The door disappeared in a heated blast of hellfire.

CHAPTER FOURTEEN

"*This* is Hell?"

Somehow, Mac hadn't imagined the Great Inferno looking like the lobby of a two-star hotel.

Dingy wallpaper, uncomfortable-looking vinyl-upholstered chairs. Dim lighting. Threadbare carpeting. Cigarette smoke hung like a nasty promise in the air. On a whole, the scene was decidedly unposh. But eternal damnation? Mac rather thought not.

"It's just the antechamber, I think," Artemis said.

"Ah."

He looked to the left and right. The ruined elevator from which he and Artemis had emerged wasn't the only one of its type. Similar tarnished silver portals marched along one long wall of a room filled with walking dead. Some corpses were old and frail, trailing hospital intravenous towers behind them. Others were younger, with visible fatal wounds and stumbling gaits. Misery etched pasty faces. Dead souls burned in hopeless eyes. All the moaning, wailing, and gnashing of teeth was decidedly annoying.

The damned hadn't come to Hell empty-handed. Each corpse was laden with baggage: suitcases, backpacks, purses, steamer trunks. Some yanked their luggage along, cursing. Others shuffled as if in a trance, tugging their burdens behind them. Still others fought for the few vacant chairs, or, giving up on the struggle, slumped on the floor atop their bags.

"Poor slobs," Mac murmured.

"I don't understand," Artemis whispered, though no one seemed to be paying them much attention. "I thought only the souls of the dead went to Hell. Not their bodies, too. Why aren't they still in their graves?"

"Most likely they are," Mac said. "But they seem to be here, as well." He shrugged. "Magic."

"Of course," Artemis murmured.

Whether dazed or determined, quick or slow, the corpses seemed generally headed toward the same goal: the hotel checkout desk and the single, harried demon toiling there. Thousands of corpses, if not more, had already arranged themselves into a snaking line, which folded back and forth upon itself, like some kind of hellish Disneyland queue.

Artemis started forward. Mac placed a cautioning hand on her arm and drew her back against the grimy flowered wallpaper. Despite the surroundings, which were beyond depressing, the brief physical contact made him go hard. Bloody hell. They'd made love not ten minutes earlier— but he wanted her again. She was quickly becoming his favorite addiction. Their first time, at his estate, had been good, but what they'd just shared in that dark, suffocating elevator? *That* had left him stunned.

It was due to the death magic. It had to be. The dark shield Artemis had conjured had amplified their combined life magic—the effect had been something like cranking up a thousand-watt concert speaker inside a squash court. For one fleeting instant, he'd held the essence of Artemis's unique soul inside his mind. The result? His mind was now officially blown.

He sidled a glance at Artemis. She'd been with him all the way. But despite the psychic connection they'd made, he couldn't be sure if the experience had been unique for her, too. Death magic was familiar territory to Artemis, after all.

Had it affected her as it had him? Was she thinking of it, even now, as he was? He couldn't be sure. Her mind seemed light-years away, her expression troubled. Most likely, she was thinking of her son. Mac was just a means to an end, after all.

What would she say if he told her his child was growing inside her?

No doubt she wouldn't be pleased, to put it mildly. A modern woman liked to be in control of such decisions. She'd even been taking birth control pills. It was going to be damned difficult to tell her he'd overridden her precautions on a whim.

Another problem: He didn't want Artemis or his child to be here in Hell. Every instinct he had screamed to get them both out. Immediately. But he knew there wasn't a chance she would go. She loved her son that fiercely.

Would she love Mac's child with equal fervor?

A bell rang. They both turned toward the sound, which had come from one of the elevators. The door slid open; a dead man wearing a dark business suit walked out. A bloody hole gaped in the center of his chest. He seemed unconcerned with the wound; he was too busy trying to maneuver three large suitcases into the lobby.

"Where's an effing porter when you need one?" The corpse hefted a suitcase in each hand, kicking the third before him as he inched across the lobby.

"You'd think he'd just abandon them," Artemis said.

"If he'd've been able to do that, I suspect he wouldn't have ended up here in the first place."

"I suppose you're right." Her gaze touched his, briefly. He wondered what she was thinking.

"Let's go, love." He steered her into the center of the lobby, avoiding the line of corpses waiting for checkout. The clerk handed a scroll to a dead man at the front of the line. The bloke picked up an enormous backpack and staggered away.

"Look," Artemis said. "He's heading toward those glass doors on the other side of the room. Beneath the flashing lights."

The corpse pushed through the exit and disappeared. Others watched, but didn't follow. A few minutes later, a female corpse left the front of the checkout line and made her way out the glass doors.

"Should we get in line?" Artemis wondered.

"No. We're not dead."

"How else are we to get out?"

"We'll just walk out. Come on."

He threaded his fingers with Artemis's and drew her toward the exit. Their progress was slow. Corpses blocked their path, forcing Mac to shove them aside. Finally, disgusted, he stopped and called a death glamour.

Invisibility made the trek a bit easier. Finally, they stood before the double glass doors. The flashing lights Artemis had noted earlier were illuminated letters, running across a screen. The same three words, over and over and over.

Abandon all hope . . . Abandon all hope . . . Abandon all hope . . .

Artemis made a choking sound.

She was far paler than Mac thought was healthy. "Chin up, love. The message's not for us."

"How can you be sure?"

"Because we're not dead. And we're not damned, either." He strode forward and pushed the door. He'd expected some resistance, but to his surprise it gave way easily.

The air inside Hell's antechamber had been foul, but at least it'd been relatively cool. Outside, a solid wall of heat greeted them. Mac and Artemis stepped onto a wide sidewalk, crowded with corpses and luggage. Beyond the curb, blurred lanes of high-speed traffic whizzed past. Heated exhaust blasted his face.

He inhaled and gagged on the fumes. His second

breath, which he kept shallow, came easier. Beside him, Artemis wasn't faring so well. Bent double, hands on her thighs, she gasped for breath, but could only manage a wheeze.

Alarmed, Mac rubbed her back. "Come on, love, don't pass out on me. Take slow breaths. That's it."

Artemis's red-rimmed eyes streamed tears, but her next breath was quieter. She raised her head, clutching his arm for a moment before trusting her balance.

Straightening, she glanced up and down the sidewalk. She even managed a short laugh when she looked behind them and saw the sign over the door they'd just come through.

"Hotel California?"

"Satan must have a sense of humor."

He surveyed the crowded sidewalk. Corpses milled about, alternately dragging their bags and engaging in fist-fights. There seemed to be nowhere to go; the hellish race of cars and lorries prevented anyone from stepping off the curb. A thick haze of smog obscured the far side of the highway.

Mac nodded toward an overhead signpost. "Styx Boulevard."

"It's supposed to be a river. All the ancient texts say so."

"Apparently, times have changed."

Some corpses had managed to secure a position at the curb. They waved at the passing traffic, but not one vehicle slowed, let alone stopped. Artemis gasped as one of the dead, apparently fed up with waiting, stepped off the curb and made a dash for it. Brakes squealed; the corpse hit the front bumper of a canary yellow Hummer. The dead man's body sailed through the air; corpses on the sidewalk scurried out of the way. The cadaver landed on the concrete with a sickening thud.

After a moment, the dead man got up, shook himself off, and started shoving his way back to the curb.

"Gods," Artemis said, shaken. "I guess crossing on foot is out. Any ideas on how we're going to get across?"

Mac eyed the traffic. "There's supposed to be a boatman, right? To ferry the damned souls to their punishments?"

"Yes. Charon."

"Well, then. He's got to show up sooner or later. When he does, we'll hit him up for a ride."

Time was an uncertain concept in Hell, but Mac thought about an hour passed before the sound of an unmuffled motorcycle engine snared his attention. His jaw dropped as a familiar vehicle careened out of the near lane and screeched to a halt at the curb. "Bloody wanking hell! That's my Norton."

His baby. His love. The classic cycle had gone up in flames; he thought he'd never see it again. Now here it was, in Hell, its chrome flashing with blinding, heart-breaking brilliance. Mac's custom leather saddle sagged under the weight of a grotesquely muscular giant clad in chains and black leather.

Bulging triceps ripped through the driver's sleeves; his thighs bulged so thickly his leather pants had split their seams. A metallic helmet, face shield down, only added to the creature's aura of menace.

Excitement rippled through the crowd. "Charon," one corpse whispered. Others repeated the name, until the sylla-bles became a chant. "Charon . . . Charon . . . Charon."

Charon gunned the Norton's motor. The roar ripped through the crowd like machine-gun fire. Straddling the cycle, the giant surveyed his supplicants.

Mac grabbed Artemis's hand. "Come on. The next ride's ours."

"We're not the only ones with that idea."

True enough. The corpses had mobilized, surging to-ward the boatman, dragging their bags behind them. A male wrapped in a white sheet fought toward the curb, only to trip over the trailing edge of his shroud and land facefirst in the gutter. A pair of shrieking women yanked tufts of hair from each other's skulls in their frenzy to be the first to reach Hell's guardian. A bald bloke with a huge gut and tattooed arms launched himself at the Norton. He even managed to wrap his sausagelike fingers around the handlebars before Charon planted the sole of his boot on the man's chest.

"Please," the corpse croaked. "Please, sir, I'm begging . . . take me across." He jabbed his free hand into his pocket. Gold glinted between his fingers. He waved the coin in front of Charon's visor. "See? I got the fare!"

The boatman's mouth opened. His breath exuded sulfur, his voice rumbled like an earthquake. "No. Not you."

He shoved the corpse back into the crowd. Charon's thick leg swung over the saddle in a dismount. "Only one may cross," the boatman intoned. "One of my choosing."

He took a swaggering step; the crowd gave a collective gasp and shrank back. Charon's head swiveled. Searched. He waded into the throng.

As the distance between the boatman and the Norton increased, Mac maneuvered Artemis toward the cycle's front tire. Brilliant. Charon had left the Norton idling.

The demon let out a roar. Mac's head snapped toward the demon, but luckily, the blighter wasn't looking in Mac's direction. As he watched, Charon ripped off his helmet, revealing a visage shining with death magic. Coarse white hair stuck out in all directions, like an old bristled scrub brush. Thin pink lips pulled back to reveal sharpened yellow teeth; a hawklike nose curved in a sharp slash. But it was Charon's eyes, Mac thought, that most inspired the terrified sobs and whimpers rippled through the cowering corpses. The sockets ran red with blood.

"I will take only one," Charon boomed. "*Who?*"

The corpses, still and silent, quivered in anticipation.

"Ready?" Mac whispered to Artemis.

"When you are."

Charon's arm rose. One long, white finger extended, pointing at a shaking corpse. "You. Come—"

"Now!" Mac leaped into the Norton's saddle. Artemis jumped on behind, wrapping her arms around his midsection.

Charon jerked as if stung, an unholy shriek on his lips. Mac gunned the engine; Charon spun about and lunged. His massive hand closed on Mac's forearm. Mac put the cycle in gear and stomped on the accelerator. Tires spun, the Norton shook, but the vehicle didn't move.

Mac bit off a curse as Charon's death magic assaulted Artemis's shielding. He could feel Artemis probing, searching for a weak spot in the demon's power. There wasn't one—at least Mac, with his amateur death-magic skills, couldn't detect any vulnerability. He willed a blast of hellfire in the brute's direction. He managed an anemic stream of red sparks that fizzled almost as soon as it ignited.

Bugger it all. He hadn't felt this helpless since he was a child. Seven centuries ago. He hoped like hell that Artemis could knock the blighter on his arse, because it was all Mac could do to keep Charon from ripping the motorcycle out from under them. He could feel her weaving a complicated death spell. She needed time.

He fisted his free hand and smashed it square in the middle of Charon's ugly face.

Blood and flames shot from the demon's eyes. His mouth gaped open, spewing an odor like rotten anchovies.

"You," he roared. "You are not dead!"

"Bingo, mate."

The demon's grip on Mac's arm tightened. His gaze flicked to Artemis. "She is also alive."

"So what if we are?" Mac said, desperate to distract Charon's attention from Artemis and her burgeoning death spell. Gods in Annwyn. Couldn't she work a bit faster?

He winced as another blast of Charon's breath bathed his face.

"The living are not allowed on the far bank of the Styx."

"Thanks for the notice, mate. Now get your hands off me."

"Insolent slug." Charon's free hand shot out and clamped on Mac's neck. "You cannot cross. It is not permitted."

A hot wave of death magic hit Mac's shielding; the barrier rippled dangerously. For one heart-stopping moment, he thought it would shatter. *Any time now, Artemis, love.*

Charon's pink lips parted on a cackle of laughter. Red eyes blazed; yellow teeth glinted. Fleshy fingers crushed Mac's windpipe. Mac gave up on breathing. He was immortal; he could hold his breath indefinitely. What really had him worried was the possibility of Charon's ire turning on Artemis.

Damn it, woman, what's taking so bloody long with that spell?

He felt her bristle and almost laughed, despite their precarious predicament. She might not have heard his precise thought, but their lingering psychic connection had transmitted his frustration loud and clear. In answer, her spell notched up a level, the tension winding tighter, and tighter, until . . .

Finally.

She shouted a truly hideous word—it felt like a nail driving through bone. Bloody hell. Could he ever bring himself to even *think* such a syllable, let alone utter it?

The spell exploded in Charon's face. The demon let out a piercing shriek, and his magic wavered. It was all the opening Mac needed. "Hold on, love!"

The Norton's motor whined. Mac shot into the nearest lane of traffic like a bullet. It was like being sucked into a vortex around a drain. Artemis clung to his neck.

If it were possible, he thought she might have climbed into his skin.

"Steady, love. We've got, what—?" He peered to his right, counting. "Twelve more lanes to cross."

Her forehead pressed against his spine. "I'm okay. Just . . . hurry."

He banked around the endless curve, spinning a counterclockwise circle. After a minute or two, they completed the circuit, whizzing past the hotel. Charon stood at the curb, shaking a fiery fist.

Mac gave up on waiting for a gap in the traffic. Bending low over the handlebars, he flung the Norton into the next lane. Horns wailed, brakes screeched, but at least he completed the maneuver without crashing. The next lane change went worse, sparks flying as a low-slung Lamborghini scraped metal. Mac accelerated, hot wind whistling in his ears. His speedometer topped out, and still he was in danger of getting run over.

He gunned the Norton for all it was worth, giddy excitement pouring through his veins. He was flying in a tornado—in Hell—and he was actually enjoying himself. What did that say about the state of his soul? He wasn't sure he wanted to know.

One by one, he conquered the next nine lanes, laughing out loud at one exhilarating near-miss. The speed boggled his mind. Behind him, Artemis groaned.

"Just one lane to go," he shouted over his shoulder.

"Thank the gods."

The Norton shuddered between his thighs, emitting a bloodcurdling, almost human whine. Mac's excitement bled into anxiety. It wouldn't do to have the machine come apart in his hands. He eyed an inch-wide gap between a Ferrari Scuderia and an Alfa Romeo Spider. Releasing a prayer, he launched the Norton through it.

Metal flashed and sparks showered, and then they were

skidding across an expanse of black asphalt, tires smoking. He hit the brakes hard and spun a tight three-sixty. Artemis slammed into his back as the Norton squealed to a halt. Mac grabbed her arm an instant before she pitched head-first onto the macadam. "You okay, love?"

"Just dandy," she muttered, scrambling back into the saddle behind him. "Gods. What is this place?"

A dingy sea of cars, aligned head to head in arrow-straight rows, stretched into the distance.

"Looks like a car park."

Artemis shot him a look. "No kidding. It looks like the mall parking lot back home. On Black Friday."

"Ah yes. You Yanks do love your automobiles, don't you?"

"There has to be a million spaces!"

"And every one of them taken." Countless cars circulated the aisles at a snail's pace, as if searching for an empty parking spot. A red Ford Pinto reached the turnabout nearest Mac and Artemis. The driver's face was a study in hopelessness.

"This must be Limbo," Artemis said. "A place for souls not corrupt enough for Hell. Can you imagine? Looking for a parking space for all eternity?"

"It's not so bad. The drivers aren't in any pain, at least."

"That's something, I guess. Does that look like a building on the other side of all these cars? What do you suppose it is?"

"Harrod's? Marks and Spencer?"

Artemis snorted. "You're right. Not exactly what I'd expected."

He regarded her with interest. "What *did* you expect, love?"

"Hard to say. So few living humans have been to Hell, let alone returned to tell about it. As far as I could determine, Dante Alighieri was the last human to make the journey, in the 1300s."

"Ah yes. That bloke. I saw his book in your car. I met him once, you know. Bloody depressed wanker, he was, living in exile. Personally, I wouldn't trust a word he wrote. Dipped into the church wine a bit too much, in my opinion."

"No. I believe Dante really did visit Hell. He drew the definitive map of Satan's realm. Nine circles, each deeper level worse than the one above it. Ptolomaea, and Satan's personal sanctuary, exist at the very bottom of the pit. That's where I have to go."

He hesitated. The dregs of Hell, a breath from Lucifer's lair, was the very last place he wanted the woman who was carrying his child to go. Mac's instinct was to take Artemis to safety, and go after her son himself. Except . . . that he didn't think he could rescue Zander. Not alone. Not with his present fledgling death-magic skills. Not without Artemis's help.

There. He'd admitted it. The great Manannán mac Lir needed help. How humiliating.

Because of his weakness, he might not be able to fully protect the child growing in Artemis's womb. That thought rankled. If he told Artemis about the pregnancy, would she turn back? Abandon her quest to save her first child in favor of protecting her unborn one? He already knew the answer to that. She would never abandon her firstborn. She was going to Ptolomaea regardless. And Mac wasn't about to let her make the trip alone.

He weighed his options. Tell Artemis about the pregnancy? No. That would only stir up her anger, making her less likely to trust Mac during their journey. And she needed to trust him, if they were all going to get out of this trek alive.

"All right, then, love. If Ptolomaea is at the bottom of the pit, that's where we're headed."

"Thank you," she said quietly. "You can't know what it means to me to have your help."

He searched her gaze. "You should have accepted it a lot sooner, love. That was quite a close escape you made from the Sidhe Council chamber."

"I know."

"You should have confided in me from the first. What were you thinking, going to Malachi? Dealing with Old Ones is a thousand kinds of deadly."

She bit her lip. "I thought I could handle him."

"Demons can't be handled," Mac said. "My sister learned that lesson," he added bitterly.

"You have a sister?"

A ripple of tension ran through him. "A half sister. Leanna. Niniane is her mother, but her father was a human. Her Sidhe magic was potent, and her human blood allowed her to call death magic. She . . . became quite adept at it. She summoned a demon, the same Old One the Immortals and I fought last year. She thought she had the upper hand."

"She didn't, did she?"

"No. She turned demonwhore, and worse. No human ever wins against an Old One. Remember that."

Artemis was silent, but he sensed her disagreement, and it angered him. She was strong, but Leanna had been strong as well. Demons were bound by the contracts they made with humans, but they were masters of deceit. In the end, they always twisted the agreement to the detriment of the human party.

That part of Artemis's life was over, though. Once they returned to the human world, she wouldn't come in contact with another demon ever again. He'd personally ensure it.

He gunned the motor and set off down the nearest aisle. "No more loitering. Faster down, faster out."

The lane must have been a mile long. Mac slowed as he neared the end of it. An ugly, squat building rose before them. A bank of doors glazed with reflective glass provided the only break in the facade.

Mac abandoned the Norton at the curb, directly under a NO PARKING sign. He gave the cycle one last loving glance. He didn't expect to see it again. Crossing the sidewalk, Mac and Artemis confronted their distorted reflections on the face of the entry doors. Mac tried each in turn, until he came to one that wasn't locked.

He paused and looked at Artemis. "Ready?"

"No."

"Me, neither." He yanked the door open.

CHAPTER FIFTEEN

Artemis walked into a darkened movie theater.

Heat wafted from a noisy overhead vent. Thick, cloying perfume, slightly rotten, seeped into her nostrils. She and Mac stood in the back of the theater, behind rows and rows of seats, all taken.

A movie was running—a porn flick. Hard-core. Brutal. Naked figures, copulating grotesquely. Surround-sound speakers blared a sickening combination of moans, curses, sobs, and cracking whips.

"A bit over the top, if you ask me," Mac commented.

A bit over the top? More like far into the depths of depravity. Pure revulsion closed her throat. In mute defense, she shifted her attention from the screen and concentrated on the audience. Not much of an improvement. The corpses were naked, writhing and moaning with the actors on the screen. The damned were clearly aroused, almost to the point of insanity. But with their arms and legs chained to their chairs, they could do nothing but watch the film.

Artemis's stomach gurgled. For a split second, she thought she'd heave. She spun around, needing to get out. Away. Somewhere, anywhere. Even back to that hellish parking lot.

But the door they'd just passed through was gone.

"Bloody hell," Mac muttered. "Nowhere to go but forward. Just keep your head down. We'll get through it."

He pulled her forward, down one of the aisles. She followed in a blind stumble, embarrassed to be so freaked out. She'd thought she was ready for this. For Hell. She wasn't.

Too late for second thoughts now.

Mac's arm encircled her shoulder. His touch reminded her of what they'd done in the elevator. That had been as beautiful as the acts on the massive theater screen were horrible.

"Steady, love. I see an exit."

"Where?"

"There. See the red light just near the screen?"

"How do you know that's the right way out?"

"Don't, really," he replied briefly.

The sounds of sex grew louder, and more disturbing, the closer they got to the front of the theater. With it came heat, and bitter, unwanted arousal. Trembling, Artemis tried to ignore the lust smoldering between her thighs. *It's not real.* But it felt as if it were. Tingling heat caressed her breasts, her belly, her buttocks. Mac's arm tightened around her. He'd felt it, too.

She sucked in a breath, suddenly aware that she'd forgotten to inhale for several long seconds. "Sex. It's all I can think of."

Mac's voice was warm and low in her ear. "I want you, too, love, but I hardly think this is the time, or the place."

"Dante wrote about this. Hell's second level is reserved for souls whose lives were consumed by lust."

The exit light loomed above them, the outline of a door below. Mac pushed the lever; thank the gods, the door opened. He shoved her over the threshold so violently that she stumbled. She righted herself and turned just in time to see the door snap closed with a resounding thud.

Mac was still on the other side.

"No!" She grabbed the handle and heaved with all her strength. The door didn't budge. Desperate, she pounded with both her fists. "Mac! Are you there? Can you hear me?"

Nothing.

She blasted the door with an unlocking spell. A melting spell. An explosive spell. Her magic had no effect. If Mac was on the other side, trying to get in, she couldn't hear him. Finally, she sank to the floor, her throat spasming on a sob. Gods. How could she have let the door close between them? Stupid, stupid, stupid.

What had happened to Mac? And what was she to do without him?

She raised her head, suddenly aware of buzzing. The noise came from a flickering fluorescent light directly over her head. Identical fixtures marched down the ceiling of a long access corridor. Slowly, Artemis stood. The hallway's walls were blank, and the passage seemed deserted. She couldn't see the end.

With nowhere to go but forward, she started walking. After a time, a light appeared in the distance. An exit?

It was a slim beacon of hope, but she fixed her eyes on the glow and plowed toward it. The light grew steadily. The outline of a human form took shape within the glow.

The figure stepped toward her. Recognition hit like a slap across the face.

Artemis halted. "Malachi."

The demon bowed. "Miss Black."

"Where's Mac?"

Vivid anger simmered red in the Old One's black eyes. "Do not speak to me of the Sidhe."

He took another step forward. The odor of rotten eggs surged with his movement. Artemis fought the urge to retreat.

"It was clever of you, I admit, to lure a tainted demigod into your service." The demon smiled, revealing a row of even, white teeth. "So clever, in fact, that I may be encouraged to forgive you for the infraction. This new negotiation you've opened promises to be even more interesting than the last."

"We're not in negotiation."

"Oh, I think we are, my dear. Your immortal lover might have brought you across the Styx, rather than I, but that doesn't mean our contract has been voided. You'll uphold your end of our agreement. Especially now that the Sidhe is . . ." His grin widened. ". . . gone."

Gods. "What have you done to him?"

Malachi shrugged. "I suggest you think of yourself, and your quest. Or have you forgotten your son?"

Artemis went very still. "No. Of course, I haven't."

"Your protector is no longer here to guide you to Ptolomaea. Or even out of this corridor. Only I can do that."

She was only too afraid Malachi spoke the truth. She sucked in a breath. "All right. If . . . if you're still willing to help me, I'll uphold my side of the bargain. Once my son is safe in the human world, I'll become your whore."

Malachi's white teeth flashed. "I adore human mother love. It's so deliciously . . . inconvenient."

"Do your part, then. Show me the way."

"Oh, not so quickly, I think. You ran out on a blood contract. Embarrassed me in front of my thralls. Damaged my elevator. All that, Miss Black, calls for a renegotiation."

A bad taste burned Artemis's palate. "What kind of renegotiation?"

"One you'll welcome, I suspect. It has the potential to end in a much better scenario for you. Your son, safe in the human world. And you, safe with him. No need to prostitute yourself."

She stared. "You would help me? And let me go free afterward? With Zander?"

"Yes."

Hope sparked to life, but it was a cautious flame. A favor granted by an Old One came with a steep price.

"What would I have to do in return?"

"A simple thing, really, for a witch of your unique abilities."

"Just tell me what it is."

Malachi's eyes blazed red. "Deliver your immortal lover into my power."

Artemis raised her brows. "Ah, so you don't have Mac, after all."

Flames shot from Malachi's fingertips, striking the ground at Artemis's feet. She leaped back, heart pounding.

"It matters not. You will imprison him for me."

"And just how do you expect me to do that? I've got no idea where he is, and neither do you. And even if I could find him, how the hell could I imprison him? Mac's a demigod. I'm . . . just a human. There's no way I could entrap him."

Malachi threw back his head and laughed. "Ah, but you've ensnared the great Manannán mac Lir already. You lured him into Shadowhaven. Into Hell. No god would follow a human to this place. Not unless that human wielded great power over him."

"You're wrong. I don't have any power over Mac. Not at all."

"Come, now, do not lie to me. I do not pretend to understand the disgusting life-magic insanity humans call love, but I recognize it readily enough."

"Love?" Her heart pounded in her ribs. "That's absurd. Mac doesn't love me."

But, she realized with sudden clarity, she was dangerously close to loving him.

"If Mac Lir doesn't love you yet, you'd better pray you can rouse that elusive emotion in his immortal soul . . . or, failing that, a sentiment close enough to love as to make no difference. Lust will do, I think. He's half Sidhe, after all."

"But . . . Mac has nothing to do with our original contract." Artemis knew she was grasping at straws. "Leave him out of it. I don't want to renegotiate."

"You've broken two contracts. Your only hope is to

negotiate a third. Those are my terms. The stakes rise. Deliver the sea god's son to me, and you and your own son go free. Refuse to cooperate . . ." The smooth voice trailed off, leaving malice lingering in the air.

Artemis's gut twisted. "What will you do if I don't agree?"

"Ah." Malachi crossed his arms. "Finally, we advance. If you refuse to cooperate, I will personally see that your son's body joins his soul in Hell. For all eternity."

It was only by a supreme effort of will that Artemis remained standing. "No. That would please Hecate too well. You hate her. You wouldn't want to—"

"Silence! Do not presume, witch, to guess what I would or would not do. I have presented you with your choices. All that remains is for you to choose whom you will betray, your lover or your child."

Gods. She was going to be sick. Choice? She had no choice. Mac was a demigod; Zander was an innocent. She couldn't condemn her son to eternal damnation. But Mac . . . Pain knotted her chest at the thought of betraying him. Again. But Mac's power was vast. He was learning to transmute his life magic into death magic. His skills were new, but as he'd said, he was a good student. She had to believe he could come up with a few tricks in a fight with a demon like Malachi.

Malachi snapped his fingers. A long scroll appeared in his hand, the curled end of the parchment brushing the scuffed vinyl tiles at his feet. Row after row of tightly scrawled black lettering ended in a bold slashing line, marked with an X.

"Your new contract, my dear. Will you sign?"

A quill appeared in his hand. The nub was a sharp, pointed blade. With shaking hands, Artemis accepted it. Slashing the quill's tip across her forefinger, she waited, light-headed, as her blood welled.

Malachi watched with satisfaction as she smeared her

name at the bottom of the cursed document. When she was done, he rolled the scroll with a flourish and tucked it under his arm. "You will deliver the immortal into my power."

"I'll . . . try."

The demon raised one sleek eyebrow. "I hope, for your son's sake, that you succeed."

Artemis clenched her bloody finger inside her fist. "Where is Mac now? How do I find him?"

"That, unfortunately, I do not know. He may be on this level, or he may have found his way to the one below. But fear not. Your human love, it is said, conquers all. You will find him." He paused. "I suggest you do it quickly. My patience wears thin. Bring Mac Lir to Hell's fifth level. I'll await you there."

"But—"

"No more questions. Be warned, lest you are tempted to deceive me yet again. I have chosen a very slow, very painful method of death for your son if you betray me a third time." He flicked an invisible speck of lint from his suit. "You will not, I think, enjoy watching the boy die."

"Artemis! Damn it, woman, are you there?"

Mac pounded on the door. Not a sound came from the other side. Long minutes had passed since Artemis had disappeared behind the intractable steel barrier—perhaps as much as a half hour. She could be anywhere by now.

He drew back, considering his options. He'd conjured a few decent blasts of hellfire, his most powerful to date, to no effect. Now, as he watched, the outline of the door wavered. Melted. Streamed down the wall into a puddle at his feet, leaving nothing but dusty, faded wall fabric in its placc.

The exit light winked out of existence.

The door was gone.

Cursing soundly, Mac spun about and stalked back up

the aisle to the rear of the theater. As he'd suspected, a new set of doors had appeared. They opened easily. He found himself in a deserted theater concessions area, staring at a bank of Coming Attractions posters. The odor of stale popcorn hung in the air.

He paced to the center of the room, his boots clinging to a thin film of dried, spilled soda. At least he hoped it was soda.

"Mac? Brother?"

He spun around, heart lurching. "Leanna?"

He saw nothing but an arrangement of battered café tables.

The voice sounded, again from behind.

"Mac . . ."

He whirled about and ran a few steps in the new direction. Leanna's whisper drifted to somewhere on his right. He barely had time to turn before the plea shifted to his left. Then behind him, and in front, and from every direction at once, like a badly mixed sound track.

He halted, pulse pounding double time. It was a trick. It had to be. An echo of his guilt and his regret, plucked from his brain. Culsu hadn't brought Leanna to Hell, but to her own demon realm.

But what if Leanna were here, now?

It was possible. When the Immortals had destroyed Culsu, Mac had wondered if his sister would be set free. When she hadn't appeared in the human world, he feared she was dead. But what if she'd survived? What if she'd been trapped in the death realms? Or here, in Hell? If he found her, he could bring her home.

He prowled the theater lobby looking for answers. There were none. The door leading into the theater had vanished, and no others had appeared. He sank down in one of the café chairs. Sooner of later, he suspected, his next move would find him.

He was right. Even so, the sudden flash nearly toppled

him off his seat. Regaining his balance, he raised an arm against a blinding glare of dirty light that put him in mind of a rainbow dragged through mud.

The chaos gradually resolved into the form of a naked human woman. A demon. He remained sprawled in his chair, regarding her impassively. Her guise was exquisite. Long, vivid red hair framed slim shoulders, abundant breasts, flat stomach, and shapely hips. The ends curled against her long, firm thighs.

Unwanted lust pooled hot and heavy in his groin. Coherent thought slipped away. Hell's version of Lady Godiva inflamed his every nerve. *She's a demon*, a small, disgusted corner of his mind ranted. *Have some pride*. Did his unruly cock listen? No.

The demon smiled, lashes fluttering as she eyed the bulge in his jeans. In retaliation, Mac called an image of his mother to mind. Immediately, his shaft shriveled.

The demon's brows collided.

Mac almost laughed. Better. Much better.

He met her gaze. Her eyes were blue, he noted, without a trace of red. An Old One, then.

"Who are you?" he asked.

Her ruby lips pouted. "Don't you recognize me, Mac? It hasn't been so long, has it?"

He smiled grimly. "Ah, Hecate. The last time I saw you, you were a hag."

"My hag guise is very useful at times, I admit. But I prefer this body." She struck a pose. "Don't you?"

Despite his best intentions, Mac couldn't stop his gaze from dropping to her breasts.

"You do," she purred. "You're a male, after all."

"A male who isn't interested."

She smirked at the hard-on that had returned to his jeans. "Oh yes, I see how 'disinterested' you are. So, tell me, Mac. How's your father? Your mother? Your dim-witted cousins? It's been so long since I've seen them."

"Doing all the better for their lack of interaction with you, I'm sure."

"And your sister? She's not so well, is she? Turned demonwhore, I heard. Well, every family has its skeletons, I suppose." Hecate studied him. "Leanna resembles you quite closely, I see. Though lately she's been looking more . . . tired."

Mac tensed. "What do you know of Leanna? Do you know where she is?"

Hecate's elegant hands fluttered. "I may."

"You *may*?" He infused his words with contempt. "What kind of answer is that?" He sat up abruptly, snapping his fingers. "Ah, I've got it. It's the answer of someone who doesn't know."

Angry red dots appeared in the center of Hecate's pupils. "I am well aware of every hour of your sister's torment, Mac Lir. Do not think otherwise."

"I doubt it. You exaggerate your power." He stood and gave her his back. Strolling toward the concessions counter, he idly examined a candy display.

Hecate's taunting voice pursued him. "Another demon claimed Leanna as whore after her first master's demise. His name is Malachi."

Mac pivoted slowly, fighting to keep his expression neutral. "Did he? How nice for him."

"You are not so disinterested as you imply."

"I don't know why you would imagine that I care. Leanna caused me nothing but trouble when she lived in the human world."

"Malachi enjoys your sister very much. He uses her body, and feasts on her soul."

Mac clung to his temper. "Is there a point to this conversation? If so, get to it."

"So demanding!" Hecate chided. "I'm only telling you all this because you might be interested to know that Malachi is here in Hell. And since he never travels without a whore or two in tow, you might be interested to know that he's brought your sister with him."

Mac eyed the demon, trying to figure out her game. "Even if that is true, why tell me?"

"Because Malachi is my enemy. He slaughtered my clan, destroyed my upper realm. I've sworn to take vengeance. A vengeance that you will help me achieve."

"Don't be so sure of that. It's you I'm after, not Malachi. You stole a living soul from a human child. A witch's son. I want it back."

Hecate laughed. "And perhaps I will give it to you. Your lover's brat is only one innocent soul in my vast collection. I gather them, you see. The souls of children. They are so much sweeter than the souls of older, jaded humans."

"You're disgusting."

Hecate's hand fluttered to her throat. "Why, thank you, Mac Lir. The compliment means so much, coming from you." She slid her palms down her torso, lifting her breasts in offering. "Perhaps you would like to taste my glory?"

Despite his revulsion, Mac felt a surge of desire. He swallowed, hard. "I think not."

"Faithful to your little witch, are you? How touching."

"You tricked Artemis."

"Tricked Lieutenant Black? Never. She sought me out, requesting service. Protection for paltry humans mired in death magic. If she didn't anticipate the worst outcome of her association with me, it's no fault of mine." She shook her head, the long fall of her hair shimmering like a red satin curtain.

"She left the military and forgot I knew her magic. She became complacent, you see, after the balance of magic shifted toward life. Her protections on her son grew lax. It was so easy to snatch him. But what I don't understand is your involvement in the witch's affairs. Why would an immortal demigod trouble himself with a mongrel human death witch of highly questionable ancestry?"

"I have my reasons."

"All of which have to do with your cock, I'm sure. Darkness has gained a foothold in your soul, Mac Lir. It will never let go. Tell me . . . don't you find that death magic makes sex so much more . . . interesting, shall we say?"

"No."

Hecate threw back her head and laughed. "Oh, do not lie to me! It's far too amusing. Death always defeats life. Always. But the surrender can be so sweet. As you've begun to realize. You, a creature of life, have been dabbling with death. With death magic. Has it been . . . good for you? Exhilarating? Do you want more?" She glided forward, and suddenly he found her in his lap. Her lush bottom ground against his erection.

"I can show you so much."

With one fluid motion he stood and broke contact. "No, thank you. Demon sex isn't my thing."

Her eyes dropping to the blatant bulge in his jeans.

"No?" she taunted. "Ah well, pleasant as it would be—for both of us—sex is not what I require from you. I have a more difficult task in mind. I want you to destroy Malachi."

"The old wanker's too much for you, eh? Can't beat him on your own?"

Hecate bristled. "Malachi," she hissed, "is *nothing*. I could crush him under my bare heel. *If* he had the courage to face me, which he does not. The bastard has eluded me for centuries. He's afraid to fight me. But a battle with you? Here in Hell? That he will not fear."

"No doubt. Not sure if you've noticed, but my death-magic skills leave something to be desired."

She made a dismissive gesture. "That can be remedied."

He eyed her. "What do you mean?"

"Power is power, as you have begun to realize. Life magic, death magic—like all opposites, the two forces are more similar than they are different. Your life-magic talents may seem useless here in Hell, but they are not. They can be transformed."

"At what price?"

"You are wise. There is always a price. A piece of your soul, of course. But what does that matter? You are immortal. Your soul is endless."

When he made no immediate reply, Hecate stepped closer. "Here. I will show you."

She lifted a hand. A high-pitched whine vibrated Mac's eardrums. Sulfurous fog escaped from the cracks in the tiled floor. The yellow mist rose quickly, blotting out the concessions counter, the café tables, the posters.

The fog enveloped him. Death magic rode on the mist. He felt it probe for flaws in the death-magic shield Artemis had erected around his soul. In less time than it took for Mac to realize what was happening, Hecate's noxious vapor had homed in on the weakest part of his protections. A tiny crack gave way.

Death magic seeped inside, flooding Mac's consciousness. His stomach lurched; his head exploded with pain. Instinctively, he countered with the most powerful life-magic defense he knew—if he'd been facing Hecate in the human world, the demon bitch wouldn't have known what hit her. Here in Hell, however, the assault only caused Hecate to laugh.

Greedily, she lapped up his power. Her vitality shone. "Life is useless in Hell, Mac Lir. You must fight me with death. The death that is in your soul."

Hellfire rolled off her fingers. It struck Mac in the stomach, dropping him to his knees. Scorching heat ran up his esophagus. Choking, he was stunned to see flames shoot from between his parted lips.

His shirt caught fire. He rolled, smothering the flames, his anger blazing hotter than Hecate's attack. Without thought, without plan, he leaped to his feet and whirled to face the demon. A truly noxious word—one he'd heard Artemis utter—erupted from his lips.

Two balls of hellfire, hotter and denser than anything he'd yet conjured, burst from his palms. He flung both at Hecate. The demon batted the attack away.

Mac took a defensive posture, his chest heaving, his mind reeling with the horror of the spell he'd just cast. He'd paid for it with a portion of his life essence. The dark wound in his soul widened. Sickened, he readied himself to call the spell a second time. But to his surprise, Hecate didn't attack again.

Instead, she applauded, her palms connecting in a loud staccato. "Well done, Mac Lir. You've learned even more quickly than I hoped. Your death power will only grow, as you give up more and more of your soul to Hell. By the time you find Malachi, your power may even be equal to the task I've set for you."

Mac crossed his arms. "And when my death magic exceeds yours? What will you do then?"

Hecate waved a hand. "Absurd. That will never happen. My power is inviolate. I am the consort of the Lord of Hell."

Mac started. "Of Lucifer, you mean?"

"Lucifer, Old Nick, Beelzebub, Satan . . . my mate has many names. He created Hell and is its supreme ruler. In the end, when death wins the final battle with life, he will rule the upper worlds as well."

"Sounds like a nice guy. Why don't you ask him to take care of your little problem with Malachi?"

Hecate's red lips twisted. "The Lord of Darkness no longer ascends to Hell's upper levels. He prefers to remain in his sanctuary, while his thralls carry on his work above. In the upper reaches of Hell and in the demon realms—it is left to the Old Ones to battle for supremacy."

She snapped her fingers. A long scroll, covered with spidery script, appeared in her hand. "No more questions. It is time to conclude our business. Your contract, Mac Lir. You will sign in blood. I make you a generous offer. Destroy Malachi for me, and you may take one living soul back to the human world. Your sister, your lover, or her child. It makes no difference to me which you chose."

Mac took the scroll. Holding Hecate's gaze, he ripped the parchment in two. The halves fluttered to the floor. "I think not."

Hecate snarled. "You are arrogant, Mac Lir."

"Gods do tend to be."

"This game you play is foolish."

"Call me a fool, then. Gods don't make deals with demons."

"You are only half a god, and far from your base of power. I could destroy you now, easily. But I think I will not. This game will be much more interesting with you and your newfound darkness in it."

She spread her arms. Fire broke out along her bare skin. "Be gone, Mac Lir. You may have refused to sign, but our contract stands. Destroy Malachi, and I will reward you. Fail me, and you will regret it."

She flung her head back, and the long fall of her hair erupted in flames. Fire and sulfur rose; a clap of thunder resounded. Dark light flashed, and when the smoke cleared, Hecate was gone.

Mac dragged a hand down his face. "Bloody drama queen."

A crack appeared on the tile Hecate had just vacated. Mac watched as the fissure widened and split, spreading outward in all directions. He jumped backward as the floor crumbled, chunks of terra-cotta and concrete disappearing into a black void. As the crashing abated, a mechanical whir took its place.

Cautiously, Mac advanced to the edge of the hole. A moving stair, such as one might find in a department store, rose to greet him. Mac glanced around the lobby. No doors had appeared. It looked like this was his path to Hell's next level down.

He thought of Artemis, trapped behind the door on the other side of the theater. Had she found a way out? There seemed to be no other option but to step on the stair and hope that she had. He gripped the rubber railing. It carried him swiftly downward.

The ride was steep, but not terribly long. The escalator ended in a sort of vestibule, before a set of automatic sliding doors. Mac made out a light on the other side of the glass, but not much else. The surface was fogged.

He stepped up to the doors. They swished open. He walked through. A blast of arctic air slapped him in the face; he blinked against a sudden fluorescent glare. When his new surroundings finally swam into focus, he stared at it, bemused.

If Lucifer had created this place, Mac'd say one thing for the old wanker.

He had a hell of a sense of humor.

CHAPTER SIXTEEN

Artemis was shivering in front of a display of breakfast cereals when Mac suddenly appeared at the end of the aisle, right next to the sliced bread and English muffins.

His jeans were torn, his shirt singed, and his face was smudged with soot. But he was *there*, in front of her. Relief pounded through her veins so fiercely that for several long moments she couldn't move. Then he caught sight of her and waved. She raced down the aisle and threw herself into his arms before she remembered she'd just signed a contract to betray him.

She ripped her lips from his kiss.

A frown wrinkled his forehead. "What is it, love? Are you hurt?"

"No." Her gaze fell on his shoulder, where a patch of blistered skin showed through a singed hole. "But you are! What happened?"

Anger flashed in his green eyes. "Had a little run-in with a demon. Don't worry—no permanent damage. See?" He rolled his injured arm, his gaze taking in the stocked shelves on either side of the aisle. "So. Hell's third level is . . . an American supermarket?"

"Yeah. Funny, huh? Been here long?"

"No. You?"

She shook her head. Formless music drifted from unseen

speakers. Mac winced. "Smooth jazz. Now I know I'm in Hell."

"What's wrong with smooth jazz? Could be worse. Could be disco."

"Right."

They started down the aisle. The aroma of fresh-baked bread filled the air. "Can't understand what's so hellish about a food market," Mac commented. "Damn cold in here, but other than that . . ."

They rounded an end cap piled high with packaged pies. "Hey, look," Artemis said. "Checkout lanes."

"No one at the registers, though. And the exit doors behind them are false. Just paint on concrete."

Artemis sagged against a tabloid rack and sighed. "Another dead end."

"The *Tartarus Tattler*," Mac read over her shoulder. "Elvis spotted water-skiing on a tributary of the Styx . . . Aliens have landed on Level Seven . . . bloody hell!" He reached past her and snatched up the paper.

Artemis turned. "What?"

Grimly, Mac shoved the newspaper into her hands. "Bottom of the page, love."

She took one look at the headline and groaned. "Oh no."

HELL'S BOATMAN ASLEEP ON THE JOB?

Numerous eyewitnesses have called the *Tattler* offices with reports of a shocking breach in Hell's Level One security. Charon, legendary boatman of the Styx, proved unable to stop two living creatures from crossing Hell's outer boundary on a stolen motorcycle. The interlopers, a human female and a male Sidhe, were last seen in Limbo. The *Tattler* is offering a reward of fifty years of life essence for information leading to their arrest. According to witnesses, the male is tall, blond . . .

"This is terrible," Artemis whispered, gaping in horror at a blurry photo of her and Mac astride the Norton. "Every demon in Hell's going to be gunning for us now." She darted a glance at the nearest aisle, half expecting one to rush out and suck her soul dry.

Mac was already constructing a new death glamour, his green eyes struggling to mask his revulsion at the spell he was crafting. Casting death magic cost him. Dearly. But since glamour was one area in which Artemis did not excel, she said nothing. When he was done, she raised her eyebrows. "That's a much stronger spell than the one you cast in Malachi's realm."

"I know. I'm getting the hang of it." He didn't sound pleased about it. "There," he said, swinging the glamour around both of them like a cloak. "That should hold for a while. Stay alert, though. No telling what we'll encounter next."

She nodded, her heart troubled. She was grateful for Mac's newfound skills, of course, but watching him cast death magic just seemed so *wrong*. Like blasphemy. What would it do to his soul?

She studied the scuffed vinyl tile beneath her feet. Mac was so good, so loyal, and she was so afraid she was falling in love with him. How could she even consider betraying him to Malachi? If she had any honor at all, she'd tell him everything. Maybe together, they could come up with a strategy to beat Malachi, outwit Hecate, and rescue Zander.

But even as she grasped at the slim hope, it slipped away. Who was she fooling? Malachi was surely watching. If he suspected treachery, it would be such a simple thing for an Old One to ascend to the human world, cast aside Artemis's protective wards, and smother the life out of Zander's helpless body. And Artemis, trapped here in Hell, wouldn't be able to do a thing to prevent it.

Mac was pacing back and forth at the end of the check-out rows. "What I don't understand is why this market is so bloody deserted. Isn't there anyone—"

He broke off as a figure emerged from one of the aisles. Artemis braced for a fight—she wasn't sure Mac's glamour would fool a really powerful demon—but to her relief the newcomer was only a corpse. No threat there. The dead were beyond the craving for life essence.

The corpse was sunken-eyed, with rotting flesh dripping from his bones. He pushed a shopping cart before him, loaded to overflowing. Bread, pasta, soda, ice cream, chips. A bakery cake. Several kinds of meats and cheeses.

The dead man passed without a look toward Mac and Artemis. Exchanging glances, they followed him as he turned down one of the aisles. Cookies lined the shelves. The dead man paused, extending a shaky arm toward a package of double-stuffed Oreos.

"So hungry . . . so hungry . . . so hungry . . ." He chanted the mantra over and over, his sunken eyes devouring the prize.

"What's his sin?" Mac whispered in Artemis's ear.

"Level Three punishes gluttony." She inhaled a steadying breath and looked away from the corpse's misery. "So, where do you think the exit leading to Level Four might be?"

"I don't care!" the corpse shouted.

Artemis jumped, but the dead man's outburst hadn't been directed at her. He was staring at the Oreos, muttering under his breath.

"I don't care. I *don't*. What can he do to me? I'm already dead. A man's gotta eat, doesn't he?"

Darting furtive glances right and left, the corpse snatched up a bag. The packaging crackled loudly in his skeletal fist. "God, I miss these. I used to eat a whole bag, every day. With a full gallon of milk." He shook his fist at the ceiling. "Nothing wrong with that, is there? Is there?

No! Of course not! A man's gotta eat. Well, this time, he's not going to stop me."

With a savage motion, he tore open the package and launched a fistful of cookies toward his open mouth. As the first crumb hit, alarm bells clanged.

Heavy footsteps shook the ground, accompanied by vicious snarls and barking.

"Ballocks." Mac's arm shot out. He pressed Artemis up against a tower of Nutter Butter cookies as three slavering hell dogs rounded the end of the aisle, barely restrained by an enormous demon dressed in a security guard's uniform.

"Stop! Thief!"

Dogs and guards streaked past the edges of Mac's glamour. No. Not *dogs*. One dog, with three heads. Each looked more than able to snap the would-be cookie thief in two.

"Cerberus," Artemis whispered.

The corpse shrieked; Oreos flew into the air. One struck Artemis on the cheek. Abandoning his cart, the dead man fled down the aisle. Dog and guard gave chase. They cornered their prey in front of a Pepperidge Farm display.

The corpse cowered in front of the Milanos, arms raised. "Please, no. Don't hurt me. I was only going to eat one. Just one! I'm so hungry. . . ."

"Payment first!" the guard barked.

"But . . . all the cashiers are closed! They're never open! And even if they were open, I don't have any money."

"That's not my problem, glutton. This is the Hell you made for yourself. I'm just the enforcer. Now get your cart and move along." The command was punctuated by three menacing growls.

"Y-yes, sir." The trembling corpse heaved himself to his feet. Oreos crunched underfoot as he stumbled to his cart. As quickly as he could manage, he shoved it to the end of the aisle and turned the corner.

The guard gave a satisfied grunt. Turning, he muscled

his three-headed dog to the opposite end of the shelving
and disappeared. Artemis sagged against Mac. "Thank the
gods he didn't see us."

Abruptly, a woman's shrill voice replaced the smooth
jazz. "Cleanup on aisle six million seven hundred twenty-
four thousand three-hundred and fifty-two."

Mac gave a low whistle. "Bloody hell."

"Great," Artemis muttered. "Just great. What do you
want to bet the exit's at aisle number one?"

Mac grabbed her hand and started walking. "Wherever
it is, we don't want to be caught in this one when the demon cleanup crew arrives."

True enough. They backtracked to the checkout lanes,
turned left, passing about twenty aisles before Mac tugged
her into one filled with pasta and jarred sauce. Following it
to the end, they emerged at the deli counter.

"Whoa. So, *this* is where everyone is," Artemis said.

Hundreds of corpses crowded the counter, waving paper tickets and shouting for service. The single demon on
duty had his head bent over a meat slicer, his arm moving
slower than a glacier in February. Artemis eyed the nearest corpse, a dead woman waving a ticket bearing the
number 2417. The NOW SERVING sign above the counter
displayed the number 0001.

"Just like back home," she muttered.

"Through here," Mac said suddenly, steering Artemis
toward a door marked EMPLOYEES ONLY.

"Are you crazy? There are probably more demons back
there."

"No pain, no gain, love."

They passed through swinging doors and by signs reading SHOPLIFTING IS STEALING—DO IT OFTEN and FORGET TO
WASH YOUR HANDS.

"There aren't any exit doors."

"Not doors, no," Mac said, forging ahead.

"Then what?"

"Garbage chute. There's got to be one somewhere."

They followed their noses past skids of wooden crates to a heap of rotting meat and produce. Two lesser demons were listlessly shoveling the stinking mess into a small, square opening. A battered steel door, swinging from one hinge, banged with every shovelful.

"This is going to be tricky," Artemis said. "How are we going to get around them? Your glamour is going to fail if we have to shove them out of the way."

"A distraction, perhaps." He called a ball of hellfire to hand, bouncing it up and down. "I'll toss this back the way we came. As soon as they run past, we head for the chute."

Artemis flattened herself against the wall. "Okay. Ready."

Mac lobbed the hellfire toward the far end of the room. It landed with a blast, toppling a tower of wooden crates. The garbage demons' heads went up. "What the f—"

They took off to investigate. Mac pressed himself against Artemis as they passed. The first loped by, eyes fixed on the fallen crates. The second wasn't so easily fooled. He drew up short an arm's length from Mac and Artemis's position, sniffing the air suspiciously. Artemis didn't dare move.

The demon sidled closer. "Hey, Rark," he yelled to his companion.

Rark turned and loped back. "Yeah, Gark?"

"Do you smell anything funny?"

Rark sniffed. "Yeah. Life essence. But it can't be. Not here."

Gark grinned. "Didn't you catch this morning's *Tattler*? Two life magic creatures slipped past Charon. And I think we've just found them. See that?" He pointed. "The edge of a glamour. Right there."

Rark peered. "I don't see it."

"Yeah, well, you couldn't find your own cock in the

dark. They're here, I tell you. Right in front of us. Feeling hungry, Rark?" He rubbed his hands, generating smoke. "I am."

"Not good," Artemis whispered to Mac.

"You take the ugly one on the right," Mac said. Hellfire sprang into his hand. "I'll take the uglier one on the left. Any time you're ready, love."

"On three," Artemis said, readying her own spell. "One, two, three!"

They hit the pair together. Rark dropped like a rock; Gark managed a blast of hellfire. It hit Mac in the thigh. Artemis dropped the demon with a kick to its knees. Mac added a stream of red fire and Gark landed atop his friend, out cold.

"Come on." Artemis gave a nervous glance toward the corridor leading to the front of the store. "We're lucky they were lesser demons. Let's get out of here before something bigger and badder turns up."

"I'm right with you, love."

Mac plowed a path to the garbage chute. The opening looked just big enough for a person to squeeze through. The fetid rot emanating from the narrow tunnel left Artemis gasping.

Mac glanced at her. "Ladies first."

She grimaced. "Age before beauty is my motto."

"Whatever you say, love." Grabbing the top edge of the frame, he hoisted his legs into the chute. "Wish me luck. Stay close behind."

Artemis stuck her head through the opening and watched him disappear down the chute. As soon as he was gone, she climbed into the shaft and followed.

The chute led to a women's clothing store. The swimwear department. Every single bathing suit on the racks was a bikini.

"Hell for certain," Artemis muttered.

"I don't get it," Mac said. "What's so hellish about buying a swimsuit?"

"Nothing at all, if you're a man." She waved a hand. "But as you'll notice, all the corpses here are women."

"So? I thought women loved clothes shopping."

"Runway models maybe. Women who exist on coffee fumes and lettuce and spend hours at the gym. The rest of us . . ." She shuddered. "And don't even get me started on cellulite. Or how pregnancy changes things around. Let's just say it should be a crime to install a lightbulb brighter than fifteen watts in any ladies' dressing room."

"The shoppers on this level shouldn't be having any angst. They're looking well enough."

It was true. Unlike the supermarket corpses up on Level Three, the dead women on Level Four weren't showing the slightest signs of decay. Except for the slight pallor of their complexions, and faint dark smudges under their eyes, the shoppers were gorgeous. Tall. Slender. Graceful. Good hair. No cellulite. In life, these women had certainly loved shopping for bikinis. Now, inexplicably, they drifted from rack to rack, wailing.

"What sin does this level punish?" Mac asked.

"Excessive love of material goods." Artemis watched, bemused, as one of the beautiful shoppers pulled a shimmery red bikini off the rack. The women checked the tag, choked, and flung it away.

"Size ten!" she howled. "This bathing suit's made for a *pig*!"

Artemis nearly choked. "What? *I'm* a size ten."

Mac snorted.

Artemis balled up a fist and punched him on his burned arm.

"Hey," he protested. "That hurt."

"It's not funny."

His eyes didn't stop laughing. "No worries, love. Personally, I like a woman with a little meat on her bones."

She slugged him again.

They left swimwear and entered the dress department, where a dead woman was pawing through a rack of slinky dresses, ripping chiffon and silk from the hangers.

"All too big! Every single one! *Arggghhhh!*" Sobbing, she staggered off toward sportswear.

The store was huge, and the scene replayed itself in every department. From jeans to outerwear, painfully thin women shopped frantically, unable to find anything that fit. Sobs of misery filled the air.

"*This* is a punishment worthy of Hell's fourth level?" Mac asked. "A bad shopping trip?"

"You wouldn't understand," Artemis said, glancing down at her not-as-flat-as-it-used-to-be stomach, framed by her not-as-slim-as-they-used-to-be hips. "You're a man. I'm still carrying ten extra pounds from my pregnancy."

He sent her an odd look. "Was it so bad? Being pregnant?"

"No," she said. "It was nice, actually. Feeling the baby move. Watching my stomach grow."

"Would you . . . ever want to do it again? Have another child?"

She stopped in front of a plus-sized manikin. "I don't know. I never thought about it. I suppose it would be nice, if it wasn't an accident the second time around."

"But you were happy, anyway, when you found out, right? Even though it was an accident?"

"Happy? Are you nuts? I was freaking furious."

Mac's cheeks flushed pink. "But after the baby was born—you were happy then, right?"

Artemis gave a wistful smile. "I fell in love with Zander, it's true. The moment I saw him open his eyes and look at me. I don't regret having him. I just don't need any more surprises in my life. If I ever get pregnant again, it's going to be because I want another child. Not because I wasn't careful enough."

"Right," Mac murmured. For a moment, she thought he was on the verge of saying more, but then he shook his head slightly and looked around. "How about customer service?" he suggested. "Seems a likely place for an exit."

He was talking about the exit to Level Five. Artemis swallowed hard. Malachi would be waiting on Level Five. And he would expect her to uphold her end of their contract. She followed Mac, her stomach churning. How could she betray him again? He didn't deserve that. Maybe she should risk telling him everything. Maybe they could take Malachi together, by surprise.

"Don't count on it."

The words came on a whisper, faintly stirred with sulfur. Artemis stopped in her tracks and looked around. Malachi smiled back at her as a wavy figure inside a full-length mirror.

With a furtive glance at Mac's back, she walked toward it. Malachi's distorted features leered from behind the glass. "Breathe a word of our . . . agreement . . . to the Sidhe and your son is dead. Bring Mac Lir to Level Five. But before you get there, be sure the shielding you erected around his soul is gone."

"Gone?" she whispered. "How am I supposed to do that? He's a lot more knowledgeable about death magic than he was. If I try anything, he's going to know."

Malachi's eyes blazed. "The 'how' is not my problem. Do as you're told, if you value your son's life."

And then he was gone.

Artemis closed her eyes, fighting a terror so sharp and painful it had her doubling over. An instant later, she felt Mac at her side, his presence comforting, his voice tinged with worry.

"What is it, love? Are you all right?"

Tell him, a small voice in her head said. *Tell him everything.*

He'll fight for you. But Artemis recognized the desperate thought for what it was. Pure delusion. If she confided in Mac, Zander would be dead in minutes.

She forced a wan smile. "It's nothing. I felt a little light-headed, is all. I'm fine now."

"Not sure I believe that, but chin up, love. I've found the next exit."

Oh gods. "Where?"

"There's an exit door behind the customer service desk. Only problem is, there's a demon at the counter in the guise of a young girl. Plenty of room to get past her, though. Shouldn't be a problem."

It shouldn't have been, but it was. The demon, as it turned out, wasn't a lesser entity. She wasn't an Old One, thank the gods, but she was ancient enough to see right through Mac's glamour.

She looked up from her magazine as they sidled past. Her chewing gum snapped like a rifle shot. "Stop right there. Did you two really imagine a paltry Level Two glamour would be any use at all here on Level Four? Who the hell are you any—" Her eyes widened. "Why, you're the pair from the *Tattler*. The human and the Sidhe!"

Mac eyed her. "What if we are?"

Her ponytail bobbed. "I'll turn you in. I'll get the re-ward! Fifty years of life essence."

He snorted. "You really don't think the blighters at the *Tattler* will give it to you, do you?"

"What do you mean?"

"They want us for themselves. They'll never pay off a Level Four demon like yourself."

"Mac," Artemis whispered. "What do you think you're doing?"

The demon's jaw stopped working her gum. "You know what? You're right. The bastards will probably screw me. I should capture you myself."

"I wouldn't advise trying. My friend here is a talented

death witch, and I'm a demigod. We'll put up a damned inconvenient fight."

She regarded him new interest. "A demigod, you say? I didn't read that in the *Tattler*."

"They didn't want the public to know, obviously. But now that you do, I've got a proposition for you."

"A contract?" The demon propped her elbows on the counter, her eyes all aglow. "I love contracts. What is it?"

Artemis stared at him. "Mac. I don't think—"

"Not a contract," Mac told the demon. "A simple swap. See that door over there? Is there a stair behind it? Does it lead to Level Five?"

"There is and it sure does."

"We want to go there. What do you say I give you fifty years of life essence, and you let us pass?"

Artemis gasped. Only Mac's grip on her arm kept her from protesting.

"Fifty years?" The demon chewed, her gum snapping. She blew a pink bubble. It popped and she sucked it back in. "Not nearly enough."

"Not enough? It's the same as the *Tattler*'s reward."

"But that was before I knew you were a demigod." She smiled. "A little more won't hurt you. Say, like a millennium or so?"

Artemis did protest then. "No way, Mac! I'd rather fight her."

"You'll do nothing of the kind," Mac said. He turned back to the demon. "A century."

"Five hundred years."

"One-fifty."

"Three-fifty," the demon countered.

"Two-fifty."

"Three hundred."

"Done," Mac said.

"Mac, no," Artemis whispered. "It'll weaken you too much."

He met her gaze steadily. "That's just it, Artemis. I don't think that it will." He brushed a kiss by her ear. "My soul is infinite. I can lose three hundred years, easily. It'll make no difference. And I'll receive death magic in return."

"And your soul will become darker because of it. I don't like it at all."

"It's our best option, love." He stepped toward the counter. "Let's have it done, then," he told the demon.

She smiled, showing a wad of gum between her teeth. She plucked it out and set it on the counter. "Pucker up."

Artemis's stomach turned. Still, she couldn't seem to turn away as Mac leaned over the counter. The demon met him halfway, her arms coming up to encircle his neck. Their lips touched.

The kiss went on and on, until Artemis thought she might very well throw up. Finally, Mac broke contact and took a step back.

"That was wonderful." The demon smiled, a dreamy look in her eyes.

Mac's eyes, by contrast, were colder than Artemis had ever seen them. She could sense the darkening of his aura, the spike in his death-magic powers. A shiver ran up her spine. What was he becoming, because of her?

Without speaking, or touching her, he strode to the stair. Artemis followed. Mac yanked the door open.

"Seems empty enough." His voice was flat and carried a metallic ring.

Artemis stepped into the stairwell. The walls were bare concrete, washed with faint illumination from an obscure source. The air smelled of urine, but at least the floor was dry and clear of debris. She peered over the metal railing. She couldn't see the bottom.

Six steps down, a left turn, six more steps. Left again. There were no doors.

Her boots thudded after Mac's. She was afraid to let him get too far ahead. Would Malachi greet them at the bottom of the stair? What would the demon do when he discovered Mac was more powerful, not less, than he'd been before? But Mac's death-magic powers hadn't grown so much that Mac would be able to defeat an Old One, even with Artemis's help. She really had no choice. She was going to have to uphold her contract with Malachi.

Quickly, before she had a chance to change her mind, she cast her senses toward the death shield surrounding Mac's soul. He could construct his own barrier now, she was sure, but he hadn't thought to do it. The shield Artemis had constructed in the elevator still protected his soul. It was easy enough to slip inside.

Six steps down, a left turn, six more steps. Left again. Still no door.

Subtly, she picked up a thread of the shielding spell. Fear jittered her senses. Would Mac sense what she was doing? Her stomach burned, and the taste of her betrayal was bitter in her throat. At that moment, she loathed herself. But this was for Zander. For her son, she'd do anything.

"Ballocks," Mac muttered as they turned yet another corner. "How bloody much farther does this stair go?"

Six steps down, a left turn, six more steps. Left again. The temperature in the stairwell was rising.

Working subtly, Artemis drew the thread of the shielding spell taut. Mac didn't seem to notice, but she sensed his anxiety rising. He took the next flight of stairs two at a time.

She increased the tension on the psychic thread. One whispered syllable, aimed just so, would snap it. The spell would dissolve slowly after that. By the time Mac realized what was happening, it would be too late.

Her lips parted; she sucked air into her lungs. She steeled herself to utter the spell word, but before she could speak it, something deep inside her—something that felt like a foreign force—rebelled. Dizziness struck.

Her toe caught on the edge of the step. She grabbed at the railing and missed. She fell. . . .

Mac spun about and caught her. "Artemis! You okay, love?"

Hardly. Her head was still spinning. Her mind was fuzzy, her tongue dry. The concrete walls around her swayed. What the hell had just happened? "I . . . I'm not sure. Can I sit down? Just for a minute?"

"Whatever you want."

She could hear the genuine concern in his tone. It twisted a knife of guilt in her gut. She didn't deserve him.

He eased her into a sitting position on the bottom step. She pressed her head to her knees. The position helped the spinning walls slow. But the heat in the stairwell was all but unbearable now. The stench had grown as well, riding on crests of hot anger. Sweat trickled down the side of her face, making her jaw itch.

There were new sounds, too. Muffled shouts, violent thuds. The roar of a jeering crowd. Hatred—boiling waves of it—scalded her mind.

Dread thudded with every heartbeat. "Do you feel that . . . that rage?"

"I do. It's coming from the other side of that door."

She raised her head and saw they'd reached the bottom of the stair. Directly in front of her stood a battered metal door.

"We don't have to go through right away," Mac said. "I'm worried about you, Artemis. You don't look quite right. I felt you . . . *fade* a moment ago. Something to do with your magic." His eyes narrowed. "Were you preparing a spell?"

Oh gods. She couldn't answer that. She grabbed the railing and hauled herself to her feet. "It's not important. I'm fine now."

She could tell he didn't believe her. "Let me flood you with life essence. You look like you need it."

Make love, here? Amid all the rage seeping from under the door? After what she'd just tried to do to him? "No. You gave enough to that demon. I'm fine. Really."

"Artemis—"

"I *am*. There's no point in waiting. Open the door."

But instead of moving toward the door, he speared his fingers into her hair and covered her mouth with a hard, bruising kiss. "Damn it all, Artemis, why did I have to fall in love with such a stubborn woman?"

She stared at him, stunned. "Fall in *love*? No. No, you can't. It's not possible. You don't know—"

"I know plenty, Artemis. For once, just don't argue."

"But—"

He stepped away and put his shoulder to the door. "Ready?"

Mutely, she nodded.

The hinges creaked. "Welcome to Level Five," a mechanical voice intoned.

Mac peered through. "Damn. And here I was, hoping for ladies' lingerie."

CHAPTER SEVENTEEN

Level Five wasn't ladies' lingerie, but there was certainly a lot of naked flesh on display. Unfortunately, that flesh was hairy, sweaty, bulging, and male. Mac would've paid good money not to have seen it.

The aftereffects of his exchange with the gum-chewing demon still burned in his gut. Despite what he'd told Artemis, the drain of three hundred years of life essence hadn't been a picnic. The resulting surge of death magic had rubbed his soul raw. He'd felt his power growing, and then he'd felt something else. Artemis, trying to dismantle the death shield she'd put on his soul. His heart had taken a hit then. He'd almost called her on it, but then, abruptly, she'd pulled back and the spell had gone uncast.

But she was up to something. Something he was damned sure he wasn't going to like.

Bugger it all. He should have taken his mother's advice and gone for a nice Sidhe girl. If he had, he wouldn't be here now, in Hell's Level Five, watching naked, snarling corpses beat each other into bloody lumps.

The dead men wrestled in pairs, atop shoulder-high floating stages, to the wild delight of an audience of lesser demons crowded on the floor below. Standing in the shadows at the rear of the crowd, wrapped in a tight death glamour, Artemis and Mac endured wave after wave of the combatants' rage. The foul emotion was so strong it nearly knocked Mac off his feet. He didn't need to ask Artemis what earthly sin was punished on this level. It was all too obvious: wrath.

"How—" What Artemis was about to say was lost in the blare of a loudspeaker.

"Demons and ghouls! Your attention please! Now appearing in ring thirteen—Hell's newest gladiators! The Basher aaaaaand . . . *Leprechaun*!"

Mac angled his gaze toward a square platform, ringed with ropes, hovering about fifty feet away. The Basher was a massive male corpse—at least seven feet of solid muscle. Leprechaun, a lean, snarling dead man who stood no higher than his opponent's navel, put Mac in mind of a vicious dog. At the clang of a bell, the combatants emerged from their respective corners, amid the roaring approval of the crowd.

For several moments the pair circled, spitting insults. Then the Basher hit a nerve.

"Whatcha gonna do, little man? Bite my kneecap?"

"Damn right." Leprechaun bared his teeth and flew at the Basher's knees, slamming skull into bone with a sickening crunch.

"Oof!" The Basher toppled, hitting the stage so hard the platform tilted.

The crowd went wild.

The Basher heaved to his feet, spewing curses. Leprechaun dodged, but not quickly enough. The Basher clamped one arm around his head, squeezing until the little man's eyes had all but popped out of his skull. Leprechaun clawed at the Basher's forearm, gasping.

Similar scenes played out on each of the other floating platforms. Hatred rolled over the audience in visible waves, like steam from a garbage pit. The sea of demon spectators cheered. How the bloody hell were he and Artemis to get through the lot of them undetected?

A new wave of anger rolled and struck. Instinctively, the

dark stain on Mac's soul responded with a hit of pure adrenaline. Raw excitement pumped through Mac's veins. His soul-darkness, enhanced by the gum-chewing demon's kiss, soaked up the anger in the air. It seeped into his body and his mind.

He rounded on Artemis. So she thought to double-cross him, did she? He stared at her. Her hair, wet with perspiration, was plastered against her scalp. Her shirt was soaked, clinging to every curve. His gaze absorbed the shadow of her bra beneath wet cotton. One thin black strap was visible on her bare shoulder.

The sight made him go rock-hard. "Let's have sex."

She gaped at him. "What?"

"You heard me. Let's do it. Now. Here. Take off your jeans."

"You're out of your mind!"

"Why? We did it in the elevator. You liked that well enough." He grabbed her lovely arse in both hands and pulled her flush against his body, groin to groin. *Yes.* He ground his erection against her mound.

Gods, she felt good. And she'd feel that much better, once he had her naked. He'd throw her down on the ground, right here, and drill her in front of all these demons.

Instead of disgusting him, as it certainly should have, the thought only inflamed Mac's lust. He wasn't himself; that much he realized even through the slough of death magic clogging his senses. He couldn't seem to care.

He sank his teeth into Artemis's neck and tasted blood. "Get naked. Now. Or I'll do it for you."

"Mac—" Artemis's struggles only succeeded in making him harder. "Let me go! You don't really want to do this. That's the demon's kiss talking."

"No, it's not. I wanted to screw you from the first moment I saw you. No," he amended. "Even before that. The first time I felt your magic. And all your backstabbing since then has only gotten me hornier." He grasped her chin and forced her to meet his gaze. The fear in her eyes made him go even harder. "Shall I prove it to you, love?"

"No. You're hurting me. Let me go."

His hands went to the waistband of her jeans, springing the snap. "You owe me this, Artemis. You know you do. After what you tried to do in that stairwell—"

Her eyes flared with alarm. Her voice took on a desperate note. "I . . . I don't know what you're talking about!"

"Do you think I'm stupid, Artemis?"

"No. Of course not. But . . . this isn't you, Mac. This place—it's getting to you. You're new to death magic. You don't know how to control it."

"I don't want to control it." He ripped at her zipper and shoved his hands down her pants. "It feels too good. *You* feel too good."

"No—"

She tried to twist out of his grip. He didn't allow it. Her fist swung at his head. He grabbed her wrist. She bit off a spell word, one that should have knocked him on his arse. He laughed as he flicked it aside. With one swift, brutal motion, he yanked down her pants.

Mac watched the struggle as if outside himself, looking down at a foreign being. Death magic had taken control of his mind, his muscles, his soul—he barely recognized himself in the cruel man assaulting Artemis. Vainly, the part of his psyche that was still linked to light and life fought to gain the upper hand.

It was losing the battle.

Twisting Artemis's arm, he forced her to the ground. He'd dropped the death glamour minutes before; now the closest demons had begun to take note of their struggle. Red, glowing eyes turned on them. Drooling mouths opened wide and cheered.

He came down on top of her, hands roaming under her shirt. She thrashed violently, kicking and biting, balling her fists and striking anywhere she could reach. Her tears

brought a sick pleasure to the dark recesses of his soul.
Death magic had overwhelmed his being; the light inside
him had gone dim. He had to be inside her. Now.

He fumbled with his belt, then went to work on the zipper of his jeans. Artemis had gone very, very still. She
stared up at him through a wash of tears. "Mac. No . . ."

Her gaze flicked behind him. Her eyes went wide.

A hot hand gripped Mac's shoulder. Mac's life essence
rushed to the point of contact like iron shards to a magnet.
Pure malevolence sapped strength from his body. Power
hemorrhaged from his soul. A measure of sanity returned,
slamming into his fogged brain like a demented freight
train.

He stared down at Artemis. She was half naked and
shivering with fear. *He'd* done that to her. Gods in Annwyn, what was happening to him?

Slowly, he took his hands from her. She scrambled to
her feet, sobbing as she yanked up her jeans.

The next instant, Mac found himself lifted into the air,
and set on his feet. His gaze collided with Malachi's smug
sneer.

"You," Mac spat.

"Yes. It is I. And just in time, I think." He smiled thinly.
"I did not give you permission to use my whore."

Mac's gaze shot to Artemis. He didn't care what she'd
tried to do in the stairwell—after what he'd almost done
to her, she should have been looking at him with pure hatred. She wasn't. Guilt shone in her beautiful dark eyes.
He didn't have to wonder why. It was clear enough what
she'd done.

Malachi's arm encircled her waist. She stiffened, but did
nothing to escape the possessive embrace. Artemis had
cast her lot with a demon. Not with Mac.

"You knew he'd be here," Mac said. "You tried to dismantle my shielding, so as to make things easier for him."

"Oh, Mac." Her throat worked. "I'm sorry. He . . . he threatened to kill Zander. There was nothing you or I could have done to stop him."

"You don't think much of my power, do you?"

Her silence was answer enough.

A primal roar from stage thirteen broke into their exchange. The crowd responded with an answering roar. The Basher, battered and missing a good chunk of torso, heaved Leprechaun's bloodied body over his head. With a snarl, the wrestler launched his defeated opponent into the crowd.

The body landed with a thud at Malachi's feet. Malachi toed it with an air of disgust.

"Weak bastard. Get up and get out of my sight."

With a groan, Leprechaun half crawled, half scrambled into the crowd, demons clawing him as he disappeared.

"He'll fight again," Malachi said with a laugh. "It's his eternal punishment. But right now, the Basher is in need of a new opponent, and I think you will do quite nicely."

In the next instant, Mac found himself atop stage thirteen, facing the Basher. A cold, deadly fury, unlike anything he'd ever experienced took hold.

The Basher jeered, pawing the ground like a bull. Smoke poured from his nose and ears. His eyes glowed a deep, unholy red. And Mac's rage-enflamed brain registered one sobering fact.

The Basher wasn't a corpse. He was a demon.

The creature charged. Mac shifted his stance, whipping up a blast of hellfire into the Basher's face. The demon howled his fury and countered with a hot blast to Mac's chest. Mac staggered back. The pain was blinding.

Foul words sprang into Mac mind and erupted from his lips. A short, brutal death spell caught his opponent squarely in the gut. The Basher crashed to the ground, twitched once, then lay still.

Victory. But the winning spell had cost Mac dearly. Artemis's shielding on his soul had broken wide open. White sparks poured through the fissure and floated over the audience. Shrieking demons clawed each other in an attempt to snatch Mac's life essence.

Mac staggered backward. His limbs refused to obey his mental commands. His legs buckled, and the platform rushed up to meet him.

He landed hard. He raised his head almost immediately, his gaze seeking and finding Artemis. She stood at Malachi's side, rigid, anguished. Gods in Annwyn. If only she'd had more faith in him. But then, if she had, maybe that faith would have been misplaced. After all, he'd lost the fight.

For the first time in his life, Mac felt immeasurably old.

Malachi's teeth flashed in a grin. His charcoal suit was crisp and unruffled, the Windsor knot of his tie a perfect square. Every strand of dark, shining hair lay precisely in place.

The demon extended a casual finger. A thin beam of red light arched from the tip, striking the center of Mac's chest.

"Aaaaaaah." He couldn't suppress a howl of agony. The searing hot bolt drilled into his soul, sucking life essence like a siphon hose. Faintly, he heard Artemis sobbing, but his vision had blurred and he couldn't make out her face.

Malachi's sneer found him. "Not so proud now, are we, Sidhe?"

Light and life continued to drain from Mac's soul. The pain was unbearable. Would it ever stop? Perhaps not; his essence was infinite. Was this to be his fate? An eternity of helpless humiliation, here in Hell, at the hands of death?

How had he ever thought death could be beautiful? There was nothing beautiful about this. It was ugly. Worse, it had the taint of finality. Perhaps death, not life, was the ultimate victor. Life was the travesty, the aberration.

How had he ever thought it could be otherwise? Old Saraid's warning echoed in his mind. *I ask you, Manannán.*

Do not do this. Death . . . it is strong. In the end, it cannot be denied.

He ignored the wisdom of the Sidhe elder—for what? Artemis and the child she carried were in the power of a demon. He should have told her about the baby, he realized now. If she'd known . . .

Abruptly, Malachi's red beam cut off. Mac slumped, shuddering. The sudden absence of pain and despair was the most absolute bliss he'd ever known.

Malachi called a stairway and ascended the stage, Artemis tucked against his side. With a groan, Mac heaved himself onto his back and stared up at the demon. Hatred boiled like lava in his gut. But this time, far from making him strong, it only weakened him further.

"Enough, I think, for now," the demon said. "But do not get used to my benevolence. I use my slaves often and hard. Sadly, the human ones do not give much pleasure. Sidhe, on the other hand . . . well, the agony of a Sidhe is quite refreshing."

"So glad . . . to be . . . of service."

Malachi grinned. "Spirit unbroken, I see. I will attend to that. With your divine soul, I am quite sure that you will soon surpass your sister as my favorite whore. Yes," he added. "I have Leanna with me in Hell. Miss Black even saw her in Shadowhaven. Did she not tell you?"

Artemis's eyes were wide. "I . . . saw a Sidhe female in Malachi's realm. I never thought—"

Malachi chuckled. "Yes, my dear, I'm sure he believes you. After all, you've been so honest with him, at every turn."

He turned to Mac. "I will never understand humans. This witch loves you and you her, yet she betrays you over and over. She knows you cannot keep me from destroying her son."

Somehow, Mac shoved himself into a sitting position. The world around him spun dizzily as he looked into

Artemis's tear-streaked face. He should be angry with her. He wanted to be angry. But he was sick to death of anger and darkness. "You might have trusted me, love."

"I did. I *do*. Trust has nothing to do with this—"

"Faith, then."

She buried her face in her hands.

His gaze shifted to Malachi. "You have what you want, I presume. Me. You don't need her. Let her go now. To her son."

Malachi inclined his head. "That was our bargain. Miss Black has fulfilled her role in delivering you into my power. She is free to descend deeper into the pit. Whether she will succeed in her quest—" He spread his hands. "I cannot say."

"But you won't interfere?"

The demon smiled. "I think not. I plan to be very busy with my newest toy."

Mac smiled thinly. "How nice for you. Artemis?" He waited until she looked up. "Get out. As quickly as you can. Find Zander and don't look back."

"But you—"

He shook his head. "Not your problem, love."

Tears streamed down her face. "Mac, I'm sorry."

"Don't be. Just go."

They were the last words he managed before Malachi's hand lifted and consciousness left him.

CHAPTER EIGHTEEN

At Malachi's nod, two foul-breathed demons grabbed Artemis by the upper arms. She cast one last anguished look at Mac's motionless body before the thugs dragged her off the stage. They didn't stop until they'd reached a blank metal door. Wrenching it open, they tossed her through.

She experienced a brief, sickening moment of weightlessness; then her stomach was left behind as she plummeted through inky darkness. Frantic, arms flailing, she tried to brace for impact.

To her great relief, she landed in water—or something similar, but thicker. She inhaled a gasp of something sour before the substance closed over her head. Lungs bursting, she gave a furious kick. Her feet encountered slick mud; she propelled herself upward. Her head broke the surface, her lungs seizing on thick oily mist.

All around, sparks rained from a glowing red sky, sizzling as they struck the surface of the lake. Kicking to keep herself afloat, she squinted through the gloom. Sheer walls rose from a dark lake. A splash not too far off to her right sent a shiver down her spine. She wasn't the only swimmer.

She stroked toward the rocky shore. Hauling herself up on slippery stone, she fought her tears. She hated herself. Hated what she'd done to Mac. Hated every choice she'd made that had led her to this horrible place.

Stupid, stupid, stupid.

She clung to the hope of Mac's increasing death magic. He'd taken out the Basher in minutes. Perhaps, given time to plot a strategy, he could find a way to escape Malachi. She fervently hoped he could. As for herself, difficulties loomed large. Malachi had promised not to interfere with her quest, but his previous offer of assistance in fighting Hecate was not part of the new deal. She'd protected Zander's body from immediate harm, but if she couldn't figure out a way to free his soul from Ptolomaea, her betrayal of Mac would have been for nothing.

She heaved herself to her feet. Her right knee throbbed, and her neck was stiff. Try as she might, she couldn't slough off the swamp's oily waters. Great winged creatures circled overhead, black silhouettes against the bloodred sky.

She knew where she was. The walled city of Dis, Hell's sixth level. Tilting her head, she could just make out the top of the city wall. More winged creatures, aligned like sentinels, sat atop the battlement.

Two of the creatures swooped low, diving on ravens' wings. The monsters were ravenlike in their lower bodies, but their heads and chests, far from being birdlike, had the aspect of a hag—wrinkled skin, coarse hair, sagging breasts. Their odor fell on her like a shower of ash.

Artemis shuddered. Harpies.

She shrank against the wall. The harpies circled low, then blessedly flew off. Her lungs relaxed. Setting a shaking hand to the wall, she started moving, following the city's curving perimeter. The passage to the next level had to be on the other side. Surely there was a gate somewhere.

Her progress on the slippery rock was slow. Sparks rained down around her. High above, harpies circled, seemingly disinterested in her progress. She didn't trust them to stay that way. Focusing her magic, she conjured the best death glamour she could manage. It wasn't much.

She wasn't sure it could fool a blind ogre. But it was the best she could do.

When at last she reached an arched portal, she was surprised to find its massive iron gates standing open and unguarded. On the other side of the archway, flames snapped, human figures darting between sheets of fire. None of the corpses looked her way. Her entry to Dis seemed unimpeded.

Could it really be that easy?

She inched along the wall, until she reached the wide path of red stone, a raw red tongue that led from a deserted dock into the gaping maw of the city.

She stepped on its polished surface. It was as if she'd set off an alarm. The harpies screeched. The closest one dove, its ragged teeth grazing Artemis's arm. She ducked her head and ran toward the portal.

She didn't get far. The bird-hags fell on her en masse, screaming obscenities. Artemis fell back, shielding her head with her forearms. Sharp teeth gouged skin. A tuft of hair was torn from her scalp.

Her defensive spells had little effect. She spat out one last curse before rolling hard to the left, off the path.

Immediately, the harpies drew back. Wings flapping, they rose and alighted on a deep ledge above the open gate. One sent a taunting cackle in Artemis's direction before setting to preening her dirty feathers.

Artemis rose to her knees, breathing hard. Blood trickled down her arms. The portal of Dis loomed tall, the rusted spikes of its raised portcullis aligned like rotten teeth. She eyed the harpy, pulling at a wing with thick red lips. One black raven feather fluttered to the ground. A gust of hot wind swept it away from the path. It landed near Artemis's knee.

She stared at the feather, the beginnings of a plan forming in her mind. Anxiety skittered along her nerve endings.

Did she dare cast such a dangerous spell? The capacity was in her ancestry, but she'd never before attempted to draw it out. It was difficult, and could be deadly, even under the best of circumstances.

Here in Hell, she had precious little to protect her. No consecrated anthame, no purifying salt. The ground beneath her knees was slick with oil. Above the gate, the harpies waited. She'd never be able to fight her way past them.

She reached out and grasped the feather. A harpy stretched, flapping its wings, its pendulous breasts swaying. For one heart-stopping moment, she thought it would take to the air. Then it settled its wings and pecked at something near its feet.

There was no need for Artemis to cut her flesh; the harpies' attack had drawn more than enough blood. The spell called for fire, too. Ripping a scrap of fabric from the hem of her shirt, she caught one of the falling sparks and willed it to burn. Placing the infant flames on the oily ground, she set the feather atop it, and watched it burn.

Extending her arm, she dripped a circle of blood around herself and the fire, forming a tight ring of protection. Within it, she croaked the words of the spell. They were hateful syllables, twisted and ugly, culled from a language so ancient that only a few living humans—mostly psy-ops officers—knew it had existed. Her body shuddered with each successive verse. Her gorge rose, her stomach knotted. Every drop of light in her essence rose in protest.

The harpies, perhaps sensing a subtle change in the atmosphere, flapped their wings. The leader craned its neck, searching. Artemis spat the next verse of the spell. A pulse sprang up inside her circle, a malicious heartbeat. Her resolve faltered. It wasn't too late. She could still abort the spell. But she knew she wouldn't. She'd come too far to turn back now.

The spell's concluding syllable fell from her lips. Air

rushed from the circle. Her lungs spasmed in the vacuum left behind. Her body went numb.

Panic turned her blood to ice. She wanted to scream, wanted to run, wanted to claw her skin—anything to prove she was still alive. But her limbs were frozen, her mind blank. Flames of death ripped through her soul. Her vision went red, then black.

Her life essence expanded, then shattered.

In the aftermath of the explosion, several long seconds passed during which Artemis wasn't sure she still existed—at least not in any form she could comprehend. Then her eyes blinked open, and the gates of Dis came into view.

The harpies were nodding and conversing among themselves in horrid squeaks and grunts. Not one of the creatures looked toward Artemis, though the protection of the blood circle had dissolved. Her fire and her dark spell had burned out.

Cautiously, she lifted her arm. A dark wing rose in its place. She peered down at a black-feathered chest and bird's claws. Her raven's beak opened on a triumphant cry.

She'd done it. She'd shifted into raven form.

She gave a few experimental flaps of her wings. Her body lifted into the hot air. Amazing, how instinctive the act of flight was. She eyed the gate, guarded by the harpies. With a flick of her tail feathers, she turned and flew in the opposite direction, out over the swamp.

The oily surface of the bog stretched into a dark eternity. Banking hard to the left, she flew along the curving wall of Dis, leaving the gate far behind. When she thought she'd put enough distance between herself and the harpies, she climbed high on an updraft. Wings outstretched, she glided over the walls.

The city of Dis, spread out below her, was vast. From her bird's-eye vantage, she made out the division between the city's upper and lower regions—Hell's sixth and seventh levels. Fire consumed the upper reaches, flames bursting from charred structures. The stench of burning excrement rode on rolling waves of soot. The damned of this level, hundreds of thousands of burning corpses, darted through the flames, shrieking their never-ending agony. When alive, they'd been blasphemers who had cursed and defiled everything sacred in their lives. The searing flames of Dis would never burn hot enough to cleanse them.

An inner wall ringed the city's lower level. Artemis flew over it and swooped low into a wide pit. Deep niches pockmarked the cliff's face. Wailing corpses, imprisoned inside these cells of pain and misery, cried out to Artemis as she passed. Flagellated by laughing demons, gouged by cackling harpies, or beaten by hunched gargoyles, the violent endured the acts they'd committed in life.

Any sympathy she might have had evaporated abruptly when she flew close to one of the niches, where two chained corpses, male and female, writhed under the iron-pronged whip of a green-scaled demon.

"This is your fault!" The man's face contorted with rage. He yanked on the chain binding his wrists to the woman's, jerking her to her knees.

The woman kicked out, snarling curses. "You bastard! If it hadn't been for you and your death magic—" Her teeth sank into his thigh.

The man brought his bound fists down on her shoulders with crushing force. "Fucking demonwhore. I should have dumped you in the gutter. I knew you'd drag me dow—aaah!" He arched his spine, gasping as the demon's whip cracked across his back.

"Up yours, you loser!" The woman's hair stuck out in wild, greasy snarls. Using the chain for leverage, she struggled to her feet and clawed the man's bloody back with her long, jagged fingernails. "The gods only know what I ever saw in you!"

"Why, you stinking bitch—"

The male corpse lunged for the female's throat just as

the demon's whip landed on her buttocks. They fell together in a biting, punching tangle. The demon rose above them, laughing.

Nauseated, Artemis banked toward the center of the pit, as far from the damned as possible. Malice and hopelessness worsened the farther she descended. She couldn't repress a shudder as she dove deeper into the morass of suffering.

The next level could only be worse.

CHAPTER NINETEEN

Mac felt like hell.

And if Hell didn't feel so bloody bad, he would've laughed out loud at such a feeble joke. As it was, he managed only the slightest amused grunt. His body felt as though it had been put through a meat grinder. No, he amended. A meat grinder would have been kinder.

He opened his eyes on utter darkness. The surface upon which he lay was hard, wet, and slimy. His nostrils contracted against the stench—something akin to fresh blood and rotten flesh.

He couldn't suppress a groan as he shoved himself up on his elbows. Mud and death coated his life essence; he couldn't get a firm grasp on his mind or his magic. The effort to find himself left him nauseated. His limbs were leaden. His skin burned as if it were on fire, though no flames were apparent.

Too bad. A bit of light would've been welcome.

His last firm memories were his surrender to Malachi, and Artemis's tormented gaze. Then a sensation of falling, through fire, wailing, and despair. He'd landed hard, then blanked out completely.

Where was he?

He managed a seated position. At least he wasn't chained, either physically or magically. There was no sign of Malachi, thank the gods. He'd need time to recover before he attempted another fight with that wanker.

And fight he would. Now that Malachi had let Artemis go, Mac intended to keep the demon too busy to change his mind and go after her.

He contemplated standing and exploring his prison. He even tried it, but his balance was so bad he sank down to the floor again rather than fall over.

Crouching on one knee, he peered into the darkness. A futile exercise; the stygian blackness was absolute. Muted wailing drifted within the gloom. He closed his eyes—though it made no difference at all in what he saw—and let his nonphysical senses take over.

The limits to his prison cell weren't large. He was in a niche or an alcove of some kind. One side was open, giving off into empty space. There was a slight hissing, off to his left. He'd almost resolved to stand and make his way toward it when a new sound from the right caught his attention.

A soft, barely audible female whimper.

"Artemis?"

No answer.

He bit off a curse. Had Malachi, the bloody bastard, reneged on his promise to let Artemis go? Mac stood, fighting vertigo as he inched toward the sobs. The closer he came to the source of the sound, the more certain he became that the distraught woman was not Artemis.

He swallowed hard. Not Artemis, but another woman he knew very well. The sound twisted his heart. Mac had experienced Leanna's anger, her contempt, her laughter. But never—not in the two centuries he'd known her—had he heard his sister cry.

"Leanna?"

The sobs abruptly ceased. Deafening silence ensued.

"Leanna. It's me, Mac. Where are you?"

A cough, and a brief, startled silence, then, tentatively . . . "Mac?"

"Yes." He inched closer and came up against a solid barrier, flat and smooth like glass, but hot. He ran his hands over it, searching for a seam, until the heat forced him to draw back.

"Leanna," he said, louder this time. "Talk to me."

"Mac? You're really here? That wasn't a dream, when I saw you in the theater?"

"No dream. I was there."

Her voice dropped to a whisper. "No. That's insane. Mac would never come to Hell."

The soft sobs began again.

"It is me, Leanna. I'm real. I'm in Hell because—well, never mind all that. The important thing is, I'm getting you out of here."

Exactly how that was to be done, he didn't know yet.

"That sounds just like something Mac would say. He's always so . . . hopeful."

Mac pounded on the hot wall separating them. "I *am* Mac, damn it! Your brother!"

Leanna continued as if she hadn't heard. "Mac thought he could get me to love him. But . . . I never did. I hated him. I blamed him for Niniane's rejection. But that was never his fault. I wish . . . I wish . . ."

What Leanna might have wished faded to nothing.

Mac pitched his voice low. "Leanna, listen to me carefully. This isn't a trick. I'm Mac. I'm real."

"You're not." At least she was addressing him directly this time. "You're just a memory Malachi pulled from my mind. He loves awakening my deepest regrets. He feeds on my pain, my grief, my guilt. But especially my hopelessness. That's what Hell is, you know. A place without hope."

"Then we're not really in Hell, love, because we've got a hope of getting out of here."

"I used to dream of that. When Culsu was destroyed . . .

I dared to hope. I thought I could go home. But then Malachi came. He claimed me—"

She broke off as a bone-grating sound of metal on metal scraped in the darkness. A key in a lock? Perhaps, because a moment later, the unoiled hinges squealed and a door abraded a rough floor.

"Oh gods," Leanna breathed. "No. No."

Her voice was very close. Just inches away, and yet Mac couldn't reach her. Frustration had him growling. Footsteps approached—steady, implacable.

"No, Malachi. Not now. Maybe later—"

Genuine amusement laced Malachi's even tone. "You know better than to plead with me, whore. On your feet. Come to me."

Mac heard her rise and stumble.

"No!" He joined his fists and swung them with all his strength against the wall. The jolt sent a fiery pain up his arms to his shoulders. Backing off, he gathered his weakened magic and released a bolt of hellfire. It spattered and died.

A ghastly red glow sprang up, and Mac realized the barrier between him and Leanna was transparent. The new illumination bathed Leanna and Malachi in murky light, an iron-studded door set in the rough stone wall behind them. Mac's teeth clenched at the sight of Leanna, naked, standing before her master with head bowed.

Malachi ran his hands over her shoulders. A sheen of bright white flickered on Leanna's bare skin. Her life essence. The Old One's lips drew back in a sudden smile. Lowering his head, he pressed his lips to Leanna's flesh.

Leanna cried out; Mac pounded on the barrier, watching with horror as his sister fought to retain her life essence. She clawed at her captor's face, kicked at his shins. Twisted as far as his grip allowed. He held her as easily as if she were made of rags. He raised his head only when Leanna's light subsided.

He dropped Leanna to the floor, where she lay, limp and unmoving. Malachi's vitality shone, enhanced by Leanna's life essence.

The demon turned and addressed Mac. "Your sister's Sidhe soul is quite invigorating, even after a year in the death realms, Mac Lir. She will last several centuries at least."

"You're despicable."

"Of course. Vile, corrupt, and lewd, as well."

"Let her go."

"But she is so very . . . inspiring. Leanna was a Sidhe muse in the upper world, I understand. She inspired artists with her body and her magic. Drank their life essence in return. I'm merely doing to her what she did to so many. A fitting punishment, don't you think?"

"Her true master is gone. You had no right to claim her."

"I had every right."

"You'll tire of her soon enough. Why not let her go now? She's not what you truly want."

Malachi eyed him. "How would you know what I truly want?"

"You want Hecate's destruction. I can give you that."

Malachi threw back his head and laughed. "Ah, but this is rich! You think you can defeat Lucifer's consort? When you could not even give me a satisfying fight? Your power is nothing here, Mac Lir. You cannot even pierce the paltry shield that separates you from your sister. Do you not understand? You are not in control here. Even the witch who betrayed you is more powerful than you are in Hell."

"Leave Artemis out of this."

"Ah, but how can I? Without her assistance, you would not be mine. She and I are allies."

"Hardly. You tricked her."

"Of course. She will help me bring about Hecate's destruction. As will you, though not in the way you imagine."

"How, then?"

Malachi toed Leanna's motionless body. "This whore's life essence is strong. But yours—yours is eternal. A feast that will never end. You will make me strong beyond my wildest dreams. Strong enough to defeat Hecate." His eyes flashed red. "Perhaps even strong enough to challenge Lucifer himself."

Mac's brows rose. "I had no idea you were so ambitious."

"Ambition is the spice of existence."

He sauntered forward. The barrier between Leanna's cell and Mac's fell away. Mac tensed, marshaling his paltry defenses. His strength was returning, though not as quickly as he would have liked.

Malachi's attack came so quickly there was barely time to react. A red beam shot from the demon's hand to Mac's chest. Fire flashed over Mac's skin; he felt as though he'd erupted in flames. Death magic seeped into his limbs, weighting them like lead. His knees buckled, and he couldn't even break his fall.

Malachi's leering grin loomed above him. "Ah, Mac Lir. You should have known. Not even a god can best an Old One in Hell."

There was no answer that wouldn't sound pathetic, so Mac kept his lips pressed together.

"There's no escape. I am your master now. You are my whore. And I will make you beg for your own defilement."

Abruptly, the demon's guise changed into that of a beautiful human woman. Lush breasts strained against a form-fitting gown of purple satin; shining hair streamed over ivory shoulders. The scent of sex, temptation, and dark, secret pleasures teased Mac's nostrils. Leaning forward, the demon provided Mac with a magnificent view of deep cleavage. A black-lacquered fingernail reached out and traced a line down Mac's chest. It didn't stop until it reached his groin.

Against his will, he felt his body respond.

Malachi's sultry feminine voice drifted lazily to Mac's ears. "I can give you pleasure. I could make you beg for me. I could make you love me."

An abrupt hiss, a swirling cloud of smoke, and the demon reverted to Malachi's familiar male guise. When he spoke, his tone was pure acid.

"I could drive you to the heights of ecstasy, but, personally, I find an unwilling whore much more gratifying. The humiliation. The pain. The anger. It's quite invigorating." He smiled thinly. "So I believe I'll remain male, and give you the buggering you so richly deserve. But first, a taste of your eternity."

The red beam moved from Mac's chest to his skull. Raw, dementing pain slammed into his brain. He curled knees to chest and rolled, trying to escape. Useless. The agony came from within.

Malachi let out an excited growl. Mac's pain was the demon's path to his immortal soul. Life essence seeped through Mac's pores, lighting his skin with a phosphorescent glow. Malachi held out a hand; Mac's body rose into the air. The demon's eyes grew bright as he placed his lips on Mac skin and absorbed the white light.

Utter revulsion ate at Mac's heart, his soul. "You really get off on this, huh?"

"Oh yes. A human soul's anguish is pleasant, and your sister's Sidhe soul is more than gratifying, but an immortal soul? Nothing can compare."

Malachi bent his head and drank more. Each sip brought searing pain. Mac felt his vision waver. When the demon finished at last, Mac barely felt the short fall back to the floor.

Malachi staggered, his gait that of a drunken human. "Oh yes." His eyes closed on a sigh; his hand waved an upholstered armchair into existence. He sank into the cushions with a sigh. "Oh yes . . ."

The sated whispers continued. Disgust churned in Mac's gut. Death magic clawed at his life essence; how had he ever thought such magic would make him strong? Hecate had tricked him. Embracing death magic had given Mac temporary power, yes, but it had bled his soul. Far from making him strong, his acceptance of his darkness had only depleted his real strength—his life magic. Evil was something to fight, not to befriend.

And now, because of his folly, he was trapped in a landscape of endless despair. Endless death. Because his life magic was useless, and the thought of casting death magic again ate at his soul.

"Not so cocky now, are we?" Malachi's eyes remained closed, but his full lips parted in a smile. His breathing slowed. Deepened.

A flicker of movement caught his attention. Mac raised his head. Leanna. She had lifted her naked body into a crouch. Arms wrapped around her knees, she was staring at him.

"It really is you," she whispered.

"Yes."

He shoved himself into a sitting position. His sister sidled closer, giving the sleeping demon a wide berth. Her haggard face carried only a shadow of her former beauty and youth. A year in Hell had aged her.

But her gaze was steady. Clear.

She inched toward him. Mac moved as well, away from Malachi. They met as far from the demon as possible within the confines of the cell. Wordlessly, Mac removed his shirt and offered the sorry garment to his sister. Cheeks heating, she pulled it over her head. It covered her body to midthigh.

She glanced at Malachi. "He took too much from you," she whispered. "He always does. Makes him too drunk to stand. He'll sleep for a while now." She reached out and touched Mac's hand, as if reassuring herself he was real. "You came for me? Why? How did you know I was here with Malachi?"

He shook his head. "I didn't come for you, Leanna. I . . . didn't know what had happened to you after Culsu's destruction. I came to Hell for another reason. As for how I can survive here—it's because my soul's no longer pure. I caught a shard of death magic while battling Culsu."

Leanna looked down at her crossed arms. "I see."

"Leanna, look at me." When she didn't, he tucked his finger under her chin and raised her gaze. "Leanna, I may not have come to Hell looking for you, but I swear, I'll get you out of here."

A tear glistened on her cheek. "I'm not sure I deserve it, Mac. But . . . at least I can tell you I'm sorry. For everything I did to you, and to Kalen, and Christine. It's been one of my greatest regrets that I can't tell them how ashamed I am."

Old, familiar guilt swamped him. "It would have been different if I'd taken you when you were born. If I'd raised you after Niniane threw you away."

"How could you have? You didn't even know I existed. And by the time you found out about me, I already hated you. I wouldn't let you care."

"I did, anyway. I do now. Let me help you. I have death magic, Leanna. So do you. Perhaps neither one of us can take on Malachi alone, but together? We can try, at least."

"Death magic, Mac? You?" Horror etched her face.

He grimaced. "Yes, I've learned to cast death. It was . . . necessary. I'll do it again if I have to."

"But why, Mac? Why not use your life magic?"

His gaze snapped to her face. "Life magic doesn't work in Hell, Leanna."

Her brows rose. "That's an old wives' tale, Mac. I'm surprised you believe it. Just think for a moment. You're a creature of life magic. If it were true that life magic can't exist in Hell, you'd be dead. But you're not."

He stared at her. "I tried to cast life magic. It didn't work."

"You have to set a circle of protection first. Something you've probably never done. That's a trick for human witches, not Sidhe. Or demigods. You're used to having unlimited power, Mac. In Hell, life magic has boundaries. You have to choose your position carefully."

He examined her intently. "Have you done it? Have you cast life magic here?"

She sent a nervous glance toward Malachi. Her voice dipped to the barest whisper. "I've tried. And if I hadn't delved so deeply into death magic before Culsu took me to her realm, I might have been able to escape after she fell, before Malachi caught me. But I've done so much damage to my soul during my life. My soul isn't infinite, and with my masters constantly draining my life essence . . ." A sheen of sweat appeared on her temple. "I didn't get far. But you—that's another matter entirely. Your life essence never ends. You could do some real damage here with it."

"And Hecate knows it," Mac whispered, half to himself. "The bitch! That's why she encouraged me toward death magic. She knew if I embraced darkness fully, I'd be no threat. I should have realized she would never have helped me."

He grasped his sister's hand. "Leanna. How do witches make a circle?"

"In the human world, they use salt. Or holy water. Neither substance exists in Hell, except within a living body. Tears work."

"Or sweat."

"Yes."

"No problem there. It's hot as . . . well, hot as Hell in this place." He stood, glancing at Malachi, still sunk in his drunken slumber. A filament of oily drool hung from the corner of the demon's mouth.

"Draw a circle around him," Leanna whispered. "With us inside. Quickly, before he senses what we're doing."

Mac nodded. Rising on silent feet, he paced a wide circle around both Leanna and the sleeping demon, leaving drops of sweat in his wake.

When he was done, he approached Leanna. "Touch me, Leanna. Let me give you back some of what you've lost."

"I don't deserve it, Mac."

"That's not true. Everyone deserves a second chance at life."

She hesitated, then nodded. She laid a hand on his arm; he covered it with his own.

With a fierce burst of will, he sent his immortal life essence flooding into his sister's body. Before Mac's eyes, Leanna transformed. The lines on her face smoothed; the shadows disappeared. Her spine straightened, her shoulders went back. Her red hair became lush and thick, every trace of white vanishing. It was as if fifty human years had dropped from her body in a matter of seconds.

"What the—" Malachi's eyes snapped open. The demon catapulted from his armchair, hellfire blazing from his fingertips.

Leanna ducked, splinters of death singeing her hair. Mac met the attack with arms raised. Elfshot burst from his hands, exploding in Malachi's astonished face. Leanna added a second burst of green sparks.

Malachi howled his outrage. The demon struggled to call a defense, floundering as Mac forced him to the floor. Muttering a life magic spell, a verse of healing and cleansing, Mac directed it full force at the Old One. Elfshot exploded.

Malachi gasped a curse. Turning, the demon fled to the iron-studded door. He didn't bother opening it this time. He merely turned to smoke and seeped beneath it.

Leanna's gray eyes were wide. "I don't believe it! We ran him off."

"Not permanently, I'd wager. That would be far too convenient. I suspect we just caught him by surprise. He'll regroup soon enough. We've got to get out of here before that happens."

"You're right, of course."

"But not through that door, preferably. Malachi might be waiting on the other side. Do you know of any other exits?" He ignited a blaze of elflight overhead, eyeing the open side of the cell. "Besides the sheer drop into that pit?"

"Yes. Up," Leanna said, pointing to the ceiling. A hole, just large enough for a slim woman to wriggle through, pierced the rock.

"Hell is riddled with secret passages," she explained. "And Malachi's created portals between Hell and Shadowhaven on almost every level. This is Level Seven. That tunnel leads to Level Six. There's another portal to Shadowhaven there."

"Will you be able to escape to the human world from Shadowhaven?"

"I'm sure I can, now that my life essence is high."

"Then go, and be careful."

"But—aren't you coming with me?"

"No. I'm going in the other direction. Down."

"Gods in Annwyn, Mac! Why?"

He huffed a laugh. "Why else? A woman. A human witch."

Understanding dawned in Leanna's eyes. "That's why you're here in Hell. A damsel in distress, and you're her knight in shining armor."

He grimaced. "I wouldn't put it exactly that way, but yes. I came to Hell with a witch named Artemis Black. Her son's soul was stolen by an Old One called Hecate, and she's determined to get it back."

Leanna gasped. "Hecate? Bloody hell, Mac. Hecate isn't just any Old One. She's Lucifer's consort!"

"I know that. Artemis won't be able to face her alone."

"I should think not. Hecate's power is off the charts. Only Lucifer's is greater. No one would willingly challenge her, not even Malachi." She eyed him. "But you mean to, don't you?"

"I have to. I love Artemis, Leanna. And I promised her I'd do everything I could to save her son. But . . ." He sighed. "That's not even the whole story. Artemis doesn't know it yet, but she's carrying my child."

"Mac," Leanna said seriously. "Fighting Hecate under any circumstances is pure folly, even with an immortal soul and the ability to fight with life magic. We're talking about facing Hell's most depraved demon, in the Underworld's deepest level. The evil on Level Nine . . . it's inviolate. It would be a pure miracle if you were able to save Artemis and her son. And miracles don't happen in Hell."

"That may be," Mac said. "But I'm still going."

Leanna was silent a moment, then sighed. "I wouldn't expect anything less from you. You're so . . . so *good*, Mac. It hurts to know how much I've disappointed you all these years."

"Leanna, that's—"

"It's true, and . . . I know it's inadequate, but I'm so sorry for it. For everything. All the people I've hurt, the lives I destroyed. You believe me, don't you?"

Mac reached out an arm and pulled her into his embrace. "Leanna. You don't have to keep asking for my forgiveness. You're my sister, and you've just given me more hope than I dreamed possible. Because of you, I have a fighting chance to save Artemis, without destroying my own soul in the process. Yes, I believe you."

"But . . . I hated you so. Because our mother loved you and threw me away."

"Niniane's full Sidhe. She's not capable of love. Not really."

"Do you . . . oh, Mac, do you think *I'm* capable of love?"

He kissed her forehead. "I know you are." He set her at arm's length and gave her shoulders one last squeeze. "Now go, quickly, Leanna, and don't worry about me. I'll knock off Hecate, snag Artemis and her son, and be home before sunrise."

"Mac. Maybe I should come w—"

"No, Leanna. Forget it. You've been through enough. You're going. Now."

"But—"

"Go, Leanna. Now. That's an order, from a demigod. Come on, I'll give you a boost."

She let out a long breath and nodded. "All right."

He laced his fingers together. Gripping his shoulders, she stepped into his laced hand. He lifted her to the tunnel entrance and watched her disappear.

CHAPTER TWENTY

Gods, the stench was foul.

Artemis had been afraid she'd be trapped at the bottom of the great pit, but when she flew into the depths of the shaft, she discovered there was no floor. She found herself flying high in the sky of Hell's eighth level.

Swooping low in her raven form, she followed the bank of a putrid brown river. Bubbles rose thickly to the surface, spewing flame into smoky air. The profound stink left a disgusting taste in the back of her mouth. There was little doubt in her mind as to the river's contents: thick, boiling excrement.

The shore over which she flew was nothing more than a narrow strip of rocky land backed by a sheer cliff with no visible summit. The sky above was a stormy charcoal. Hot wind whipped from the low-hanging clouds. Each breath was sheer torture. But her own agony was nothing compared to that of the corpses swimming in the fetid river.

The damned fought against the river's current. Flying on, Artemis understood what they so desperately wished to avoid. The river widened and flattened around sharp-edged rocks, strewn with broken bodies. The damned caught on the rocks cried out, their raised arms scant defense against the diving attacks of what looked like birds and sounded like pure evil.

Furies. Hideous winged demons. And they'd already noted Artemis's approach.

One darted in her direction, its pointed tail cracking like a whip. The movement drew more of its kind. They gathered, red eyes blazing, beaks dripping blood.

Thank the gods, they didn't attack. There seemed to be an invisible line beyond which they would not fly. Artemis had no doubt that the moment she crossed it, she'd be shredded to pieces.

Wings tiring, she fluttered to the shore, backing up as far from the oozing river as possible as she considered her predicament. The passage to Hell's deepest level surely lay within the Furies' territory. There had to be a way to get past. She turned the dilemma over and over in her mind. Some time later, after mentally proposing and discarding more than a dozen scenarios, she still had no answer.

And then a small demon materialized beside her. For a moment, all she could do was stare at the creature. If Artemis had been in human form, she doubted the demon would have stood much higher than her knee. It looked very much like an imp or a sprite, only bald, with brown, scaly skin and a slender rattail that never completely stopped moving.

Recognition dawned. She opened her beak. Her bird voice squeaked, but formed human words easily enough. "You were in Shadowhaven. You're one of Malachi's minions."

The demon spat. "Minion. Huh. Slave, more like. Thrall." He waved a hand toward the river. "But at least I'm not as bad off as those idiots. Fitting, isn't it?"

"What is?"

"You know who's here? Seducers, con men, politicians, and bigamists." He grinned. "Advertising executives. All experts in shoveling crap. Now they're drowning in it."

"Poor fools."

"Don't bother feeling sorry for them. Believe me, each

and every one of them would pull you in there with him, if he could. My advice? Obey Hell's number-one rule. Look out for yourself. That's what everyone else does."

Artemis ruffled her wings. "Then why are you here, giving me advice?"

The demon winced. "Don't have much choice, do I? Malachi says 'jump,' I say 'how high?' He says 'help the human witch get to Level Nine,' I've got to do that, too. As distasteful as it may be."

"Malachi sent you?"

"I just said he did, didn't I? Damn, but you humans are dense."

"And he told you to help me."

The demon crossed his stubby arms and glared.

"All right, all right," Artemis muttered. She supposed she should be grateful for help in any form at this point. "Do you have a name?"

The little demon sighed. "Damn it, yes. Malachi calls me Angel."

"You're kidding."

"Malachi has a warped sense of humor. Now, do you want my help or not?"

"I want it. Can you get me downriver?"

"I could, but that's not where you want to go."

"It's not?"

"No." He pointed his tail at the river's far bank. "You want to go across."

Right past the Furies. "How?"

He looked her up and down. "Not by flying, that's for certain. Those Furies will tear you apart in half a second."

"Are you saying I have to *swim* across?"

"Wouldn't survive that, either."

"Is there a boat, then?"

Angel scratched an armpit. "Nope. No boat."

Artemis's patience was growing thin. "Then how?"

The little demon grinned. "Thought you'd never ask!

You've got to jump from rock to rock. Shouldn't be all that difficult with that bird body you've got."

"But . . . there are corpses on every rock! And Furies attacking them! There's no way they'll just let me by."

"Yes, well, I admit, you'll likely get a nasty gouge or two. But it's really your only hope. Keep your head down and don't let them blind you. That would be unfortunate."

Gods. "And after I get across? What do I do then?"

"There's a cave. A tunnel, really, in the cliff on the other side of the river. You'll see it. It leads to Level Nine. The pit of the betrayers." He grinned. "Ready?"

Not by half. She flapped a wing. "Lead on."

"Oh, I'm not going."

"What? I thought you said Malachi told you to lead me—"

"No. He said to *help* you. Which I've done. I'm not holding your hand on the way across. What do I look like, a damned nursemaid?"

"All right. Just tell me, where's the best place to start the crossing?"

"There." A sweep of his tail indicated a flat boulder near shore. Three mauled corpses clung to it. "No sudden movements, though. The Furies see motion more than anything else. They're not the most intelligent of creatures. But beware," he added with a smirk. "Not all the damned are idiots."

With that, the little demon vanished.

Artemis blinked at the place where he'd been. All that was left of the bizarre little creature was a puff of smoke. Shaking her head, she inched her way to the riverbank, her raven's claws slipping on slime-covered rock. Angel was right; when she moved at a snail's pace, the Furies took little notice.

She approached the bubbling shoreline gingerly. The flat boulder was too far for a human to jump, but one flap of her wings would be enough to get her there. She grimaced. So much for "no sudden movements."

No sense in waiting, either. Spreading her wings, she made the jump.

The nearest Fury screeched. Artemis hunched motionless on the rock until the air-bound demon turned its attention elsewhere. Only then did she begin to move, with excruciating slowness, to the far end of the boulder.

One of the corpses clinging to the rock spat an obscenity in her direction. She steered as far from the damned man as she could; a moment later, he became preoccupied with beating off a Fury. Artemis's short hop to the next rock landed her within reach of a snarling female corpse. She rolled, but not before losing a handful of tail feathers.

Tail unbalanced, leaping to the third and fourth stones was difficult. She was halfway across the river now. She navigated the fifth stone without incident, but on the sixth she landed badly. The awkward movement caught the attention of a diving Fury. It darted toward her, its sharp beak stabbing her under her ribs. Desperate, she jabbed her raven's beak into the demon-bird's eye. Yes. The thing took off, hooting in pain.

But the wound the Fury had inflicted burned. As she jumped the next few stones, the pain only amplified, making it harder and harder to dodge the grasping corpses. The damned men clutched at her legs, her wings, her neck. Freed, she thrust her beak right and left, and even managed to squeak a death spell. She jumped to the next stone—blessedly vacant—and crouched, gasping.

The Fury's gash seeped poison into her soul, disrupting Artemis's own magic. Her shape-shifting spell began to unravel. She still had a distance to go to reach the opposite shore—two stone, three jumps. Damn. If she lost her raven shape, she'd have to swim the distance between them.

She lurched on and off the first stone, narrowly avoiding

a Fury's bite. Her landing on the second stone fell short. As she scrabbled to avoid the boiling river, a rough hand closed on her flapping wing.

She heard a sickening crack. The next instant, she nearly passed out on a rush of pain.

"Gotcha, birdie!"

The corpse that had caught her let out a barking laugh. Panicked, Artemis snapped at her new attacker. The damned man was hideous—rotten, ragged, blackened. Skeletal fingers crushed fragile raven's bones.

The pain snapped the last strands of the shape-shifting spell. The change came quickly, stunning the corpse into sputtering silence. Taking advantage of his shock, Artemis kicked hard, smashing the sole of her boot into the corpse's face.

The blow snapped the man's neck. His skull, mouth open and screaming, rolled into the river with a thick plop. His body dove after it. Artemis's sigh of relief didn't last. Her struggle with the corpse had attracted a trio of Furies.

The monsters dove. Artemis gasped a repulse spell. Cradling her useless arm, she dropped into a defensive roll and came up in a crouch.

The fiery pain in her side nearly caused her to topple into the river. She held firm, eyeing the last jump to the shore. Not so very far—on a good day, with a running start, she could've made it easily. In her present condition . . .

Gritting her teeth, she summoned every last ounce of strength and jumped. Her boots splashed on the edge of the filth lapping the shore. Staggering forward, she collapsed on relatively clean ground. The Furies, howling, drew up short at the river's edge.

She dragged herself across the rocky beach, intent on leaving the Furies' territory behind. A steep cliff face loomed before her. Just as Angel promised, there was a cave.

Not allowing herself time to think, she crawled into the opening. Darkness enfolded her like a moldy cloak. Rising to her feet, she leaned her left arm against the cave wall. Her right arm hung heavily at her side. Broken. The wound under her ribs burned. Fiery pain stabbed with every breath.

She stumbled forward, the cave growing darker and darker with each step. Her magic was gone. She couldn't even call the faintest glow of hellfire. The path went on and on, twisting and turning, always descending. For a long stretch of time, she encountered no impediment to her slow, painful progress.

Then she turned one sharp corner and drew up short.

A pair of glowing red eyes lit the darkness before her.

CHAPTER TWENTY-ONE

Artemis screamed as the creature charged. She flung herself to one side, her body slamming hard against stone. The thing thundered past, the heat of its massive body snapping like a whip. She fell, gasping out a curse when she rolled onto her injured arm.

She tried to gain her feet, but fell back to her knees. Her strength was gone. Her magic was spent. The death shield protecting her life essence had crumbled.

The creature pounded to a halt in the darkness. She heard it turn back, snorting. Its red eyes blinked into view.

And she didn't even have enough strength left to move.

Was this how she was fated to die? Alone, in pain, trapped in the bowels of Hell, so close to Zander, yet powerless to reach him? Not knowing what had happened to Mac?

A growl vibrated; the ground shook as the monster advanced. And still she couldn't move. She closed her eyes and braced for the blow. . . .

A grunt, and an enraged howl. Then a thundering crash, and the monster slammed into the ground. A spurt of flames burst from the creature's mouth. She caught a glimpse of a grotesque figure, muscled legs and torso of a man, hideous head of a bull. Steam hissed from the Minotaur's snout. Blood spurted from its skull; Artemis caught a glimpse of an open gash on the side of its head. A bloody boulder lay nearby. Someone—or something—had attacked the beast from behind.

The monster lurched to its feet and spun to face the threat. With a roar, it spewed fire into the passage. Artemis could see nothing beyond the Minotaur's massive body. When there was no immediate riposte, Artemis feared that whoever—or whatever—had assaulted the monster from behind had been burned to a crisp. Grunting satisfaction, the Minotaur swung to face Artemis.

Too soon.

Again the beast was struck from behind. It staggered, howling. It fell to its knees, then pitched forward with a crash. It shuddered once, then lay still.

Without the Minotaur's fiery breath to light the cavern, Artemis was plunged back into darkness. She strained to hear the creature who'd felled the bull; whatever it was, she had no doubt it would soon come for her. Residual adrenaline shot into her limbs. She lurched to her feet and stumbled deeper into the cave.

Quick footsteps followed. A familiar male voice bit off a curse. "Bugger it all, Artemis, is that you? Are you hurt?"

She stopped dead. "Mac?"

His voice traveled as if from a great distance. "Yes, it's me. Hold on a bit. This bloody great beast is in my way. . . ."

She listened as he jumped down from the Minotaur's body. Then he was sprawled on the ground beside her, drawing her into the circle of his arms. An orb of green light appeared above his head, bathing him with a muted glow. His beautiful face, streaked with grime, swam in the sheen of tears that suddenly welled in her eyes. He'd lost his shirt somewhere. He felt warm and safe and alive. All the things she thought she would never be again.

"Damn, but that thing was ugly." His tone was light, but he scanned her with a worried gaze. "Not even a mother could love a face like that."

"Oh, Mac."

He squeezed her, then drew back when she cried out. "You're hurt."

"A corpse broke my arm. And a Fury gouged my side. It burns like anything."

He ran an assessing hand over her injuries, then touched her head. She felt him searching, inside. When he spoke, his voice was grave. "I got here just in time, then."

"But . . . *how* did you get here? Malachi—?"

His expression hardened. "Bloody unpleasant bloke, that demon friend of yours."

"He's not my friend."

"No? The two of you seemed chummy enough."

She hugged her torso with her good arm. "I hoped you'd get away from him."

"But you really didn't believe it. You have more faith in that twisted demon's powers than you do in mine."

"Mac, I—"

"And you would have been right," he continued quietly. "I'd still be Malachi's prisoner if not for Leanna."

"Your sister? I don't understand."

"Malachi thought to taunt me by assaulting Leanna in front of me. He'd thought he'd broken her, but my sister is half Sidhe. She knows more about magic than he realized. More than I realized. Together, we drove Malachi off."

"You defeated him?"

"No. He slunk back to Shadowhaven."

"And Leanna?"

"She's on her way back to the human world."

"You could have gone with her."

"Yes. I might have."

She could feel his gaze on her. She couldn't bring herself to look up. "Why didn't you?"

"You're a smart lass. You tell me."

She did look at him then. "Pity?"

He laughed. "Come on, love, you can do better than that."

"Duty?"

"No."

"Then . . . I have no idea, Mac. The gods know you didn't follow me because I deserve your help. And you're too sane to have saved me just to enact some crazed plan of revenge for all I've done to you. So . . . I really have no idea why you came after my sorry butt."

"Artemis." He grasped her hands and gently unclenched her fist. Once he'd succeeded, he threaded their fingers together.

His touch made her guilt burn. She tried to tug her hand away, but he only tightened his grip. With his free hand, he tilted her chin, forcing her to look at him. The green of his eyes deepened. She felt the brush of his magic against hers.

His expression turned grave. "You've been in Hell too long, Artemis. Far too long. You could lose the—" He cut off. "You could lose your life essence. Completely. It's bleeding from your soul."

"I know. My shielding broke. I don't have enough strength to erect a new one."

"It's all right now. I'm here. I'll protect you." He murmured a word, and she felt a cocoon of well-being wrap around her. She sighed and let herself lean against his strength. It was only then that she'd realized what he'd done.

She went still. "That . . . that light over our heads . . . that's elflight, isn't it? And that spell you just cast—it's a life-magic spell. A healing charm."

He grinned. "I was wondering when you'd notice, love."

"But . . . how?" she whispered.

"Leanna," he answered. "She showed me what was possible. Showed me that what I'd thought was the right thing—casting death magic—had actually been making me weaker. Despite the darkness in my soul, I'm a creature of life magic. And if I establish the right protections, I can cast life magic even here."

"I don't understand."

"You don't have to understand, Artemis. That's just the point. Death magic is logical enough, but life magic defies understanding. What's needed is faith."

She bit her lip. "I've never been good at faith, Mac."

He cupped her face in his hand, his thumb brushing her lip. "I don't believe that for a moment, Artemis. This entire journey has been an act of faith. You couldn't have gotten this far without it."

"But I've made so many mistakes. I've broken your trust, over and over. You shouldn't have come after me. I wouldn't blame you if you left me here to die."

His hand smoothed down her neck and arm, his palm flattening on her belly. Something inside her leaped to meet him. When he spoke, his voice was hoarse. "Come, now, love. None of that depressing talk. I need you to be strong."

He spoke a word. Life magic flowed from his hand into her body, flooding her senses, her heart, her soul. She nearly cried at its beauty. She hadn't until that moment realized how familiar with death and darkness her soul had become.

The pain in her arm and her side vanished. She lifted her arm. The bone had mended. Looking down, she realized the grime and sweat had vanished from her skin and her clothes. The scent of a bright forest glen teased her nostrils.

And she was trembling.

Mac was looking at her with an infinitely tender expression. "How's your arm feel now, love?"

She lifted it. "Fine. No—better than fine. It's perfect."

"And the wound in your side?"

She smoothed a hand down her flank. "Gone."

"Good. But not quite good enough. Your life essence is still low. I need to be sure you won't fade on me again. Will you open up your soul, Artemis? And your body? Let me flood you with as much life essence as you can hold?"

Her eyes widened. "Open up—? Just what are you saying, Mac?"

He sent her a wolfish grin. "I think you can guess, love. I'm half Sidhe, after all."

CHAPTER TWENTY-TWO

Artemis stared. "Mac. You . . . you can't mean what I'm thinking you mean."

"Try me, love."

"You want to have sex? Here? Now? You're crazy!"

Mac's tone sobered. "Artemis. You were hurt. Badly."

"Was. You've already healed me."

"Your body, perhaps. But your soul? I don't want to take any chances. I need you strong. The balance your magic had in the human world—that's gone. You're becoming far too familiar with death magic. It's not good, love. It could destroy you."

Artemis nodded. Mac was right. A low, sick hum underlay her every thought and action. It had become so familiar it almost wasn't disturbing her anymore.

"Mac." Her voice shook. "I—"

He gripped her hand. "Do you love me, Artemis?"

She swallowed. "You don't want me to love you, Mac. I'm a mess. I hurt everyone I love. Sometimes I think my life is cursed."

"Don't ever say that." His voice was uncharacteristically sharp. "You're not cursed. You're everything that's loyal and good and true."

"Are you cra—?"

Her protest died when his lips came down on hers. "I love you, too, Artemis."

"Oh, Mac . . ."

His mouth was warm and firm. Gentle, yet demanding. She knew she should push him away, but she had no strength left for that. She needed him, needed this. She gave a small moan and melted.

He took her mouth, his tongue stroking deeply. She splayed her fingers on his bare back, relishing the flex of his muscles. His hands roamed under her shirt, cupping her breast. His head finally came up, and he looked down at her. The tenderness in his gaze nearly undid her.

"Mac. I've made so many mistakes."

"So you think only perfection is worthy of love?"

"No, of course n—" She cut off abruptly, biting her lip. Yes, that was exactly what she thought. Only perfection deserved love. At least when it came to someone loving *her*.

"If perfection bred love," Mac said, "Annwyn would be flooded with the emotion. It's not. Why do you think I make my home in the human world? Because I want what humans have. Love, in all its messy imperfection. I looked for it for centuries, but I didn't find it, until I found you. Do you know what I love about you, Artemis?"

She shook her head, her eyes burning with unshed tears.

"Your bravery. Your loyalty. Your tenacity. Your independence. Your infuriating tendency to hide things from me. I've never been so bloody angry with anyone as I've been with you, Artemis."

A reluctant laugh left her lips. "I'm not sure that's a compliment."

"It's not. I want to strangle you with alarming frequency. And I just might if you ever try to sell me out to a demon again."

She pressed her forehead to his chest. "Oh gods, Mac, I'm so sorry. I—"

He dropped a kiss on the top of her head. "There's only one apology I want, Artemis." He kneaded her breast. "Make love with me."

"Yes."

With eager hands, she tugged at his belt and unbuttoned his jeans, slipping her hands inside the waistband. He eased her shirt and bra over her head; with a few more deft moves, he had her naked. Shucking off his jeans, he lowered her to the ground, to lay atop their discarded clothing. He stretched out over her, supporting his weight on his elbows, his arousal hot and hard against her belly.

She threaded her fingers through his golden hair. Fear almost kept the words unspoken. But how could she be such a coward? He'd given her so much.

"I love you, Mac."

He lifted his head and flashed her a cocky grin. "Do you? Prove it."

A laugh bubbled up. "Only you, Mac, could make jokes in Hell."

"Beats the alternative, love."

His knee parted her thighs. She opened for him gladly. With a tilt of his hips, he pushed inside, entering her on a long, slow glide, and then she wasn't laughing anymore. Not at all.

He spoke soft, lilting words of magic. A circle of life sprang up around them. When he moved inside her, nothing outside mattered. Life and healing flooded her soul. When he sought to claim every part of her, she held nothing back. Deep in her belly, she felt something vital turn toward Mac's light, like a flower toward the sun. And when the final pleasure came, it swept her into a place so beautiful she wept.

Mac awoke to find Artemis entwined tightly around his body. He lay on his back; she was nestled against him, her body stuck to him as if with glue. Her right arm was locked in a stranglehold around his neck, and she'd flung her right leg over both of his as if she were afraid he'd get away. The vulnerable position was so unlike her he found himself fighting a laugh.

A laugh that faded to a deep, burning contentment when he remembered their lovemaking. Once again, the connection they'd found went beyond anything he'd ever experienced. Fantastic sex, yes, but so much more. Love. And the experience of touching his unborn son's soul.

Now he had to take both Artemis and that new, precious life into the deepest level of Hell. Because there was no other path to take. His immortal arse was hanging out the window on this one, and he didn't like it one bit. But he could see no other way.

He allowed himself one last look at Artemis's peaceful expression before he shook her awake. "Come on, love. Time to get up."

"Wha—?"

The dreamy fog in her blinking eyes made him smile. All too soon it vanished, replaced by a spark of anxiety.

"Gods. I fell asleep? I don't believe it."

She retracted her limbs from his body, crimson painting her cheeks as she realized how tightly she'd been clutching him.

He felt all the poorer for the loss of her arms around him. "You needed the sleep. How do you feel?"

"Fine." She paused, twin lines appearing between her eyes. "Great, in fact. Better than I've felt in . . . well, in I don't know how long. I'm almost . . ." She looked up at him. "Hopeful."

"Good. Hold that thought."

Her hand came to rest on her belly, as if she sensed the life growing there. He rose and extended her a hand. She took it. They didn't speak as they shook out their clothes and dressed.

"Are my jeans and shirt really clean?" Artemis asked. "Or is this some kind of life glamour?"

"No, they're clean. Though they probably won't be by the time we get home."

"Home." Her fingers paused in combing the knots from

her hair. "Right. Only one more level to go, but it's the worst of all."

He flexed his fist. Should he tell her now? It was past time, but even after what they'd just shared, he still wasn't sure how she'd react.

"Ptolomaea's adjacent to Satan's lair," she was saying. "We should stay as far away from that as possible. Hopefully—"

"Artemis."

She blinked at him. "Yes?"

"I need to tell you something. Before we go another step."

She frowned. "What is it?"

"When we reach Ptolomaea, I want you to leave Zander's rescue to me. Whatever it takes, I'll handle it. Please. I need to know that you're safe."

"I can't promise you that, Mac. If Zander needs me—if you need me—I won't just stand by and watch."

He picked up her hand and turned it palm up. Bending his head, he traced the lines there. "I need you to stay safe, Artemis, because there's another life at stake." He raised his head and met her gaze. "I didn't tell you this before, because I didn't know how you'd take it. I imagined you'd be furious. Perhaps you still will be. But when I found you here, half dead—I thought my own heart would stop. You're carrying my son, Artemis. And I won't let any harm come to him."

Her eyes widened; her nostrils flared. Her mouth opened, but no words came out.

He placed her palm on her stomach. "He's barely a day old, but if you look inward, love, I think you'll be able to feel him."

The oddest expression crossed her face. "I'm . . . pregnant?"

He swallowed, and nodded.

"When . . . How . . . ?" The words emerged as croaks.

"At my estate. I went a little crazy, lost control."

"But . . . that's impossible! I'm on the pill."

He almost laughed at that. "Do you honestly believe the pill has any effect on a god?"

"You're only half a god," she whispered.

He shrugged. "Half is good enough, I suppose."

"And you knew? Right when it happened?"

"I had a good idea. I wasn't completely sure until I caught up to you in Shadowhaven."

A shadow passed over her eyes. "So that's why you came after me. Why you argued for my life before the Sidhe Council. Why you followed me to Malachi's realm and into Hell. I wondered. I knew . . ." She hugged her torso. "I knew it couldn't be because of me."

"Artemis, love, look at me."

She studied the ground.

"Damn it, Artemis, that might have been the first reason I went after you. But it was by no means the last."

She held herself very, very still.

Bloody hell. He hated when she did that. "Artemis, love—"

"No. Don't call me that. It's not me you love. It's—oh gods. A baby? Will he . . . will he . . . or she . . . be immortal?"

"He. And yes, he'll be immortal. If he's delivered safely. Until then, he could die."

She turned her back on him, both hands splayed on her stomach. "And when . . . if . . . he's born? Will you take him from me?"

"What?" Mac dragged both hands through his hair. "No! Of course not. Not unless . . . unless you don't want him."

She didn't answer.

He paced a circle around her, until he was standing in front of her again. "Would you want me to take him, Artemis? Would you not want to raise our child?"

She closed her eyes, her head tilting back as she expelled

an angry breath. "Gods. A baby. How could you do this to me, Mac? I need all my strength for Zander. How can I protect another child in Hell?"

"You won't have to, Artemis. I will."

"And if you can't? If it comes down to a choice? How am I ever supposed to make that call?"

He gave her a long, even look. "It won't come to that. I swear it." He held out a hand. "Trust me, Artemis."

She swallowed and looked away. She didn't, he noticed, dip her head in a nod. His chest hurt. He had no right to promise her everything would be all right. He didn't know if it would be. He stared at her, mutely, willing her to look at him.

After a time, she squared her shoulders. She didn't quite meet his eye when she spoke. "I know you'll do everything in your power to get us all out. But . . . I can't promise you anything. Now, please. Can we go?"

He nodded. He kept the orb of elflight glowing overhead as they made their way deeper into the cave. Waves of foul air and foul emotion buffeted his life shield. Casting his senses ahead, he searched for specific threats. He felt none.

A red glow marked the end of the cave. Wailing voices grated like fingernails on a chalkboard. The tunnel ended, and they looked out over Hell's ninth level.

"Oh my gods," Artemis breathed.

They stood on the edge of a large, domed cavern. The roof and walls of the cave ran with blood. Its acid drip had dissolved most of the cavern floor, leaving only the barest network of solid surface.

Mac advanced as far as he dared. He peered through the floor to the pit below, where blood dripped, sizzling, into lava. Wailing corpses burned in boiling stone.

Betrayers, every one of them. Mac let his gaze pass over them. What he and Artemis sought wasn't in that pit of misery. Their goal lay on the opposite side of the cavern, across the treacherous floor. Two arched portals stood side by side fronted by a wide ledge of solid rock.

"One archway leads to Ptolomaea," Artemis said. "The other leads to Satan's lair."

"Which is which?"

Artemis bit her lip. "I don't know."

"Right. Well, first things first. Getting across." He studied the delicate stone tracery.

"I'll go. I'm lighter than you."

Mac grabbed her arm. "You'll do nothing of the sort. Stay here."

He slid one foot forward. As soon as he began to transfer his weight, the stone crumbled. He jumped back as a huge chunk of rock disintegrated. Long moments later, it splashed into the lava below.

"Looks like we won't be taking the obvious route," he said.

"Gods. How are we going to get across? I don't have any magic that will bridge a gap like that."

"I do."

Doubt was clear on Artemis's face. "Your magic can only be cast inside a circle. How will you ever get a circle around the entire cavern, with us stuck on this side?"

"Trust me, love."

He drew a tight circle around himself and Artemis. Closing his eyes, he called the spell. When it was ready, he lowered his protection and cast the magic out. It formed a shining white bridge, arching between the cave and the solid ledge on the other side of the cavern.

Artemis gasped. Mac took a step onto the spell's transparent surface. It dipped under his weight, but held.

"It's not going to last long," he said, jumping off and pushing Artemis before him. "We'll have to hurry."

They ran, their eyes fixed on their goal. They were halfway across when a dark wave of pure malice rose from the lava pit. Tentacles of raw evil, reaching, curling, clutching . . .

Mac's bridge cracked.

Artemis paused, looking back at him. He all but picked her up and threw her forward. "Run!"

For once, she didn't argue. Her boots pounded on the disintegrating spell as she sprinted to the other side. Mac dogged her heels, catching her once when she stumbled and shoving her on ahead.

She leaped to safety as the spell gave way completely. Mac threw himself after her, his fingers clawing slick stone. His legs kicking empty space. Blood, dripping from above, burned on his bare back. Artemis grabbed his arms and dragged him onto solid ground.

"Gods," she gasped when he was safe. "I didn't think we'd make it."

He rolled over and looked up at her. "I know."

She met his gaze, startled. "I'm sorry."

"No need." He grunted as he sat up. "I wasn't so sure of it myself."

Climbing to his feet, he peered up at the twin arched portals, looming darkly above them. Each was sealed with a monolithic black panel that resembled polished obsidian. He could see no latch, no handle, no hinge, not even a seam.

"Want to hazard a guess which is Ptolomaea?" he asked Artemis. "Perhaps you can sense your son's soul?"

"Maybe . . ." Her eyes closed. A moment later they opened, with her no wiser than before. "No. I can't feel a thing."

Mac shrugged and chose the door on the right. He cast his senses toward it. It was sealed with death; his psychic brush against it burned his mind. The weave was flawless, stronger than any magic he'd ever encountered on earth. As strong in death as magic in Annwyn was strong in life.

He laid his hand on the panel. Ignoring its heat, he traced a circle on its surface. Casting deep, he called his brightest elfshot into his palm.

Light blazed, causing Artemis to shield her eyes. He poured his soul into the green fire, willing the wall to melt under its power.

It did not.

Perhaps if he put some force behind it? He stepped back and traced a circle on the ground around himself and Artemis. Gathering his magic within it, he launched a blast of elfshot at the door.

A woman's laugh sounded behind him. "It doesn't matter what you try, you know. You'll never get in."

Artemis made a strangled sound. Slowly, Mac turned, not at all surprised to find Hecate standing behind them. The demon wore a shining black gown, its long train trailing into the lava pit. A lacey corset cinched her tiny waist, offering her breasts like a deadly gift. Her scent, thickly floral with a touch of dung, contracted his nostrils.

"You." Artemis tensed like a spring about to snap. Mac put a cautioning hand on her arm.

"Surely you're not surprised," Hecate scoffed. "Ptolomaea is my realm. If you wish to enter, all you have to do is ask. It's leaving that will pose a problem."

Artemis let out a sound akin to a growl. "Where is my son?"

Hecate smiled. "Safe."

She waved a hand. The blank face of the right portal lightened, revealing wisps of light floating behind it. Human souls. Children.

Artemis covered her mouth with her hand. "Oh gods. Zander. I see him."

Mac followed her gaze. He caught only a glimpse of the lad before Hecate dimmed the panel. An animal sound of distress emerged from Artemis's throat. She pitched forward, arms outstretched, only to have Hecate knock her back into Mac's arms with a flick of her finger.

"No! Please! Bring him back. What do you want? I'll . . . I'll do anything, if only you'll let him go free."

This time it was Mac's hand that covered her mouth. "Damn it, Artemis, shut up. Don't you know by now that bartering with demons is useless?"

Hecate laughed. "Wisdom for the ages. Come, now, witch, even if I were disposed to trade, what could you offer? Your soul is hardly equal to that of a sweet child." Her gaze moved to Mac. "But your immortal lover . . . if his soul is part of the bargain, I may be inclined to negotiate."

"Sorry," Mac said. "I'm not for sale."

He punctuated his rejection with a blast of elfshot.

Hecate repulsed the attack easily. "Ah yes, clever of you to realize your life magic isn't so useless here in Hell after all. But if you should step out of that circle . . ."

Mac responded with a second round of elfshot—swift, precise, and stronger than his first shot. Artemis, inside his protective circle, added her own spell to his attack.

Mac scowled. "Damn it, Artemis," he snapped. "Get behind me and let me deal with this bitch."

With a grimace, she obeyed.

"Protecting your whore?" Hecate taunted. "How touching."

The demon launched hellfire at Mac's legs, intent on blasting him out of his circle of protection. "Fight as long as you can, Mac Lir. It will do you no good. Death cannot be denied."

Saraid's words. Mac couldn't accept them. "We'll see about that." He gathered a new assault on his fingertips.

But even as he launched it, he knew his chances of destroying Hecate, in her own realm were slim. He was discovering that casting life magic in Hell was wrenchingly difficult. Hecate, by contrast, didn't seem to be exerting herself at all. For now the battle remained relatively even, but for how long? He had a sickening feeling that Hecate was toying with him.

Artemis knew it as well as he. He felt her step outside his circle of protection; felt her gather her death magic, preparing to enter the fight with the most powerful weapon she had at her disposal. Damn it. He didn't want that—didn't want her risking his child.

Artemis's spell unfurled in ugly strands, wrapping itself about Hecate's ankles. Demon snare. Hecate cursed, kicking. Her struggle only caused the strands to tighten. "Insolent witch . . ."

The demon launched hellfire at Artemis. Artemis ducked. Mac, growling, grabbed Artemis and pulled her back into his circle of protection. He strengthened his defenses as Hecate, spitting curses, disentangled herself from Artemis's spell.

"Don't you dare do that again," he hissed at Artemis.

"You needed my help. She's stronger than you, Mac. You're not going to be able to take her alone."

As much as he didn't want to admit it, he knew Artemis was right. "What do you suggest, then?"

"A melded life/death spell," Artemis said. "Like the ones I cast in the human world. My death magic, your life magic. Together."

Mac cursed. "Damn it, Artemis, I don't want you casting death magic. A spell that strong could—" Could kill his child. But he didn't say it. He knew they had no choice.

"All right," he said tightly. "Tell me what to do."

"Here. It's easier to show you."

She laid her hand on his arm. Their minds touched. He felt what she needed from him; felt the death magic he would have to balance.

A blast of hellfire shook his protections. Hecate had returned to the fight.

"Ignore her," Artemis whispered. "Fighting her now will destroy our balance."

Mac nodded. The ground shook as Hecate exploded her next spell. He focused on Artemis, on her power, on her death magic. They built the spell strand by strand, death magic, then life, dark, then light. Perfect balance, interwoven in a perfect pattern. Truly a terrifying work of art.

They loosed the spell together. It hit with a tsunami roar. A whirling symphony of dark and light, dissonance and harmony, evil and beauty, it demanded as much as it gave. The tension it exerted on Mac's soul was fierce. Balancing Artemis's death magic, he fed his life magic into the maelstrom. The spell descended on Hecate, surrounding the demon like a storm.

The spell sucked power from the Old One with the ease of the sea accepting the flow of a river. Hecate fought; Mac and Artemis fed the spell, drawing it tight around her. The demon writhed, and cursed, and launched spell after spell in defense. Mac, with his infinite life essence, countered Hecate's every attempt to break free.

The demon howled. "This cannot be! No god can defeat a demon in Hell!"

"I'm only half a god," Mac muttered.

Hecate's human guise wavered. Her cold beauty withered. Her young woman's form faded into that of a withered hag. But even that guise could not hold. Her human form slipped away entirely, revealing a misshapen, tentacled monster.

The creature's gelatinous maw gaped, spewing filth and rage. Artemis, caught in the trance of her magic, didn't react; Mac grabbed her and pulled her to the ground as the vomit flew overhead. Grunts spilled into the air as Hecate's demon form melted into an oily blob.

For a long moment, Mac lay motionless, Artemis wrapped in his arms. Her heart hammered against his ribs.

He delved deeper, seeking the spark of new life in her womb.

He let out a long breath. Thank the gods. His son was alive. But the scent of death on Artemis was strong.

"Bloody hell," he said. "I'm sorry."

She lifted her head and stared at the mess that had once been Hecate. "I had to do it."

"I know."

He helped her to her feet; she could barely stand on shaking legs. He flooded her soul with life essence; some of her color returned. But she was unsteady. The spell had almost been too much for her. He lowered her back to the ground.

She looked up at him. "Mac?"

"Yes, love?"

"Do you . . . do you really think we'll be able to get Zander out from behind that door?"

"No worries, love. I'll see to it." He hoped it wasn't a lie. "Just rest a moment first."

"No, I'm fine. See—" She tried to sit up, then moaned and sank back into his arms.

Alarmed, he fed her more life essence. "Give it a minute, love."

Weakly, she nodded. But a minute passed, then two, and Artemis didn't improve. Her defenses were gone. The life essence Mac channeled to her slipped through the cracks in her soul and disappeared.

Mac shifted his focus, reinforcing the circle of life around her. But it was as if an unseen hand snatched each thread of the spell before he could tighten it. He stood as the barrier crumpled completely and turned to face his new foe.

"Malachi."

The Old One dipped his perfect chin. "Surely you anticipated my return."

Mac said nothing. Malachi toed the oily remains of

Hecate's body. "So. She is gone." Satisfaction gleamed in his eyes. "Ptolomaea and all its delights are mine. I claim your whore as well, Mac Lir."

"No. She fulfilled her contact with you. You'll let her go, and free her son as well."

Malachi heaved an exaggerated sigh. "Oh, but the contract terms have changed once again. Because of this witch, I've lost your sister. I'm due compensation. I claim Miss Black's soul and that of her son as recompense."

The demon's index finger tapped his lips once, as if a thought had just occurred. "Of course, I may be induced to consider alternate reparation. Your own soul, for example."

"Hardly an equal exchange," Mac said evenly. "My soul is infinite." He paused. "I would, however, consent to a duel for the right to take Artemis and her son out of this place."

Malachi's eyes lit with interest. "A duel? And what will you surrender when you lose?"

"*If* I lose, Artemis and her son will go to the human world. I will stay in Hell."

A smile played on Malachi's lips. "Then let us fight, by all means. Life against death. There can be only one outcome. Death cannot be denied."

Saraid's words again.

"Mac, no." Artemis's whisper was fierce. "This isn't your fight."

He spoke without turning. "Stay out of this, love."

"No."

Malachi laughed. "Why not let your whore fight for you? It may delay the inevita—"

The demon's words were lost in a fire blaze, as Mac landed a ball of elfshot in his handsome, leering face. Building on the advantage, he drilled another shot into Malachi's stomach.

Malachi screamed his rage. Flames erupted from his fingers. A sizzling stream of hellfire struck Mac's right shoulder. Cursing, Mac countered the attack. But Malachi had recovered quickly from Mac's opening maneuvers. The demon advanced, gazing death into Mac's face. When the next assault came, it was all Mac could do to hold his defensive position in front of Artemis.

And then things went from bad to worse.

Malachi spoke a word; the air behind him ripped in two. "Come," the demon commanded.

The tear widened. Mac recognized the first demon to emerge from the portal—the bouncer from Shadowhaven. Travis the cowboy came next, tipping his ten-gallon hat. A small, implike demon with a curved tail rode on his shoulder—the little blighter blew a kiss at Mac, then gave him the finger. More of Malachi's thralls followed—strong demons and lesser ones, human demonwhores, and even a few undead.

Malachi faced Mac with a broad smile. "My army. Defeat them, and you may leave Hell with your whore. Fall to them, and become my slave for all eternity."

Mac's stomach clenched. He could never defeat such a throng. Not here in Hell. Not even with Artemis's help.

"What's the matter, Malachi?" he taunted. "Afraid to fight your own battles?"

Malachi's eyes blazed. "You tricked me once, Mac Lir. Never again."

Mac felt Artemis trembling at his side. He eased her behind him. The odds were firmly against them. Much as he loathed the thought, Artemis would have to fight.

He met her gaze. "Ready, love?"

She nodded. He readied for the first wave of attack.

Malachi waved his army forward. "Go!"

Mac tensed. But not one demon moved.

Malachi rounded on his thralls. "Well? Get on with it! Now! Attack the immortal!"

The cowboy and bouncer demons exchanged glances. Travis shuffled a step forward, hat in hand. "Well, now, Malachi, about that? We're not so sure . . ."

Malachi released an oath and a bolt of hellfire. Travis's boots danced.

And one final figure stepped from the portal.

A woman. A slender red-haired wraith.

Leanna.

Mac stared at his sister. She was dressed in vaguely medieval garb—tunic, breeches, and knee-high boots, with chain mail and a hammered breastplate covering her torso. Her red hair was slicked back, showing her pointed ears. Advancing, she came to stand between the cowboy and the bouncer.

She smiled. "Hello, Malachi."

"Seize her," Malachi snarled.

Neither the cowboy nor the bouncer moved.

Leanna's gray eyes glinted. "They no longer answer to you."

"That's right," Travis drawled. "That's what I was about to tell y'all. Drager and I . . . well, shucks, ain't no pretty way to say it. Truth is, we've decided to go our own way. And take all your thralls with us."

"Damn right," the little demon on his shoulder chipped in.

"You've cast your lot with a pitiful, half-Sidhe demon-whore?" Disbelief rang in Malachi's voice.

"Well, ya see," Travis said, "there's those of us been thinking for a while now that a change in management in Shadowhaven would be a good thing."

Malachi snorted. "And you, Drager?" he demanded of the bouncer. "You've joined this slack-witted slug?"

"Yeah," Drager grunted. He lowered his beefy arms. "I have."

Malachi's voice was deadly soft. "Traitors. I will destroy you utterly. Right here. Right now."

He launched a ball of hellfire. Leanna and her unlikely allies met the attack together. The fire fizzled even before it struck.

Leanna laughed. "Looks like your little empire is crumbling, Malachi. It was rotten at the core, after all. That's what happens when you reward loyalty with pain and humiliation."

"Demonwhore." Malachi hissed the word. "You dare challenge your master?"

"You're not my master anymore."

A blast of hellfire punctuated the declaration. The bolt struck Malachi in the chest; the demon staggered backward. Recovering quickly, he flicked a finger and returned the attack. But with Travis and Drager intercepting, the blast was neatly put down.

Malachi let out a snarl. Black smoke swirled from beneath his feet. His arms rose, and the stone platform trembled. Brimstone fell like hail. The lesser demons, arrayed behind their leaders, traded nervous glances.

"I give you one chance to choose," Malachi told his minions. "Fight for me, or for these pitiful upstarts. But beware. There will be no mercy for any who stand against me."

Mac tugged Artemis into the shelter of Ptolomaea's archway. Quickly, he cast a circle of protection around her. "Stay here," he told her. "No matter what happens. This is going to get ugly. I've got to help Leanna."

"Mac—"

He silenced her with a look. "No arguments, Artemis."

She pursed her lips, then nodded. "Be careful. Remember, you're only half a god."

He quirked a smile. "I rarely forget it, love."

About a third of the demons glided to Malachi's side. The rest aligned themselves behind Leanna and her demon partners. Malachi watched the dispersal with hawk's eyes. He seemed to have forgotten all about Mac and Artemis. Mac liked that just fine.

A blast was fired—Mac wasn't sure which side started the fight. It hardly mattered; the next instant, pure chaos erupted. Mac, working from within his own circle of protection, sent beams of elfshot to aid Leanna's cause, but he dared not stray too far from Artemis, for fear Malachi or one of his minions would attack the protections he'd placed around her.

The scene disintegrated into smoke and fire. Grunts, shouts, and curses. A howl of defeat was followed by the sound of a body splashing into lava. The battle raged, shaking the ledge upon which they stood. At any moment, Mac expected the entire platform to disintegrate into dust, pitching them all into the pit.

Slowly, more and more of the lesser demons defected to Travis and Drager. If the tide maintained its shift, soon Malachi would be fighting alone.

The Old One knew it; he tried to morph into mist, but the transformation didn't take. Desperate, he made a run for the portal leading to Shadowhaven. With a curse, Leanna ran to intercept him. Mac caught a glimpse of her red hair as she dashed through the thick of the fray, cutting off Malachi's path of escape.

Mac plunged after her.

She cornered the Old One—suit torn, face bloodied, hair gone wild—in front of the lava pit. Malachi's human guise wavered. As Mac watched in disgust, the demon's virile form and handsome face melted into a squat reptile body and bulbous head. A flattened snout breathed fire. But after an initial blast, the flames sputtered and died.

Leanna pressed forward, forcing her former master to the very edge of the platform. One backward step would drop him into boiling lava. Malachi curled his spiked tail around an outcropping of rock.

A blast of hellfire landed at his front feet. The demon skittered back, the rear half of his lizard body skidding over the ledge.

"Here are your choices," Leanna said. "Jump. Or be pushed."

Mac came to stand at his sister's side. Her face was

streaked with soot, a gash on her right arm was bleeding freely, and her hair was a tangled mess. But triumph blazed in her eyes.

"Sounds like a fine choice," he said.

Malachi's eyes burned. His snout opened. A forked tongue emerged, bearing rasping human words. "You don't want this, Leanna."

"Oh, I find that I do."

"No. Remember the pleasure I'm able to give. I offer that to you—on your own terms. Enslave me. Use me. I'll service you gladly, in any guise you wish."

Disgust shuddered through Leanna's body. "I find I've lost my taste for slavery. In any form."

"Not slavery. Pleasure. Freedom."

"Jump," Leanna commanded, taking a step forward.

Red eyes gleamed. "No. If I'm to die, I want to feel your hands on me one last time. . . ." He smiled. "Push me, my whore."

With a snarl, Leanna lunged, a kick aimed at Malachi's hideous face. The Old One's tail whipped toward her.

"Leanna! No!" Mac sprang for his sister, but his warning came too late. His fingers snatched air as the demon yanked Leanna out of Mac's reach.

"Nooooo! Mac, help!"

Demon and woman vanished over the edge of the platform.

Mac threw himself after them.

CHAPTER TWENTY-THREE

"Mac!"

Artemis launched herself toward the empty ledge. The distance seemed immense, her limbs moving in slow motion, her lungs squeezing against oxygen-sucking panic. She stumbled as she reached the edge, nearly pitching over it into the blinding heat. Only Travis's hot grip on her arm prevented her from falling.

She blinked up at the cowboy demon. "What—?"

"Won't do y'all any good to throw yourself after your lover, sweet thang." Travis's thick brows waggled. "Not when there are so many of us shy fellows willing to take his filly for a ride, if ya'll know what I mean."

A sharp retort died on her lips. He was lewd, but his eyes looked . . . kind? She gave her head a shake. She was losing it, big time. "Let me go. I need to—"

His grip didn't loosen. "Ain't nothing down there y'all want to see, sugar, I can tell you that right now. Best come with me and the rest of the crew." He nodded to the shimmering portal, into which Malachi's former thralls, guided by Drager, were disappearing one by one. "We'll sort everything out upstairs." He raised his voice. "Dollar blackjack and drinks on the house!"

The demon army cheered. Travis tugged her farther from the edge of the pit.

"Thank you, but no," Artemis said through gritted teeth.

She tried to hobble a few words together for a spell, but she couldn't reach through her fatigue to her magic. "Let. Me. Go."

Cowboy grinned and wrapped his arm around her shoulder. "Ah, come, now, sugar. Is that any way to treat the demon who saved you from an eternity in Hell?"

"You had your own reasons for going after Malachi."

"That's sure 'nuff the truth, little lady, but that don't mean y'all didn't benefit. Why, I—"

"The lady said *no*, cowboy. Is there a part of that word you don't understand? Let her go."

Travis's head jerked up. His red eyes flashed with fear as he eyed a point past Artemis's head. His grip loosened. "Sure thing, friend. She's all yours."

Artemis's heart stalled. Slowly, not wanting to risk shattering the hallucination, she turned.

"Mac." The single word—a name, a question, and a prayer of gratitude all at once—was all she could utter. He stood before her, his golden hair a halo against the flames leaping from the pit behind him. He was alive and—as far as she could see—unharmed.

The same couldn't be said of Leanna. Her body hung limp in Mac's arms. Angry burns blistered her lower extremities.

"Gods. Is she—"

"No," he said sharply. "At least, not yet." Kneeling, he laid his sister gently on the ground. "Little idiot," he murmured. "I don't believe you came back for me."

Leanna's eyelids fluttered, but didn't open. "Couldn't . . . let . . . my big brother . . . have all the fun. Now . . . can die . . . in peace."

"You're not going to die, Leanna. I'm getting you out of here."

Artemis glanced toward the portal to Shadowhaven. The last of the lesser demons had disappeared through it. Only Travis, Drager, and Angel remained.

"Take her to Malachi's realm," Artemis told Mac. "You can reach the human world from there."

Mac raised his head. "I will. Once we open Ptolomaea and rescue Zander."

Travis and Drager exchanged glances. Angel started chuckling.

Artemis glared at the little demon. "What's so funny?"

"Open the gates of Ptolomaea?" he chortled. "That's the funniest thing I've heard in centuries!"

"Why?"

"Only an Old One can open Ptolomaea. But most Old Ones don't even want to, because whoever controls Ptolomaea has to deal with . . ." He sent a meaningful glance to the second, silent archway. *"Him."*

"Satan," Drager clarified. "Ptolomaea's master becomes the devil's consort. And let me tell you, Lucifer's tastes are . . . deviant . . . even for a demon. Hecate might have enjoyed that sort of thing, but as for me . . . even if I were an Old One, an eternity of life essence couldn't persuade me to become Satan's bitch."

"Me, neither," Travis professed. "And as for freeing a soul from Ptolomaea? Shucks, that needs an okay from the big man himself. Satan."

Angel hooted. "The witch could try throwing herself on Lucifer's mercy."

"Except we all know he has none," Drager said grimly.

"None at all." Travis looked slightly ill. "You know, I reckon I've had enough of Hell. This place gives me the willies."

"Agreed," Drager said. "Let's get back to my realm."

Travis's eyebrows shot up. "Excuse me? *Your* realm? I believe Shadowhaven is mine now."

Drager grunted. "Like hell. Is that a challenge?"

Travis smiled thinly. "Sure as hell is."

Angel whipped his tail. "Oh, good! Another fight!"

Drager cracked his knuckles. "Let's get to it, then."

The trio ducked through the portal. Artemis met Mac's gaze. "Go after them."

"And leave you here, to deal with Satan? I think not, love."

"Zander . . . he isn't your concern. Leanna is."

"Both of them are," Mac said. "And you are." His gaze fell on her stomach. "And our son is as well."

Tears crowded Artemis's eyes. "You might not be able to save us all, Mac."

He stood. "I mean to try."

He tried first to open Ptolomaea. But the odd little demon hadn't lied. The door wouldn't budge. In contrast, the merest touch set the door to Lucifer's inner sanctum swinging. The darkness beyond was thick. When Mac stepped into it, he actually felt the absence of light on his skin.

"Mac—"

He looked back at Artemis, cradling Leanna's head on her lap. Her dark eyes were wide. "Be careful."

He nearly laughed. *Careful* kept people safe in their beds at night. It didn't take them into the presence of pure evil. "No worries, love. I'll be back before you know it."

He hoped.

He plunged into the darkness. He hadn't taken more than a half dozen steps when he came to a narrow, circular stair. There were no handrails that he could discern; gripping the center vertical bar, he began his descent. Six hundred sixty-six steps later, he reached the bottom.

A faint yellow light appeared, illuminating a polished wood door. The iron latch bore no lock. Briefly, Mac considered knocking, then decided against it. He didn't imagine Lucifer was unaware of his approach.

He pushed the door open. His eyes met the dancing light of a fire, contained in a civilized manner by a stone mantel and hearth. The blaze cast its light on a cozy library that had none of the appearance of a hellhole. Mahogany bookcases lined the walls from floor to gallery above. Rows upon rows of leather-bound volumes filled the shelves, gold lettering gleaming in the soft light.

A desk was all but bare, ink and quill set neatly to one side, its comfortable-looking leather chair unoccupied. A large globe rested on a stand in one corner, a sideboard with decanter and glasses stood ready in another. A thick-pile Persian carpet spread the length and width of the room, its fringe on either end dusting polished hardwood.

A high, wingback chair faced the fire. A small table next to it held a blue china bowl. A poker and bellows lay against an iron stand on one side of the hearth; a toasting fork hung on the other. A brass spittoon rested between hearth and chair.

The mantel bore a black lacquered clock, gently ticking.

No voice greeted Mac's entry. No welcome. No threat, either. He called a spark of elfshot to his fingers.

Nothing happened.

Frowning, he advanced to the center of the room.

"Hello?"

No answer. Was the Lord of Hell abroad? Mac dragged a hand through his hair. If Lucifer wasn't in his lair, where could Mac begin to look for him?

He started as a skeletal hand and arm emerged from the shelter of the wingback chair, reaching for the china bowl. Dipping inside, it withdrew a small morsel. A peanut, perhaps? The owner of the arm retracted the limb. It disappeared behind the chair. Mac heard a pop as teeth crunched and chewed.

Then silence.

Mac strode to the hearth. Pivoting to face the chair, he inclined his head.

Lucifer did not look up.

Mac studied the Lord of Hell. Satan, Mac decided, looked less like evil incarnate than he did someone's eccentric elderly uncle. His features were angular—eyes set deeply under slashing brows, a hawk's nose, a thin-lipped mouth and jutting chin. Despite the generous heat thrown off by the fireplace, the devil's withered frame was swathed in an argyle cardigan sweater. Brown trousers hung on his bony legs. His stockinged feet were propped on an ottoman. Slippers waited nearby.

The devil's throat emitted a scraping sound. A moment later, he spat, the chewed morsel striking the spittoon with a clang.

Mac cleared his throat. "Sir—?"

"Silence." The command was softly given, but no less forceful for its lack of volume. Lucifer raised his hand again, his fingers dipping into the china bowl. Mac glanced inside it.

What he saw inside the bowl made his stomach heave.

Not peanuts. Not at all.

Lucifer's fingers fished inside the basin. Mac was close enough now to hear the faint, terrified squeals of the devil's prey. Corpses—once alive and human, now dead and shrunk to the size of candied nuts—scrambled to avoid Lucifer's claws. One did not succeed. Lifted high, pinned between the devil's thumb and forefinger, the damned man's limbs waved frantically. His cries, all but unintelligible, squeaked.

Lucifer held his victim up to the light, a smile stretching his thin lips as he peered at the squirming, pleading soul before plopping it into his mouth. Mac stared, horrified, as the devil's teeth popped the corpse. His jaw worked. A blissful expression washed over his face. At last, long after the corpse's cries had faded, Lucifer leaned forward and spat.

His victim hit the spittoon. For a moment the dead man just lay there, groaning. A moment later, he heaved himself to his feet and disappeared.

Satan spoke. "Do you wonder what happened to him?"

He waved a hand toward the china bowl. "He's back with the others now. Waiting and wondering when he'll be chosen again."

Mac swallowed. "Ingenious."

The devil met his gaze. "Do you pity him?"

"Yes."

"Don't bother. He deserves his punishment. All of them do."

Mac nodded. He had no doubt but it was true.

Lucifer eyed him. "You don't belong in Hell, Manannán mac Lir. Let alone in my private den. Why are you here?"

"I'm sure you know."

Lucifer's lips twitched. "That is the correct answer. For that, I will not dispose of you immediately." He paused. "You thought to fight me."

"I thought to try."

"Put the notion from your mind. You cannot. Outside magic has no power here."

Mac had already realized that. When he cast his senses inward, he felt nothing. No life magic. No death magic. Just . . . mortality.

"You seek a soul ensconced at present in Ptolomaea," the devil went on. "And safe passage to the upper world for yourself and the two women under your care."

"Yes."

"You are not unintelligent. You know there will be a price."

"I do."

"You will not like it."

Mac crossed his arms and met Satan's gaze squarely. "I'm sure that's true. Nevertheless, I will pay."

The devil smiled. "Excellent."

What was taking so long?

Artemis hardly dared drag her eyes from the archway leading to Lucifer's lair. Mac had been gone for . . . well, she didn't know how long. She'd lost all sense of time. But she wanted him back—now.

Leanna wasn't going to last much longer. Angry burns covered her legs. She was only semiconscious.

Mac's sister let out a soft moan. The sound melded horribly with the wails rising from the lava pit. Leanna's eyes moved behind closed lids; she clutched at air, muttering. Caught in a nightmare. Artemis owed her so much. She didn't even want to contemplate what might have happened if Leanna hadn't returned with an army of Malachi's thralls.

Artemis leaned close. "Leanna? Can you hear me? It's just a dream. Wake up."

Leanna answered with a moan.

"Come on. Wake up!"

She shook Leanna's shoulders, gently, until her gray eyes opened. For a moment she just stared, dazed. Then recognition sparked.

"You. You're . . . the witch . . . that Mac loves."

"Yes."

Leanna tried to sit up, grimaced, and sank down again, stirring a fine dusting of ash. "Mac . . . he pulled me out of the pit. Where is he? Where is my brother?"

Artemis swallowed. "He's gone to fight."

"Fight? With whom? We won the battle. We were supposed to follow Travis and the others—"

"The portal to Shadowhaven is closed now."

"I don't understand. Why didn't we go through?"

Artemis bit her lip. "I told Mac to go. With you. He . . . he wouldn't. I came to Hell to rescue my son. But . . ." She made a helpless gesture toward Ptolomaea. "We couldn't open the gate. No one can, except Satan himself."

Leanna jerked upright, gasping—whether from pain or outrage, Artemis couldn't tell.

"You said he's gone to fight. With Lucifer?"

Artemis nodded.

"Gods. He'll never win. He'll never even get a chance to try. Life magic can't be cast in Satan's private sanctuary."

It was as if a tight hand had reached out and clamped Artemis's throat. No life magic, and Mac had sworn never to cast death magic again. "I couldn't stop him. I tried to go after him, to help, but the door closed behind him. That was hours ago. I think. I can't tell how much time has passed—"

A tremor shook the cavern.

"Gods in Annwyn," Leanna whispered. "Do you feel that?"

She wasn't talking about the vibrations, but the magic. Death magic woven from pure malice. Hatred stretching from eternity, into eternity.

The platform upon which they sat trembled, like a living thing consumed with fear. A crack appeared, widening as it raced across solid rock. Artemis scrambled to one side, heaving Leanna with her. Clinging together, they watched the fissure hurtle straight as an arrow, toward Ptolomaea.

It hit the portal with a deafening crash. Shock waves reverberated, knocking Artemis and Leanna flat. It was all Artemis could do to keep them both from being swept backward into the pit.

"Look!" Leanna whispered. "The door's cracking!"

Artemis's heart leaped. It was true—a network of cracks spread across the blank face of Ptolomaea's archway. She watched, heart pounding, as the fragments separated and fell. They crashed to the ground and shattered to dust.

Wisps of white emerged.

Souls. Innocent souls. Children, dancing in a stream of pure joy. And there, in the midst of the laughing torrent, was Zander.

His form, already indistinct, blurred even more.

"Mommy!"

She leaped to her feet and stretched out her hand. "Zander! Come here!"

"I can't, Mommy—not yet. I have to go with the others—"

Artemis's gaze followed the path of the white, shining river of souls. Winding a graceful arc, it cascaded into the fissure in a constant, downward flow. The movement generated a swift, suctioning wind. Artemis found herself and Leanna being drawn into it.

"But where?" she shouted. "Where are you going?"

"Don't you know, Mommy? We're going home! And you're coming, too!"

Leanna, still sprawled on the ground, was trying to struggle to her feet. "No! We can't leave Mac! He's—"

"Right here," a voice said.

Artemis turned, gasping, as Mac's arm came hard around her shoulders.

"Mac. You're alive." Her gaze shot to the door leading to Satan's lair, gaping open now. "But how? Did you fight Lucifer?"

An odd expression flitted across Mac's face. "No. That's not possible. Details later, love. Once we're out of this place." Bending, he scooped Leanna into his arms.

"Mac." Leanna's voice was thready. "I was afraid . . . you were gone for good."

"Not so easy to get rid of me, love."

"I'm . . . glad. . . ." Her eyes closed, her head lolling to one side.

Mac set his jaw. "Artemis. Let's get out of here."

"Of course. Do you . . . do you know how?"

He nodded at the stream of souls. "Follow them."

They stepped into the river of souls. Brilliant light enveloped them; Artemis could do nothing but let it take her, body and soul. She was aware of a rapid downward rush, like the free fall of a roller coaster. Then a long, sustained glide of upward movement. A sound like an explosion. Then . . .

No motion at all.

Just blessed ground cradling her hip and the tickle of

grass on her bare arm. Nearby, the bleat of a sheep sounded like a gentle laugh. Artemis opened her eyes and looked up into a brilliant blue sky, dotted with clouds. A cool breeze caressed her skin.

The sun, bright and loving, peeked from behind a cloud to add a touch of warmth to her face. The rays poured through a dancing, shimmering current of air.

The souls from Ptolomaea.

"Zander!" She shoved herself to her feet, her hand coming up to shade her eyes as she scanned the vibrant stream overhead. Like a river pouring into the ocean, the freed souls were separating, floating to and fro, some purposefully, others more uncertain. Several oriented themselves quickly, darting into the distance, others drifted away more slowly. Artemis searched, desperately, for the one soul that belonged to her son.

And then he was *there*, swooping low. "Zander!"

"Hello, Mommy!"

He grinned, showing his new front teeth. Then his ethereal form executed a back flip.

She laughed. Gods, had anything ever felt as wonderful as this moment? "Come closer."

"No, Mommy, I can't." He glanced behind him. *"I have to go. I feel it calling."*

"Feel what?"

"My body. It needs me. I have to go." His wide eyes found hers. He was already drifting away, higher and higher. *"You'll be there when I wake up, won't you, Mommy?"*

"Yes. At least . . . I'll try to be."

He flashed her another grin. She watched, heart bursting with emotion, as he floated out of sight. Only then did she become aware of a hand on her arm. She turned to find Mac sitting beside her.

He looked awful. His fair complexion was tinged with gray, and dark smudges marred the skin under his eyes. Leanna, sprawled in his arms, looked even worse. The burns on her legs were ringed with blackened skin. Her face was as pale as a corpse's. Was she even breathing? Artemis couldn't be sure. "Is she . . . alive?"

"Only just." Mac scanned the landscape. "Good. We landed near the cairns. The barrow entrance is just over that rise. I've got to get her to someone who can help."

He stood, staggering under Leanna's weight. He was weak, Artemis realized. Much weaker than she'd ever seen him.

A shiver of dread chased down her spine. "Mac."

He didn't turn to look at her. "Yes, love?"

"What happened in Lucifer's lair? You didn't fight, you said. Did you make a bargain?"

He started walking. "I did."

She fell into step beside him. "What was it?"

His breathing roughened as they started up a steep hill. "If you don't mind, Artemis, I'd rather not go into it right now. Perhaps after Leanna is safe in Kalen's castle . . ."

"Is that where we're going?"

"Yes. Despite Kalen's history with my sister, I'm hoping he'll allow Leanna refuge there. And Christine . . ." He grimaced. "I'm hoping she's not the vindictive type."

"I don't understand."

"Leanna was Kalen's lover, before he threw her over for Christine. Leanna didn't take it well. She tried to eliminate her competition. Permanently."

"Oh." Artemis paused. "In that case, maybe you should take your sister someplace else."

Mac halted before the barrow entrance. Artemis touched the ancient oak. Had it been only a day since Niniane had dragged her through that door? It seemed like a lifetime ago.

Mac brushed aside a hanging vine, shifting Leanna in his arms as he touched the tarnished brass latch. The door swung open. He didn't speak until they'd descended the narrow stair.

"There's nowhere else I can take her." The dirt walls and hanging roots muted his worry. "She needs a place saturated with life magic in which to heal. Annwyn would be ideal, of course, but Niniane would never let her in."

"But . . . Leanna is her daughter! Of course she would."

His voice turned hard. "Not every mother is like you, love. Trust me, Niniane wants nothing to do with Leanna. She wouldn't care if she died. In fact, she'd probably be relieved."

The tunnel branched. Without hesitation, Mac chose the left fork. His steps were slow and plodding, his breathing labored.

"Mac. Are you all right?"

He ignored the question. "There's another reason we need to get to Kalen's. You want to get to Zander's bedside quickly, don't you? So you can be there when he wakes?"

"Well, yes, of course, but—"

"Kalen can get you there quicker than anyone. He can translocate at will, to anywhere in the human world, and he can take one other person with him. Shouldn't take him more than fifteen minutes or so to get you to Philadelphia."

"Fifteen *minutes*? You're joking."

He looked back at her, the ghost of one of his old grins on his face. "Me? Joke?"

She lifted her brows.

"No joke this time, love. Very soon, you'll be holding your son in your arms."

CHAPTER TWENTY-FOUR

Mac felt older than the oldest Sidhe elder who had ever lived. No, he amended. Older than that. From where he sat, on the armchair in Kalen's library, he could practically see the boat to the West sailing up to his soul's shore.

Saraid's words drifted in the back of mind. *Death is strong. In the end, it cannot be denied.*

He was all too uncomfortably aware of Christine's worried presence. She was on to him, he knew. He couldn't summon any ire, though. Christine hadn't even blinked when Mac showed up on her doorstep asking her to take in Kalen's former lover. She'd only nodded and set about seeing to Leanna's care, had even performed a powerful healing ritual. And that had been *before* Mac had told her how Leanna had saved his arse, not once, but twice. Truly, Christine was a rare woman.

His gaze drifted to another rare woman. Artemis, thankfully, was consumed with her need to get to her son. She hadn't peppered him with any more difficult questions about what had transpired in Lucifer's sanctuary. At the moment, she was completely absorbed with Kalen's description of the process of translocation, a very rare magical talent in which the Immortal excelled.

Dressed in a hastily borrowed outfit of jeans and sweater from Christine, she looked beautiful. Her dark eyes were wide with trepidation, despite Kalen's assurances that diving in and out of holes ripped in space was perfectly harmless. He wanted to laugh. This, from a woman who had been to Hell and back.

"Really," Kalen said. "Christine doesn't care for translocation—makes her nauseated—but there's no danger at all. You're much more likely to be injured hurtling around London on the M25."

Somehow, Mac summoned a smile and a jaunty tone. "That's right, love. There's nothing to it, really, especially after what you've been through lately. Just close your eyes and remember to breathe. Kalen will take you directly to Zander's hospital room."

"You can land that precisely?" Artemis asked Kalen.

The Immortal nodded. "We can go right now, if you'd like."

"Yes! I'm ready. Except . . ." Her gaze sought Mac's. "Will you come, later? Once Leanna doesn't need you?"

"Of course, love." He hoped the lie didn't show in his eyes.

Apparently, it didn't, because Artemis nodded. Padding toward his chair, she leaned into his body and entwined her arms about his neck.

"I'll miss you every second until you come," she said. Her hand went to her stomach. "And so will your son. Zander's going to love having a little brother."

His fingers tightened on her hips. He closed his eyes, fighting tears. He breathed in her scent, imprinting it on his mind. Her lips met his, and for a moment he forgot his fatigue, forgot his bleak future, forgot everything except what it felt like to have the woman he loved in his arms.

The embrace was unbearably sweet, because he knew it was to be their last.

Artemis drew back. Her fingers rose to smooth a lock of hair from his temple. She searched his eyes, and couldn't disguise the worry in hers. "You still haven't told me what happened in Lucifer's lair."

Damn. He'd really been hoping he wouldn't have to lie to her again. "Nothing for you to worry about," he said. "Now, off with you. Zander's waiting."

She gave him one last kiss. "All *three* of us will be waiting for you."

Not trusting himself to speak, he only nodded.

She turned to Kalen. "I'm ready now." She looked at Christine. "Thank you for everything."

"No need. It wasn't any trouble at all."

Mac watched as Kalen let his power drop. A rift in space appeared. Unlike a demon portal, the doorway shone with a muted white light. Wrapping his arm firmly around Artemis's waist, the Immortal pulled her inside.

And they were gone.

Several moments passed. Mac stared at the place where Artemis had been, waiting for Christine to speak.

He didn't have to wait long. "Now," she said in a tone that brooked no argument. "Tell me what happened. All of it. None of this silent macho stuff men are so fond of."

Mac let his head fall back on the cushions. "Macho" was about the last thing he felt at the moment. "Not much to tell, love."

Christine only pursed her lips and crossed her arms.

He sighed. She already knew the basics of his and Artemis's journey into the Underworld. She might as well know the rest.

"The deepest level of Hell, as you know, is reserved for betrayers. Except for the realm known as Ptolomaea. There, it's not the betrayers who are tormented, but the betrayed."

His fingers stroked the leaf pattern on the carved arm of the chair. "Living souls. Mostly children, snatched by Hecate. That's where the demon took Zander's soul."

Christine edged closer, her blue eyes sober as she sank down on an ottoman just beyond Mac's knees. "You freed Zander, along with all the others. You opened the door to Ptolomaea."

"No. Not me. Lucifer opened Ptolomaea's gates. He's he only one who can. He freed Zander and the others, af-er I negotiated an exchange." He closed his eyes.

He could feel Christine's anxiety, radiating in waves. "What . . . did you trade?"

"My immortality, Christine."

He heard her swallow. He opened his eyes. Her blue eyes, deep as the sea, looked infinitely sad, but not, he thought, so very surprised.

"You knew."

She shook her head. "No. But I suspected, as soon as I saw you, and heard what you'd been through. I hoped I was wrong."

He leaned forward in his seat, his forearms on his thighs, his hands dangling uselessly between his knees. "You weren't wrong. I'm no longer immortal. And my life essence is none too strong at the moment." A ripple of fear washed through him, deep and surreal. "I think . . . I think I'm dying, Christine."

She took his hands in both of his. They were very warm. Or perhaps his were very cold. It was hard to tell. "Mac. Look at me."

He did.

"You're not dying. At least not—" Her voice hitched, but she regained control quickly. "At least not for a very long time. You may not be immortal, but you're still a god."

He smiled faintly. "Only half."

"Sidhe live for centuries as well."

"Normal Sidhe. Not Sidhe who have been to Hell and back, and dealt with the devil himself. I'm hardly holding it together at the moment. I'm not sure . . . I not sure I could even stand up without pitching to the carpet."

She squeezed his fingers. "Your life essence is low, true, and stained with death magic. If you stay in the human world, you could very well die. But there's somewhere else you can go. A place that will heal you."

His head dropped forward. "Gods, Christine, no. Please don't tell me Annwyn is my last hope."

"Not only your last hope, Mac. It might very well be Leanna's as well. She's worse off than you are. She needs to get to the Otherworld as soon as possible. It's the only thing that will save her."

Mac closed his eyes with a groan. "Splendid. Looks like Niniane's fondest dream and worst nightmare will be coming true all at once."

"Mackie—oh, Mackie, you wretch! You idiot! I can't believe you could *do* this to me!"

Mac opened his eyes. He lay on a bed in one of Kalen's many guest rooms. Every muscle in his body ached. And now his brain hurt as well, because his mother stood frowning down at him. He caught a glimpse of his cousins hovering behind her.

He'd never seen the pair look quite so somber.

He forced a grin. "Hello, Mum. Nice to see you, too." He nodded at his cousins. "Niall. Ronan."

Niall returned the nod, and Ronan raised a hand. Neither cracked a smile.

Niniane's lips trembled. A tear slipped down her cheek. "Oh, Mac." She swallowed. "Kalen told me the whole sorry tale. How you freed all those innocent souls. Your father . . . Lir is very proud of you."

"And you?"

"I'm just glad you're safe. Or at least, you will be, once we get you back to Annwyn. The gates are open and waiting. All we have to do is cross the Channel to the mainland and sail through. Niall and Ronan will carry you to the boat."

"On one condition."

Niniane's brows shot up. "Condition? What condition could you possibly have? Frankly, Mac, you're in no shape to be issuing orders. You're half dead!"

"Nonetheless, I have one. I am not going through those gates without my sister. Leanna is coming to Annwyn with me."

Several seconds passed, during which the only sounds were the ticking of Kalen's Louis XIV clock and the shuffling of Niall's and Ronan's feet.

At last, Niniane found her voice. "But, Mac, she's half human! She belongs here, in the human world."

His jaw tensed. A spike of pain shot through it, making him feel as if he'd taken a left hook. "She's half Sidhe as well. Your own daughter."

Panic flashed through Niniane's eyes. "But . . . what will I tell your father?"

"You think Lir doesn't know you were unfaithful all those years ago?" Mac almost laughed at the alarmed expression on his mother's face. "Da is a bloody god! Believe me, he knows all about your little indiscretion with that bonny Highlander. If he didn't throw you over back in the eighteenth century, he's not going to do it now."

He surprised himself by reaching out and taking his mother's hand. "I know Leanna reminds you of the biggest mistake you've ever made, Mum, but it's not her fault, after all. Can't you welcome her in Annwyn—if not for her own sake, then for mine? She fought for me in Hell. Nearly died for me. She needs Annwyn's magic now."

Niniane looked down at their joined hands. After a long moment, she looked up and nodded. "All right, Mac. Anything to get you home."

CHAPTER TWENTY-FIVE

Artemis looked up from her magazine and sighed. Zander was resting peacefully in his hospital bed, even smiling a little in his sleep. She was grateful for that blessing, really she was. Her son's soul was obviously back in his body where it belonged.

But he had yet to awaken.

It's only been three days, she reminded herself for the thousandth time. She closed the magazine—she wasn't reading it, anyway—and tossed it on the wheeled tray table with the others.

She wished Mac were here.

He'd said he'd come, and with Kalen's neat trick of translocation, the trip from Scotland only took minutes. Three days had passed, and Mac hadn't yet appeared. It made her uneasy. Had Leanna worsened? Had *Mac*? He'd neatly evaded all her questions about what had happened in Lucifer's lair. And he'd looked so wan and tired, despite his jokes and smiles.

Her hand drifted to her stomach. Even if Mac had changed his mind about loving her, surely he would have come because of his son. Something was wrong, terribly wrong. She stood and paced the tiny room. In her haste to get to Zander, she hadn't thought to ask Mac how she could contact him. He'd said he would come, and she'd taken him at his word. She had no phone number, no

-mail address. She didn't even have a good idea of exactly
here Kalen's island castle lay. Short of getting on a plane
nd beginning a survey of the northern Scottish coast, she
ad no way to connect with Mac at all.

A small sound, like the mew of a kitten, broke through
er churning thoughts. Her gaze flew to the bed.

Zander's tossed his head, mussing his dark curls. She
/as at his side in an instant, lowering the bed's side rail
nd chafing his small hand. His fingers were warm. They
urled into hers. Dark eyelashes fluttered, and then his
•eautiful eyes opened. He blinked, his forehead wrinkling.

She smoothed the lines with her fingers. "Zander?"

"Mommy?"

"Yes, love, I'm here."

He turned his head to one side. "Where's here?"

She sat down on the bed. "A hospital, baby."

He wrinkled his nose. "Don't call me that. I'm not a
•aby." Then, "Am I sick?"

"Not sick, exactly." She paused. "Don't you remember?"

"I remember you went out. I didn't want you to go. Mrs.
Clark stayed with me. She read me a story and I went
o bed."

Artemis cupped the side of his head. His skin was so
mooth, so perfect. Tears crowded her eyes. "Do you re-
nember what happened after that?"

He shook his head slowly. "A bad dream, I think. Bad
nagic. It's all fuzzy, though." He peered up at her. "Is it
mportant that I remember, Mommy?"

She leaned close and kissed his cheek. "No, Zander, it's
1ot. In fact, I think . . . I think it's best if you just let the
nemory fade away."

He entwined his thin arms around her neck. "All right,
Mommy. I will. I don't like it much, anyway."

"Oh, Zander." She lost the battle with her tears.

Zander patted her arm. "Don't cry, Mommy."

His attempt to console her only made her cry harder.

Heedless of the intravenous drip, she pulled her so
into her lap and wrapped her arms tightly around hi
small body. The plastic tubing pulled free; an alarm ligh
flashed. She didn't care. She brushed Zander's soul with
her magic. No surge of lingering darkness met her psychi
touch. Her son's soul was strong and innocent, just as i
had been before he'd been snatched.

Her tears came harder. She couldn't seem to make then
stop.

A round-faced nurse popped her head in the door. He
gaze took in Artemis and Zander entwined on the bed
and a broad smile appeared on her face.

"Looks like my favorite patient is awake." She bustle
into the room. Reluctantly, Artemis relinquished her so
while the woman recorded Zander's vitals.

"Everything looks good," the nurse said, smiling as sh
headed out the door. "I'll just let the doctor know."

The next hours went by in a blur of consultations and
opinions. By evening she and Zander were back in thei
own tiny apartment. Zander giggled over cartoons on ca
ble, while Artemis made a mental note to call his school'
principal in the morning.

It all seemed so surreal. As if the last six months had beer
nothing but a long, terrible nightmare.

Except for Mac. And the fact that in nine short months
she'd be giving birth to his child. She'd have to tell Zan
der. Would Mac be here with her when she did?

Where *was* he?

Fighting a deep sense of unease, she found the remote
and switched off the television. "Time for bed."

"Aw, Mommy, I'm not tired!"

She smiled. "Too bad."

Zander rolled his eyes, but changed into his pajama
with a minimum of fuss. He fell asleep during his bedtime
story, his head drooping onto Artemis's shoulder. For a
long time, Artemis savored the feel of his soft, trusting

body. Then she lowered his head to the pillow, pulled up the covers, and kissed him good night.

Maybe Mac would come tomorrow. She could hope, anyway. She walked across the living room and entered the kitchen.

And stopped dead. A very large man sat at her table. His bare legs, covered to the knee by a tartan kilt, stretched halfway into the center of the small room.

"Kalen. What are you doing here?" Then, more fearfully, "Where's Mac?"

The Immortal stood and inclined his head in a brief greeting. "Mac's in Annwyn."

"Annwyn? But he hates it there."

"So he does. But it was . . . necessary."

"Necessary?" Why did the word sound so ominous? "Necessary in what way?"

Kalen hesitated. "Mac didn't want you to know. But once he left, Christine started hounding me about making the trip here to tell you. She thought you had the right to know. We argued for three days." He smiled ruefully. "You can see who won."

His smile faded.

Artemis's hand found the edge of the counter. "Tell me what?"

Kalen nodded to the empty chair beside him. "Sit down, Artemis. I don't think you want to hear this standing up."

Numbly, she dropped into the chair. "What's wrong, Kalen? What's happened to Mac?"

Kalen rose and paced the length of the narrow kitchen. When he reached the doorway, he pivoted to face her. "Mac's gone to Annwyn in the hope . . . that the life magic of the Celtic Otherworld can heal his soul well enough to hold back the inevitable. For a time, at least. Exactly how long, I have no idea. He's not human, after all. It's possible—even probable—that the end won't come for centuries. But it will come, eventually."

"The end?" Artemis was aware of a chill seeping into her extremities. "What . . . end? I don't understand."

"Death."

The word fell like a curse. Air rushed from her lungs. She went very still. "But . . . Mac can't die. He's immortal."

"He *was* immortal. No longer." Kalen's dark eyes bored into her hers. "He traded his immortality to Lucifer, in exchange for the souls in Ptolomaea. For your son, and the other innocents. Mac's soul is mortal now. When his life essence is depleted, he'll die."

An image of Mac, lying still and pale as a corpse, burned panic into Artemis's brain. All that life, all that humor and vibrancy—gone? A shudder ran through her.

"No. That's not right. He's a *god*. Gods can't die."

Kalen shook his head. "Gods can do anything they want. Even sacrifice their lives."

Kalen's broad form wavered through Artemis's tears. Gods, she never used to cry. Now it seemed like all she could do. "This is my fault."

Kalen was feigning a fascination with her coffeemaker. "I can't pretend you didn't play a major role in what happened, Artemis, but in the end, the choice was Mac's."

The assessment did little to relieve Artemis's crushing guilt. "Will he live the rest of his life in Annwyn, then?"

"Perhaps. He'll live longer there."

"But he hates Annwyn."

Kalen sighed. "I know."

CHAPTER TWENTY-SIX

The summer sun was warm, and the air carried a hint of perfume. The mid-July breeze gathered in a cluster of wild roses before running across the playground. Artemis sat on a wooden bench, her hands folded atop a very round belly as she watched three lads scale a ladder leading to a spiral tube slide. Two of the boys, strapping blond-haired twins, reached the top first. A smaller, darker lad, hair kissed with gold, was close behind.

Mac returned his attention to Artemis. Her stomach was so large he was sure she'd lost sight of her feet some months prior. She looked like a Madonna, round and filled with life magic. It almost hurt to look at her. It had been so long since he'd kissed her good-bye.

He was glad he'd gotten here in time. Time was a highly distorted commodity in Annwyn, and he wasn't at all sure until he'd cleared the gates just how many months had passed since he'd last walked on human ground.

He smiled. It was good to be home. Despite his new mortality, his heart was lighter than it had ever been. He loped forward on silent feet. He couldn't resist the temptation to sneak up on her. "Hey, love, is this a private bench? Or is that far end available?"

Her head jerked up. Her face was fuller than he remembered it, her cheeks a bit blotchy. For a moment, he thought she hadn't recognized him. He knew he looked older than when she'd seen him last—perhaps a human decade or so. But surely he didn't look so different as all that.

He sat on the far end of the bench, one arm extended along the backrest. His hand dangled scant inches from her shoulder. "What's wrong, love? Cat got your tongue?"

She glanced at him quickly, then looked away. "It's . . . really you? Alive? You're not . . . dead?"

"Dead?" He frowned. "Did you think I was?"

"I wondered. Kalen . . . he told me what you'd given up. When I didn't hear from you . . ."

"I'm sorry, Artemis. I should have gotten word to you. And it was touch-and-go there for a while. I came very close to dying. But in the end, the magic of Annwyn came through for me. For me and for Leanna."

She still wouldn't look at him. "But . . . you're not immortal."

He exhaled. "No. But neither are you, love."

She did look at him then. "But . . . I never was immortal. I never expected to live forever. You were a god!"

His lips quirked. "Only half a god."

Tears shone in her eyes. "How can you joke about it?"

He scooted a few inches closer. He wanted to gather her into his arms, wanted to feel his son's life essence in her belly. He contented himself with playing a little rhythm on her shoulder. "I gave up my immortality, love, not my sense of humor."

She met his gaze, stricken. "Stop joking, please."

"I'm not joking," he said quietly. "Technically, I'm still a demigod. Just not an immortal one. All my powers are intact. It's just my longevity that's changed. Does it mean so much to you, Artemis?"

"You must be so angry with me."

"Oh, I've been angry with you. For a lot of reasons. But not for the one you imagine." He looked toward the playground. "Zander's doing well?"

"Yes. He doesn't remember his time in Hell. It's gone,

like a bad dream. There are no lingering effects that I can tell."

"Excellent."

She cleared her throat. "I've given up death magic. For good. I don't care if it means I'm less powerful than I was. I've had enough death magic to last me three lifetimes."

"Me, too." He shifted on the bench, bringing his fingers in contact with the back of her neck.

She startled, but didn't move away.

"I didn't do it only for Zander, you know," he continued. "There were the others."

"You never even would have been in Hell if it weren't for me."

"True." He paused, picking his words carefully. "If not for you, all those innocent children would still be suffering."

"On no. Don't, Mac. Don't try to make me out as a hero."

He walked his fingers to her opposite shoulder. "Suit yourself, love. I'm just pointing out the facts."

"The fact is, you'd be better off if you'd never met me."

"Ah, now, there I have to argue. That's not a fact, but an opinion. One I don't share, as it happens." He scooted down the bench until his left thigh pressed firmly against her right. He stroked down her bare arm, then fitted her against his side.

"Much better." The fingers of his opposite hand caught her chin and turned her face toward him. His gaze dropped to her lips.

He dipped his head and kissed her.

Her lips were soft and plaint. They moved beneath his, flooding his soul with her warmth. And her fear. She still wasn't sure of her welcome in his heart.

He'd have to work on that.

He speared his fingers through her hair as he plundered her mouth. She tasted so sweet. Like ripe summer peaches. Like—

"Ooh!" She stiffened in his arms.

His head came up. "What? What is it, love?"

She glanced up at him almost shyly, her hand coming to rest on her stomach. "Your son," she said. "He just kicked me."

A slow grin spread across Mac's face. "Did he, now?"

"Yes. Hard."

He couldn't take his eyes off Artemis's stomach. "Can I feel?"

"Of course."

She took his hand and guided it to a spot on one side of her belly. "Feel that lump? That's his foot."

He pressed the taut skin, amazed to feel the outline of a small foot beneath a layer of muscle. He closed his eyes and cast his senses deep. His son's heartbeat pulsed in his mind. The spark of the infant's soul was beautiful. It leaped in recognition, flashing bright.

The lad gave a hard kick against Mac's palm.

He opened his eyes and grinned down at Artemis. "Been giving you a bit of trouble, has he?"

For the first time since he'd approached her, Artemis smiled. "That's an understatement. I think he's going to be a soccer player."

"Better get him signed up for a team, then." He chuckled. "Sign me up for coach if you'd like."

Her smile drained away. "That would be . . . nice. But . . . are you sure you should? Stay with me, I mean?"

He sent her a hard look. "Don't you want me, Artemis?"

"Of course I do! But maybe you should go back. To Annwyn, I mean. You'll live a longer life there."

"A longer, more miserable life, you mean."

"Mac—"

"Artemis, I hate Annwyn. Every bloody perfect inch of it. I just spent the better part of nine months there, and damned if I'm going back for anything longer than a weekend holiday. You think I'd live there permanently, just so I could add a few years to my life? I'll let you in on a little secret, love. Immortality is vastly overrated."

"You can't possibly mean that."

"I can and I do. I knew it even before we met. What was my old life like? Year after year, stretching into blurry infinity, no real emotion attached to any of it. A meandering song that had no hope of ever achieving that last, beautiful note. The final tone that gives the whole melody a deeper meaning."

He slid his palm on her belly, following his son's movement. "But now? Now that I know there'll be an end to it all? Now everything's come into focus. I can see what I want now, Artemis. Clearly. And do you know what that is?"

Mutely, she shook her head.

"You. You and Zander, and our child. And maybe more young ones later on. If you'll agree." He drew a breath. "Marry me, love."

Her eyes were wet. "Mac. I . . . I don't know what to say."

"What about 'yes'? Really, Artemis, it's not such a difficult word. Go ahead. Try it. 'Yes, Mac, I'll marry you. And once I'm your wife, I'll do you the honor of being happy. No regrets. No guilt. Only love and life, together.'" He grinned. "There. Now you try it."

Tears spilled over her lashes. She reached up and touched his temple, his cheek, his jaw. "Oh, Mac, I love you so."

"And I love you, Artemis. Now, will you please say you'll be my wife as well as the mother of my child?"

She entwined her arms around his neck. "Of course I'll marry you. Gods, it's like a dream come true."

He touched her lips with his, in a brief exchange of emotion that no doubt would have gone deeper if not for a small, childish voice. Mac looked up to find Artemis's son staring up at him with his mother's dark, serious eyes. He felt something in his heart catch.

"Mommy? Who's he?"

"I'm Manannán mac Lir," he told the lad, surprising himself with his formal tone.

The boy nodded. "My brother's father."

Mac shot a look at Artemis. "Yes."

Zander's brows drew together. "Do I know you? Have we met before? I feel like . . . I know you. Like we're friends."

Mac regarded him seriously. "We are friends, Zander. Very good friends, in fact. And what's more, I'm going to marry your mother, so we'll be even more to each other. We'll be family."

"Oh!" A spark leaped in the lad's dark eyes. "Will you be my father, too, as well as my new brother's?"

"Do you want me to be?"

Zander nodded.

"Then I will be," Mac pledged. "For as long as I live."

He hoisted the lad onto his lap, then shot a glance at Artemis. Love and joy shone bright in her eyes. His child grew inside her body.

And Mac knew it would be a very good life indeed.

For centuries they have walked among us—vampires, shape-shifters, the Celtic Sidhe, demons, and other magical beings. Their battle to reign supreme is constant, but one force holds them in check, a race of powerful woarriors known as the

IMMORTALS

The USA Today *Bestselling Series Continues*

Immortals: THE REDEEMING
Coming September 2008

Immortals: THE CROSSING
Coming October 2008

Immortals: THE HAUNTING
Coming November 2008

Immortals: THE RECKONING
Coming Spring 2009

New York Times Bestselling Author

C. L. WILSON

Only one enemy could destroy them.
Only one love could unite them.
Only one power could lead their people to victory...

TAIREN SOUL

The magical tairen were dying, and none but the Fey King's bride could save them. Rain had defied the nobles of Celieria to claim her, battled demons and Elden mages to wed her. Now, with magic, steel, and scorching flame he would risk everything to protect his kingdom, help his truemate embrace her magic and forge the unbreakable bond that alone could save her soul.

KING OF SWORD AND SKY

COMING THIS FALL!

ISBN 13: 978-0-8439-6059-4

To order a book or to request a catalog call:
1-800-481-9191
This book is also available at your local bookstore, or you can check out our Web site **www.dorchesterpub.com** where you can look up your favorite authors, read excerpts, or glance at our discussion forum to see what people have to say about your favorite books.

☐ **YES!**

Sign me up for the Love Spell Book Club and send my
REE BOOKS! If I choose to stay in the club, I will pay only
$8.50* each month, a savings of $6.48!

AME: _____

DDRESS: _____

ELEPHONE: _____

MAIL: _____

☐ I want to pay by credit card.

☐ VISA   ☐ MasterCard.   ☐ DISCOVER

CCOUNT #: _____

XPIRATION DATE: _____

GNATURE: _____

Mail this page along with $2.00 shipping and handling to:
Love Spell Book Club
PO Box 6640
Wayne, PA 19087
Or fax (must include credit card information) to:
610-995-9274

You can also sign up online at **www.dorchesterpub.com**.
lus $2.00 for shipping. Offer open to residents of the U.S. and Canada only. Canadian
residents please call 1-800-481-9191 for pricing information.
f under 18, a parent or guardian must sign. Terms, prices and conditions subject to
ange. Subscription subject to acceptance. Dorchester Publishing reserves the right to
reject any order or cancel any subscription.